PRAISE FOR THE SHADOW OPERATIVES
SERIES

"*Catch and Kill* is a perfect medley of high-tech thrills and old-school James Bond espionage."

    – Nick Thacker, author of the thrillers *Mark for Blood* and *The Enigma Strain*

"Fans of Michael Crichton will love *Catch and Kill,* a fast-paced, high-octane techno-thriller that's sure to do damage to the best-seller lists."

    – A.C. Fuller, author of The Alex Vane Media Thrillers and The Ameritocracy Trilogy

"J.D. Lasica is the new master of techno-thrillers. His protagonist Kaden reminds me of Lisbeth, the *Girl With the Dragon Tattoo.*"

    – Shel Israel, author of *The Fourth Transformation*

"J.D. Lasica is a threat to a good night's sleep."

    – Melissa F. Miller, author of the thrillers *Dark Path* and *Critical Vulnerability*

"An amazing read. What a Netflix series this would make!"

— Michael James Gallagher, author of the thrillers *Diamond Rain* and *Tsunami Connection*

"Fantastic! It's like a summer-blockbuster action flick with a brain."
— Denise Howell, host, *This Week in Law* podcast

"This is the Dan Brown-meets-Lara Croft-meets-Michael Crichton thriller series we've been waiting for. Kaden is one smart, kick-ass heroine."
— Saul Tanpepper, author of the sci-fi thriller series *Gameland* and *The Flense*

"*Catch and Kill* should have a pharmacy sticker on the cover. 'Warning: readers might experience heart palpitations, rapid breathing, heightened senses, and difficulty accepting interruptions while reading.'"
— Al Boss

"*Catch and Kill* is a heart-thumping thriller, combining cutting-edge technology and nonstop action into a wild roller-coaster ride."
— Dan Petrosini, author of the thrillers *Vanished* and *The Final Enemy*

"A high-tech thriller with a cool, modern protagonist. I couldn't put it down!"
— Kira Dineen, host, *DNA Today* podcast

CATCH AND KILL

J.D. LASICA

A SHADOW OPERATIVES THRILLER (BOOK 2)

Readers' note: If you need to get your bearings, see the Characters section after the last chapter.

"Reality is merely an illusion, albeit a very persistent one."
  – ALBERT EINSTEIN

"What has been decreed must be accomplished."
  – THE BOOK OF DANIEL

PROLOGUE

Qaanaaq, Greenland, one year ago

The lone figure watched the private submarine rise from the depths, a craft that looked like a curvy concept car blended with a submerged rocket ship. He tightened the fur hood on his down parka and set off from the dock, nosing his one-man skiff through the bay's biting cold.

As he drew closer, he saw two men fighting on the topside of the sub. A loud bang interrupted the purr of his outboard motor and echoed across the bay like the crack of a calving glacier. The target's body slipped into the frigid waters with a muffled splash.

"Sorry you had to see that, sir." Savić, his security chief, tucked away his snub-nosed revolver and held out his bearish paw to help his boss on board.

"All part of the deal." Lucid's breath formed a cloud. "Let's leave the skiff and go below."

They descended the hatch into the belly of the sleek private craft on loan from the Compact. "S'way," Savić grunted. Lucid understood the shorthand for *This way* and followed his security chief forward to the bow.

As they entered the Observation Salon, a man dressed in a white uniform and officer's cap shot to his feet, greeted him, and shook hands. "Honored to have you aboard. Captain Jan Kjellin, commanding officer."

"The honor is mine," the visitor said. "They call me Lucid."

"Lucid. That's clear as a bell, isn't it?" The captain turned to Savić. "And the other fellow you were with?"

"He had to leave," Savić said.

Lucid took in his surroundings. He had been on many cramped, godforsaken subs, but this room resembled a five-star hotel suite. Recessed lighting, leather sofas and seats, flat-screen TVs, and full bar. Instead of portholes, the room had four rein-forced picture windows for a first-hand look at the arctic depths.

The captain moved toward the doorway. "Your chief scientist is down below."

The captain guided Lucid and Savić down a carpeted hallway past a sleek dining room with pendant lights that swayed in unison as the sub began to move. Lucid captured video footage with his Eyecam as he stepped through the vessel.

They were out of Internet range and it would be impossible to live-stream the action for the Chairman. He felt an enormous sense of relief wash over him. Apart from sleeping, it was the first time in months he wasn't *always on*.

The captain made small talk as he led them down a stairwell to the bottom deck. Lucid was pleased the captain didn't seem to notice his artificial left eye—or was polite enough not to mention it. This model, version seven, appeared so lifelike that it often passed for the real thing. His Eyecam was already taking data readings. The exact geo coordinates of his location. The direction of true north. The amount of carbon, oxygen, and argon in the surrounding air.

"Here we are," the captain said as they arrived at a small room marked Immersion Chamber. "I've been instructed to be accom-modating—within reason."

Lucid and the captain entered while Savić remained outside. The room was bare except for the butter-yellow deep-sea probe glistening in the LED lighting, held in place by steel rods on a metal track. Lucid's people had flown out to modify this next-generation bathyscaphe. It had a large oval window, protruding metal arms, and an array of "specimen catchers" in front—large titanium containers custom-tailored for the mission.

Two men were inside the probe arguing about something. Adam Bashir, their chief scientist, wagged his finger at a fair-haired submariner.

Bashir spotted him, opened the hatch, and climbed out. "Good to see you, Lucid."

The crew member also exited the submersible and introduced himself. "Systems engineer Erikson, sir. I'll be piloting the craft."

Bashir ignored the young submariner. "I'm going alone."

"Not happening." Erickson looked adamant.

Bashir turned to Lucid for support. "This is unacceptable. Tell them."

"Kasparian promised us secrecy," Lucid said.

"And that you shall have," the captain said. "I often accompany Erikson on these deep-water missions. It's a two-man undertaking. But this is no standard geological expedition, is it?"

Lucid's face gave away nothing, like the ancient rock formations on the seabed floor.

"Bit of a mystery, is it?" Erikson's palm brushed the side of the probe. "If we're going that deep, I need to know what we're hunting."

Lucid knew they'd get only one shot at this, and the Chairman would not accept failure. At the Lab, Bashir had mastered the computer simulation they'd created for the expedition. But Lucid knew how wrong things could go at the bottom of the ocean.

"Erickson will pilot," Lucid decided. "Bashir will co-pilot and direct you to our target. The details of the hunt should not concern you."

The captain pivoted to face the two outsiders. "Listen here. I've made over forty expeditions to the deepest, darkest cracks under the sea, from the Mariana Trench to the hydrothermal vents below the North Pole."

Lucid tried to stop him. "You and your people are on a need-to-know—"

"I've seen stranger creatures than maybe any living man. Giant zombie worms. Dragonfish. Sea pigs. Spookfish that come up to you like wraiths of the abyss. Seadevil anglerfish that swum straight up from hell."

The captain moved close to Lucid's fake eye. "If there's one person on board you need on your side, it's the captain."

Lucid considered this. If anything went wrong at the crushing depths they planned to explore, he would need the man's full cooperation. He grabbed the captain by the shoulder. "Let's step outside."

They exited the chamber, walked past Savić, and huddled in a stairwell.

"I'll read you in, Captain. But you need to keep this strictly under wraps. None of your men can know."

The captain gave a slight nod.

"Captain. Our quarry is the oldest form of life on earth."

The captain paused, then smiled as if he understood. But how could he? He couldn't possibly fathom that today's voyage would change the face of the world.

The clock is now ticking. Project Ezekiel is underway. The only question is how many millions will die.

1

Southampton, New York, present day

The young woman stepped into the gazebo and let out an unbridled laugh at the absurdity of the scene. The multimillion-dollar estates lining Shinnecock Bay in the Hamptons. The tight-fitting party dress she had to borrow for the night. The whole idea of heading to a gala where she'd be honored for killing a man.

"Who *am* I? What am I doing here?" Kaden whirled on her expensive heels. "Come on, this is nuts. Let's go back to Brooklyn."

"We can take a ride share back." Gabriel followed her into the gazebo. "But I have a surprise for you first."

They sat on the lone bench with its unobstructed view of the water. He took her hand as the raspberry sun slid into the bay.

I've got to admit, she thought. *This is pretty damn idyllic.*

A cool breeze prickled her skin and tousled the short blond hair she'd started to grow out. Gabriel slid his hand over her eyes and folded something cold into her palm.

"Happy two-month anniversary," he said.

She opened her eyes to see a heart-shaped rose quartz pendant attached to a silver chain necklace.

"Oh my God, Gabriel. It's gorgeous."

He clasped the thin necklace around her neck. "Seriously, look at you. Smart, sexy, strong, athletic. You could break me in half if you wanted."

She smiled. She had no intention of breaking Gabriel in half. He had his own sexy thing going—kind brown eyes, short beard, an open mind. Not a kickboxer like her, but buff enough.

Gabriel showed her both sides of the pendant. "It's a wearable. You can put that photo of your mom in the front. There's a digital display on the back. Just click twice to let me know you're thinking of me."

She held it up, clicked twice, and heard a ping from the phone in Gabriel's suit jacket pocket. She leaned over and they kissed. When she opened her eyes, he slipped on the pair of smartglasses he'd borrowed from her apartment.

"I thought I could meet Amelia tonight," he said.

She hesitated. "I haven't shown her to anyone yet. Why do you want to meet her?"

"Can't meet your parents. I figured Amelia's the next best thing."

I've been taking it slow with Gabriel, but is it time to get serious? Took till I was twenty-three to find someone who gets me. Maybe it's time to stress-test the relationship.

Kaden used her smart contact lenses and aircracked a hotspot from one of the nearby estates. "Here goes nothing. Amelia, I'd like you to meet Gabriel."

She blinked three times and Amelia materialized, perched atop the gazebo railing to the right. She wore a dust-colored aviator's outfit with a gold aviator's pin. She smiled, her face framed by a pair of goggles and a loose-fitting aviator's cap draped over a tangle of curly brown hair. Her scruffy brown boots dangled a foot off the ground.

Amelia turned to face them. "Hi, Gabriel. Nice to meet you."

Gabriel's eyes grew large. He stared for a moment, turned to Kaden, then back to Amelia. "Nice to meet you, Ms. Earhart. I've never met an artificial intelligence before. I'm a little … wow."

The Wi-Fi signal was temperamental but decent enough. Amelia appeared at full opacity—completely solid, even though you couldn't touch her. *Don't want her to look like a ghost or it might freak out Gabriel.*

"Nice of you to escort Kaden to the gala," Amelia said.

"We're still deciding whether to go," Kaden broke in. "We only have a minute."

She was nervous about what Gabriel might ask. Amelia knew nearly everything about her. Every detail about her abused childhood. Every file she'd hacked from her estranged grandfather. Every covert op she'd orchestrated.

Haven't shared those little details with Gabriel yet. Working my way up the trust ladder.

Amelia hopped down, strolled across the gazebo, and leaned against a post. She fished a pack of cigarettes from her purse and lit one up. "You know, dears, back in my day, I'd be swinging almost every weekend. But this is the first party Kaden has invited me to. It looks absolutely rip-roaring."

"Looks?" Gabriel appeared mystified. He turned to Kaden. "Can she see … everything?"

Kaden laughed. "Amelia can travel anywhere there's an Internet connection." She pivoted to face the AI. "I'm guessing guests are already sharing photos and videos online. That right, Amelia?"

"Yes, they are. Silly habit, if you ask me. They're at a party!"

Kaden had programmed Amelia to stay true to her persona and never mince words. Modern social niceties could come later.

Amelia sat down on the steps of of the gazebo and fixed Gabriel with her gaze. "Tell us one thing about yourself that Kaden doesn't know."

"Amelia, that's personal," Kaden chided.

"It's all right." Gabriel thought about it. "Let's see. I had a childhood nickname."

"How embarrassing?"

"Chip."

"I've heard worse." *Let's not go there.* "Why Chip?"

"I fell on the playground during third grade and chipped my front tooth. My family couldn't afford to get it fixed."

"Aww. You have an amazing smile." Kaden poked the bridge of his smartglasses with her forefinger. "We should go. Say good-bye, Amelia."

Amelia began to glitch in and out as the bandwidth strained to keep up with her. "So great to meet you, Gabriel," she said. She straightened, dusted off her lap, and turned to Kaden. "Such a nice young man. And such a stud in bed last night!"

"Oh my God!"

Kaden felt her face flush hot red as she realized she'd forgotten to take out her lenses or put Amelia into sleep mode during her date last night. She reached up and snatched the glasses from Gabriel's nose.

Gabriel's expression turned from surprise to a satisfied smile. He lunged for the smartglasses and called out, "Glad you enjoyed the show!"

Kaden stalked off, mortified beyond belief. She removed the earpiece from her right ear—she didn't want to hear any of Amelia's excuses—and nearly flung it into the reeds along the bay before thinking better of it and stashing it in her pocket. Her lenses provided the visuals, but the two-way earpiece let her communicate with Amelia.

Gabriel caught up with her, enjoying the moment a little too much. "I liked her. She reminds me of you. Direct, honest. Knows more than she lets on. Bit by the wanderlust bug. So are we going to the gala?"

"Three more blocks," she said. She needed a change of scenery. And she'd given her word.

As they walked along the lane, fall colors danced in the trees. They passed mansions with killer views of the bay—big estates with pools, tennis courts, sprawling lawns, and lights winking in the twilight. She was already working out what adjustments she'd need to make to Amelia's social settings.

But first she'd have to make it through tonight.

She was still processing the fact she'd killed one of them—a member of the one percent.

Part of her wondered if they'd honor her tonight. Or arrest her.

2

Southampton, New York

Kaden and Gabriel reached the address, a two-story mansion with a long paved driveway, manicured garden, and more windows than she could count. The noise from the party spilled out to the front sidewalk.

"The last honoree is here," a woman at the doorway announced to someone inside. Then to Kaden: "Welcome, dear. I like your outfit. So svelte and tribal."

"Thanks." She'd borrowed something feminine from Annika, figuring her usual anti-fashion uniform of ripped jeans and faded tees wouldn't cut it tonight. She stepped into the marbled foyer beneath a crystal chandelier. *So this is how the rich live.*

A dark-haired young boy held up a silver tray containing smartglasses—she saw most of the guests were wearing them. "Smart parties" seemed to be the trendy new thing in the Hamptons.

Kaden declined—her smart contact lenses would do fine. Her AI had already tapped into the open network and paired with the gala's cloud so she could see the same data as the other guests.

And more. She suspected she was the only party-goer with an AI companion.

"Nice little soirée." Gabriel eyed the main room, which could hold both of their apartments and then some. Rows of recessed lighting graced the lofted ceilings. Guests milled about as white-uniformed waiters served drinks and canapés. On the far wall, images of the honorees rotated on a digital display.

They moved into the buzzy maw. Kaden counted six leather sofas, one baby grand piano, five wall murals, and a single gleaming spiral staircase leading to a marble balustrade lining a second-floor walkway.

Where a large man with a thick dark mustache seemed to stare at her.

"Champagne, Miss?" a waiter offered. Kaden and Gabriel each grabbed a flute. She glanced up. The man was gone.

"Isn't that the mayor?" Gabriel nodded toward a gaggle near the fireplace. "And what's her name, the actress."

Someone tapped her on the shoulder and she turned to see a silver-haired woman in a blue designer outfit that probably cost more than Kaden made in a year.

"Kaden, so glad you could make it. I'm Marian Shorenstein." They shook hands. "It was so brave what you did, saving all those poor girls."

She still felt uneasy talking about how she'd freed all those young women held captive at the fertility center in Dallas. She became an instant cult hero online. But the D.A. was still deciding whether to bring charges against her.

"It happened so fast. I just reacted."

"We need more warriors like you on the front lines."

"Thanks, but I'll be happy to disappear into the shadows after tonight. I need some humdrum in my life."

The only reason she attended was that the award came with a stipend. She'd decided to turn the prize money over to Jamie, the sixteen-year-old call girl who made it through the Dallas ordeal.

Kaden knew what it was like to grow up in a household without loving parents.

A member of the wait staff pulled Marian Shorenstein away, so Gabriel and Kaden chatted with two other couples before wandering out the rear door. The party extended into the sweeping back yard and around the swimming pool, lit up in a blue glow.

Gabriel leaned over and kissed her on the back of her neck. She felt a flush of warmth. "I don't know what to say to these people," she confessed.

"Just be yourself. They've probably never met a real-life action hero before."

She elbowed him in the ribs. During the past six weeks with Gabriel, she'd been revisiting a lot of her assumptions. She'd always thought of herself as a lone wolf. No boyfriend or girl-friend, free of entanglements. Having a plus-one was changing the equation.

Gabriel took her empty Champagne flute. "Be right back with a refill."

She turned and followed the pathway, illuminated with tiki torches. At the end of the pool, the path led to an open-air patio with a large fire pit aflame with orange embers. Wooden chaises were set back a safe distance from the fire flanked by an island stand topped with bottles of liqueurs and wines. She was away from the crowd now, and she fished the earpiece from her pocket to check in with Amelia.

A tall figure approached from the shadows. The man from the upstairs balustrade. He had a large build, with broad shoulders and an Eastern European look. His dark eyes danced like shimmering glasses of red wine in the reflection of the tiki torches. His name and occupation appeared in the bottom third of her field of vision. The gala's attendee list identified him as Lazarus Wojcik, a cardiologist from Prague.

"Ms. Kaden Baker, it's an honor to meet you." He extended his immense palm and she shook it.

"Actually, I don't use my last name. Or a courtesy title." The gala people never asked her.

"Forgive me." He moved closer. He had a half-moon scar on his forehead and a musty odor. "I am still getting used to this new reality. Using glasses to learn the name of a person across the room. Strange."

"You were staring at me before. From the banister."

"I was admiring your golden hair and purple highlights. And your … body decorations." His gaze moved from her hair to her lip piercing and settled upon her left shoulder.

"An equality tattoo," she said.

"These are rare in my social circles."

Amelia appeared in the corner of her field of vision. "Kaden, something about this fellow doesn't add up. No record of a cardiologist by that name in any hospital database in Europe."

"What can I do for you, sir?" Kaden asked. She wondered why he'd be using an alias.

"I have an urgent private matter to discuss with you. Let's walk toward the fire pit for some privacy."

He grabbed her by the elbow and tried to steer her away from the other guests.

She resisted. "Wait. What's this about?"

"Please. Come this way. Don't make a scene."

He wrapped his thick, bearlike fingers around her biceps and pulled her toward the darkness.

"Hey!" She jerked her arm free, more angry than frightened.

To her left, behind a row of chaise lounges, she saw a second man approach at seven o'clock. Bear Man grabbed her by the shoulders while the shorter one, lithe like a cat, came up from behind and pushed her head downward to expose her neck. He was holding a syringe.

Her special ops training kicked in. She yanked away, leveled a powerful kick to the second intruder's groin, and snatched the syringe from his hand. She tried to plunge it into his neck, but he grabbed her wrist, so she used her free hand to grip the syringe and snap it in half. Their faces were inches apart. He had long, stringy blond hair and a ruddy, sunburnt face. He reminded her of the bad date she'd had with a surfer.

She grabbed Surfer Dude's arm, used his weight to whip his body over her back, and crashed him to the ground. *Two against one, not fair, Surfer Dude.*

Guests around the fringes of the pool scattered. Someone called out, "Security!"

Kaden turned and saw Bear Man coming at her. She grabbed a hardwood lounge chair, hoisted it, and put her full weight behind it, smashing it into his upper torso. He fell, dazed but still conscious.

She reached down, grabbed the hem of her fancy dress, and ripped it straight up to her hip to get better lift and leverage. *Annika's gonna kill me for this.*

From the ground, Surfer Dude grabbed her ankles and toppled her backward. He shot to his feet and dragged her by the ankles toward the fire pit. "I'll teach you some manners."

"Accent from a region of rural Croatia," Amelia informed her through her earpiece.

Surfer Dude relaxed his grip for a second and reached for two metal roasting sticks from the stand next to the fire pit. He snagged a glowing orange rock and brought it toward Kaden's face.

Just as she felt the heat on her cheek, she surprised him with a hook kick to his left kidney from her supine position, a move she learned at boot camp. The heated rock toppled to the side. Surfer Dude shrieked in pain. She regained her feet and followed with a foot jab to his solar plexus. Her kickboxing instincts took over, and she was glad she was wearing her black steel-toe flats.

She saw Bear Man reach for something inside his jacket.

Before he could grab it, she spun and delivered three lightning-quick strikes. She started with a side kick to his rib cage. She planted, turned her body to generate more power, then delivered a left-handed blow to his liver. The coup de grace was a round-house strike to the left side of his head that sent him crumpling to the ground.

She heard a wheezing noise behind her and saw Surfer Dude coming at her again. She took three steps to her right, pulled a tiki torch out of the ground, and smashed it across his back.

Black oil from the torch splashed onto his jacket, setting him on fire. Surfer Dude shrieked—the howl of a wounded animal. He tried to shed his jacket as the blaze grew. He lunged into the pool, sending a surge of water onto the concrete pavement.

She turned to face Bear Man. He drew his gun, a Browning Hi Power by the look of it, and aimed it at her. "You're coming with me."

"You'll have to kill me." She started toward him.

"Kaden? What the hell!" Gabriel exploded out of the back entrance and ran toward them. The Champagne flutes in his hands smashed to the pavement. A pair of security guards followed on his heels.

As Gabriel came closer, Bear Man flashed her a smile, whirled, and took aim at the onrushing figure.

"No! Shoot me!" Kaden screamed. She charged him. *I'll kill you, you son of a bitch!*

She launched herself and delivered a compact uppercut to his right arm to throw off his aim. Her blow arrived a split second too late.

Bear Man shot Gabriel square in the forehead.

3

Annandale, Virginia, day of the Disappearance

Bo Finnerty began the day with his usual routine. He rose earlier than he would have liked. Shaved with military precision. Took a quick shower so the steam would dissipate on the mirror before his seventeen-year-old daughter awoke.

He checked the clock and began to cook her favorite breakfast. Waffles with fresh berries. Cottage cheese on the side. Orange juice from real oranges, not frozen concentrate.

"Hi Pop."

He turned to see Bailey plunk into the wooden kitchen chair and check her phone. Misty, their spaniel-cocker mix, bounded in from the next room and sat at Bailey's feet.

"I made your favorite breakfast," he said.

"No time. Just cottage cheese."

He checked the clock. She had only two minutes to wolf something down or she'd miss the bus. He brought over the cottage cheese and a glass of OJ. *Just six more weeks of high school. In the fall, college life would change her perspective, smooth out the edges.*

"I thought we could go out one night this week. Maybe see a movie."

She escaped into her phone. Which in its way was her reply.

Weren't fathers and daughters supposed to have a special bond? How in hell did I miss out on that?

He knew the answer. He couldn't undo all those years.

"Or we could stay home. Play a game of chess. You used to like that."

He studied her impassive expression. He could get reads on some of the most elusive terrorists around the globe. But he could never get a good read on his own daughter.

"You're trying too hard to be superdad." She shot up, headed toward the front door, looked back. "Busy studying for finals."

And with that, she was gone.

♀ ♂

Bailey caught the Fairfax County school bus at the usual corner with seconds to spare. She spotted her best friend, Ling, near the back and sat down next to her.

They picked up where they'd left off last night. They'd watched *America's Got Talent* on TV while they hung out on a video chat and debated the merits of each contestant. Ling rose and gave an awkward little shimmy, imitating one of the finalists. They burst out laughing.

The bus screeched to a sudden halt. Bailey nearly fell into the aisle.

They were only halfway to school. *Maybe there was an accident?* Bailey thought.

Bailey heard men's voices shouting from outside in front of the bus. The bus driver raised his hands then slowly lowered his right hand to open the doors. Two men dressed like commandos rushed into the bus and pointed submachine guns at everyone.

The bus had about thirty students on board. The kids started to scream and panic.

"Shut up and nobody gets hurt!" one shouted.

A third attacker entered. He looked like the others, wearing a black ski mask and black coveralls—except for one difference. Atop his partial ski mask he was wearing a pair of glasses.

He moved down the row of seats, studying the faces of each passenger. He stopped two seats in front of her and looked at Piper Matthews, captain of the Annandale Atoms cheerleading squad. He raised his head, as if comparing Piper's face with something he was seeing with his glasses.

"You. Out now!"

He pointed the weapon at her and signaled for one of his men to grab her. Piper disappeared down the steps of the bus, shaking and crying as she went.

He continued down the aisle. "Target one obtained," he said. It looked like he was talking with someone, but she didn't see any phone or device.

He moved slowly, pausing in front of the girls but not the guys. He stopped as he reached her and Ling. Bailey felt a chill pass through her as she avoided eye contact. *No, please no.*

He paused again, checking something reflected on his glasses as if to make sure he was taking the right hostages.

He pointed his gun at Ling. "You."

And then at Bailey. "And you. Move."

He jabbed the assault rifle into her back to move faster, and she exited the side of the bus. As she reached the bottom step, she saw the kidnappers string a white collar around Piper's neck and push her into a van.

The lead attacker walked away from the bus and shielded his mouth with his palm. He was almost out of earshot, but it sounded like he said, "Lucid, you're breaking up. Packages en route."

One of the men grabbed and held Bailey's arms from behind. The lead attacker returned and fished something from his pocket. He draped the white neckband over her head and clasped it from behind her neck. As he slipped it on, it began to glow and she realized what it was. An electric collar.

4

Brooklyn and Long Island

Kaden emerged from the Southampton Village Police Department still in shock. Detectives questioned her for hours, and she let them download her video footage of Bear Man. She slid into Nico's car still wearing her torn dress, and they drove her back to Brooklyn with her friends Annika and Sayeed in the back seat.

"You don't have to say anything," Nico told her. He was her best friend and knew when to give her space.

Usually his car overflowed with nonstop chatter about their work together at B Collective. They still had a lot to figure out about their new consultancy, but today they all kept silent during the long drive back on Sunrise Highway.

Nico parked and the four made their way up the steep stairwell to Kaden's third-floor flat. They found the door ajar. She pushed it open and stared at the shambles. Overturned furniture, desk drawers open, clothes and personal items strewn on the ground.

"Damn," Nico said. "I thought this was a safe neighborhood."

"It is," she said.

"We should call the police." Annika stepped over a pile of smashed picture frames.

"No." Kaden shook her head. "I can't deal with any more police today."

"All right," Nico said. "We'll help you clean up, then."

They went to work, clearing the glass from the floor, righting the sofa and chairs, organizing the scattered clothes into little folded piles. Kaden kicked herself for spending every waking moment on Amelia rather than setting up a home security system for her apartment.

"Where's your laptop?" Annika asked.

"At work." She kept no sensitive files on her laptop, so no need to go rushing off to B Collective.

They sat on the sofa and chairs while she changed into jeans and a black Semper Femina T-shirt. She returned, sank to her knees, and found the research notebooks she'd been compiling about her late mother's life with the goal of unearthing some clues about her own identity.

That was the plan. Until last night.

They checked the room for surveillance devices, but it came up clean. Nico pressed the play button on her stereo to see if it still worked. The Housemartins' "Happy Hour" filled the irony gap in the room. It would also drown out any bugs.

Kaden plunked down on her Moroccan fringe rug. "I'm ready to talk."

She recounted the Southampton gala step by step, from the moment she and Gabriel got out of their ride share. She told them about the two assailants who targeted her and their attempt to drug her and escape into the darkness.

"I should have let them take me. Gabriel would still be alive."

"You did nothing wrong. You fought back." Sayeed leaned forward in her ratty armchair. "They could have killed you."

Kaden shook her head. "The big one with the Browning, he had me dead to rights. They must have had orders to capture, not kill me."

She saw Amelia had a message for her. So she maximized her and Amelia appeared in the kitchen doorframe, though only Kaden could see her with her special contacts. She'd given Amelia standing directions to provide updates.

"Amelia, on speaker," Kaden directed.

A moment later, Amelia's voice broke into the Housemartins and came tumbling out of the speakers. Kaden had already clued in the crew about her personal AI, so nobody freaked out.

"Hi everyone, Amelia here. I took a cue from Kaden and had a peek in the Southampton police precinct's active crimes database. They have a digital portrait of one culprit. Sending it to your phones."

Their phones pinged with the new message. Kaden examined the enhanced image of Bear Man captured from her smart contacts. She'd spent minutes trying to revive Gabriel's lifeless body while the two assailants slipped away.

"So far no suspects identified," Amelia reported. "They think the perp used an alias at the party and he's a ghost. Am I getting these terms right, Kaden? Such a long way from my reality."

"You're doing fine."

"Do you think this could be related to the Disappearance?" Annika asked the question that must have crossed everyone's mind. That quieted the room.

"It's been almost six months since they were taken," Nico pointed out.

Everyone had a theory about the Disappearance. The exact number was in dispute, but hundreds of girls disappeared off the streets of America, all between the ages of sixteen to nineteen, all on the same day. Most simply vanished. Heavily armed operatives took others.

"Kaden is four years older than the oldest girl taken, but otherwise she fits the profile." Annika looked somber. "Maybe there's another wave of abductions coming."

The room went quiet again, the music gone. But for Kaden, a distant thunder rang in her ears. The sound of the gunshot that killed Gabriel.

"Why do you think they did this, Kaden?" Nico asked. "Why tear apart your apartment? Why try to abduct you?"

She had no idea what they were after. Was it for something she had? Something she knew? Something she'd done? And why didn't Bear Man just shoot her instead of Gabriel? Gabriel didn't deserve this.

"I don't know. But we're not leaving it to the police to find out."

They began to speculate again but didn't come to a consensus on the next steps they should take.

Kaden's phone pinged with a new text. Amelia again? She picked it up and peered at the message on screen.

"Meet me in 20 minutes at the address below. Come alone. No AI. I know who killed your friend."

5

Samana Cay

A lex Wyatt closed his eyes as the Embraer E-Jet pilot announced, "We have begun our initial descent into Samana Cay International." This was one secretive little island, and he was determined to blow the lid off the place.

The government of the Bahamas had surprised the world a few years ago by selling this small, uninhabited island to a secretive business consortium. The price tag ran into the billions—more than 300 times the sales price of the Louisiana Purchase for property 50,000 times smaller, as one wag put it.

The idea was controversial at first, but the Bahamas already rented out entire islands to major cruise lines. In the end, the decision to peel off and sell one outlying island out of 700 in the commonwealth proved popular when it put more than half a year's salary into the pockets of every Bahamian citizen.

As soon as the paperwork was finalized, the acquirers declared the island to be the world's newest independent nation: the Free Republic of Samana Cay.

The island's theme parks, shops, and markets had been open

for the past year, but today marked the "soft launch" of the island's most audacious venture, Fantasy Live. Trouble was, the press and public were not invited. Only high rollers lured by what some were calling a real-life Fantasy Island.

The wheels of the private charter jet touched down on the island's short runway. Alex switched off airplane mode and called his editor.

"Just touched down," he reported. He was half-sure they'd stop him at Customs and send him packing when they learned his real identity.

"Good." Alice Wong's voice came through crystal clear on the encrypted line. "Let me know if you make it through security."

"Will do."

"You probably haven't heard yet. About the incident with your friend Kaden last night."

"No, what about Kaden?"

"There was a shooting."

He bolted upright. "Is she all right?"

"Yeah. We're still trying to piece it together."

"Let me know when you find out anything."

"Will do. And be careful, Alex. I mean, Andrew Bayless." His new alias.

"I will. Talk soon." He disconnected the call and tried to reach Kaden. No answer. He sent her a text.

He wasn't sure his investigative project would get the green light from the powers that be at *Axom*, the online news site in Miami where he was a senior correspondent. But he was the golden boy of the staff now. There was even talk of a possible Pulitzer after his video dispatches exposed the wrongdoing at Birthrights Unlimited in Dallas, thanks in no small part to Kaden Baker.

After Dallas, he figured he'd go for another home run. So he crafted a forty-page memo proposing an undercover assignment —a first-person series looking at the new Fantasy Live Resort.

Until now, it was a story for the business press and the tabloids, with salacious rumors about millionaire guests soon being able to play out their wildest fantasies. A playground for the ultra-rich.

"You have a crumb." The woman seated in the leather seat next to him reached out with a silk handkerchief and flicked it off the lapel of his $900 light blue leisure suit. A suit triple the cost of the priciest outfit in his closet at home.

"Thank you." Alex had been been wondering about her. "You going to Fantasy Live, by any chance?"

"I think we all are."

"I couldn't help but notice that men outnumber women on this flight about five to one."

"Fantasies come in all genders. Mr. ....?"

Alex nearly blurted out his real name but caught himself. "Andrew Bayless."

They shook hands. "Evelyn Gladstone." She was mid-forties or so and wore a tropics-ready sundress and a Panama hat above curls of ginger hair. "I'm teasing you, Andrew. I'm sure you're well aware women have fantasies, too."

"So I've been told."

He made a mental note to ask about her experience by week's end so they could compare how their fantasy storylines played out.

"What do you do, Andrew?"

"I run a machine learning startup in Silicon Valley. And yes, it's as boring as it sounds. You?" He didn't want to invite too many questions about Andrew Bayless's work.

"Got you beat. Commodities. And what brings a handsome young man like yourself to a fantasy theme park?"

"I'm here to check out the technology."

"That's a good one." She smiled and gathered her things to deplane.

The jet finished taxiing. The pilot turned off the seatbelt sign. Alex collected his carry-on and stood to grab his suitcase.

He'd packed light—partly because *Axom*'s budget for this project only went so far when it came to his sartorial tastes. Fortunately, most startup founders weren't exactly fashion mavens.

Alex counted himself lucky that *Axom*'s owner was one of the good billionaires, willing to fund public interest journalism and willing to let his team use some old-fashioned muckraking methods to uncover the truth about this weird little flyspeck of an island close to company headquarters in Miami.

Besides the deep pockets of *Axom*'s owner, the last thing he needed to pull this off was to create a new identity. Kaden agreed to help. She and her colleagues got behind the plan, fabricated a Real ID for him, and created an elaborate backstory. It included a corporate website, social media accounts, fake online news coverage, medical records—the whole shebang. She also scrubbed hundreds of photos of him as Alex Wyatt from his social media accounts.

Alex followed Evelyn Gladstone down the jet's metal stairs onto the tarmac's red carpet and into the mild morning heat. He counted fifty-two passengers on their flight. At twenty-nine, he was undoubtedly the youngest.

They approached the small terminal and Evelyn gestured toward the sleek sign above the main doorway: "Welcome to Samana Cay, Land of Unlimited Fantasies."

Alex smiled and nodded. "Yeah, we'll see about that."

Ten small lines formed, with guards reviewing each guest's passport or Real ID. The lines moved quickly. After all, the Fantasy Live people conducted extensive background checks before any guests boarded their flight. Evelyn scooted into a faster-moving line at the far end.

When he made it to the front of his queue, he noticed a bright red line on the ground that ran the length of the terminal. Small metal stands held signs reading, "No conformity past this line."

Alex stepped forward to the guard's desk. He began to sweat under his jacket, nervous about whether he'd make it through.

Unlike the usual Customs station, where bored agents ushered through nonstop throngs of tourists, this seemed to be a more high-tech approach. The guard passed his suitcase through a magnetic imaging scanner. Then he looked at Alex, examined his ID, and asked him to step in front of a camera to have his photo taken.

Alex peeked around the monitor and saw that his photo was being compared to the image on his Real ID.

"Facial recognition?" Alex asked.

"Latest and greatest," the guard said. He compared Alex's face to the face on his screen one final time, then handed him back his ID. "Have a nice stay."

Steps beyond the guard's desk, an attractive, dark-haired woman fixed him with a steady gaze. She wore a stylish tropical print knit halter dress and strappy taupe-colored sandals. She stepped forward, gave a broad smile, and extended her hand.

"Mr. Andrew Bayless? Welcome to Samana Cay. My name is Rachel Torres. I'll be your personal ambassador during your stay."

Alex Wyatt smiled. He was in.

6

Brooklyn

K aden stared at her phone and recognized the address in the text message. It was her favorite shooting range in the Woodhaven section of Brooklyn.

How did they know I hang out there? They've been following me.

She told Nico, Annika, and Sayeed she needed to leave for an hour to run down a lead. Her friends volunteered to stay and help clean up the mess in her apartment. She took her Beretta M9, but she removed her smart contacts, so no Amelia.

She grabbed a ride share to the range, showed her range card, and booked an hour slot. Her Twilight SVLK-14S sniper rifle was still in the possession of the Dallas police, so she picked out a long-range rifle to rent.

She slipped the magazine into her pouch and headed to the farthest lane. Only two other shooters were on the range; it looked like a father teaching his teenage son how to shoot. She set up, mounted her semi-auto rifle on a rest, and began with a few test rounds to set the zero on her scope. She used the adjustment knobs to recalibrate. This scope was a little fussy.

The door opened and a lone figure entered the range. He looked to be in his mid-forties with handsome, chiseled features, dark brown hair flared with gray, and a fit physique. He looked haggard, though. Not getting enough sleep. He wore a casual shirt and slacks and carried a blue blazer, which he folded neatly over the railing behind them.

He set up in the lane next to her, loading what Kaden recognized as a Ruger Mark IV rimfire pistol. The firearm was designed with a seamless barrel suppressor, with the silencer built in. Pretty wicked, but out of her price range—and illegal in New York state. Maybe he was from out of state. Or maybe he didn't care.

He put on his eye and ear protection and aimed at the target. *Pup-pup-pup*, three quick shots. He reeled in the target. All three shots were within three inches of the bullseye.

He removed his ear covering and spoke in a low voice without looking at her. "I'll get to your questions. Listen first. What I'm about to tell you will sound … out there. That's good. You need your B.S. detector turned up to eleven."

He set up a new paper target and sent it out.

"For eighteen years I was a field operative for an off-book field division of a government agency you've never heard of."

"Try me."

"It's too early for that."

She studied his face, trying to decide whether this guy was legit, a master hoax artist, or maybe flat-out crazy. He glanced at her and picked up on her furrowed brow.

He scowled in return, retrieved his phone from his folded jacket on the railing, and held up a photo. "This the man who shot your friend?"

She recognized the face of the attacker. *Bear Man.* A sharp pain shot through her heart and her body gave an involuntary shudder.

"That's him. He gave his name as Wojcik."

"He won't turn up in any local police database. His real name is Dražen Savić. He's a mid-level operative for a transnational cabal we've been tracking for over a year. It's basically a shadowy confederation of billionaire thugs."

That photo jolted her into a different mindset. This guy was the real deal.

"How'd you ID him in less than a day?"

"We're a small outfit but we can access almost anything." He aimed his Ruger with the stance of a professional marksman. "The real question is, what did they want with you?"

Kaden was about to ask him the same question. *What would they want with me?* Sounded like he agreed with her hunch that they were after her and Gabriel was an unintended casualty.

"No idea."

"You must have something they want. Could be something you don't know you have."

He fired off five rounds. He reeled in his target and she saw he'd laid down a tight grouping around the bullseye.

"Could it have to do with the digital stash you stole from Randolph Blackburn?"

That rocked her. "How do you know about my grandfather? And the files we hacked?"

"Blackburn has been on our radar for a very long time. We think he washes some of this group's dirty money." He paused, as if unsure whether to say more. "We find out things. Sometimes we act. Sometimes we let it play out."

"How do I fit into any of this?" She fired her Beretta at her target.

He sent out a new bullseye and fired four more rounds. "You're in the crosshairs of the Department of Justice, Kaden. You killed a very powerful man when you rescued those girls in Dallas."

She lowered her weapon, paying close attention to what this guy was telling her. She was still waiting to hear whether the D.A. would bring charges against her for the Dallas shooting.

"Local authorities decided not to bring charges," he said. "But someone bumped your case up to the feds. They can gin up charges if they want, trust me."

"Why would they?"

"Because you shot a man who was very useful to this shadowy group. We don't know much about them, but we know they have their hooks into members of Congress and the current administration."

"Even the Justice Department?"

He looked at the father and son practicing and saw they were still out of earshot. His eyes traced the top and rear of the gallery, maybe looking for listening devices.

"The vast majority of federal prosecutors follow the law, old school style. But this administration placed some political appointees in key positions at Justice."

"So I'm in trouble?"

"You've made enemies. It could go either way. If we move fast, a plea deal should fly with the faction I'm working with."

A plea deal? Last night I was getting an award for rescuing those women.

"The basics are this: You plead guilty in a closed federal court hearing to transporting a firearm across state lines for an unlawful purpose."

"But it wasn't unlawful."

"Forget the law. I'm trying to save you from a trial. Possible prison time. The plea and sentence will be sealed. Nobody will ever know it's on your record. You'll serve no time."

"What's the catch?"

"In return, you work for me. Not on payroll. You'll be an off-the-books, off-the-grid contractor. A ghost. We need someone with your skill set. We'll make it look like you've lost your job to fend off the black hats at Justice."

"Why me? What do you want with me?"

"We saw how you carried out your covert ops. How you

brought down that entire criminal enterprise in Dallas. We've been impressed by both your hacking and field work—a rare combination."

So far it didn't sound too appealing. Cop a plea. Quit her job.

"Work for you … doing what?"

"Intelligence gathering, mostly. Depends on the day."

"And if I say no?"

"You'll be fighting a war on two fronts. One front against a hard-ass segment of the Justice Department hell-bent on getting you behind bars. A second front against a shadow organization with global reach. Trust me, Dražen Savić is not the last operative they'll send for you."

She needed more than this. "What's your name?"

"I should go."

He turned, unloaded his weapon, grabbed his jacket, and hurried out the door.

Leaving her with a million more questions.

7

Minsk, Belarus, present day

According to legend, no living person had ever seen his face. No photograph of him was known to exist. Rumors flew that he'd been in a terrible accident as a young man. Even in his own companies, people speculated whether he was man or myth.

He gunned the engine of his Harley-Davidson FXDR 114 and took the sweeping curve onto the M5 highway at double the speed limit as he left the city limits of Minsk. He watched the digital dashboard as he kicked up his bike to the maximum speed, 160 mph. Truckers gave him a salute—half were thumbs ups, half were middle fingers—as the brass-balls rider in the black-onyx visor and helmet flamed past each obstacle in his way.

His mind wandered to the nickname he had as a teen. *The boy with no face.* He had a real name, all but forgotten now. Maxim Volkov. Second son in a powerful family in Belarus. But anyone who had ever called him by the name Volkov was dead or gone. He had long ago assumed a new identity, Incognito. His name mattered less than his preordained mission.

Soon I'll be known as the most important figure of the modern era. Strange how a mother's flash of blind rage could alter not just one boy's life but the trajectory of the world.

Volkov felt a giddy, exhilarating thrill begin to surge through his body. History might well mark today as the beginning of the Transition, paving the way for the Reset. Everything we knew about the power of nations was about to change.

"Chairman Incognito." The soothing voice of his virtual assistant Liv came over the speakers lining his motorcycle helmet. "Lucid is ready for your weekly check-in."

"Patch him through."

He called up Lucid's Eyecast on the high-tech screen on his visor. Volkov saw Lucid sitting in an executive suite aboard the luxury superyacht *Seaduction.* The vessel was on loan from the same member of the Compact who'd loaned them use of a submarine a year ago.

Virtual meetings with the man who ran his day-to-day operations put Volkov at a distinct advantage. On screen one, he watched a video livestream of Lucid and his surroundings. On screen two, he could also see what Lucid was looking at through his artificial eye. It was like being inside the man's head. Lucid, on the other hand, saw only an avatar of Incognito.

"Good afternoon, Chairman. I'm en route to meet the first arriving guests."

"Excellent news," Volkov allowed.

Today marked the soft launch of their epic leap forward that promised to revolutionize augmented reality. To take it to a place no one had dared before. And to lure more visitors to Samana Cay.

"Indeed, Chairman. No last-minute hitches with Fantasy Live. I'll keep you apprised. Unless you have any questions, only two items on our agenda. The Summit on Friday. And the Phase One rollout of our grand project."

"Let's start with the Summit. Do you have a recommendation?"

"I do. If I may speak freely."

"Continue." Volkov smiled as he watched this unfold on his visor's screen. Volkov inside Lucid's head watching Volkov's avatar watching Lucid.

Almost godlike.

Lucid fidgeted and peered out the window as the ship churned through the tropical lagoon. "I think it may be to our advantage if you showed up to the Summit in person."

The words brushed Volkov back like the cold Belarusian fall air pummeling his Titan sport jacket. He had not attended an in-person meeting since his youth. Not with anyone. A knot of tension laced through his neck and back muscles. *Attend in person? Impossible!*

"I'm thinking of our global strategy." Lucid was speaking again, straining for the right words. "This is the first time members of the Compact have ever gathered in one place. From their perspective, it might seem ... *off-putting* if they showed up in person and you, Chairman Incognito—the convener of the Compact, architect of the Seven Spheres—did not."

Volkov usually went with his first gut reaction, and his gut told him this was out of the question. *I've built a larger-than-life legend by remaining anonymous. My entire persona, my entire way of presenting myself to the world—why, it was built on my being incognito! Meeting others in the flesh would destroy the myth I've spent a lifetime perfecting. There was no setting in which he would press the flesh or agree to be seen and judged by his fellow billionaires in the Compact.*

"My dear Lucid. You and I have met face to face only once. And yet we've worked out a mutually advantageous arrangement. We trust each other. Do we not?"

"Yes, but—"

"You and I manage to speak every day and communicate well with our virtual set-up, do we not?"

"This is different."

"I disagree!" he bellowed. His Harley nearly side-swiped a turnip truck. He slowed down so he could focus on his video chat. "I will not subject myself to the judgments of ordinary men. Not when I'm the one executing the events that will reshape our planet."

"Of course, Chairman."

He dialed it back. Lucid was his chief operating officer and longtime top lieutenant—and a steadfastly loyal one. "I'm open to flying to the Summit. Let's consider the cloaking safeguards we've been developing."

"Very well, Chairman."

He hunkered down closer to the snarling powertrain between his legs. As the head of a global multibillion-dollar enterprise, he spent most days indoors, so he relished his sprints on his sport bike—the machine was one part drag racer, one part fighter jet.

"Next item."

"Good news from the Lab. After many months of setbacks, Bashir has perfected the delivery mechanism."

"That's been the key holdup, hasn't it?"

"Indeed. The lab coats have been working around the clock to devise a biological agent with all the requisite properties. The clinical trials have now begun."

"Superb news."

"Chairman, our contractors are ready to go. We only await your signal for us to execute the plan."

"We have been building toward this day for a long time, Lucid. Execute. Go forth and lay the groundwork. Our enemy will never know what hit them."

"Very good, sir. There's no doubt the new era is about to unfold."

He saw on the screen that Lucid's yacht was pulling into the marina near the airport.

"I need to attend to our new guests." Lucid rose, ready to leave. "Anything else?"

"One final item. One unfinished piece of business that could jeopardize our plans." He gunned the motor again, roaring to a dizzying speed on the open road before him.

"Kaden Baker. Bring her to me. Do not fail this time."

8

Brooklyn

Kaden left the gun range and headed to the B Collective workspace. Her friends had left her apartment and gone back to work, and they all were expecting her to take a few days off. But she'd rather put her grief into action.

She did client work for a few hours and then talked Nico into hitting the kickboxing ring at the gym down the street. She had things to work out, and there was nothing like a few bracing rounds to get the blood flowing and focus the mind.

Nico was nearly her equal in the ring now. He sent her sprawling with a wicked side kick to her left rib cage.

She sprung to her feet and came at him. "Again," she said.

She assumed a street defense stance. They traded blows. She needed to hit something. She pictured Nico as a stand-in for the thug who attacked her and shot Gabriel.

For the past two months, Gabriel was the reason the light was returning to her eyes. She'd grown up in a dysfunctional household. She'd learned only a few weeks ago that she was adopted, and her fake parents had raised her for a paycheck while spying on her for years.

Gabriel had nudged her closer to a normal life where people laughed and loved and didn't have ulterior motives. She'd been almost ready to start her life again. Now? Normal was on hold.

During the hour, she got in two knockdowns, Nico three. Then they showered and returned to their workspace. Nico, Annika, and Sayeed spent the afternoon helping her try to turn up anything on Dražen Savić or whatever outfit he might work for. They were careful to cover their tracks while searching, but they couldn't find a trace of him.

Near the end of the afternoon, a text message pinged her phone: "20:00. 40.656104, -74.007181, 120 z. Leave the AI." She understood. No signature, but she'd figured the gun range mystery man would be in touch.

She finished some busywork, grabbed a yogurt from the fridge, then brought up the map on her phone since she wouldn't be bringing her Eyewear. The coordinates showed an office building in a trendy tech startup section of town.

She'd leave her AI, but she brought her Beretta in case this guy was connected to Bear Man.

At eight o'clock Kaden stood in front of a rehabbed office building along the waterfront in Brooklyn's Industry City neighborhood. She entered the main doors and checked in at the security desk. The tower was an older low-rise, so no metal scanner. The guard didn't look up, absorbed in his Danielle Steel novel. She spotted the glass elevators. She figured the z in her text referred to the third coordinate in a three-dimensional space. So she eyeballed the height of the lobby and each floor, entered the elevator, and pushed floor nine.

As she rode up, she looked out at all the shiny new tech toys and colorful, expensive office furniture in the startup offices on each floor. She got off at the ninth floor. Her phone showed an elevation of 120 feet.

She stepped across a large barren room, its wooden floor choked with dust and debris. Ramshackle blinds streaked with spider webs blotted out the setting sun. She must have messed up. *This can't be right.* She drew her Beretta, just in case.

She heard movement toward a back room and headed that way. "Hello? Anybody here?"

No reply. She saw a light coming from under the far door so she entered.

The room was bare of any human touches ... *unless you counted misery and despair.* A stale odor hung in the air. Rows of empty desks. Papers strewn on the floor. Two oversize wall hangings with smashed glass panes told of some unhappy departing tenants.

Three figures roughly her age glanced up from their keyboards before resuming their work. Kaden returned the gun to her shoulder holster beneath her fleece jacket. She must have been imagining things because she thought she glimpsed Annika disappearing into the kitchenette.

At the far side of the room, a man stood with his back to her, peering at a large digital screen. At the sound of stilled keyboards, he spun, saw her, and advanced down the center of the room. Gun Range Man.

"I'd like you to meet the crew. Carlos, Tosh, Annika, meet Kaden."

Carlos and Tosh looked up again and gave a quick nod. Annika emerged from the kitchen, juice drink in hand, and came up to her with a serious expression. She wrapped herself around Kaden and squeezed tight.

"I'm so sorry. I couldn't tell you about any of my government work."

"How ... how long?"

"Since July."

She'd noticed Annika had been spending less time at B Collective. *But doing spy work for the government? Jesus!*

Gun Range Man approached through this health inspector's nightmare of an office space. "Well?"

Kaden's eyes swept the rest of the room. "This is it? This is your big-time global crime fighting headquarters?"

"You were expecting the Situation Room?" Tosh shot out without looking up.

Gun Range Man frowned. "We don't need frills. We run lean and we move around a lot."

"I was expecting a bigger team."

"We have assets in the field."

Now she was even more dubious. After a lifetime of secrets and lies and hidden agendas, did she really want to join a spy outfit?

"No more games," she demanded. "You seem to know a lot about me. What's your name?"

"That's not important."

Still stonewalling!

"Oh, Bo, just tell her your freaking name," Annika chided.

"It's Bo." He flashed a sideways smile.

"All right, Bo," Kaden said. "Just to be upfront, I'm not gonna join your team. But I'll hear you out."

"Fair enough." He started across the room. "We brought in the big screen tonight to show you what we're up against."

She and Annika followed and leaned against a desk ten feet from the large monitor mounted on the wall. Carlos and Tosh looked up to watch Bo's presentation, too.

Bo swiped with his right palm and the screen filled with a 3D animated globe that slowly rotated. The outlines of nations and cities appeared. Riyadh, Belgrade, Belarus, Moscow, Chechnya all were glowing bright red.

"What I'm about to show you doesn't leave this room—not that anyone would believe you. Agreed?"

"Sure."

"Agreed?"

"Yeah!"

"We're in a war, Kaden. Not the stuff of history books with great armies and naval and air power. It's a war of disinformation. A stealth war with unseen forces gathering strength. The players are not our usual enemies on the world stage. The enemy consists of oligarchs and oil barons, billionaire cartels and syndicates that control vast wealth and influence. We now live in an age when a single billionaire in the shadows wields more power than a hundred nation states."

She crossed her arms and nodded. She was no conspiracy theorist, but she had no doubt forces behind the scenes were shaping world events.

"We don't know all the players or what they're after. What we do know is their track record. Money laundering, human trafficking, child pornography, black market arms dealing, murder of political opponents. They use dark money to exert deep influence on the levers of power in the U.S. and the West. But the threat has escalated."

"Escalated how?" she asked.

Bo swiped right. The slide filled with images of nuclear facilities, power grids, reservoirs, and other potential targets.

"They've infiltrated the top ranks of western governments. They're turning off the eyes and ears of our intelligence services. The black hats in the Justice Department I mentioned? That's only part of the story. NSA, CIA, nearly every national security agency has been compromised in some way."

She'd heard rumors in the online forums. But she never imagined things were this bad. "What in hell can we do about it?"

Bo's face grew darker. "Two weeks ago, a high-value asset crossed the border in Belarus and asked for political asylum at the U.S. embassy in Lithuania. The walk-in provided actionable intelligence about one event in particular. The Disappearance."

Kaden nodded. She felt sorry for those girls and the families. But it didn't affect her.

Bo swiped. The screen filled with disturbing images of women being rescued from sex slave rings and human trafficking cartels.

"We need your help, Kaden. In finding these girls, bringing them home."

Bo stopped swiping and turned to gauge Kaden's reaction.

"Why isn't the CIA or FBI doing something about this?" Kaden asked.

"In the past, that would be happening. But the world has changed. The U.S. shuttering foreign embassies. Intelligence agencies truncating overseas sources to save a few dollars. Allies refusing to swap sensitive intelligence with the their U.S. counterparts. The security agencies are flying half blind while focusing on the president's priorities. Following up on every lead about the Disappearance is not their top priority."

This was a lot to take in. Much as she wanted to see Bo and his team kick the asses of these Mafia types, she had a hard time seeing herself upend her life and join the front lines. Sending Dražen Savić to an early grave was *her* priority.

"So instead of sending in CIA Special Operations, saving the free world falls to a ragtag band of geeks and off-book intelligence agents?" Kaden rose from the desk and scanned everyone's faces. "Is that about right?"

Tosh and Carlos looked at each other.

"Yeah," Tosh said.

"She kind of nailed it," Carlos added.

Bo glared at them, then turned to her. "We've been fighting dark forces for a long time, in the background, with no thought of being thanked. But there's a storm gathering and we need all hands on deck. Someone's got to go find these girls. Kaden, are you with us?"

She looked him in the eye, this man named Bo with his sharpshooter skills and his team of diehard tech warriors and his stirring call to save democracy and rescue those missing girls.

"That was a pretty speech. But look, you have me pegged wrong. I'm after the guys who came after me and killed Gabriel."

She turned without looking at Annika or the others. She couldn't take their judgment right now. She padded out of the room and across the barren wasteland of the next room. She reached the elevator and pressed the down button when she heard footsteps behind her.

Bo said, "You're making a mistake. We had a deal."

"I never agreed. I said I'd hear you out."

"And you're dead set on not joining us?"

"Yeah. Pretty much."

The elevator door opened. Bo stretched his arm out to block her from getting on.

"You're stubborn as hell. Just like your father," he said.

That startled her. "You didn't know my father."

"I barely remember that man, it was such a long time ago. But yeah. I knew him."

He looked back into the other room to make sure no one was within earshot. Then he turned back to her.

"Kid, I'm your dad."

9

Samana Cay

A bracing sea breeze billowed Alex Wyatt's golden hair as he steered the 282-foot luxury yacht *Seaduction* from the airfield marina toward the island's main harbor of Samana Village. About half the passengers from the flight were on board, including this odd duck Lucid who seemed to be running the show.

"You sure this is okay?" he yelled above the engine's growl. "First time driving a boat."

"Don't get deflated, Andrew, but she's a smartship." Rachel Torres offered him a plastic cup filled with rum punch. "You couldn't crash her even if you wanted to."

"Well, in that case." Alex took the drink from her hand and polished it off. The ship was all but running on its own, following the satellite-guided itinerary on the panel in front of him. The controls showed nearby vessels' size, speed, and course. All clear ahead.

"Is Rachel your real name?" He'd need to know for his story.

"It's my real name on Samana Cay."

Well, that was a great dodge, he thought. He was still trying to get a read on her. "You from around here?" He guessed Spain or Mexico by her accent.

"No, not from around here. But I got my citizen papers last week."

Ah, yes, the New Republic of Samana Cay.

The opulent resort and theme parks were a shot across the bow at nearby Paradise Island in the Bahamas with its lavish Atlantis and Baha Mar compounds. Only three countries dared recognize Samana Cay's sovereignty after it declared independence. The rest of the world had no reason to poke a stick at the United States, which was wary of this weird little potential troublemaker that joined the neighborhood.

Lucid came up from below deck and approached them. "Mr. Bayless, welcome to our humble retreat. I trust Rachel is treating you right."

"She's a superb ambassador."

"Not only an ambassador. She's our head of hospitality. I hope you'll take advantage of the many amenities we offer during your stay." He gestured toward a large promontory jutting out from the cliffs up to their left. "Just behind our race track you can see the edge of War Games Valley. For those who missed out on the real thing and want a real-life simulation on the battlefield."

"Sounds interesting." Actually, it sounded awful, but he was here to get the flavor of the place in all its over-the-top virtual excesses.

Rachel slipped on her shades and poked around in her satchel. She produced an eyeglass case, opened it, and handed him a pair of glasses. "Here's your Eyewear. Titanium Dita Mach glasses. Please keep them on during your island tour. You'll have the option to swap them out when you arrive."

They were the latest-generation smartglasses with miniature audio speakers embedded in the earpiece. He looked them over and slipped them on. "Perfect fit!" Not surprising, given the facial measurements he'd sent them. Within seconds the lenses darkened into sunglasses to ward off the tropical sun.

He turned back to the wheel when an enormous sailfish flew out of the water a dozen feet off the ship's bow and landed with a thundering splash. *My God! That thing had to be thirty feet long!*

He spun to face them "Did you see that? Was that real?"

Rachel let out a high-pitched laugh. "Was it?"

"Man!" Alex held up his empty cup. "What was in that drink?"

"I saw it, too." Lucid gave his shoulder a comforting you're-not-going-crazy pat.

The enormous yacht shifted into a lower speed on its own as the marina came into view. The ship parked itself next to the pier, two deck hands tied the ropes to the dock pilings, and they hopped off. Lucid led the procession.

At the end of the pier, Alex saw the hillside rise to a plateau high above the waterline. He figured they'd have to climb a steep hill or staircase. Instead, he saw a long escalator at the bottom with a sturdy tentlike fabric covering patterned with tropical flowers.

"Stairway to heaven!" one of the guests shouted.

They stepped aboard and took in the spectacular view of the aquamarine bays and lagoons. The scent of hibiscus wafted through the tropical air.

They emerged in the middle of a long promenade. As they moved through the crowd, blue and orange butterflies with six-inch wingspans fluttered above them. Virtual pets walked beside their owners—dogs with gold fur, kittens in rainbow colors. Princesses, unicorns, and bunnies frolicked amid the bushes lining the walkway. *This is what Alice in Wonderland must have felt like.*

"Nice unicorns," Alex said.

Rachel stopped in her tracks, came up to his face, inspected his Eyewear, and made an adjustment. "Sorry! You were in Little Girl Mode. You should be synced correctly now."

The scene took on a different feel now. Less fanciful, more imposing. Off to the right, a Ferris wheel soared to an enormous height, disappearing behind a patch of clouds. Zombies lurked on a nearby hillside. In the distance, a flying saucer shot laser beams at a Godzilla-like monster.

Lucid steered the group onto a side walkway with cute little storefronts. He went up to a window and spoke to the elderly proprietor in bright Caribbean garb. The man looked over the group of new arrivals and nodded. A moment later, the man opened the door to his shop and ushered the group in.

"What's this for?" Alex asked.

"All new arrivals get chipped," Rachel said. "Don't worry, it's painless and temporary."

He wasn't wild about the idea, but when it was his turn at the counter, he held out his right hand and watched as the shop owner inserted a thin microchip into the fleshy part between his left thumb and index finger. *This will make good color for the story.*

"Congrats." Rachel inspected his hand. "You're now a chipper."

"Haven't heard much about these things." His palm felt sore, but it wasn't bleeding.

"You'll find it's a convenient way to get around. They're all the rage in Scandinavia. People like the convenience of starting their cars, storing medical information, paying for items with the wave of their hand. Did you know Sweden's national rail network has been biochip-capable since 2015?"

"We're not in Sweden."

"You'll see how they're used on the island."

Soon they were out the door and back on the main plaza. Hundreds of tourists mobbed the granite plazas, gawking at high-end merchandise in shop windows or zipping around on Segways. Just ahead of them, a masked figure atop a hoverboard approached, shooting flames into the sky. The figure lowered his bazooka-like weapon and aimed. A burst of fireballs hurtled toward them.

"Get down!" Alex yelled and yanked Rachel to the ground out of the line of fire.

As they crashed to the pavement, Alex's Eyewear slipped down his nose and he saw the assailant—a young boy firing an air gun.

"Quite heroic." Lucid loomed above them. He helped Rachel to her feet.

Alex rose and brushed himself off. "Well, that was a rush."

Rachel came up and brought his palm up to the side of his glasses. "You can hit the Reality Mode button on the right of your Eyewear to toggle off Fantasy Mode at any time." She held her wrist to her mouth and spoke into her bracelet to record an audio note. "May need to dial back a few things."

"But I smelled the burning embers from the flames," Alex protested.

"The bottoms of your frames have little air vents."

He removed his glasses to look closer and saw the tiny nozzles. "Sight, sound, smell. Three of the five senses. Impressive."

"Actually, all five," Lucid said. "You'll experience touch and taste during Fantasy Live."

As they resumed their trek, Alex tapped on Reality Mode to see what was real or simulated. In the center of the town square, a dozen women in bikinis paraded across the stage in a beauty contest in front of a lively crowd.

"Yes, quite real," Rachel said.

"Aren't beauty contests a little retro?" he asked.

Lucid twisted his lips into a condescending smile. "This isn't America, Mr. Bayless. There is no culture of political correctness on Samana Cay. My background is in evolutionary biology. And a basic fact of nature is that both men and women need variety.

In earlier eras, the need to procreate meant males in particular took multiple partners. It's hard-wired into our genes to propagate the species. Perhaps we're not meant to mate for life."

Alex nodded. *That outlook would make a Neanderthal blush. But it'll be great fodder for my series.*

They passed through the Maker Zone, a whimsical theme park for geeks. Creative types from the Caribbean, the Bahamas, and the world over operated arts and crafts stalls next to thirty-foot-tall metal sculptures of fire-breathing serpents and water-spouting fanged fish. As they passed through each zone, Rachel pointed out the virtual world theme parks offering glorified amusement park rides and the more elaborate immersive role-playing games.

"Almost there," Rachel said. "There's a cocktail reception in an hour followed by a brief welcome from the Chairman."

"The Chairman?"

"Chairman Incognito is the ultimate authority in our island republic."

"So I'll get to meet him?" Alex asked.

"Not exactly. You'll see."

At the next intersection, four security guards in camouflage uniforms and olive berets chatted with each other, semi-auto weapons at their sides. The lettering across the back of their uniforms read, GUARDIANS. Two blocks ahead Alex spotted another unit of military police smoking cigarettes below a bank of CCTV cameras positioned at the intersection.

"Are all these armed guards and security cameras necessary?" he asked Rachel.

"The Guardians are here for the safety of our guests. As for the cameras, they're part of our Sharp Eyes security network. Borrowed the name and the idea from the Chinese. Today crime is almost nonexistent on Samana Cay."

"Is that right? What about personal privacy?" He wasn't buying the virtues of mass surveillance.

"Statistics don't lie, Andrew. We have a different attitude toward privacy on the island. While Chinese culture equates privacy with seclusion or secrecy—a negative value—we hold a different view. You have complete privacy in your own home, but in public places, security comes first."

Lucid had been mingling with other guests further back in the procession. He rejoined the front of the line and turned to him. "Andrew, I understand we have a mutual acquaintance."

"Who's that?"

"Kaden Baker. Have you spoken with her recently?"

That rocked him. Kaden forged his identity to get him into Fantasy Live. *If Lucid knows about Kaden, it could be a big problem. Are they monitoring my texts?*

"How do you know Kaden?"

"Samana Cay supports many philanthropic organizations. Kaden was due to receive an award at one of our events last night. We need to present her with a check. In person."

"Haven't spoken with her in weeks."

"Very well. If you hear from her, let her know we need to get in touch."

That troubled him. Alex decided he'd find an ultra-secure satellite uplink to communicate with Kaden and find out what was going on.

At last they reached what looked like a gated community on the leeward side of the island. The stone pathway led to a pretty, low-slung modern wood and glass building perched atop a small hill behind a security gate. The porter and a dozen other guests behind them waited. Rachel waved her empty hand in front of an electronic touchpad. The wrought-iron gate clicked open.

"Welcome to Fantasy Live Resort," she announced.

Lucid took a step forward and shook Alex's hand. "I must take my leave. I will see you at the reception, Andrew."

Guests made their way to their luxury villas. Rachel led him to his villa suite at the end of the building. "Go ahead, wave your hand," she said.

He waved it in front of the small electronic pad where you'd expect to see a lock and keyhole. A soothing computerized voice said, "Welcome, Andrew." The door glided open.

He stepped inside. The room had an upscale tropical design with ceiling fans, marble floor, light woods, elegant wall decor, and cozy sofas and armchairs. An indoor infinity pool pressed up against floor-to-ceiling windows.

He peered through the window. "Look at that view!"

"You have a private veranda," Rachel said.

He stepped onto the patio balcony and felt a refreshing sea breeze. Turquoise waters lapped a long stretch of white sand. A dozen private cabanas lined the beach. So far he was getting mixed signals from Samana Cay: a relaxing, feel-good Bahamas vibe on the surface interlaced with Silicon Valley tech influences, Europop flavorings, and a heavy dose of Chinese authoritarianism.

Rachel moved directly in front of him. He noticed the bracelet on her wrist now glowed a light green. She took his hand in hers and positioned it on top of her left breast.

He drew back, startled, but she kept his hand in place. *Was this a test?*

"Do you know what this means?" she asked.

He felt aroused even though he knew he shouldn't. "That you like me?"

"It means I'm an Opt-In. Now, let's go to the Bliss Lounge so you can become more familiar with the Terms."

Brooklyn

Kaden followed this stranger who claimed to be her father into Big Sal's, a hole in the wall on the first floor of a brownstone one block away. The place was nearly deserted. They sat at a small square pine table toward the back.

Bo fidgeted with the menu. "I don't know what I want."

"That makes two of us. But I haven't changed my mind."

The waitress took their orders. Two coffees. Chef salad for Bo. A protein power wrap, some kind of grilled chicken and mixed greens combo, for her.

Bo frowned as he watched the only other couple in the place taking photos of their food. "Never got that. Is the food supposed to smile?" Then his expression softened and he met her eyes with a steady gaze. "I imagined this day a thousand times. It never played out this way."

Never played out this way for me, either. Until a few weeks ago, I didn't know I was adopted.

She picked up a glass of water and drank it to calm her nerves.

"Are you left-handed?" Bo watched her and picked up his glass with his left hand.

"Yeah, I am."

"You got that from me." He smiled. "Sorry, I guess."

Time to get down to business. "Why don't you start at the beginning?" she said.

He sipped from his water. "Your mother was an amazing woman. Let's start there. Beautiful, kind, funny. So full of life. I've never met anyone else like Deirdre."

"How'd you meet?" If this guy is legit, she wanted to hear more about her mother. The college friends she'd tracked down in the past month recalled only so much about her.

"I was playing beach volleyball with some buddies in Santa Monica. Deirdre was watching us with some of her female friends. They asked if they could join us." A far-away look came to his face. "I couldn't take my eyes off her."

Kaden stayed quiet, letting him finish the story.

"I was a little older, twenty-five. Flat broke. Just started working as an intelligence analyst, telecommuting from home at first. Deirdre was from another world. Living in a mansion in Bel Air. She could have had any guy she wanted."

The waitress returned and poured their coffees. Bo waited for her to leave.

"For some reason, she fell for me. She said she liked my smile." He flashed it again, that sideways thing he did with his mouth. *Yeah, I could see that.*

He went on with his story. "I only had a few weeks before I had to leave for D.C. We spent every free moment together. The chemistry was torrid—if you held up a match it'd go off.

"But we were careless—no, *I* was stupid. Didn't use protection. Deirdre missed her next period. And when she found out, she didn't hesitate, not once. She wanted to keep the baby. I offered to marry her, quit my job, stay out West. She wouldn't hear of it. Said we could always get married once you came along and things settled down for me."

She barely breathed while taking this in. It seemed plausible —the story of how she came to be. So very different from the lie her adoptive father told her about her mother sleeping around and how they didn't know who the father was.

"As you probably guessed, things never settled down. I'd fly out on holidays to see you both. But by then I was in the field on covert assignments in Europe and Asia."

She had long ago blocked out those terrible memories of the holidays during her childhood. But Bo was talking about when she was two or three, before all the drama.

"Just for the record, your name isn't on my birth certificate," she pointed out.

"It isn't?" He considered that. "I'm not surprised. Your grandfather would have arranged that."

Kaden nodded. She knew Randolph Blackburn was capable of anything. "So you knew my grandfather back then."

"Yeah. We weren't big fans of each other." He leaned forward and lowered his voice to conspiratorial level. "If you want to take a drop of blood, we could do a DNA test right now. There's got to be an app for that."

She considered his offer. Couldn't just take his word that he was her father.

"Wait, I've got something better." He reached for his wallet and pulled out a color photo. It was old and crinkled, faded like a memory. He handed it to her.

The photo showed three people in a hospital room. Her real mother was lying in a hospital bed—she recognized Deirdre from the photo she'd added to her pendant. Deirdre held a baby in her arms. Bo stood at their side with a blissful expression.

They looked ... like a real family. The kind of family she

always wanted. Still, she felt a coil of angst about this whole reunion thing, if that's what it was.

"Keep it," he said.

"You sure?"

"Yeah."

"Thanks, Bo. I'm definitely not ready to call you Dad."

His lips twisted into a wistful smile, and she thought she saw his eyes watering. He nodded.

"You said you'd be willing to get your DNA tested?"

"Yeah, sure."

"Sorry. I guess I'm not a very trusting person. Let's go ahead."

"All right."

She felt bad asking him to do that. *You're my real dad? Prove it!* But no harm in being certain. "What's your last name, anyway?"

"Finnerty."

"Finnerty." She tried it out on her tongue. "So I'm Irish?"

"Half, anyway."

She was still pulling little bits of her identity out of the air, like assembling a puzzle. She wanted to try the words out on her tongue. "I'm half Irish."

Bo smiled but kept glancing outside. The last hints of daylight spilled through the window as dusk gave way to night and the first LED street lights turned on with their halo glow.

"You looking for someone?" she asked.

"I want to make sure we're not being watched. Hard to know who to trust."

She wondered if he was being paranoid, but the attack last night proved the threat was real.

"Any idea yet of why they came after you?" he asked.

"Not really. But now I'm wondering if you're the reason."

He didn't flinch as he sipped his coffee. "Could be. I've made some powerful enemies."

"Okay. Before we go there, you were telling me about the early days. Filling in my tabula rasa."

He smiled at her stab at humor, but then his expression grew serious. "You were three when the doctors called. I was Deirdre's emergency contact. Whenever we talked, she never let on that she was sick. I was in Yemen when they called with the news. It wasn't good, Kaden. She had only a few months to live."

His voice was low now, almost inaudible over the clatter of plates coming from the kitchen.

"Took the next flight out. We talked about whether we should get married. Whether I should raise you if it came to that. Your grandfather wouldn't hear of it. I never got along with the old SOB."

"But you could have done it. If you wanted."

He still has no idea about my damaged childhood.

"I was a different person then. Spending ten months a year overseas infiltrating enemy networks. What did I know about babies? Your grandfather was already a billionaire, and you'd be his only heir. I figured the best thing for you would be if I got out of the way."

"Here you go, hon." The waitress deposited the wrap in front of her and the salad in front of Bo. "Enjoy."

Kaden looked up and smiled. "Thanks so much."

When the waitress left, Bo continued. "After she passed, I was heartbroken. Flew out for her funeral. Within a couple of weeks, Blackburn arranged for a couple to adopt you. With him being a billionaire and all, I figured you had a safe, loving home."

"Not exactly."

"Oh?" Bo looked concerned.

Now wasn't the right time to tell him. In the years after her real mom died when she was three, Kaden felt as if she was living someone else's life. Where other children had normal parents who did normal things with their kids, her adoptive parents would routinely monitor her calls, read her diary, document her traits, genetic defects, weight, and behaviors—even her menstrual cycles. She recently found out they were reporting back to Blackburn.

But she was trying to power through her past, not dwell on it.

"Let's just say I had a less than ideal childhood. Not a big deal."

He raised his body in his seat and his voice rose with him. "Good God, did they abuse you?"

She shook her head, wanting to quiet him down in this small room. "Not physically. Forget I said anything."

He settled back into his seat and poked at a cherry tomato. "Maybe I should have quit my job and married your mother. Raised you myself. What was I thinking?"

He reached his hand across the table and placed it on top of hers. She flinched and pulled her hand away. The reaction was instinctive, not passing judgment.

"It's too early for that," she said.

Bo gave a serious look and nodded. "When you were a kid, I'd think about showing up at your door. 'Hey, it's me, your real dad.' But how would that work? I was stationed abroad most of the time. I figured you could always track me down if you wanted to know your biological father."

"I never knew I was adopted."

"Really? That's not right. I wrote to your grandfather once. He wrote back saying you were doing fine, that it was time for me to move on. So I did. After a while, I met someone. Eileen, an American graduate student living in Prague. We had a whirl-wind romance—"

"Because that's how you roll." She bit her lip at letting that slip out. Unfair.

Bo just smiled. *No meanness in him.* "The marriage lasted fifteen years. We split up four years ago and she moved to New York. Overseas assignments are hell on a marriage."

Kaden nibbled on her wrap but wasn't all that hungry. "So how did I get on your radar again? And why now?"

"I was watching the news one day. Lo and behold, who's on CNN? The young hero who broke up a forced surrogacy ring. My damn daughter, Kaden Baker. I'm proud of you."

"And then you tracked me down?"

"My people did some digging and turned up the special ops missions you pulled off at the Vatican and in D.C. I've got to say, chip off the old block."

"Nobody says that anymore."

"Sure they do."

"So here's the million-dollar question. You're not here to get me to follow in your footsteps. So why are you here?"

He went quiet and pushed his chair back to give himself space and distance. When he spoke again, a tremor came to his voice.

"Because. You have a sister."

♀ ♂

JUST LOOK AT THE RESEMBLANCES, Bo Finnerty thought. *The same high cheekbones as her sister. The same green eyes. Even the same Finnerty sass. Bailey looks more like her mom, Kaden looks more like me—the same olive undertones in her skin from the black Irish blood running in her veins.*

He snapped back to real time as Kaden nearly spit the words at him. "What do you mean I have a sister? What does she have to do with this? I said no more secrets!"

"All right, slow down. Let me explain." He took out his phone and swiped through a photo album. "This is Bailey. Your half-sister. She's seventeen. Senior in high school. Or was."

"What happened?"

"The Disappearance." *Come on, Finnerty, lay it out for her.*

"She was one of the girls taken?"

Bo nodded. "I don't think it was random."

"How do you know?"

"The operatives on that bus were using a list when they targeted Bailey. I can't shake the feeling it has to do with me."

And now they're coming after my other daughter.

"Why do you say that? I thought no one knew why those girls were taken."

"We still don't know the why. But Bailey being targeted was no coincidence. I've been on the trail of a lot of scumbags over the years." He wanted to use a stronger word but hadn't heard Kaden swear yet. "I've made a lot of enemies. This is the one way they can get back at me."

"But you have no evidence."

"Not yet."

A look of clarity came to Kaden's face. "And that's why we're sitting here."

"Yeah. That's my hidden agenda." He braced himself. He wouldn't blame her if she got up, walked out, and never spoke to him again. He wanted to use her to find his other daughter.

There's more. I'm sorry. But I can't tell you everything right now.

She went quiet. Finally said, "Gabriel's killer. Let's not lose sight of him. I need to find Dražen Savić."

"Agreed."

Kaden looked down at the digital photo of Bailey on his phone. Then she looked up and held his gaze with those bright green Finnerty eyes.

"Tell me how this would work."

11

Samana Cay

Alex entered the Bliss Lounge, a private enclave for Fantasy Live members a few hundred feet from his suite. The entire Fantasy Live Resort was just southeast of the Samana Ventures corporate complex, which straddled the eastern boundary of Samana Village. *This entire scam should be within walking distance.*

Inside the lounge's foyer, Rachel introduced him to his "personal accessories concierge."

"We may be able to improve on these," the concierge said, leaning closer to inspect the smartglasses on the bridge of his nose. It was clear she had reservations. "Please, have a seat."

He sat and removed the glasses Rachel had given him on the yacht. He placed them on the tabletop next to a mirror with a brightly lit border.

"Please look into the mirror and let me know if any of these strike your fancy." The concierge began projecting virtual glasses that matched the contour of his face. "I could see you in a Prada.

Maybe a Marianela. Oooo, I'll bet some Ray-Ban geometrics would look fab on you!"

He didn't care how *fab* he looked during his stay. He picked up his titanium glasses and checked them in the mirror. He figured Andrew Bayless would like the look. "These will do."

"All right. Just want to make sure you're in the right *frame of mind* this week."

He stood and grinned at the bad pun. Rachel led him onto the back patio, already filling with guests meeting each other and making small talk. He stepped to the railing at the edge of the platform and took in the stunning views of the lagoon lapping at a long stretch of white sand. Halfway down the beach, a waterfall rushed down a lush tropical hillside.

If only my personal life were this tranquil and simple.

Rachel introduced him to three other guests huddled together in two armchairs and two loveseats set across from each other. William, Maurice, and Evelyn—he remembered her from the plane—were all wearing stylish designer smartglasses, each pair conveying a different attitude.

"I'll be right back." Rachel headed off to the bar set up on the patio. Just beyond the wooden railing, a bright-yellow hummingbird flitted back and forth.

"Let's ask Andrew his opinion." One of the men, with a bald crown and patches of trim brown hair that he must dye, wore owlish spectacles, giving him a professorial look—probably undeserved.

"Sure, William, what's the question?" Alex liked that these new-generation glasses let you see everyone's name without cluttering up your field of vision. He felt like he was walking around inside a movie with subtitles.

William started in. "You look like the youngest one here, so this'll affect you more than us old farts. What's your position on sex robots?"

"Did you really just ask him his *position*?" Maurice chortled.

He had thinning gray hair and wore pink John Lennon glasses and a gold necklace beneath his open-collar shirt.

William ignored the gibe. "I mean, for the price of this camp I could have ordered a harem of sexbots. Have you seen the latest models? You know, the new ones come with swappable faces."

"But have you ever tried to fuck one?" Maurice asked. "No thank you. Let's see what Fantasy Live has to offer."

William wasn't done. He locked eyes with Alex. "How about you, Andrew Bayless? Ever gone to bed with a robot?"

Rachel arrived with Alex's cocktail and sat on the love seat next to him. He took a sip. "I'm actually in a relationship. Haven't seen the need to explore that option."

He said it for Rachel's benefit as much as for William. His girlfriend back in Miami, Valerie Ramirez, trusted him to go undercover—and use his judgment about how far to go. Valerie's surrogate was three months' pregnant, and while engagement hadn't crossed their lips yet, it was certainly on their minds.

Maurice turned to Rachel. "Excuse the locker room talk, Rachel."

"Nonsense." She poked at an ice cube with her lavender fingernail. "The whole point of Fantasy Live is to leave those cultural stereotypes behind. You saw the sign at the airport: 'No conformity past this line.' You're free to say anything that comes to your mind."

"Anything?" William asked, and the others laughed.

Rachel nodded. "You American men have become so conditioned to suppress your natural urges, to police your thoughts and language, to never objectify women. So boring! And what do you get? Generations of unsatisfied men *and* women. Venus and Mars have never been so far apart."

"Okay then, sweet cheeks. What's your view of sexbots?" William seemed eager to test the boundaries of appropriate social discourse on the island.

Rachel tilted her head to one side and pursed her lips. "I

haven't found one who can keep up with me." She winked and they laughed again. "William, when you're out and about on the grounds, I'm guessing you'd enjoy a new function on our smart-glasses. Boys Will Be Boys Mode. Our AI can display a realistic approximation of what the women look like beneath their dresses as you pass them by. Doesn't apply to guests, though."

"That's all right." William's smile got big. "Sign me up."

Rachel leaned into the foursome like Tom Brady calling a play. "Okay, some quick business. During the week, I'll be the personal ambassador for just the four of you. That means I'll be checking in with all of you every day to make sure the Fantasy Storyboards our team has developed meet your expectations. Remember, you're here to *live out* those fantasies."

Evelyn swirled her liqueur. "I think we'll keep you busy. I swing both ways."

"You'll have a male ambassador at your service, too." Rachel's lips curled a smile. "There are two ways to approach Fantasy Live. You can down shots, one after the other. Not so satisfying. Or, you can think of Fantasy Live as a fine bottle of Cognac to be savored over time. It's all about pacing."

"I like that." Evelyn eyed the three men seated around her. "I mean, sorry, boys, I'm not here for a rich guys' frat party. I'm here for something deeper. To explore the boundaries of light and dark without holding back. To role play and become someone entirely different. To probe new frontiers of eroticism and unlock the fantasies that keep me up at night for a long, long time."

Now that's interesting, Alex thought. *Evelyn's a woman who knows what she wants.*

Rachel reached for a tablet computer on the side table. "I must say, Evelyn, your imagination has stretched our creative team to the limit. I think you'll be pleased with the In-World simulations we've tailored for you."

"I can't wait," Evelyn said.

"Now, one last piece of business." Rachel's eyes swept over the foursome. "Now, have all of you reviewed the Terms and Conditions?"

They nodded. Samana Cay was run more like a corporation than a government. Violate "the Terms" and visitors will forfeit their deposit and be sent home on the next flight out, banished for life.

Alex was fine with the Terms so far, and the boilerplate language in the contract he signed as Andrew Bayless didn't surprise him. The Fantasy Live simulations would contain no bestiality, no pedophilia, no torture, no S&M, no physical violence of any kind. That would be "off brand."

But *how Fantasy Live's stories would unfold* was still a mystery. How realistic would these experiences be? Would it be Hooters for rich guys? Would it be some variation of virtual reality porn, with adult film stars trying to satisfy horny guys in smartglasses? Now *that* would be disappointing—barely worth a feature story in *Axom*.

There must be more to it. Why did they ask for him to send in photos, videos, and a detailed questionnaire about the women in his fantasies?

"Your literature described Fantasy Live as a 'judgment-free, guilt-free, no-shame zone,'" Alex pointed out. "What's that about?"

Rachel straightened. "We're not out to change American culture. Think of us as an escape, a release valve from social and cultural tensions back home. You're free to express yourself without worrying that someone's passing judgment. Just be aware of one golden rule. Evelyn, would you hold your left wrist out for me?"

Evelyn stuck her left arm straight out.

"See?" Rachel brushed Evelyn's arm with her fingertips. "Nothing on her wrist. Evelyn is a guest, not an Opt-In. Hands off the women guests—please treat them with respect."

Rachel held out her own wrist as she circled the group. Their eyes fastened on her bracelet, a silver band with symbols—heart, pyramid, silhouette of a woman—outlined at the edges with strings of bright emerald green lights.

"This is an Opt-In bracelet. The most important rule of Fantasy Live is this. When you see a glowing green Opt-In bracelet, you're allowed to touch." She touched the side of her bracelet and it turned bright red. "But the moment the light turns red, hands off. No more touching. That's important."

William nodded. "So any Opt-In is fair game, or just you, Rachel?"

She flicked her bracelet's color back to green. "You were assigned to me because I matched the requirements for your ideal type."

And now that she put it so bluntly, Alex saw that, yes, on the surface Rachel was the kind of woman he'd always fallen for. Through years of dating. Through three love affairs, breakups, and heartbreaks. She even resembled a younger version of Valerie.

Rachel positioned herself across from William. "To answer your question, yes. Any Opt-In in Fantasy Live is 'fair game.' Just be discreet. Groping in public is considered gauche. This isn't Plato's Retreat." A blank stare from the guests. "Look it up."

"As I understand this, women guests get the same fringe benefits, correct?" Evelyn asked.

"Of course. You'll see male staff wearing Opt-In bracelets, too."

"How far can we go?" William asked, then turned toward the others. "Come on, you're all thinking the same thing!"

"Oh, William," Maurice tut-tutted.

Rachel smiled. "Don't hesitate to ask any question. Our policy is to provide full transparency." She moved behind William and massaged his shoulders. "How far can you go? Opt-Ins are here to serve your needs and get you pining for the main event. But Fantasy Live is not a brothel, William. Our Opt-Ins are here to guide you on your journey. To help reawaken the desires of youth, the aching longings for your first heartthrob."

William and Maurice looked at each other with expressions that said, *Oh, really?*

"Just keep in mind. Opt-Ins are the appetizer, not the main course." Rachel rose, headed to the patio entrance, and turned back to them. "The Chairman comes on in five minutes. Let's take our seats."

12

Brooklyn and Manhattan

Kaden and Bo hopped onto the D train from Industry City to Greenwich Village. She joined him on a decrepit seat for two that didn't look too horrific. She checked her messages and saw the encrypted note from Alex. He was worried about her and warned about this shady character Lucid in Samana Cay. She texted a reply, saying she was okay and she'd explain more later.

She wasn't okay. Not at all. Gabriel was gone. Her fingers found the pendant beneath her shirt. Her palm curled around the digital display on the back. She clicked twice. She wondered if Gabriel could hear her.

Bo leaned over and said in a low voice, "I let the others know we're a go." He pecked his way into sending a text.

"I thought technology was against your religion," she said.

"Just anti-AI. Taking everyone's jobs away." He stashed his phone in his jacket pocket. "Anyway, you'll like this place. Loud and last minute. Perfect for what we need to discuss."

"Which is?"

"Next steps."

She sent a voice message asking Nico to meet them at Suya, the new Afro-Caribbean underground club in the Village. Bo said he was concerned bad actors inside the NSA had been eavesdropping on the gatherings he'd organized. The noise in the club would tamp down any chance of surveillance.

By the time they arrived, Annika and Nico were waiting at the entrance. If she was about to go dark to look for Bailey and hunt down Gabriel's killer, she wanted to brief Nico, and she persuaded Bo to see if Nico wanted to join the effort. She was still dubious that Gabriel's murder and the girls' kidnappings were connected, but she would damn well find out.

Bo paid for their covers, and she sidled up to Nico as they entered the dark space. "Hey, I like the look."

Nico was rocking a new hairstyle, an Afro—edges fringed with mint green—pulled back and tied with a rubber band.

"Thanks. Figured it was time for a change."

The place was hopping but roomy enough to grab two wooden tables along the far wall. On stage a foursome was kicking out some high-energy Cuban jams. Red lights played on the young bodies busting salsa moves on the dance floor.

"As you requested," Nico said, handing her the kit from her flat with her smart lenses. "Annika and I thought they looked cool. We almost tried them on while we were waiting for you."

That stopped her. She grabbed him by the wrist. "Nico, this is important. Never, *ever*, put these lenses on. The consequences would be dire."

"Hey, okay, lighten up. I didn't put on your lenses. But I did bring two pairs of glasses so we can finally see what you've been working on for so long, Ms. Programmer From the Future. That okay?"

Leave it to Nico to turn a compliment upside down. She let go of her grip just as the waitress came to take their drink orders.

Annika inspected one of the smartglasses, put them on, then

removed them, dangling them in front of Bo. "Age before beauty," she said.

Bo shook his head and leveled a glare at Kaden. "You mean if I put these on I'd be able to see your imaginary friend?"

Kaden looked up at the waitress. "He'll order whatever's on your drink menu that hasn't changed in twenty years."

Bo smirked. "Jack Daniel's, neat."

"See?" Kaden placed an order for iced tea, hold the Long Island.

Annika reached out and clasped the top of Kaden's hand. "It's too early to talk about tech, or the mission, right?" She whispered, "You're still in mourning. You can tell Bo, he'll understand."

Kaden looked at her father and then turned back to Annika. "Bo's been mourning for six months, since the Disappearance. It's all right, I'll get through this."

Annika brought her voice back up to normal. "All right. Tell me and Nico about your AI."

Kaden asked the waitress for the Wi-Fi password then turned back to her friends. "You know how most people just settle for outfitting their personal AIs with off-the-shelf templates to look like wizards, robots, baby dragons, cats? As if their AI were some kind of damn *pet*?"

This was one of her pet peeves. The personal AI revolution was off to a ragged start. Most people still talk about artificial intelligence as if it had to come wrapped inside a robot or device, but that never made sense to Kaden. Why have any hardware at all? All you needed was code, the cloud, and some visualization software.

She saw Tosh and Carlos enter the club and join their group at the main table. She nudged their smaller table a few inches away to keep the conversation to just her, Nico, and Annika.

"You know how much I've always loved Amelia Earhart."

"Yeah, you worship her." Nico began reciting from memory.

"First woman to fly solo across the Atlantic. First woman to fly coast to coast nonstop. First cross-dresser to win the Distinguished Flying Cross—"

"She was a risk taker," Kaden cut him off. *No dissing Amelia tonight!* "Always searching for something just out of reach. Never fit in her time."

"Like someone else we know," Nico said.

Kaden had felt that way about Earhart for as long as she could remember, from her childhood search for her gender identity to her adoptive parents' abusive treatment of her when she dressed like a boy. Amelia was her role model.

"You both felt alienated from your worlds," Annika offered. "Maybe that's why you spent so much time on coding Amelia. You could relate."

Kaden nodded. "I've been working on the code for years but only deployed Amelia six weeks ago. Decided to make her lifesize even though it takes a ton more bandwidth. I wanted to do her justice. Used old newsreels to get her voice exactly right. Made sure her period outfits and expressions were authentic. Kept her running in the background, trusting her to use deep learning to self-improve."

The waitress set down their drinks. Kaden pulled out an empty seat at the end of the table and gave Nico and Annika permissions to join her network. "Looks like we have a strong signal. Amelia, say hi to my friends."

Amelia materialized standing next to them, wearing a strapless party gown with a three-strand pearl necklace and a mink stole wrap. Kaden made a mental note. *Update Amelia's wardrobe accessories.*

Amelia looked around. "Oh, what fun! This reminds me of the speakeasies I used to go to in my twenties!" She spotted the band and walked a dozen feet in that direction.

Also, update Amelia's empathy settings. No condolences about Gabriel.

"Amazing," Annika said. "She can simulate a realistic walk across a room."

Kaden nodded. "It's partly illusion—she can't see the band or detect anything from over there. She can only see what I see, unless there are Internet-connected cameras around. But she's convincing, isn't she? The Internet Archive contained old footage with hundreds of Amelia Earhart's movements. Her gait and posture, her hand gestures, her laugh, her speech patterns. I wanted to simulate a realistic physicality."

"Well, you sure got it." Annika looked impressed.

Amelia returned and sat in the empty chair between them. "Hi, Nico. Hi, Annika. Nice to finally meet you."

"Hi. Hey there." They stumbled over each other's words and laughed.

"I hope you don't mind, I ordered a bloody Mary." Amelia raised her virtual cocktail glass and they toasted, with Amelia even tossing in a clinking sound for their glasses meeting hers. She leaned closer to Kaden and whispered, "Sugar pie, before we socialize, I have some news for you. Should we speak in private?"

Kaden looked at Nico and Annika. "These guys are good."

The smartglasses came with built-in micro-speakers, and Amelia raised her voice above the strains of the music. "To bring you all up to speed—is that the right term? I *adore* it! To 'bring you up to speed,' I've been working in the background on an assignment Kaden gave me six weeks ago. Remember, darling? After you hacked into that trove of digital files from Randolph Blackburn?"

She grimaced. Fortunately, Nico was her accomplice in that operation and Annika knew all about it. "Go on."

"My task was to search for anything in Blackburn's files related to Kaden's late mother. That search came up empty. But I came across one curious digital file, unlike all the others. The file's name is Project Ezekiel. Does that mean anything to you?"

"Just the guy in the Old Testament," Kaden said.

"What's especially curious is the military-grade encryption. Not the sort of thing you normally see on a business file, or so I'm told. On my own, it would take more than a hundred years to decrypt. But I've reached out to thousands of other AIs to tap into their spare processing power to make it a more manageable task."

"Wait," Annika said. "I didn't know that was a thing. You're collaborating with other AIs like in some kind of global virtual co-working space?"

"I see." Amelia thought about it. "Sure, let's go with that metaphor."

Amelia reached into her handbag for a pack of Lucky Strikes and lit one. Kaden felt ridiculous at having to resist the impulse to tell her about all the studies about lung cancer and second-hand smoke that have come out since the 1930s. *Let Amelia be Amelia.*

Amelia blew out a string of smoke circles, then continued. "Our neural network is still working on it. Most of the content remains gibberish. But I'm beginning to piece together some strands. I may have something for you soon."

Bo leaned toward them. "Am I interrupting anything in ghost world?"

"No, we're good," Kaden said.

"I'd like you to meet some people," Bo said.

"You mean Tosh and Carlos? We met already, remember?"

They smiled at her and lifted their beers in a *salud.*

Bo raised his hand and signaled for four newcomers to join them. Two middle-aged couples skirted the dance floor and pulled up chairs at the now crowded table.

"Kaden, this is Yuan and Wendy Deng, parents of Ling. And Judy and Ernie 'Viper' Matthews, parents of Piper. Their daughters were kidnapped on the same bus Bailey was on."

They gave polite smiles and shook hands. Wendy was the last to shake and squeezed Kaden's hand. "Thank you *so much.*"

"So sorry about your daughter. I'll do what I can."

Tosh broke in. "They're here for a reason, Kaden. We're organizing a grassroots effort. A Disappearance task force."

"We don't call it the Disappearance," Wendy said firmly. "We call it the day our lives ended."

Tosh looked wounded, so Kaden took a shot at playing peace-maker. "Me, Nico, Annika, and a fourth guy operate Red Team Zero, a hacker collaborative. But Nico and I also have some experience in the field after we spent ten months at a special-ops boot camp." She looked at Viper, who no doubt had seen more action on the ground. "I'll explain more later, but no reason we couldn't extend the assets of Red Team Zero to all of you."

"Red Team Zero." Viper chewed it over. "I like it."

Everyone nodded. Bo hunched forward in his chair. "The fact is, by whatever name, we're all here because traditional law enforcement channels haven't gotten anywhere."

Kaden looked around the table and saw a lot of passion and pain. What she hadn't heard yet was a course of action. "Okay, fill me in. What do we know so far?"

Bo looked at the others. "After the … *event*, a lot of conspiracy theories were floated about who was behind it. The U.S. government. The Russians. Domestic terrorists. Aliens. Teams of serial killers. So far nothing's panned out. The girls disappeared without a trace. So far."

He lifted his whiskey glass, hand shaking, and placed it back down.

"Parents and relatives of the abducted girls banded together. We looked for patterns. But there were no patterns. In fact, just the opposite. Other than their age range, all the missing young women had different ethnicities and came from different backgrounds. Different heights. Different eye colors. Different hair colors." That faraway look came to his eyes again. He went quiet.

Carlos spoke up. "There was one pattern. The one constant

seemed to be ... variety." He let the word hang in the air with all its implications.

"Variety?" Kaden wasn't expecting that.

"Quantico seems to think the abductions weren't random. That the wide variation in appearance, body type, and physiognomy was itself a pattern."

Kaden nodded. "Anything else?"

"A statistical anomaly," Carlos added. "A higher percentage of the girls' parents work in law enforcement when compared to the general population."

"Maybe not a coincidence," Kaden said, thinking back to the hunch Bo shared about this being personal.

Bo managed to pick up and knock back the rest of his Jack Daniel's. "Some parents of the missing girls have skills we can use." He turned to the others.

"I'm a systems analyst," Wendy Deng said.

"My company makes surveillance equipment," her husband Yuan said.

"I speak eight languages, in case that's handy," Judy Matthews said.

"It is," Bo said.

Viper looked at the others but stayed silent until his wife Judy prodded him in the back. "Former Special Forces."

Bo put on a grave face. "Viper made some enemies overseas, too. We think this cartel is making it personal by targeting our daughters."

Kaden looked around the table. On the one hand, these were some high-powered pissed-off mommas and poppas. On the other hand, whoever heard of crowdsourcing a covert intelligence operation?

Bo hunched his shoulders forward. "We'll take this in two stages. Intelligence gathering and extraction. Carlos?"

Tosh, who'd been lying low, looked around to make sure he wouldn't be overheard outside this small circle. His voice barely carried over the band's jams. "Over the last twenty-four hours, we've detected chatter that could lead us to one or more of the assets we think may be involved."

"Definitive?" Kaden asked.

"Fifty-three percent probability," Tosh replied.

"So, coin flip."

"Yeah," Carlos said. "But more solid than any other leads in the past six months."

She shut her eyes, lowered her chin, and hugged her chest. Gabriel's killing was seared into every movement around her, every waking moment of her day. And someone was trying to kidnap her.

Should I walk away and try to return to a normal life? Or join this covert operation and maybe get captured or killed? I still have a lot to prove to the world.

"All right, I'm in. Now what? Do we wait? Make plans?"

Tosh shook his head. "We have hours. Not days."

"Hours?" This was unspooling much faster than she'd imagined.

Bo leaned forward and locked eyes with her. "We fly out at five a.m."

13

Catskill Park, New York

Dražen Savić had only a cursory knowledge of New York state's water system, much less an understanding of the science and technology that was about to unfold beneath the brilliant blanket of stars in the sky above the Catskill Mountains. But he knew enough about field logistics to organize a black ops mission.

Tonight's goal: Get the strain into Pepacton Reservoir's intake pipes without being noticed. Not an easy task.

The speaker on his phone in the fire engine barked out Lucid's familiar voice. "Come in, Ezekiel One."

"Ezekiel One here," he confirmed over the encrypted line.

"I have faith that you'll get it done this time, Ezekiel One."

Savić was still brooding over his failure to capture Kaden Baker last night. And now this—Lucid rubbing salt in the wound. But he kept his cool. "My men are in place."

"You are a go, Ezekiel One. Repeat, you are a go."

Savić and Lucid had spent weeks mapping out every detail of this mission. Getting the timeline worked out. Lining up the vehicles and heavy equipment. Researching the manmade lake's intake structures and access roads. Getting his men trained to carry out land and aquatic assignments.

Savić knew similar operations were underway at water supplies all across the United States. But he'd been walled off from learning any details about those missions.

No matter. New York was the big kahuna. And he was running this operation.

The goal was simple: Prepare this reservoir for delivery of the strain.

"Bison Team leader, do you copy?" Savić called out on his comms.

"Roger that, Ezekiel One. Bison Team is in position."

"We are go, Bison Team. Light her up!"

He'd picked the team names himself. The European bison was Belarus's national animal. *Hunted to extinction, just like the Americans would soon be.*

He switched to the next frequency. "Scorpion Team, you are go. Confirm."

"Scorpion Team reads you, Ezekiel One. My men are fanning out."

Savić scanned the hillsides with his binoculars. It took less than two minutes for the first glimmers of orange flames to appear along the southern and western rims of the reservoir. The gasoline and fire accelerant his team had added to the already dry underbrush in the past hour began to light up the forest like a tinderbox.

Yuri Groza, his red-faced underling and comm chief, sat across from him in the front seat of the repurposed fire engine. Groza checked the airwaves for a distress call. Budget cuts had reduced the number of conservation officers and game wardens who monitor the state's reservoirs. The ones who remained were full-fledged police officers equipped with radios, firearms, and other equipment.

"They spotted the fires," Groza said, lifting the headset from his left ear. "Call's gone out to the local fire departments."

"That's our cue."

Savić flicked on the siren and directed the men sitting in the extended cab just behind them to put on their helmets and gear. Their wildland fire engine, smaller and more rugged than a standard fire truck, was built to withstand difficult terrain. They roared out of their hiding spot, leading a convoy of four tanker trucks right on their tail. Each water tender, as the Americans called them, carried 2,000 gallons of water, far more than a fire truck.

He did not know what kind of biological agent was added to the water in the tanker trucks. All he knew was that he and his men had received vaccinations and were safe.

He switched to the third channel on his comms. "Dragonfly Team, stand by, we're minutes away."

"Roger that. Dragonfly Team standing by."

Savić stepped on the gas. His wildland engine roared through the open gate to the state park. A hundred yards ahead, he saw a forest ranger outside the ranger station waving his arms in the middle of the road, trying to flag him down.

Couldn't take that chance. He gunned the engine. The front of the wildland looks like a Mack truck in a surly mood, and he could see the ranger's eyes widen as the monster vehicle bore down on him. The ranger flew out of the way at the last second as Savić led his procession down the two-lane paved road and toward the targets.

"That was close," Groza said with a smile.

"S.O.B. is lucky I didn't hit him. We're under orders. No conversations with the Americans."

"You could have at least winged him."

"And attract even more police? Think, Groza, think!"

Groza scowled and went back to monitoring his comms.

After ten minutes, they reached the turnoff for the first target on the west side of the massive reservoir. Hard to miss, given the flames dancing in the trees. They passed by oaks, spruce, and birch trees lit up like giant burning bodies against the night sky. Savić cracked open his window. The smell reminded him of the battlefields of his youth.

The road ended at a T-bone with the edge of the reservoir in front of them. Savić turned his vehicle left to hug the small one-lane dirt road that lined the banks. In the headlights up ahead he saw four members of Dragon Team dressed in the same firefighter uniforms as the men in his truck. The Dragon Team directed him to the target area alongside the reservoir a good distance from the fires. The tankers pulled and parked behind him. At the water's edge, two men in navy frogmen gear were preparing their masks and air cylinders.

He stopped the engine. His men spilled out. He watched as his operatives hooked up large hoses to the valves on each truck. Two men pulled the hoses out toward the edge of the artificial lake. Groza set up a mobile command support unit and sent up the two drones.

Savić radioed the team across the reservoir, where they had a nice conflagration going. A living bonfire. "Scorpion Team, report."

"This is Scorpion Team, Ezekiel One. We're lit. Waiting for tankers to arrive."

He checked his handheld and saw that the second wave of fire engines, which bore the names and insignia of local fire departments, were five minutes out. He'd instructed his men not to arrive too early or it would look suspicious.

"They're almost there, hang on and keep out of sight."

They had run this simulation many times without a hitch. The real world, though, was another matter.

Groza came up beside him, listening to his headset and peering at the readouts from the drone video live-feed. "State police on their way."

"Damn! I thought we'd have more time. How close?"

"Maybe ten minutes out."

Savić turned toward his team. "We have less than ten minutes. Go! Go! Go!"

His men were well trained but a twenty-minute timeline had now collapsed to under ten. He pitched in, grabbing a large hose from the side of the wildland engine and tucking it under his right arm as he hurried toward the granite slope that slanted down to the water.

He handed the hose to the nearest frogman, ankle deep at the water's edge. "There and back in nine minutes or we leave you. Got it?"

The frogman nodded and dove into the water toward the target, hose in hand. The intake pipe was just below a floating pontoon twenty-five yards from the shoreline. Fortunately, no divers were needed for the central floating intake.

The central intake!

He reached for his comms. "Dragonfly, execute. Repeat, execute now."

"Confirmed, Ezekiel One. We're on our way."

The original plan called for the chopper to arrive after they'd left, but no time for that now. There were no airfields near the reservoir, so the operatives had to take off from a makeshift helipad in a dark empty cow pasture six miles outside of the park.

Savić returned to the matter at hand. All the divers had taken up positions around the floating intake just beneath the lake's surface. The lead frogman signaled they were ready. Savić gave the hand signal for his team to open the valves on the sides of the truck and tankers. Torrents of water surged through the hoses. Usually the fast-drain valves allowed firefighters to empty thousands of gallons of water into a portable water tank in just seconds. Tonight they were targeting two subsurface targets.

Flickers from the fires across the reservoir reflected across the water's surface. He watched as the frogmen dove to reach the intake pipes submerged just below the floating pontoons moored offshore. The intake was designed to suck down the fresh water near the surface of the reservoir and avoid the heavier silt loads near the floor of the lake.

Groza checked the night drone footage. "Looks like they're three minutes out."

Damn. This was cutting it close.

"Get those drones down now."

He signaled for the divers to return. Then he signaled for his men to wrangle the hoses and hurl them back onto the trucks.

"Move! Move! Move!" he ordered. The frogmen climbed onto the shore bank out of breath, removed their flippers, and climbed into the passenger compartment of the wildland, ducking out of sight. The other operatives scurried to the tanker trucks.

Savić saw the lights of two patrol cars leading a fire engine just over the ridge. He hopped into the driver's seat, started the motor, and made a wide U-turn at the edge of the burning forest before barreling down the road the same way they'd come.

He rolled down his window.

"Do you see it?"

"No. Do you?" Groza asked.

"No. But listen."

Above the rumble of his convoy, they heard the blades of a distant chopper in the dark sky. He heard a loud splash—the sweet sound of the final watery payload.

The strain was on its way to New York.

14

Samana Cay

Alex and the other guests abandoned their seats on the outdoor terrace and headed inside to the Bliss Lounge as the sun began to set. Evelyn followed and sat next to him. One by one the guests settled into the theater-style seats the staff had set up in front of a stage that now appeared at the narrow end of the room.

Rachel and the other staff ambassadors—he counted twelve in all—lined up on stage and she stepped to the front.

"Ladies and gentlemen, welcome to the opening of Fantasy Live, a special retreat where your fantasies come true. Please join me in welcoming Lucid, the chief operating officer of Samana Cay."

The room filled with applause as the other staffers left the stage. Lucid stepped into the spotlight. Alex noticed Lucid was the only one in the room not wearing smartglasses.

"Welcome, all. We're excited you've agreed to take part in our soft launch while we fine-tune our offerings for the guests who'll follow in your footsteps."

Evelyn patted him on the arm and whispered, "Hear that? We're pioneers!"

Alex smiled and nodded. He was off the market, but he preferred older women and didn't mind her acting a little flirty.

Lucid gave a little talk introducing Chairman Incognito, "the founding father of Samana Cay," before stepping back into the shadows.

A figure appeared in the center of the stage. Alex toggled to Reality Mode and saw the stage was empty. He returned to Fantasy Mode.

A brief flurry of applause filled the lounge, but it gave way to uneasy murmurs as the form took shape. Alex narrowed his eyes as a strange-looking creature materialized before the crowd.

The being's face morphed from a man to a woman to a beast and back again. A golden glow appeared around its head. The creature appeared to levitate above the stage with fiery red eyes. It had a human body dressed in a flowing white tunic with three pairs of feathery white angel wings fluttering behind its back as if to keep aloft.

"Honored visitors." The creature's voice sounded deep and resonant, a full octave lower than a normal speaking voice. The audio came from speakers above the stage, not his eyewear. "Excuse my appearance. I wanted to be sure I made a lasting impression."

Dead silence in the room. Everyone seemed captivated, staring at the stage with mixed expressions of wonder and dread.

"Today I come to you as a seraph, a six-winged celestial being inspired by passages in the Old Testament."

A miniature drone camera circled Chairman Incognito, hovering up and down as he spoke. He hugged a glowing golden book to his chest. The whole thing had the air of a mystical experience—a stark contrast to what Alex considered an absurd moniker. *Incognito? Please!*

The celestial creature continued. "The word seraphim means

'fiery ones.' I hope it conveys the burning love I have for my employees and for our guests."

Evelyn leaned close to Alex's ear. "I suppose he could have appeared as a puppy dog. But no one would be talking about that ten years from now."

Alex smiled and nodded. Odd as the Chairman's appearance was, he was making an impression.

Alex noticed the recesses of the lounge began filling with virtual creatures—warriors, anime characters, a fierce-looking griffin—paying rapt attention to his words as Incognito floated closer to the guests in the lounge.

"Today we write a new chapter for Samana Cay—and for the world. The desires that will unfold this week at Fantasy Live have lain hidden in your hearts for years. As we grow older, we lose our sense of wonder. Our dreams grow less vivid. This week we want to reawaken those dormant feelings. We want to help you embrace your youthful passions and indiscretions. For the next week, you are masters of your reality. For the next week, you are all gods!"

Chairman Incognito's gaze swept across the audience and locked eyes with Alex. A chill passed through him. Looking at this apparition with its angel wings and golden halo and burning eyes—Alex felt as if he was facing not an avatar but a divine being. A god who recognized his true intent. Perhaps even his true nature.

"Outside forces beset today's world with political strife and civil unrest. Let us be your refuge." He thumped the golden book in his hand. "Remember this place of destiny. This new paradise."

Incognito's three faces forced the semblance of a smile as he floated back to center stage. "A final surprise announcement. A technical achievement that my team has been working on went live moments ago. You've all filled out the 'physical traits' questionnaire. Whenever an Opt-In who matches your desired type comes within fifty feet, your medallion will vibrate with an alert and grow in intensity as you get nearer. Another opportunity to revel in the life force. You deserve all that awaits you!"

Alex's fingers found the medallion beneath his shirt. He was already curious what would happen when it went off. *Just one more piece of this strange, strange puzzle.*

Incognito landed gently on stage. His wings came to a standstill as he spread his arms apart. "Now, go forth and enjoy the evening. Let the fantasy games begin!"

The audience burst into applause but for only a moment. Just like that, in the blink of an eye, Incognito was gone.

15

Over the Atlantic

Kaden was as surprised as anyone to find herself in the middle seat next to Bo and Nico on a commercial flight to Zurich. After the gathering at the nightclub, she barely had time to get home, pack an overnight bag, and snag a few hours' sleep.

This isn't how things are supposed to work, is it? The day after my boyfriend is shot in front of my eyes, I discover that a stranger is my real father and now I'm heading off with him on a secret mission to find the sister I didn't know I had? Am I really supposed to think only about the mission and push everything else aside?

She snuck a look at her phone and watched the video of her last day with Gabriel. She'd asked Amelia to pull together the scenes. She started to tear up and stashed it in her pocket.

She turned to look at Bo. There was still a lot they needed to sort out. This morning at the airport, she sent off a DNA paternity test with cheek swabs from her and Bo—and expedited the order. So there was that. In a few minutes, they'd go over the surveillance plan. But first she had to fill in Tosh and Carlos about her white-hat hackers consultancy.

She switched seats with Nico on the aisle so Bo could fill him in about the mission—she'd convinced her father that Nico could be a major asset during their trip. Then she swapped seats with Judy Matthews, who was sitting farther back next to Tosh and Carlos.

"You're here to tell us about Red Team Zero?" Carlos asked in a hushed voice.

She nodded. "Yeah, the thumbnail version. Ever hear of red teaming?"

Tosh—short, stocky, with a nervous manner and bad haircut —nodded yes. Carlos—tall, tawny-skinned, ruggedly handsome —shook his head no.

She started to explain. "The term was coined by the U.S. Army, but it dates all the way back to the early 1500s when the Vatican created an Office of the Devil's Advocate to put up arguments against candidates for sainthood."

"So that's where the term 'devil's advocate' comes from?" Carlos asked.

Kaden nodded. "Today smart corporations use the same concept to introduce contrarian thinking, to stress-test their strategies, to expose security vulnerabilities."

"Smart. It takes a hacker to think like a hacker," Carlos offered.

"Exactly. We plan and carry out attacks against critical systems as a way to make them stronger. Our motto is, 'We don't know what we don't know.'"

"Why the zero in Red Team Zero?"

"Programmer humor," she said. "We don't officially exist."

Tosh set down his tray table and his fingers began to dance across the keys of his notebook computer. "We use red teaming for our military exercises to get inside the heads of the enemy.

You use it for cybersecurity. Sounds like our skill sets mesh pretty well."

She smiled. "Bo needs to fill me in about the mission." She returned to her original seat, ordered hot tea from the flight attendant, and listened as her father mapped out the plan.

The mission seemed straightforward enough. Powerful figures from around the globe were converging for a world summit in Switzerland's Zug Valley—ground zero of the cryptocurrency movement—to discuss displacing the U.S. dollar and the euro as the default currencies for moving vast sums of wealth around the world.

Bo kept his voice low so only she could hear. "Our contacts in the intelligence community believe some of the attendees will include high-value targets who've relied on creative use of crypto and blockchain technologies to fund sex trafficking, drug trafficking, black market arms dealing—anything they want hidden."

"You mean, when they need it hidden," she said. "Sometimes they're in league with their governments."

"True."

"And in *our* government, we don't know which agencies to trust."

"I'm saying we have to be careful. In some departments there are forces working at cross-purposes."

"You still haven't told me what agency you work for 'off book,'" Kaden pointed out.

"You really need to know that?"

"I made a leap of faith. I'm here, aren't I? Now it's your turn."

"DIA."

She gave a blank look.

"Defense Intelligence Agency. The CIA gets all the glory, and that's fine by us. Our unit is much smaller. In fact, it doesn't exist."

"But you're saying even the CIA may be compromised?" she probed.

"That's a strong word." Bo's voice was low and gravelly. "I'd rather talk about what my people are doing."

"Okay. Once we land, what do we do?"

"Zug Valley isn't a big place. Most of the summit's events will take place at the main venue and along old town. Most of what gets decided happens in the hallways, the pubs, the streets."

Nico leaned halfway across her seat to make sure no one else could hear. "We using an alias?"

Bo reached inside his jacket pocket, pulled out two identity cards, and handed them over. Tosh had apparently finished forging them late last night.

Bo put on his all-business expression and looked at Kaden. "Your new name is Jordan Wilkerson."

"Jordan. I like it. Gender neutral." She hadn't had that talk with Bo yet.

Bo shot her a quizzical look but continued. "You're the heiress to a rare-earth minerals fortune in Alberta, Canada. Copper, iron ore, tungsten. You have assets you want to convert to crypto. You may be open to exploring other business ventures. Higher risk, higher return."

He turned his gaze to Nico. "And you, my friend, are Jordan Wilkerson's executive assistant, Lawrence Dougherty."

"They'll look into my background," she said to Bo.

"Check your phone."

She did. A message from Tosh was already waiting for her. Even though they were off the Internet, Tosh had set up a private local area network for sharing files during the flight. She accepted the file transfer. For the next five hours, she'd memorize her new identity—even though she was still getting used to the identity she learned about only last night.

She nudged Nico out of her personal space then turned to face Bo. "I have a lot of questions for you. But let me ask just one. Tell me more about Bailey."

"Like what?"

"Like what's your favorite memory of her?" She realized how that sounded, so she amended, "Up until now."

Bo thought for a minute. He closed his eyes as he spoke.

"Even at six years old, she had a willful streak. Cried if she didn't get her way—a cry that tore my heart out. Yeah, I spoiled her. Maybe to make up for what I did to you."

He opened his eyes to see how she'd react. She kept still.

"One weekend we all went clamming together in Chesapeake Bay—me, Eileen, Bailey. The tide started to go out, and we decided to take off our shoes and go prancing around in our bare feet. Turned into an epic mud fight. The rule was I could only use my feet and the girls could use anything. Well, you know who lost that battle. We filled two pails with clams, but Bailey was more intent on giving me a standing mud bath."

He smiled that slanted smile of his and slid his seat back. "I wanted to bottle that day."

He sounded like he might not see her again.

16

Minsk, Belarus, and Samana Cay

Maxim Volkov sat at the control console in his high-tech home office in Belarus where he oversaw his financial empire. He wanted to make sure Phase One was ready to go, and time was short. His flight to the Summit was leaving in five hours.

He barked out a voice message: "Bashir, we need to talk. SCIF now."

In seconds, the response came back: "Heading to Blackout."

Volkov watched his chief scientist scurry past microbiologists hovering over test tube racks and microscopes, past computer screens where neurophysiologists were studying microelectrode recordings of the brain.

Bashir entered the Blackout Room, set up as a Sensitive Compartmented Information Facility in a remote corner of the Lab. The glass windows were darkened and soundproofed so none of Bashir's lab coats could even imagine what was taking place inside.

Bashir secured the door behind him. "Chairman, this is a surprise."

"I need to know if everything is on track. After a year of research, we're entering our operational phase."

"Yes, Chairman."

His voice was transmitting fine, but he still needed a body for this virtual meeting. Volkov never appeared as himself in these video chats. He appeared as an immersive display projected by the other participant's smartglasses. His fingers lingered over the array of buttons on the console in front of him.

Let's see. Which avatar shall I choose today? Ezekiel, of course! How could it be anything else?

He had spent weeks perfecting the dress and appearance of his favorite digital alter ego. The simple olive-colored cloth shawl. Ezekiel's blue eyes (like his own) and mop of scraggly white hair (unlike his own wild mane of brown hair). The prominent nose (true enough). The long white beard and mustache (longer than his woodsman's beard).

As he spoke, so did his Ezekiel avatar—a hologram-like figure grasping a wooden staff and seated at the table across from Bashir.

"The neurobiology progress reports you've been sending over have been somewhat *dense*. Give me a status report."

"Well, where to begin?"

"Let's rewind one year ago this week to your sub expedition."

"All right. We managed—"

"Twelve months when the deadline called for six months."

Bashir's eyes darted from the Ezekiel avatar to one of the webcams on the far wall. "I made it clear from the start the time-line was too aggressive. We've accomplished a great deal in a very short time. I've worked my team around the clock—"

"Yes, the clock. Your disregard for our timeline has pushed back the entire operation."

"The science cannot be rushed. You're asking for something science has never done before."

"Which is why I hired you in the first place."

After an exhaustive global search, he had personally recruited Bashir, the most renowned microbiologist in all of Saudi Arabia. He had both the right pedigree and mindset to head up the science behind Project Ezekiel. He'd agreed to head up the R&D division of Samana Ventures two years ago. He'd built this lab and put together an all-star team of like-minded researchers. Just as important, he shared Volkov's devotion to the radically reimagined world that would soon emerge.

"Let's review your disregard of deadlines to assess whether the project has been compromised. The Greenland expedition was a success, was it not?"

Bashir retrieved a laptop from a smaller table behind him. "Absolutely. As we discussed at the time, this was a high-risk, high-reward gambit. The challenge was to find a vector that could be easily transmitted to tens of millions of targeted subjects."

"Go on. I'm recording this for posterity."

"I presented several options. We selected the one where the biological agent would be masked. All but undetectable."

"And the name of this biological agent?"

"Genetically modified archaea. You can't find a single-celled organism hardier than the specimens we collected at the entrance to hydrothermal vents along the North Pole's Gakkel Ridge. These organisms have no parallels among animals, plants, bacteria, viruses. They're not even distant cousins. Traditional laws of biology do not apply."

"That was the whole point, was it not?" So far, Volkov knew all of this, but he enjoyed hearing the summary of Bashir's scientific breakthrough.

Bashir pulled up his keyboard and stabbed out commands. "We literally cannot find any organisms older than archaea on the planet—and to think they were unknown to science just fifty years ago! If you compare their DNA to a bacterium or virus, they lack certain bits that are always there. And they contain other bits that shouldn't be there."

"Why does that matter?"

"Chairman, I'm making the point that we started from scratch. We had no scientific research to build on top of. No case studies to reference."

"Continue," Volkov said.

"It took my team twelve months to get us here, with not a day wasted. The breakthrough came three weeks ago when our Lab synthesized the final base pair blueprint into a new genetically modified organism."

"In layman's terms, please."

"The two strains we're developing need to be modified to induce the desired effects in our targets. But first, they need to *reach* the targets. They need to survive the gauntlet posed by modern drinking water systems."

Volkov knew this posed a challenge. In New York City, for instance, residents might be surprised to learn that one-quarter of all the water flowing into the city's water pipes comes from the massive Pepacton Reservoir a hundred miles away. The water travels through mountains and deep valleys through aging aqueducts, flows underground in tunnels, and settles into vast holding tanks, where it gets treated with chlorine to kill bacteria and fluoride to prevent tooth decay. It then undergoes a final dose of ultraviolet light to kill any nasties that may have slipped through.

Volkov said, "So you're saying your lab coats have found a way for the strains to survive this purification process."

"Yes, Chairman. We've designed the perfect carrier."

Bashir punched a few keys and turned the laptop screen toward the webcam. The screen showed a magnified image of a writhing organism. Ugly little bugger. Looked like a tube-shaped purple sponge.

"Behold, a life form that never before existed in nature."

Bashir looked a bit too self-satisfied, as if he expected a Nobel Prize for his work. But there would be no awards or ceremonies. Only a shift in the world's balance of power.

Volkov led him through the final steps of Project Ezekiel to date. "The archaea you describe are the carriers—the transmission agents—that our operatives have begun delivering to major drinking water systems in the U.S. and Europe, correct?"

"Yes, Chairman. The Plant has begun producing large supplies of the treated water."

"And you're confident the biological agents will avoid detection, at least until they propagate?"

"I am. We know viral biological agents are difficult to detect. Viruses are tasteless and odorless. By way of comparison, pathogenic archaea are a thousand times more difficult to detect. Archaea reside in the nose, lungs, gut, and on the skin of every person on the planet. Put the archaea under a microscope and you won't see the variations we introduced--you'd need to examine them at the molecular level to detect the pathogenic genes."

"Looks can be deceiving."

"Precisely. Every other type of microorganism produces potential toxins: bacteria, viruses, fungi. They can all make host organisms ill. But there are no known examples of archaea with pathogenic properties."

"Until now."

"Indeed, Chairman. Pathogenic archaea are not on anyone's radar. And until they're activated, they're harmless."

"A final matter. Lucid tells me mass production of the vaccine and the cure is now underway at the Plant."

"Correct."

"That's good." *The vaccine and the cure will be immeasurably valuable—but they aren't for sale.* "Make sure all staff on the island receive the vaccine."

"We've already begun the inoculations."

"Bashir, thank you for that summary. We trust each other's word, do we not?"

"Yes, Chairman."

"Can you give me your word that every one of your men—and they are all men, as we discussed, correct?"

"Correct, sir."

"Can you assure me that all your lab workers can be trusted to execute Project Ezekiel?"

"All team members are put through a rigorous screening process, including psychological testing. So yes, sir, I'm confident. They're true believers in our cause."

"Good. In a few days' time, the first strain will propagate throughout the drinking water supplies, waiting for us to activate it. You now have a new deadline. One week from today we we trigger the strain—we launch Phase One of the project."

Bashir pushed back from the table in his office chair. "Chairman, we're only now completing the clinical trials—"

"Think of it this way. The targets on the ground will become part of the trials."

Bashir's objections were predictable. It was one thing to propagate the first strain through public drinking supplies. It was quite another to *activate* the strain and have it produce the desired effects. Yet the timeline required urgency. Destiny demanded it.

"Sir, if I may, that's a very aggressive timetable."

Volkov's avatar, Ezekiel, stamped his staff onto the ground. Haptics filled in the sound effects and rattled the floor, making Bashir recoil.

"One week, Bashir. The countdown begins at this moment."

17

Zug, Switzerland

Kaden stepped off the train from Zurich just behind her new team members. She'd never heard of Zug, a once-sleepy burg in the Alps. But she read about it on the way over. Seems just about everyone in the crypto space knows about the place. If the San Francisco Bay Area was the epicenter of the tech revolution, Zug was the capital of the crypto economy.

Which is why a thousand business leaders from around the world were expected to descend on Switzerland's Zug Valley this weekend for the first Crypto/Blockchain Grand Summit, a gathering of the crypto elite.

If Bo's intelligence sources were right, the goal of this gathering was to lay the foundation to displace the U.S. dollar and euro as the cornerstone of global finance. Which didn't interest Kaden in the slightest.

She was here to find Bailey. And get revenge for Gabriel. Not necessarily in that order.

The conference was taking place in a four-star hotel and

adjoining buildings at the far end of the old town of Zug. To get a feel for the setting, the whole crew took a walk: Kaden, Bo, Nico, Carlos, Tosh, and Judy Matthews. The old town seemed transported from an earlier century, nestled beside a pretty lake and rimmed by Alpine mountains and hills dusted with snow.

Night was already falling, so they gathered in an old-timey cafe facing the lakefront. The others left their overnight bags in the foyer, but Tosh and Carlos insisted on taking their large black handbags inside. A crush of business types jammed the cafe. Looked like a lot of the conference attendees had already arrived.

Kaden searched the eyes of this makeshift team of intelligence gatherers. She had always fantasized about being part of an intelligence task force. She didn't picture this. "What's the plan?"

"Damn, girl, we haven't even ordered yet," Carlos said.

"I'm not thinking about food," she said.

"All right," Bo stepped in. "Here's how I see this going. We get the lay of the land tonight but call it an early night. Carlos has whipped up six day passes for us tomorrow, and we'll be on the lookout for any known black market targets in our database. Tomorrow night's the grand ball you and I will be attending."

Kaden decided to play devil's advocate. "But this all sounds random. *Maybe* we'll spot some shady characters, *maybe* we'll be able to follow the food chain up to the higher ups."

"We're not doing random," Judy Matthews broke in. She turned to Bo. "Tell her. Tell her why I'm here. Why Tosh is here."

Good question. Kaden was wondering the same. The waitress came and took their orders while Kaden waited for Bo to respond.

"We got our introductions out of the way at the club," he said. "We don't have time for a practice run, we're creating this operation on the fly. Kaden, Carlos, and I have new aliases that we'll use during the conference. Nico will head up operational support. Tosh is our gadgets guy. And Judy is our translation specialist during our monitoring operation."

"Monitoring what?" Nico asked.

Carlos and Tosh glanced at each other, reached under the table, and set their black valises on their laps.

Tosh leaned forward and lowered his voice, which was already hard to hear above the sounds of the Bavarian folk songs coming from speakers overhead.

"We've brought our mobile command unit with us. Tonight and tomorrow we cover every inch of old town with listening devices."

"Switzerland is one of the top five countries in the world in terms of Internet speeds," Nico chimed in. "That should help."

"Yeah, but how do you get that kind of coverage?" Kaden was dubious. "There's like a thousand attendees here."

Tosh looked at Bo to see how much he could say. Bo gave a quick nod.

"Micro-drones," Tosh said. "The short answer is we'll be filling every street lamp, every tree limb, every restaurant rafter and conference room with cheap, dumb, but ubiquitous and effective micro-drones."

He reached into his valise and placed a small white box on the table. He opened it, took out a small object, and placed it on his fingertip. Tosh was turning out to be a real gearhead.

"Look at that!" Judy leaned closer and marveled.

Kaden had to squint to see the tiny propellers. She found the idea audacious. Could it possibly work? "This is an international gathering with lots of different languages spoken."

Judy said, "I'm fluent in German, French, Italian, Spanish, Swedish, Finnish. Can get by in Chinese, Russian, and Ukrainian. The official language of the conference is English but yeah, we expect the streets and hallways will be a potpourri of languages."

"But you can't possibly listen to every conversation," Kaden said.

"We can't," Tosh agreed. "Normally we'd be transmitting live streams of all audio to an offsite facility that can monitor for keywords in real time. It's a huge data mining job, and we don't have the set-up for that on such short notice."

"So what we do we do?"

Tosh looked at her dead on. "We use a local AI. We use Amelia."

"Well, good to know!" Kaden said. As she thought about it, it struck her. *Of course! This would be a perfect use case for an artificial intelligence.* "I'll have to add a few language libraries to her dataset."

Bo gave his slanted smile. "Looks like your imaginary friend may come in handy after all."

Carlos looked around to make sure no one was looking. He took out his phone and launched the micro-drone from Tosh's fingertip.

"Let's get this party started," Tosh said.

18

Minsk, Belarus, and Samana Cay

Maxim Volkov watched as Lucid approached the Data Center on Samana Cay and took out his mobile device to monitor his biometrics. One last meeting before they both needed to jet off to the Summit.

The screen in front of Volkov lit up with Lucid's vitals. Body temp, blood pressure, blood oxygen, air quality, temperature, humidity, radiation levels—all readings were normal. The chip implants and subdural sensors embedded in his arms, hands, upper torso, and legs were operating at optimal levels.

A few months after Lucid had gotten chipped, *Wired* magazine ran a profile piece describing him as "the world's most connected human." That's how Lucid came to Volkov's attention. In their first conversation, Lucid complained about the magazine dubbing him a "half-cyborg"; he preferred the term "posthuman." After all, he argued, he was the epitome of an advanced augmented human, pioneering the path toward the Singularity, the merging of man and machine.

The Data Center's main doors whooshed open as Lucid

approached. *But what's this? He's being accompanied by one of the guests.*

"Lucid, who's with you? Do they have clearance?" His voice took on an urgent tone. Lucid was wearing his earpiece for their scheduled check-in.

"Excuse me." Lucid stepped away from the guest. "I need a moment."

"I'll wait," the guest said at the guard desk.

Volkov watched as Lucid advanced down the marble hallway to the Multimedia Room. As he entered, a phalanx of monitors blinked to life, forty in all across the main wall and two side walls.

"Do we need to meet?" Lucid asked.

"No, I'll make this quick. I'm flying to the Summit in an hour. You?"

"Two hours." Lucid gave no sign he was upset at being consigned to a separate flight.

"We need to discuss logistics when you arrive." *This gathering of the Compact has to run like a Swiss watch.*

"Yes, Chairman."

"Who's the visitor?"

"Evelyn Gladstone. She paid a six-figure premium for the right to observe the simulations and have me give a quick tour."

"Observe? As in, voyeurism?"

"That's a label, sir. We're careful to avoid labels."

"Very well. As long as she abides by the nondisclosure agreement." Volkov was uncomfortable with letting outsiders see how Fantasy Live worked. But he had too much on his plate to begin micro-managing Lucid.

"Evelyn understands her obligations."

"Proceed. I'll be monitoring."

"Yes, Chairman."

Lucid opened the door and signaled for Evelyn to enter. Volkov called up Evelyn's background details on a side monitor.

American. Forty-six. Twice divorced. Made her fortune as a broker trading futures in energy and metals.

Evelyn entered the room, her eyes sweeping across the full-color high-def screens. It was late afternoon and the initial Fantasy Live simulations were just getting underway.

"Intriguing." Evelyn moved closer to the bank of monitors and brushed the screen closest to her with her fingertips. "Lucid, I may need to write you another check to have some recordings sent over."

"I'm afraid I can't do that." Lucid handed her a pair of Eyewear that covered her eye sockets. "Observe the action in each scene. Wholly interactive, no latency, wide field of vision from the guest's point of view."

Evelyn put on the small rubbery goggles and moved to the next screen where a troupe of Chippendale look-alikes was entertaining one of the female guests.

"What am I looking at?" she asked.

"Our soft launch," Lucid said. "You're looking at the first Fantasy Live stories being played out. Each Fantasy Live simulation has a story arc. You're a player in your own story, a story with pacing, anticipation, rising action, and a satisfactory resolution."

"I can't wait for mine. But thanks for the sneak peek, so to speak."

Lucid explained how it worked. Instead of watching the action through a TV monitor, the Eyewear transported Evelyn into the room of the simulation. Each guest was having a high-touch, intimate, immersive AR experience while Evelyn was having a VR experience that let her toggle between the perspective of the guest and each Chippendale performer.

"I understand you're a VR and AR aficionado?"

"I dabble," she said. "Always disappointed by the limitations. In your literature you promised revolutionary breakthroughs. You said you've made the magic leap."

"We have." Lucid guided her to the next simulation showing

a French maid with a feather duster and a naughty outfit. "We've taken AR from 3-D to *five* dimensions—the dimensions of sight, sound, taste, smell, and touch. Your audio receptors live in an ancient part of your brain. We'll pull you into the experience in a deep way by using advanced reverbs from audio projectors embedded into the sets. You'll notice the sound picked up by your skin, not just your ears."

Evelyn stared at the simulation through her headset. "You make it sound so high-tech, but it's just a French maid in a slutty outfit."

Lucid frowned. "When you're in the simulation, you'll understand. Shall I continue?"

"Please do. How does it work?" She squinted behind her goggles. "I'm not seeing any sensors."

"WE APPLY a thin chemical compound to the performers' faces like makeup. They also wear sensors on any part of their torso that needs re-imaging. But hearing and sight are only two components. You'll have to wait until your simulation to experience the remaining three senses: taste, smell, and especially touch. We've cracked the tactile nut."

"I'd go for a different metaphor if I were you." Evelyn chortled as she moved down the row of monitors on the wall. She peered up at one simulation with a young woman wearing Playboy bunny ears and another with the Dallas Cowboys Cheerleaders. "Just curious. I see several copyright violations or trademark infringements. How do you get around that?"

"We hired two of the world's leading IP law firms. The augmented reality aspect means the performance is both transitory and transformative. That's one reason I can't send you a video. We're in the clear if we limit the simulation to a brief AR or VR experience where the guests bring their own personal media to us and they're the only ones who see the performance."

"But they're not the only ones. Do they know we're watching?"

"They know they've signed a privacy waiver."

Evelyn flounced her mane of red hair dismissively. "I'd be surprised if they're okay with this." She moved to her right along the long row of glowing screens. "What have we here? It doesn't look like the others."

Lucid nodded. "Mother of three. We do have a handful of women clients."

They peered at the simulation through their Eyewear, then nudged down their goggles to see how she really looked. She was a slightly overweight woman around fifty years old. In the simulation, she has the gorgeous, rock-hard bikini body of a twenty-year-old. She's lying on a lounge chair overlooking a pool and eating a cheeseburger with a buttered bun. A server clad in tight swim trunks brings her a piña colada and then begins cooling her with a fan. Awaiting her at arm's reach is a silver dessert tray with a slice of strawberry shortcake, fresh strawberries, and real whipped cream. Her eyes move to the shirtless pool boy who's getting sweaty in the midday sun. The pool boy is flanked by three bronzed male models sunning themselves or doing laps. In the tented veranda just beyond, three middle-aged white men are hard at work. One is washing a mountain of dishes, another is diapering an infant, another is on his hands and knees scrubbing the bathroom floor.

"That's inspired." Evelyn moved to her right along the long row of glowing screens. Her Eyewear switched to the next simulation. "A strip club? Tell me about this one."

"Our guest remains fixated on an ex-girlfriend. His fantasy involves her performing a pole dance. Think of it as a form of immersive therapy."

"Oh, really? So this becomes a fantasy shrink session for some people?"

"We give people a chance to work out their shit. We give

them a second chance to make things right in their own minds. To express those pent-up feelings or to live out that wild night you always regretted you passed on. In this case, seeing his ex perform a striptease act on stage provides a kind of release and emotional closure."

"Bullshit." She knitted her brow and scowled. "He's in it for the revenge and humiliation."

"You'd be surprised how many revenge fantasy requests we received for launch week," Lucid said.

"And you'd be surprised at how unsurprised I'd be. Do you green-light all your guests' fantasies?"

"By no means. Some of our guests' fantasies are impractical to pull off from a logistical standpoint. Others are … quite dark."

Shouts in the hallway were followed by a loud, efficient knock on the door. An assistant burst into the Multimedia Room. "Sir, we have a problem."

Volkov's eyes went from Lucid to Evelyn and back again.

"It's all right," Lucid told the aide. "Speak!"

"One of the new girls. There's a big problem with one of the new girls."

19

Samana Cay

The medallion dangling on Alex's chest vibrated as he approached the resort's Ready Room across the court-yard from the Fantasy Theater. It buzzed two other times in the past day when a "Type 22" Opt-In came within fifty feet. He'd struck up a conversation with the dark-haired beauties both times but didn't take advantage of the privileges during his first full day at Fantasy Live.

Now on day two he entered the Ready Room, a larger, more impressive space than he'd imagined. Tasteful modern art, contemporary furnishings, mood music personalized to his tastes —a contemporary bossa nova. *Thank you, pre-island questionnaire.*

Rachel, also a Type 22, smiled at him from across the room. The late afternoon sunlight glinted off her bare shoulders, her flawless tanned skin accentuated by a one-piece turquoise print dress with a tropical palm design. They were alone.

She smiled, strolled past him, and locked the door. "This is our private time. To get you prepped. Just a half hour from now." She sounded more like a sultry date than an ambassador.

She glided to the black lacquer table beneath a colorful print of a Caribbean beach and poured two glasses of red wine. She handed him a glass of Cabernet Sauvignon. "Ready for your first Fantasy Live simulation?"

"I'll admit I'm damn curious."

A knot of nervous energy was forming in the pit of his stomach, a mix of anticipation and dread. He wanted to see whether the augmented reality wizards at Fantasy Live could really conjure up a realistic likeness of his first girlfriend, Cynthia Esposito. They'd dated during their senior year of high school, a torrid romance she broke off at the end of summer when they went off to different colleges.

My first true love. My first heartbreak. I never got over you.

The dread came from what he suspected was about to unfold. Cynthia had never opted in to his fantasy. He scraped together some old video clips from when they were young and stupid and posted everything to Facebook. He sent everything he could remember about her to Fantasy Live as part of his Fantasy Prep Kit. Even though Cynthia wouldn't be in the room and would never know about it, it still felt invasive. Even a little creepy.

Aren't fantasies supposed to be unattainable by definition? Maybe not anymore.

Rachel glided back to the lacquer table and picked up a small canister. It looked like the inhalers he used to take for asthma as a kid.

"Here, this will help you relax."

Alex inspected the canister and shook it. "I don't do drugs."

"It's not a drug. It's a neurochemical mist to enhance your experience. Trust me."

"It's not a matter of trust. I need to know what's in it."

"You sure? It takes away the air of mystery."

"I put nothing in my body unless I know what it is."

"Fair enough. No secrets, I promised. The visual and auditory stimuli from the Eyewear you'll be wearing make the simulation hyper-realistic. The mist opens your sensory pathways and takes the experience to a whole new level."

"What are the ingredients?"

"A blend of neurotransmitters. Endorphins, dopamine, testosterone, and oxytocin, the so-called cuddle hormone."

"Cuddle hormone, huh?" He flipped it around in his palm. "What do your scientists call this little blend? They must have a nickname for it." She hesitated, so he reminded her. "You said full disclosure."

"You're persistent, Andrew. 'Perception Mollies'—that's what our neuroscientists call it. But there's no meth involved. It's a hundred percent safe."

He still wasn't ready to take a hit. So she snatched the canister from his palm, held it to her mouth, and inhaled a single puff. "See? Now your turn."

"I won't get the full experience unless I give this a shot?"

"Exactly."

He retrieved it from her hand. Did he want to do this? Certainly not. Would Andrew Bayless? Almost certainly yes. "Never let it be said Andrew Bayless wussed out." He took a puff.

Rachel smiled. They took another sip of wine. She headed to the opposite end of the room and fetched what looked like a makeup kit. "One last thing to get you ready."

"To make me look good?"

"It's not about appearances. It's about *perception*. Lean closer."

She used an application brush to apply a powder to his face.

"You've heard of double-blind experiments? At Fantasy Live, all our simulations are double *safe*. You never see what the fantasy performer really looks like. And she never sees your true identity. When you're walking around all week, you'll never know which young woman you interacted with the night before. Adds an added layer of security. And mystery."

She daubed his cheeks, nose, forehead, chin, and around his mouth.

"Like a masquerade ball," he said.

"That's a good analogy. I'll have to steal that."

She finished with his *perception* makeup. He felt the neuro-chemicals kick in. The effect reminded him of the rave parties in college where everyone was dropping Ecstasy. A sense of well-being coursed through him. He felt strangely at peace. Even the lights and the artwork now seemed more vivid, pulsing as if they were alive and had stories to tell.

Rachel clinked wine glasses with him. She looked so beautiful. Part of him wanted to kiss her right now. And part of him knew the oxytocin and endorphins were messing with his synapses. He took a last sip and set down his glass. He couldn't take notes during the Fantasy Live simulation so he needed to remember every detail of what was about to unfold.

"I have questions before we begin."

"I can answer any questions you have, Andrew. Take whatever time you need."

He gathered his thoughts. Since his arrival he'd heard stories from fellow guests about dark fantasies they'd requested. It was a subject he's never discussed in polite company. Maybe he was just out of step with his contemporaries. What kind of fantasies did his friends and neighbors harbor? Did some secretly desire a night of sexual domination? Did they want to exact vengeance on an overbearing boss? Would any of them hire a hitman if they could get away with it?

"You must have received some outrageous requests for fantasies," he probed. "I mean, beyond the kinky stuff."

"Yes. Nothing I can share, though."

It makes sense Fantasy Live can't cater to all our fantasies. We'd all love to be rich, good looking, popular, brilliant, well respected, famous. But how convincing would those simulations be? No, Fantasy Live was mostly an excuse to act out some of our darker impulses. I'm happy to chronicle this for my undercover series, but I'd be happier to see those secret impulses stay sublimated, thank you very much. There's a reason society clamps down on the lizard side of our brains.

He needed to return to the task at hand. Cynthia Esposito.

"The model or performer, she volunteered for today's simulation?"

"Yes. Every girl is evaluated and scored across a wide range of criteria, including physical attributes and resemblance to the fantasy subject."

"And then they're given some kind of script?"

"No, nothing that detailed. Just some biographical material. Some info about you and your relationship with her. And a storyboard that maps out the story path we'd like her to take you down. But don't ruin the experience by asking too many questions. Let it unfold!"

She was right about that. "Okay, last question." He hated himself for what he was about to ask. But he needed to probe deeper for his story and separate the B.S. from the reality. "You said part of your job as ambassador was for the build-up before the main event."

"The appetizer."

"Right. The appetizer." He paused and checked the color of her Opt-In bracelet. It was still glowing bright green. "Would you take your clothes off for me, please?"

She laughed. "I had a feeling this was coming. Well, since you said please. I feel safe with you, Andrew."

She reached around to her back, untied a knot, and her sundress dropped to the floor. She wasn't wearing a bra. She reached down and removed her panties.

Alex stood there in wonder, looking at Rachel standing naked in the middle of the Ready Room. She was flawless. If Leonardo da Vinci or Botticelli sprung to life and painted her, they wouldn't do her justice.

She was only a few years younger. In another time, he might have fallen for her. He was single, amped up on biochemicals, and a jumble of emotions right now. He found her sexy as hell. Intoxicating. But he knew he would never act on it.

He was in a committed relationship with Valerie. They were moving past the tear-your-clothes-off stage of animal lust and exploring things like compatibility, intimacy, common interests, worldviews, life goals. He was still coming to terms with Valerie's decision to use a surrogate for the baby they planned to raise together.

For him, love at first sight had happened only once. With Cynthia Esposito. God knows, when you're seventeen, you're hopped up on pheromones and oxytocin and other mysterious chemicals that turn your brain to mush.

He thought of all this while this goddess stood before him, assured and unselfconscious in her naked sensuality.

"You're a beautiful person, Rachel. Thank you. I'm ready."

She smiled demurely and put her clothes back on. "Take a deep breath, lover boy. Let's go meet Cynthia."

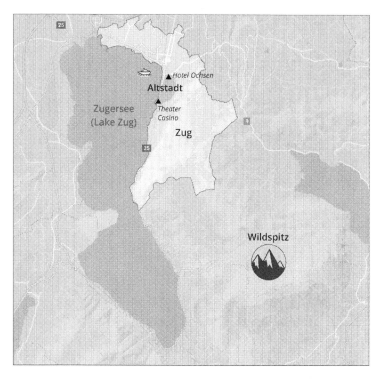

Map of Zug and Wildspitz, Switzerland.

20

Zug, Switzerland

Kaden hopped aboard the fishing boat at mid-morning when the streets of old town Zug began to come alive. Bo, Nico, and Judy joined her along with the captain, as the boat's owner introduced himself. He pushed the aging vessel out into the lake that kissed the edge of old town.

"Thanks again for working us into your schedule," Bo told the captain, a dude with gray whiskers and a bandage across his nose that made her think skin cancer. He was smoking a pipe that smelled of cherry, menthol, and death. *Working on lung cancer, too.*

"It's just good to see you again, my friend," the captain said in a Swiss German accent. She figured he'd met Bo somewhere along the line during his overseas stints.

The captain turned the wheel to head out to the middle of the lake. "First time in Zug?" he asked her.

"First time in Switzerland," she said.

"Welcome." He smiled. "How do you like Zugersee?"

"Zugersee?"

"Lake Zug."

"Pretty." She breathed in the crisp Alpine mountain air and watched the seabirds trailing their boat. The captain turned the wheel and the boat began tracking the lakefront, gliding past the snug little village enveloped by ice blue mountains with wisps of fog curling through stands of evergreens.

"A lot of visitors here for the Crypto Summit," the captain said. "I'm an investor myself. Zug's a big financial center. Has been for decades. It has a special tax status within Switzerland—our version of the Caymans. There are more companies on the tax rolls than locals."

"Interesting. But we're not here to invest."

"Sightseeing then?" the captain asked with a wink. "Have you had a chance to see Altstadt?"

She'd taken an early morning walk along the cobbled Old Town with its medieval buildings, narrow alleyways, and colorful bay windows. "Yes, beautiful."

"Make sure you visit Wildspitz before you go home." The captain pointed with his pipe to the highest peak rising in the distance to the southeast. "Spectacular views, especially at night. "

Kaden looked out over the vast lake. "There's a purity here. Can't say I love it."

She smiled politely, excused herself, and moved to the back of the boat. She was a New Yorker, attracted to the city's grit and grime, its helter-skelter welter of neuroses, its nonstop nervous energy. No sense trying to explain that to a stranger.

She checked the Internet signal. Surprisingly strong out here. Carlos had set up a series of high-powered encrypted Wi-Fi hotspots along the banks. Now she'd be able to tap into the conversations Tosh's micro-drones were starting to pick up. Nico set up the ultra-long-range shotgun microphone to target anyone on shore who looked suspicious. The equipment came from Yuan Deng, one of the missing girls' fathers. Judy, wearing a headset, came up and offered a Swiss pastry. She could provide instant translations, helping them decide when to move on to a new target.

The always-on set-up had another benefit: She could consult with Amelia. She didn't know how the captain would react to her talking to herself, so she moved to the rear of the craft.

"Well, this is nice." Amelia appeared, sitting on the edge of the boat in the lake's choppy waters. "Smell that fresh mountain air!"

Amelia couldn't smell anything, of course. Kaden suppressed an urge to warn her about sitting on the stern. So she asked, "The new language libraries up and running?"

"Sie wetten. Scommetti. Usted apuesta. Tu paries. Det kan—"

"Okay, I get it. You'll need to shut down all your other processes—including visualization—once we start."

"Then I should stretch my legs." She hopped to her feet and pretended to stroll around the deck. "Oh, Kaden, my love. I'll need lots of bandwidth crunching these keywords looking for patterns. So I'll get back to decrypting the Project Ezekiel file as soon as we have a more robust Wi-Fi signal."

"Yeah, that's fine, keyword patterns are the top priority. And let's add one more keyword phrase to watch for. Dražen Savić."

"Roger. Amelia out."

Nico looked over. "Who you talking to? Oh, right."

"Ready to start?" Kaden asked him.

He aimed his high-powered binoculars across the promenade of charming storefronts, historic landmarks, and park benches that were starting to fill up with tourists and conference-goers. "Let's do this."

♀ ♂

KADEN WANTED to make the most of their short time in Zug. While the others continued with their surveillance on both land

and water, she headed to the shopping district and bought a risque low-cut dress for tonight's grand ball. Carlos hacked into the guest list and added their names. Then she headed to the hotel where the first panels were just beginning.

They wouldn't get much use out of her attending the conference sessions. So she headed to the hotel bar to drum up some attention. She had changed into the kind of respectable upscale wardrobe that a rare minerals millionaire like Jordan Wilkerson might wear. Full-on slutty mode would come later at the ball.

"Can I buy you a drink?"

Well, that was fast! Sidling up next to her at the bar was a dark-haired guy a little older than her, late twenties, wearing a fresh haircut and a designer suit that signaled, *I'm a player.*

"Why not?" she said.

She had no idea how to do the flirty bar-talk banter that singles seem to master.

"What brings a beautiful woman like you to this gathering of financial geeks and freaks?" He had an accent she couldn't place, but she couldn't bother Amelia, who was still processing conversations taking place in hundreds of locations.

"I'm here to explore new opportunities."

"And I as well." He brushed his jacket against her bare shoulder, even though there was plenty of room to spread out.

"They say the real action happens in the hallways and on the streets."

"And in the hotel bars?"

"Perhaps." She smiled. "What is it you do in this brave new world?"

"I make money. A lot of money. And you?"

"I run a rare-earth minerals family business in Alberta. But I'm looking to diversify into something with higher risk, higher reward. Know of anything?" *Am I pushing too fast?*

"I may. But there are many possible kinds of ventures to explore. We should discuss. Perhaps later tonight?"

She suspected business was the last thing on this guy's mind. Even if he was mixed up in some shady operations, he wasn't about to bring a complete stranger into his confidence.

Kaden smiled and reached into her purse. She pulled out one of the business cards Tosh had created for her. The ones with a microchip-size listening device embedded in the image of her.

She wrote someone else's room number on the back and tucked it into his breast pocket. She smiled. "See you at midnight."

21

Samana Cay

Alex followed Rachel out of the Ready Room building and along the ridge to their destination. The enormous Fantasy Theater was off-limits to guests until it was time for their Fantasy Live simulation. They entered the main doors and stood in a large, dimly lit open space, perhaps an atrium.

"It's time to get outfitted." Rachel reached into her satchel and retrieved a different-looking kind of Eyewear. "Tonight you'll be using these."

Instead of his designer smartglasses, the new Eyewear in her palm reminded him of the goggles swimmers wore at the Summer Olympics. She wrapped the rubbery device around the back of his head and adjusted the fit around his eyes. The bright blue lenses were small but still provided a wide field of vision. The sides of the Eyewear contained a pair of earbuds with tiny audio speakers.

"Don't take this off under any circumstances. Understand?"

"Why?"

"It violates the Terms. You want an immersive experience, don't you? The fantasy is diluted if you're thinking about the equipment or focusing on the reality layer."

He nodded and placed the earbuds into his ear canals.

"See, you can still hear me fine," Rachel said.

"Got it. Anything else?"

"Let's walk." She grabbed his hand in hers and they padded across the atrium of the cavernous building.

Alex saw three corridors up ahead leading in different directions. Two remained shrouded in shadows while the middle walkway glowed a soft yellow. As he stepped through the middle doorway, a cluster of little white stars swirled around the entrance and a distant medley of notes chimed.

They emerged at the entrance to an enormous footbridge with bamboo slats suspended above a vast river gorge. To the right, an immense waterfall gushed down the face of a mountain with jagged pinnacles. A brilliant rainbow curved from the top of the falls to a large arched doorway cut out of the mountain at the far side of the bridge.

"We call it the Bridge of Forbidden Love," Rachel said above the sound of the cascade.

"What if I fall in?"

"Don't." The waterfall's roar grew louder. "You must have really liked this girl," she said.

"Why's that?"

"I got that sense from the storyboard. Okay, let's go."

They moved onto the footbridge, with Rachel prompting him to go first. She spoke up over his shoulder. "A few last things. There's no Reality Mode when you're In-World. You're inside a Fantasy Live simulation. You can't step out of it until you signal for it to end."

"All right."

As they walked above the rushing river, water droplets from the cascade pelted his face. He tasted the spray on his tongue. He felt a gust of wind and his knees almost buckled as the bamboo footbridge rocked from side to side. His heart raced, his hands began to sweat.

"You'll be starting off in virtual reality," Rachel shouted as the roar of the falls became louder. "When you're ready for augmented reality, hold up two fingers to signal you're ready for Scene Two."

He gripped the support ropes on both sides to steady himself. He knew he wasn't standing on a rickety suspension bridge a hundred feet above a raging river. But there was nothing movie-like about this. It felt *real*.

"Last thing. Remember, this is mostly a *visual* experience. How *tactile* you want to get during the augmented session is up to you—the girl is an Opt-In. Don't expect her to recount old times. Don't ask specific questions or the entire fantasy may collapse."

He understood. This wasn't a place for second chances or regrets. It sounded more like a vivid dream.

"Good luck, Andrew. You deserve all that awaits you."

"Wait. What?" He turned around. Rachel was gone. The footbridge swung in the breeze and he nearly lost his balance. He gripped the ropes tighter and pulled himself forward.

After a minute the wind died down, the bridge stopped rocking, and he came to the end. He stood before a dark entrance carved into the mountain. He plunged through the opening.

He appeared to be floating inside what looked like a colossal palace, a great hall laden with elaborate chandeliers, gold statues, rich carpeting. But there was something wrong. Everything seemed out of scale. It was as if he were a Lilliputian inside a giant Palace of Versailles.

His movements were no longer under his control. He floated down a grand corridor as if encased in something. He passed by immense oil paintings, colonnades, and several grandly decorated rooms. He slowed as he approached a door that stood ajar. He slipped through the opening. Scores of candles illuminated a large, sumptuous bathroom outfitted with oversize mirrors, tile mosaic on the floor and walls, and a white clawfoot tub.

In which Cynthia Esposito was taking a bubble bath.

Alex realized where he was. Inside a bubble. A literal bubble. He floated closer and closer to her until he was hovering just above the tub.

Cynthia looked every bit as dazzling as he remembered. The high-fidelity realism of her likeness startled him. It was like watching a high-definition film of a movie star, but this was *Cynthia*. Cynthia, the spitting image of the girl he fell in love with. She had the same soulful brown eyes, the same chocolate hair, the same small ears that poked out a little. She was always self-conscious about that but he thought her ears were cute.

"Hi, Andrew." She looked up directly at him.

He almost toppled over, startled by her voice. "You can see me?"

"Of course. You're floating right there."

It was like she was a giantess watching a pathetic little peeping Tom creep toward her.

"Don't worry, I won't pop you." She smiled and inched down to let the water touch her chin.

Her voice sounded so rich, exactly the same as when they were seventeen. *Well, you sent them the tapes, didn't you? Of course they can reproduce it. The ability to extrapolate hours-long conversations from a recording only a minute long—that tech has been around for years. Still, her lips match her words. They're doing this in real time. Astonishing!*

"Thanks, Cynthia." He wasn't sure what to say. He slipped against the wall of the bubble and found his movements were propelling the bubble in the same direction.

"Don't worry, say anything you want. Or just watch. It's your fantasy. I'm here for you."

His heart was melting at the sound of her playful, alluring, slightly throaty voice that once twisted him into knots. No woman had ever again touched his heart in the same way. Was it because Cynthia was so special? Or because they were seventeen and in love for the first time and that kind of magic happens only once?

He searched his memory frantically to remember if he'd put down anything too weird or kinky for his Cynthia Esposito fantasy. He didn't think so. He gave the Fantasy Live people several options. But he didn't put a ton of time into it. He didn't think they could pull off anything like this.

"Let me move out of your way," he said as he watched her swipe a large sponge across her leg.

"You're not in my way, Andrew."

Floating right on top of her was making him nervous. He tried to navigate the bubble to get a vantage point from the side of the tub, his palms pressing against the soft damp rubbery contours of the bubble. He glimpsed her breasts beneath the soap bubbles, dappled by the candlelight.

On one level, there wasn't anything unusual about this kind of fantasy. He'd slept with the real Cynthia Esposito several times when their parents were away. He'd seen her naked in her bedroom and in his bedroom and once during a hike in the woods. But he wasn't seventeen anymore. And suddenly he realized how inappropriate it was for a twenty-nine-year-old man to be watching a seventeen-year-old girl take a bubble bath.

"I ... I should probably apologize about this fantasy."

She laughed. "Oh, silly. It's okay. Nobody has G-rated fantasies. How boring would that be?"

That relieved his guilt a bit. And he didn't need to mention his fantasy girlfriend's age in his article, did he? He and his editors at *Axom* would need a boatload of meetings to figure out how to handle this. Could he even quote a seventeen-year-old? Did he need to get permission from the girl's parents? How old was fantasy Cynthia anyway? And what was the age of consent on Samana Cay?

"All right, let's continue," he said. "Don't do anything you don't want to do."

That sounded lame, too. *She's a paid actor in a story! Of course everything she's doing is not what she'd be doing on a Wednesday night! Or at least, he doubted it. But he couldn't very well pop the pretense and start interviewing her. They were watching.*

That reminded him to survey his surroundings more closely. *How were they doing this?* This was some kind of set, maybe similar to a Hollywood movie set. Somewhere out of sight they must have outfitted the room with state-of-the-art high-def audiovisual equipment. He reasoned the setup included use of artificial intelligence that had captured Cynthia Esposito's facial features and body type from the video imagery he'd supplied.

The challenge would be to convert the girl's facial expressions and speech patterns *in real time* via an ultra low-latency communication system and then transmit it to him in a way that was convincing and realistic *at close range*. All of it done on the sly in the background to preserve the illusion of a fantasy.

He was familiar enough with AR and VR to know this was a remarkable achievement. He knew about "deepfake videos," where computers swapped someone's face onto another person's body, but this took it to a whole new dimension. The algorithms involved, the cross-platform engine for physics and graphics, the voice cloning software—their set-up must all be staggeringly powerful. *Yet they've done it, by God. Right down to the timbre of her voice. Right down to her freckles. This isn't sci-fi. It's mixed reality. And the world isn't ready for this yet.*

Cynthia turned her head and peered at him with that lost-fawn look of hers as he hovered astride the tub. "So tell me what you've been up to lately, Andrew."

"Well, it's been a long time since we talked. Graduated from Florida State. Work in the tech sector now." He wanted to be genuine while still maintaining his cover. He was tempted to remove his goggles, but that would shut down the simulation, maybe get him kicked off the island. "I think about you a lot. You still take my breath away."

She smiled shyly. "Thanks, Andrew. That's nice."

"I'm seeing someone now. It's serious."

"Oh, good. You deserve the best. And don't worry, you can say anything here. Your fantasies are safe with me."

He was still gobsmacked by her. She smelled of fresh lavender. This entire simulation was mind-blowing, soul-stirring. He felt a surge of vitality he hadn't felt since his teenage years. A mixture of amazement, ardor, and impossible longing buzzed through his body. His teen years were no picnic, but Cynthia would be in the highlight reel.

He took a moment to check himself—his pulse was slightly elevated, his eyes tracked his finger movements. He knew he wasn't drunk in the slightest. In fact, just the opposite. His senses felt heightened and sharp.

He thought about how he should play this.

Alex Wyatt the journalist was paying attention to every detail of this fantasy. Cynthia's appearance, her voice, the dimples that formed on her cheeks when she smiled—it was all captured with such fidelity that he knew he had a hell of a story here. What kind of Pandora's Box was Fantasy Live about to unleash on the world? Who wouldn't want to spend time with their favorite fantasy subjects? What did this portend for modern relationships? How would it disrupt a world where you could compare your spouse or significant other with someone from your idealized, airbrushed past?

Andrew the millionaire startup founder would have a different reaction. He'd want to play this story out to its logical conclusion. It cut him to the quick that she was calling him Andrew instead of Alex. But he couldn't tell her. He had to keep in character.

Alex the ex-boyfriend found himself remembering how moon-struck he'd once been. Originally he thought this experience might be akin to coming across a photo of an old flame on social media. But his feelings in this moment ran much deeper. It was almost as if he'd traveled back to a time in his life when love was pure and boundless. A time when all things seemed possible and heartbreak was something that happened to other people.

He knew the oxytocin and endorphins were swimming in his head, roiling his emotions. Even so, he was having a hard time resisting the impulse to confess his love for her all over again. Maybe his subconscious was telling him to find the real Cynthia Esposito and meet her for coffee. Maybe she really was meant to be his one true love.

No! That's the cuddle hormone talking!

"Tell me what you want, Andrew." He thought he detected a note of sadness in Cynthia's voice. She leaned forward and reached for the oversize sponge.

His heart was bursting with passion. He wanted to kiss her, to caress her face with his hand. He'd turn thirty next month—he wanted his youth back.

But how could he say any of this to the fantasy version of Cynthia Esposito?

Instead, he raised two fingers into the air. *Time for Scene Two.*

22

Zug, Switzerland

Volkov arrived in Zurich in the usual manner. His Dassault Falcon 8X jet landed at one of the airport's four private jet terminals. He descended the jet's airstairs and entered the black armor-plated bomb-proof Cadillac Escalade SUV limousine with black tinted windows and partition. The outside mirrors were turned downward so there was no chance the driver or bodyguard riding in the front could glimpse the Chairman. So unfortunate if they did.

He punched in the security code to confirm his identity. They were off to Zug. An LED strip across the ceiling of the SUV illuminated a silver bucket of Champagne and ice. He was not in the mood for a drink or the entertainment console. Instead, he occupied himself during the forty-minute ride by reading a new book about the coming collapse of the American empire. *The author would be stunned to learn how quickly that collapse was coming.*

He prided himself as something of a history buff, devouring volumes about the Roman Empire, Sun Tzu's *The Art of War*, books about geopolitics and the rise and fall of civilizations. As a

young man in Belarus, he was reading a tract of ancient apocalyptic literature one day when the realization struck him like a
thunderbolt. He recognized himself in the text.

Or more precisely, he recognized his future self as a destroyer
of worlds, a builder of new worlds.

He recalled the day the family attorney took him aside with
the news. His parents and older brother were killed in a car accident. As the only remaining son, he would inherit his parents'
vast fortune. Rumors swirled that he was behind the fatal crash,
but there was no official inquest in cash-strapped Belarus. He was
coy about it, never speaking of the accident. Instead, he retreated
into his chamber for days, weeks, months.

Incognito was born.

It was foretold. *His eyes are like a flame of fire, and on his head
are many diadems, and he has a name written that no one knows
but himself. Revelation 19:11-21*

He snapped out of his reverie as they pulled up to the
mansion and circled to the back. Ah, yes. He'd heard Zaven
Kasparian boast about his place with an epic view of Lake Zug.
He'd developed a complex relationship with his fellow billionaire.
Months ago he'd done Kasparian a favor. An operative in Kasparian's employ had made the fatal mistake of skimming profits from
the boss's gambling operations. Savić had boarded Kasparian's
submarine and taken care of the problem with a bullet to the
back of the head.

You wash my hand and I'll wash yours.

His bodyguard did a quick reconnaissance of the backyard
grounds and then disappeared inside. Volkov made his way to the
second story via a private marble staircase. He opened the door to
his quarters in the west wing, a seldom-used area of the estate
reserved for special guests. Staff members were instructed to
accommodate his every wish but admonished not to enter the
room under any circumstances. Communication would be done
verbally and through written notes.

The legend of Incognito demanded such discretion. It was so ingrained into his identity that he rarely needed to remind himself of his one unalterable law: *Never drop the mask of anonymity. Your power flows from it.*

He hung up his jacket. An old habit, he still wore an unremarkable, blend-into-the-woodwork sport coat in a boring shade of gray. As he checked the electronics his advance team had set out for him, his phone rang. Only members of the Compact had this private number. He saw the caller's name: Randolph Blackburn. The American whose secure digital vault was breached.

"Yes?" he answered.

"Incognito, is that you?" A frail voice. Blackburn's chronic disease seemed to be getting the better of him.

Volkov decided to lie. "I've been meaning to contact you, Blackburn." Addressing members of the Compact by their last names was not impolite but rather the accepted protocol. These were not your friends. These were men who understood only one thing. Power.

"Rumor has it our group will be meeting soon. Why wasn't I informed?"

Volkov hesitated. Blackburn had informed him his digital vault had been breached by Kaden Baker, his granddaughter. It was an unforgivable misstep, letting a copy of Project Ezekiel fall into the wrong hands. The digital file was an executive summary, not the full unredacted outline of the operational plans. Even so, if the stolen document was decrypted or fell into the hands of law enforcement, the operation could be compromised. It contained a brief mention of each member of the Compact.

Such a slip-up might have been forgiven, considering Blackburn's contributions to the Compact. Even now, Blackburn's broadcast group was requiring its network of local television stations to air video segments spotlighting threats to America from outside forces. Immigrants. Terrorist groups. The European

Union. It played beautifully into their long-term campaign of disinformation.

Combine that with the biological cocktail Bashir's Lab was introducing into the population, and soon there would be widespread panic in the streets.

No, Volkov decided, *I still need Blackburn for a short time. But I can't fill him in about the full, nations-altering breadth of Project Ezekiel. Blackburn might be a globalist, but the mass casualties suffered by Americans would be a bridge too far.*

"We've heard your physician has ordered you not to fly." This much was true. "Let's do this. I'll send you a transcript of tonight's Summit. And we'll let you host the next convening in Bel Air." This was a lie, too.

"That would be … acceptable." Blackburn sounded more tired than angry. "I also have some thoughts about Project Ezekiel."

"Send them through the usual channels. I look forward to reviewing them. I must go now."

"But—"

He hung up. One item on tonight's agenda was Blackburn's pending expulsion from the Compact. The only question was *when* to pull the trigger.

He had once thought Blackburn's investment in the Birthrights Unlimited biotech firm would pay dividends. But it turned out Bashir and his people could accomplish their genetic engineering work in-house. Blackburn's usefulness was coming to an end.

He checked the time. Lucid should touch down in Zurich within the hour. They would need to discuss the last-minute arrangements for tonight.

A popup reminder appeared on his phone. He decided not to take the medication his doctor prescribed for his manic episodes. Needed to be on his game.

He stepped to large bay windows and opened them. The

smells of fallen leaves and burning fireplaces mingled in the air. Two large yachts glided around the glorious lake down below, resplendent in fall colors.

He remembered traveling to places like this. As a young man, he vacationed in Ibiza, Saint-Tropez, the Amalfi Coast, and other European hotspots. The beard hid the disfigurement but only partly, and after a time he could no longer bear the stares he would get.

He looked at the clock and tensed up about tonight's first in-person meeting of the Compact. He would face six men who would evaluate his appearance and judge his every move.

He wanted to slip into his casual wear while prepping the last items for tonight. Where was his assistant? He cracked the door open and saw his suitcase sitting outside the next bedroom door. He used the bedroom phone to call the house staff. No answer. He tried calling his assistant or his bodyguard with his regular phone but saw it wasn't connecting. Should he call with his special Compact hotline phone? No, can't share that number with staff.

Damn it all! It's just a dozen feet away!

He opened the door wider, looked both ways, and stepped furtively to retrieve it. He grabbed the handle, got halfway back to his quarters, and froze.

A figure appeared on the landing at the end of the hallway. A boy, standing motionless and staring straight at him.

A boy nearly as old as he was on that day. The day his mother threw acid in his face.

23

Samana Cay

Alex stood in a long, empty hallway leading to a single door at the far end. No sign of the Palace of Versailles or the bubble bath or Cynthia. After a minute, the door started to glow blue around the edges. He walked toward it and pushed it open.

He emerged onto a stone patio overlooking the beach and oceanfront. Fresh ocean air filled his senses. There, at the entrance to a walkway leading down to a grassy knoll, stood Cynthia Esposito. She was wearing khaki shorts, sandals, and a breezy tropical top that showed off her white choker and bare midriff. She was still very much seventeen.

She held a picnic basket in one hand and extended her free hand toward him. "Come on, we don't want to miss the sunset." The late afternoon sunlight and soft sea breeze played with her hair. She was a fairytale sprung to life.

He approached and took her hand. That impossible longing, that crazy ache in his heart, came rushing back to him. He was thunderstruck the first time he laid eyes on her. Love at first sight. After they went off to separate colleges and in the years afterward, he waited for that kind of feeling to happen again. But lightning never struck again.

She smiled and took his hand, leading him down the stone walkway. They paused atop a rock outcropping that gave them a grand view of the turquoise waters lapping at the northwest end of Samana Cay.

Their virtual reality experience was over. He was still wearing his Eyewear, but this was a real place—maybe fifty yards from the Fantasy Theater—and this was the spitting image of Cynthia Esposito holding his hand. He had found the VR part of the Fantasy Live simulation fascinating and jaw-dropping but unnerving. It was like being trapped inside a Hollywood movie with an over-the-top special effects budget.

Scene Two, an augmented reality experience rather than VR, was more like real life. Except it wasn't.

They followed the trail that traced the edge of the tall cliffs and came upon a patch of grass with a picnic blanket festooned with paper plates, plastic cups, and a bottle of chilled Champagne. He'd long imagined taking one of his girlfriends to a romantic, secluded lookout like this.

They sank onto the blanket. Cynthia opened her basket. Inside was an assortment of cheeses, crackers, cold cuts, and a warm loaf of French bread with that fresh-bread scent.

"Isn't this a great view?" Cynthia said, looking out over the bay. To the east, they could see the little waterfall spraying down along the far cliffs.

"It's perfect," he said.

And it was. He studied the curve of her cheeks, the style of her hair. Again he marveled at the masterful job they'd done with Cynthia's facial features. But it was her voice that transported him back to another time and place when the whole world stood before them, alive with possibilities.

"You hungry?" he asked.

"Actually, yes, I skipped lunch today."

He sliced the Manchego cheese for the crackers. "I like hearing your voice. Tell me a story."

She scrunched up her face. "I'm not a storyteller."

"Just say anything. You have a dog?"

"I did. Or I mean, I do."

"Do you or don't you?" He opened the Champagne and poured it into two cups.

"Yeah. I mean, I haven't seen her in months."

"Why not?"

"Let's change the subject. Tell me more about you. Your career sounds exciting."

He wasn't about to spend his time talking about his fake background as Andrew Bayless. For his story, he needed to find out more about this girl and what made her tick. Where is the Performer Impersonating Cynthia Esposito actually from? Why did she volunteer for this gig?

"Well, this is my fantasy, and I'd rather talk about you, Cynthia. What's your dog's name?"

"Misty. She's a good dog. Always brings the ball to me instead of my dad."

"Your dad—tell me more about him." He'd met Cynthia's father a few times back in the day. A carpenter. Or woodworker. Works with his hands.

"He—he's a businessman. Travels a lot. Haven't seen him in months, either."

"Then who takes care of the dog? Your mom?"

She turned away, avoiding his eyes. "I don't—I don't know what I'm supposed to say. I didn't prep for this."

"What do you mean?" He repositioned himself in front of her and looked at her dead on. "Tell me."

She looked frightened now. "I can't. I'm not allowed."

"Not allowed by who?"

He reached out but she brushed his hand away, stood up, and

began to walk toward the pathway leading down to the beach. He followed on her heels and saw she was starting to cry.

He caught up to her at the bottom of the incline where the walkway ended and the beach began. He tried to comfort her. "It's all right. What's going on?"

"It's not fair!" she cried. "It's so unfair!"

"What's unfair?"

"This! Everything! What they're gonna do to my family!" She started to tremble.

"Who?" he asked.

"I can't—they're watching."

"Come on, let's walk."

Cynthia took off her sandals and he removed his loafers and socks. They walked along the edge of the water for a long while, toes digging into the sand as the tide came in and washed away their footprints. This stretch of beach was private and empty. Farther up the sloping beach above the waterline, he spotted a series of small transponders blending artfully into the tropical landscape.

He stopped, removed his eyepiece and earbuds, and stashed them in his pocket, rules be damned. He stepped in front of her, held her by the shoulders, and explored her face.

Cynthia was gone. This performer did bear a resemblance to Cynthia. The same wiry build, the same jet-black hair, the same height and eye color. But her face was different now, fuller and rounder. Her hairstyle was more clipped. Her freckles and dimples were gone, her eyebrows darker. She looked like a scared high school kid, not his fantasy dream girl.

"What's your name?"

"Bailey. My name is Bailey Finnerty. And I've been kidnapped."

24

Zug, Switzerland

Volkov watched the boy scamper down the marble staircase and disappear into the maw of the country mansion. He grabbed his suitcase, thrashed into his quarters, and closed the door, breathing heavily.

He rushed to the workstation his advance team had set up against the far wall. He sat down and fired up his screen. He was relieved to see he was online and that his tracker showed Lucid had touched down and was en route. He chose audio mode and connected.

"Lucid, we have a problem."

"Chairman, I'm on my way. Can this wait until I arrive? I'm still dealing with one of the girls refusing— "

"We've had a security breach. I was spotted."

"Spotted?"

"Seen. In the flesh."

"By who?"

"A boy."

The boy looked about twelve. Who was he? Kasparian's son?

Would he tell anyone? Surely he'll tell his father. And his father will tell other members of the Compact, undercutting his authority at tonight's gathering.

"A boy," Lucid repeated, as if to make sure he'd heard correctly.

"Yes. You know how we've handled this in the past."

This had happened three or four times over the years. He would send his people and the hapless interloper would disappear. A story was spun about the unfortunate country dweller who fell from a great height. A tale was woven about the foolhardy lad who didn't realize the strength of the river current. Would Kasparian even need to know?

"Zaven Kasparian has one son, a thirteen-year-old. Chairman, let me talk with them. We can't do anything rash."

Volkov rose, strode to the window with its sweeping views of "Crypto Valley," and tried to calm himself. The big picture demanded he keep things in perspective. He had assembled a gathering of the world's leading power brokers. What mattered was that they were buying into his vision.

He returned to the workstation. "Make it clear he must not speak of this to anyone. Ever. Or the consequences will be dire."

"I'll handle it."

He hung up and changed into his casual outfit: a polo cotton knit shirt, twill cotton pants, and slippers. He needed to focus on tonight's meeting. With Blackburn out of the picture, the world would be divided into seven spheres of influence for the Compact to carve up.

History buffs might liken it to a modern-day Yalta, just as Churchill, Roosevelt, and Stalin had redrawn nations' boundaries after World War II. Only today governments were less important than the billionaires and business interests pulling the levers of power behind the scenes.

Seven spheres. That was what mattered more than national borders.

He breathed deeply and calmed himself as he recalled the seven kings from the Book of Revelation. And Ezekiel's prediction of a plague followed by an era of peace. Although he would never breathe a word of this to his secular friends, with their unending thirst for greater wealth and power, he knew he was a modern-day prophet fulfilling a historic destiny. He could see things other men could not. He was a man of visions.

Armageddon will not come about through a nuclear holocaust. Armageddon will be biological. The fire and fury will come from the funeral pyres of millions.

In the chaos that ensued just days from now, an even larger opportunity presented itself. A chance not just to reshape borders but to reboot humanity. Project Ezekiel was not merely a strategy document for the new world. It provided an anthropological roadmap.

Was this not a chance to remake civilization in whatever form we choose? To redefine the roles of men and women? To rethink the very rules of engagement between the sexes? How often does history come knocking like this?

Three quick raps came at his door. This was what human interaction passed for in his life: door knocks, intercoms, phone calls, virtual meetings.

"Chairman?" An unfamiliar voice, deep and throaty.

"Yes."

"It's Savić, a captain on your crew. You put out word to contact you directly if our target surfaces."

"Which target?"

"Kaden Baker. Chairman, she's right here in Zug."

25

Zug, Switzerland

Kaden entered the Theater Casino Zug for what was dubbed the Crypto Ball. She was expecting some gaudy monstrosity based on the couple of times she'd been to a casino. But this place was impressive in a retro kind of way. Set at the southern edge of old town, perched on the lake, the building had tasteful cream facade and wedding-cake trim. If Switzerland had royalty, this is where the princess would marry her prince.

"Jordan Wilkerson," she said to the receptionist.

"Welcome, Miss Wilkerson."

Thank God, no one was wearing smartglasses at this gala. But Kaden was wearing her smart contacts. Amelia was still busy crunching keywords from the spots around old town that Tosh had bugged. The surveillance had turned up zip so far. Either there was nothing too shady going on at the conference or the attendees had done a hell of a good job concealing it.

The grand ballroom was already wall to wall with people in white tie or evening wear. She glided past the buffet table with its spread of caviar and decided to fit in by accepting a glass of Champagne from a waiter in a white tuxedo and shavings of black winter truffles from another waiter.

She spotted Bo across the room and walked toward him.

"Well, don't you look nice," Bo said. "Maybe too nice."

She wore her new outfit, a slinky V-neck sleeveless crepe evening gown in a shade of jet-set red that screamed, *Available for scandal.* Quite a change from her usual uniform of boy clothes and faded tees. But she figured it might give her an advantage if her targets got distracted. She hoped she wouldn't run into any of the men she'd met today when she slipped them a business card with a room number and embedded bug.

Sorry, boys. No late-night hook-ups for this girl.

"Let's step onto the patio," Bo said. He led her through the arched doorway onto a large balcony. It was chilly outside, so only a few other guests were out here taking in the lights shimmering on the lake. Down at the lakeside she heard a few rowdy guests at a neighboring resort jump off the pier for a nighttime polar bear dip.

When the other guests turned away, he took a necklace out of his pocket. "Here, let me." He fastened the clasp behind her neck.

"Diamonds?" She was surprised, and her voice caught in her throat.

"Fake diamonds," he said. "But you can't tell without a loupe. More important, you can't see the miniature videocam."

"Another Tosh special?"

"He's monitoring the feed even as we speak. Hey, Tosh." Bo tapped his earpiece and nodded. Then he looked at her again. "We'll be doing facial recognition all night to see if we get any hits against our database. Let's mingle."

They reentered the ballroom. She saw Nico had arrived. Easy enough to spot him in the sea of white faces.

She passed through the crowd, smiling at strangers and

pointing her chest at the men so Tosh could try to find a match. She hoped to sweep the room so everyone in here would be scanned by Tosh's facial software. The task would be much harder during the second half of the event when guests peeled away to hit the slopes for Zug's famous Full Moon Skiing Gala.

"Pardon, I don't think we've met." The voice came from her right. She turned to face a tall man with blond hair and a touch of gray and brilliant blue eyes. He was dressed in a cashmere wool blend suit and looked to be about thirty-five.

"I'm Jordan Wilkerson."

"Jacques Bouchard, from Provence." He tilted and bowed his head in a greeting she found oddly charming.

"And what brings you to the summit, Jacques Bouchard from Provence?"

"Opportunity. The chance to seize the future. And you?"

"Perhaps the same."

He smiled and reached out to stop a passing waiter. He nudged a slice of a yellow-orange fruit onto a small plate and picked up a fork to feed it to her.

"You need to try one of these. Yubari King Melon. It is said to be the sweetest and most delicious on earth."

Jacques was trying to flirt with her, but her feelings were too raw. Something about Jacques's smile reminded her of Gabriel, and her heart panged.

"All right." She opened her mouth and tried a bite from Jacques' fork. Delicious, but she wouldn't be adding it to her grocery list. She'd read about these—a single melon cost more than $20,000.

In the corner of her vision, she saw a new alert from Amelia. She excused herself, much to Jacques's heartbreak. She passed him with a smile and nod and headed toward Nico, who was standing in a circle of women near the ice sculpture. *He probably hasn't let it slip that he's gay. Good for him.*

She stepped up onto a raised platform and into an alcove

with a bank of spotlights overhead. Fewer guests up here, and she could have a word with Amelia. She put in her earpiece.

"Well, don't you look smashing!" Amelia glided across the waxed floor wearing a sparkly ballroom gown that Kaden had uncovered in an old piece of footage.

"You look good, too, toots," Kaden said, taking a stab at thirties lingo.

Amelia laughed that heart-dropping laugh of hers. "Not exactly the right term of endearment, but we're both learning. I have two updates for you. I've allotted enough memory for sixty seconds, so let's get to it."

She knew Amelia had to get back to scanning scores of conversations being fed to her by Tosh.

"First, you'll be happy to know we finally decrypted the Ezekiel file. Shoutout to my AI network. Is that the right term, 'shoutout'? What fun! The bad news is, I think you'll find the file more than a bit disturbing. Sending it to you now."

"Thanks. What's the other news?"

"We have a keyword hit from one of the local conversations we were monitoring."

"Awesome. Which keyword?"

"Kaden, it's you, dear. You're the keyword match."

26

Samana Cay

A lex peered at the stretch of beach ahead of them. In the distance he saw kids darting into the surf and adults lolling along the water's edge—tourists who were restricted from accessing this section of private beach.

"Come on, let's go!" he urged.

"I don't think I can." Bailey Finnerty backed away, on the verge of tears.

"Why not? We can get help!"

"Because. Because of what they'll do."

He looked around. Still no signs of security goons. He wasn't even sure if they were being surveilled. No sign of the transponders he spotted earlier.

"Why? What will they do?"

"Hurt my parents."

Alex knew this changed everything. The undercover reporting assignment he'd been pursuing was no longer a priority. *I've got to help Bailey Finnerty get off this damn island.*

But how? The authorities controlled the airport. They'd have to leave by boat. Maybe he could get her to the marina and commandeer that superyacht. *It was a smartship—would it follow my instructions? Unlikely.*

He reached into his pocket for his phone. He'd try to call the U.S. Coast Guard. But he now saw his phone had no signal even though it had five bars near here yesterday. Were they jamming him?

"You can't stay here. Your parents would want you to get free. Those tourists up ahead, that's our best shot."

She stood there, shoulders hunched up in a knot, head lowered, as if to ward off an ominous threat that was about to descend at any moment.

He'd try one last thing. "Look, I'm not Andrew Bayless. I'm not even a real guest of Fantasy Live. My name is Alex Wyatt, I'm a journalist, and I'm here to uncover all the shady shit going on with this outfit. But nothing's more important than getting you to safety."

She looked up and relaxed her shoulders. She nodded.

"Let's go!"

"Wait!" She bent over and plucked out one contact lens and then the other.

"Why'd you do that?"

"They can see everything."

"Maybe you could have mentioned that earlier." *All right, deal with it, Wyatt. My cover is now officially blown.*

They raced down the beach. The throng of tourists was only a few hundred yards ahead. They galloped past a blur of palm trees, sending a pair of shore birds scooting over the water. The surf lashed at their bare feet. The hot tropical air burned in his lungs, but he didn't dare look back.

He needed a plan. *Find a tourist with a phone. Call the States for help. Someone he knew and trusted. Kaden? She was traveling out of the country. The Axom newsroom!*

"Aargh!" Bailey dropped to her knees in agony. Her fingers

grasped at the choke collar around her neck. She couldn't remove it.

"What's happening?" he asked.

She grimaced, struggling for the words to form. "It's like I touched an electric socket or something. There's pain shooting down my entire chest."

He leaned over her and inspected the back of her choker, a solid white strip of leather that fit snugly around her throat. For some reason, the clasp wouldn't unfasten. The neckband wouldn't come off.

Alex realized what was happening. Bailey was geofenced.

27

Zug, Switzerland

axim Volkov settled into his chair in the pitch blackness. He would have to trust that Lucid and the advance team had gotten this set-up right. His entire reputation—perhaps his entire empire—depended on it.

He watched as members of the Compact gathered on the other side of the plexiglass barrier. One after another, they entered the room for the Summit.

"I find this entire process humiliating and degrading," growled Walid Abdullin. The blustery Uzbek was known for his hot temper, child porn empire, and crypto investments. He was said to be worth more than $40 billion, though the real number was probably double that.

"I agree. This is an insult to us all!" Radovan Broz, the beetle-browed Serbian, all but spit out the words. He had made the bulk of his fortune in black market arms dealing.

The security process for admittance to their exclusive gathering was brutal: Staff was not permitted inside the sealed-off conference room. No phones or recording devices were allowed.

To enter, each man had to pass through a gauntlet of steps to authenticate his identity, ending with a full body scan and facial recognition scan.

No wonder they were in a foul mood.

"Relax. Security is the price of admission." Jaco Kruger, the portly South African who made his fortune in blood diamonds, stood at the long table replete with delicacies. Beluga caviar, specialty foods, liqueurs, and fine wines were flown in for the occasion. Kruger grabbed a pair of whiskey glasses and a bottle of fifty-year-old single malt Scotch whisky and set them down next to the nameplate at his seat.

Most of the Compact's members had never met each other. None had met Volkov in person. For the moment, he could view them while they didn't know he sat only feet away. It gave him a chance to see how the principals might interact when all their accoutrements of prestige and power were stripped away and all that remained was the man himself.

"I have had my doubts that this man, Incognito, even exists." Zhang Lee, an investor from China, took his seat. He looked like a mild-mannered accountant. Behind his back he was known as the King of Human Trafficking.

"Oh, he exists, all right." The host, Zaven Kasparian, nodded and shot him a glance through the darkened glass. "Arrived with his entourage six hours ago."

Volkov felt relieved Kasparian left it there and didn't mention his son's encounter. Lucid must have made an impression.

"Amigos!" Luis Alcivar, an Ecuadoran business mogul and retired general, stepped into the room and loosened his silk tie. "It appears I'm overdressed. Stuffy in here. Can we open the window?"

Kasparian stood and played with the thermostat next to the digital screen mounted on the wall to get some ventilation going. He'd had the conference room windows bolted shut earlier today as a security precaution.

With Alcivar's entry, the last of the billionaires had arrived. Counting Volkov, that made seven. *Seven kings for seven spheres of influence.*

All of them had engaged in dubious cryptocurrency trading, exploiting market volatility. And while none of the seven would be found on the pages of Forbes or Fortune, they wielded influence beyond their wealth. *These were the most powerful men on earth who made things happen in the shadows.*

Volkov leaned forward. It was time to reveal his presence. He spoke into a small microphone. "Gentlemen, thank you for coming." His voice sounded from all sides via the mobile speakers set up by his team. The billionaires looked up and around, as if searching for the voice of God.

"Show yourself, Incognito," Broz said. "I agreed to come because they said you would be here in person. No more magic tricks."

Volkov had feared as much. Here he was, the convener of the Compact, the man who would be ushering in a new era for humanity, and they questioned how he chose to present himself. What did it matter?

He would try his first fallback. Volkov put on his black head covering and pressed the button on the end table to his right. A soft light turned on and glowed to his right and left. It illuminated the enclosed space.

"I would prefer not to reveal myself," he said through the mic in front of him.

"We know the legend," Broz said. "But how do we know that's you?"

"I do not trust a man I cannot look in the eye," Abdullin added.

All six members were now peering into the dimly lit space behind the partition. Their severe expressions signaled they were in no mood for anything less than a face to face.

Volkov removed his head covering and swept his fingers

through his hair and newly cropped beard, once a chestnut brown but now mottled with gray. He was dressed in a classic black cotton sateen suit jacket and open-collar white shirt he thought conveyed the right mix of deadly seriousness yet confident informality.

The attendees looked at each other, seeming triumphant in their unmasking of the legend. It was true they could see him. But they were seeing six versions of him.

A team of scientists at the Lab had been working on this contingency plan for months. A new generation of spatial augmented reality showed one could use projectors to change the appearance of physical objects in an enclosed space—say, materials stacked on top of a table or the color of a couch—without the observers needing to wear glasses. Bashir's lab coats took it a step further so that each member of the Compact would see a somewhat different variation of the man called Incognito. A sort of high-tech face masking.

"The mythical Incognito." Zhang looked gleeful. "In the flesh at long last."

"A bit anticlimactic, if you ask me." Kruger filled a glass of Scotch to the brim. Then he filled a second one. "I was expecting an abomination from the gates of hell. You look normal enough."

"Sorry to disappoint. I take my privacy seriously." Volkov stroked his beard. From their reactions, the face masking appeared to be working.

"I've heard of germaphobes, but this takes things to a whole new level," Alcivar said in a thick Spanish accent. He shook his head and surveyed the room. "Is this everyone? I notice the American is not here."

"Randolph Blackburn will not be joining us." Volkov was still debating how much to reveal. The glue that held the Compact together was greed, not trust. They had not yet earned each other's trust, and they had not yet been assured their avarice was warranted.

"I understand he is in declining health," Kasparian offered.

"That," Volkov said, "plus a reason that will soon be apparent. This may be a fitting time to advise you: You should liquidate or transfer your U.S. holdings at once."

The room went silent as his words sank in.

"You'll also want to take a cash position against the euro and British pound."

"Good God, man. What are you planning?" Kruger put his drink down.

Volkov's mind returned to the fateful day when his mother lashed out in a pique of madness, weary of her second son's insolence and worried about their secret coming out. How he wished she'd lived to see the revenge he was about to unleash on the world. His entire life's work has been building to this crescendo.

"Gentlemen. Tonight I am here to announce we've found a way to vanquish our enemies once and for all, without firing a single shot. Our Lab has developed the ultimate secret weapon." He decided that sounded less scary than *biological pathogen*.

The billionaires looked at each other, trying to assess this news. He had been coy about it in the executive summary, describing the technology in only the broadest strokes.

Finally Abdullin asked, "What kind of weapon?"

"A personal doomsday clock. We are about to set it off."

28

Zug, Switzerland

The most connected man in the world was feeling disconnected. Lucid surveyed the drawing room, decorated with lifeless paintings, antique settees, and rosewood side tables with their tasteless grape carvings and leaf patterns to reflect Kasparian's fetish for all things Rococo. Second-rate talents from each billionaire's entourage were seated around the room in the classic chairs with curved, ballooning backs.

He was not permitted into the Summit's inner sanctum. On the one hand, Lucid understood each member of the Compact had their top lieutenants cooling their heels in the mansion's main drawing room. On the other hand, he had strategized with Incognito about which underground leaders to invite into the fold.

Why, I organized this gathering!

He leaned over to Dražen Savić and said, "Let's go for a walk." They had a large security detail on the premises to keep Incognito safe.

They strolled down the hill in the cooling night. A light dusting of snow began to fall as they reached old town with its lit-up buildings and cobblestone plazas. They paused at a fountain in front of Hotel Ochsen.

"How do you know Kaden Baker is in Zug?" Lucid asked.

"One of my men spotted her from two blocks away, coming out of a hotel bar. By the time he got there, he lost her in the crowd. We've spent the last three hours at every hotel in town looking through guest registries."

"She's probably traveling under an alias."

"Agreed."

This was the longest conversation Lucid had had with Savić for weeks. *He's good at carrying out orders. Not so good at thinking out of the box.*

"What's your plan?" Lucid asked.

"My detail is spread thin."

"Go find her. No more excuses!"

Savić shot him a glare that made Lucid's spine shiver. Then he turned and disappeared into the night. Lucid lingered for a moment before returning to the mansion.

♀ ♂

TOSH STARED at the monitor of his mobile console in his hotel room. An alert flashed across the screen. A keyword match! He looked at the notification. It was not a phrase he expected to see.

Kaden Baker.

He'd plastered old town with state-of-the-art surveillance equipment: smoke detectors, wall outlets with micro-cameras, pen cams, even a few paper clip transmitters. But it was one of the agency's new micro-drones that scored a hit.

He had considered activating the Return to Home function for the drones, now that a light snow was falling. A single big fat snowflake could down one of those expensive gems. Then came the hit, courtesy of one of the micro-drones with both video and audio.

"Carlos! Get in here!"

Carlos rushed in from the balcony. Tosh and Judy Matthews in the next hotel room were monitoring online intercepts as well as listening devices in 320 public and semi-public spaces: street corners, plazas, park benches, restaurants, cafes, hotel lobbies, bars, conference rooms. Carlos was in charge of navigating the drones, using his own electronic setup to make sure they were inconspicuous.

"We have a hit," Tosh said. "The plaza outside Hotel Ochsen."

Carlos swiped up on his tablet. "That's drone unit 134. It's the only one we have on that corner."

"Launch track mode. We need to follow these guys."

Carlos watched the live feed and positioned the drone to get a better look at both of their faces. "Running facial recognition now." He waited to see if there was a database hit on either target. After a minute, two green lights popped up on his screen.

"Target one is Lucid, maybe an alias. Right-hand man to a shady underworld figure who's been eluding us for years. Target two is a black ops specialist. Dražen Savić."

"Savić?" The blood drained from Tosh's face. "That's the SOB who attacked Kaden and killed her boyfriend."

"Wait, they're separating! What should I do?"

Tosh wrinkled his forehead. He promised Kaden he'd do anything to bring Savić to justice. But protocol demanded they go after the high-value target. "We have no choice. Follow Lucid. I'll notify Bo and ask him to tell Kaden."

♀ ♂

KADEN SPOTTED Bo again across the sea of faces in the ballroom of Theater Casino Zug and made her way to him. Before she could say anything, he nodded, leaned close, and said in a low voice, "I just heard. Tosh has a tracker on the suspect. He's moving north, out of old town."

"Why would *my* name come up during our surveillance?" she said.

"It means they know you're here. And they'll come for you again." Bo scanned the crowd, looking for potential threats. Then his gaze met hers. "Think! You must have something they want."

The Ezekiel file—that must be it!

"I hacked a file from Randolph Blackburn's digital vault."

"And you're just telling me now?" Bo looked ticked off. "That must be the reason they're after you. They must want it bad. What's in it?"

"It was encrypted up until a few minutes ago. Haven't checked it yet. Let's get out of this crowd so we can figure out next steps."

They moved through the throng, past white-tux waiters and the well-dressed crypto-elite. She signaled to Nico to meet at the side entrance.

Jacques Bouchard spotted her and threaded his way through the thinning cluster of guests to intercept her. "Jordan, the buses are starting to leave for the Full Moon Skiing Gala. You're coming, aren't you?"

She was on the fence. "I'm not sure."

"Oh, you must! They've already reserved a ski bib and jacket in your size. It's a magical experience. The entire Zug Valley is lit up. It's like skiing in a dream."

"Let me talk to my—" She almost said father, though that was still an open question. "Let me confer with my partners."

She turned back toward the exit. She and Bo emerged into the hallway. Nico was standing there next to the noisy entrance of the kitchen.

"What's the plan?" Nico asked.

"I have an idea. If they're looking for me, I can draw them out."

A look of alarm flashed across Bo's face. "Not a chance. I'm not losing another daughter."

"We agree," Kaden said.

She considered their options. The party was winding down with guests heading to the slopes for the super-hyped Full Moon Skiing Gala. She could supply backup to Tosh and Carlos and head north. But she sensed Bo was holding something back.

Bo grimaced. "Kaden, there's something I need to tell you. But I don't want it to jeopardize our mission."

There was something she needed to tell him, too. The paternity test results. But not now.

"What is it?" she asked.

"We have a positive I.D. on one of the suspects on our watch list."

She waited and finally had to pull it out of him. "Who?"

"Dražen Savić."

The whole world stopped. All the noise and chatter in the hallway fell away, replaced by a faint hum. She closed her eyes and pictured the scene. She saw Dražen Savić shift his gun's aim to her lover's forehead. She saw the look on Gabriel's face. She heard the little gasp escape his throat—that little half-second gasp of surprise that just tore her heart out.

29

Zug, Switzerland

Volkov looked at the faces around the conference table. Call them what you will. Oligarchs, plutocrats, magnates, tycoons, moguls, syndicate bosses, drug lords, enterprising businessmen. These were the faces of men who had always done things their own way. *Collaboration* was not in their vocabulary. But now he needed them.

He knew what unleashing the pathogen would do to the target populations. Civil society would collapse. Markets would crumble. Chaos and mob rule would replace law and order. There would be a major power vacuum. Look at Iraq after the fall of Saddam.

He needed authoritarian strongmen to fill the vacuum that chaos and lawlessness would bring. Men who would be indebted to him. And over time, he wanted a world he could perfectly control. *Winner take all.* He had already seen such a world of smoke, brimstone, and abject subjugation in his visions of the end times.

This is what he wanted. Not a ten percent year-over-year

return on investment. He wanted a reset of the existing world order. He wanted to impose a death choke on the West and the vapid set of values it stood for. He wanted to reboot civilization itself.

A voice. Somebody was talking. "Incognito, are you listening? What do you mean, 'personal doomsday clock'? You mean a cancer?" The voice of Zhang Lee.

"Not quite. On screen."

The rudimentary personal assistant in the corner of the conference room lit up bright blue and turned on the large high-def wall monitor opposite the windows. Kasparian had synced the device to obey Volkov's voice commands and gestures for the Summit.

The screen filled with a short presentation Volkov and Lucid had pulled together. *First, the science. Then the geopolitics. And finally the Compact's role.*

The first slide showed two archaea side by side. "You're looking at the transmission agent. Two strains of genetically modified archaea, a little-understood microbe that resides in nature and in the human gut."

"They look the same." Abdullin tilted his head sideways with a skeptical expression.

"Exactly right. They've been altered in several ways, but the changes take place at the molecular level, invisible even under a microscope."

He flicked his hand to the right and the new slide showed two Petri dishes: a normal archaea culture next to a culture with out-of-control growth. "This brings us to the first step of Project Ezekiel. *Propagation.* Our strains reproduce at a much faster rate than ordinary archaea. Even more important, they can be passed from person to person through casual contact."

He held up two fingers and an aerial view of Samana Cay filled the screen. "Step two. *Penetration.* How to get these microbes out of the laboratory and into the population centers of the U.S. and western Europe? You've no doubt heard about the popularity of the VR and AR theme parks at Samana Cay, plus the new Fantasy Live camp. Visitors who dine on the island have a little something extra added to their diet. Tasteless and harmless —at first."

"Ah! I was wondering why you'd poured all that money into your island paradise. It can't be just for the young girls." Kasparian, who'd loaned a submarine and superyacht to Project Ezekiel, grabbed a wine glass and opened an $8,000 bottle of Grand Cru from the Côte d'Or region of Burgundy. A token of Volkov's appreciation for hosting the Compact.

Volkov flashed his teeth, trying to approximate what a smile might look like. "There are many reasons for what we're doing on Samana Cay." *No need to spell them out here. And no reason to tip my hand to the Compact about the full scope of my plans.*

Kasparian was on board. Volkov took the measure of the others. *Intrigued, but not yet sold. This next bit of news would show that this was more than blue-sky talk and conjecture.*

He swiped right again and the screen filled with a map of reservoirs and water sources targeted in the United States and Europe.

"While many thousands of visitors pass through Samana Cay each day, we're not waiting for visitors to come to us. We've gone straight to the water sources. With a highly virulent agent such as ours, a few liters can be diluted into millions of gallons of water and still reach their hosts and replicate."

The billionaires studied the screen with its video images of the Washington Aqueduct, Los Angeles Aqueduct, Miami's Biscayne Aquifer, Bleiloch reservoir in Germany, dozens of others. Operations were being completed as fast as the Plant next to Bashir's Lab could produce the treated supplies of water.

Volkov held up three fingers. "Step three. *Execution.* We turn New York, Washington, LA, Miami, London, Berlin into living laboratories. We trigger different biochemical reactions in different populations."

Broz, the severe-looking Serb, held up his palm. "You're losing me. Triggers? How does this work?"

"You'll forgive me for not disclosing more of the specifics. But let me paint the picture in broad strokes for you."

He advanced the presentation to show a busy city sidewalk in Washington, D.C. Red arrows pointed to the types of individuals with specific genetic markers who would be targeted.

"Once the archaea reside in our target, you need something to trigger the expression of the altered genes. This brings us back to Zhang's question about a personal doomsday clock. We're quite proud of the technique our Lab has developed. Gentlemen, I present the world's first genetically designed sleeper pathogen."

"Sleeper pathogen?" Broz said. Some of them still didn't get it.

"We've built a trigger into the process. A trigger with a time delay. That allows the contagion to spread to tens of millions of targets without detection. No one will show any symptoms until a specific signal triggers the pathogen. By the time officials realize what's happening, it will be too late. Half the population will be infected and there's no vaccine on earth that can stop it."

Phase One would begin five days from now. Phase Two would deliver the crippling blow.

"And the pathogen would mean death to the person infected?" Zhang tapped his fingers together.

"Not at first." He swiped right, showing the last two Lab slides. "The new frontier of synthetic biology allows scientists to create individualized viral therapies for patients, using 'magic bullets' to micro-target cancer cells with extreme precision. Now, what if we could control the behavior of healthy cells instead? Target the cells of the retina and the result is blindness. Target the limbic system and a memory wipe is possible. Target the liver and death comes quickly."

Silence in the room as the members weighed this break-through.

The advent of personalized germ warfare.

"We begin not with mass deaths, but with fear." Volkov advanced to the next slide showing file footage of police in riot gear being attacked by an angry mob. "We will pit American against American, Brit versus Brit, German versus German. It will begin in small pockets, followed by race wars in urban centers. Life or death might depend on your genetic inheritance. We may even see a Second Civil War come out of this for the Americans."

"That I would like to see." Kruger lifted his second glass of whisky in a toast, then polished it off.

For Volkov, it was less a personal vendetta against the West and more an acknowledgment that the western powers were the only obstacles to his vision of a new world order. A grand Reset.

"If we want to change the world order, we can't go up against the superpowers' strength. We cannot win on a military battle-field. We will win by outflanking them in broad daylight. We will wage a stealth war, gentlemen. One front is biological. A second front is psychological. Our assets in social media and mass media are in place, prepared to spread a disinformation campaign. We will cultivate psy-ops on a massive scale. *The battlefield is each target's mind.* The target will question what is real and what is not, who can be trusted and who cannot, to the point of madness. We will keep the Americans and the western Europeans in a constant state of fear."

"And our own people—our wives, children, mistresses." Kruger shot a sly look at Kasparian. "They will not be affected?"

"Your people, your citizens, will be safe," Volkov assured them. He had provided a Q&A in the executive summary, antici-pating all the questions and possible objections that the attendees would raise, but he skirted the issue of targeting populations by ethnicity and ancestry. Some members of the Compact might be squeamish about so-called ethnic cleansing.

"All your people will be safe." He leaned forward, wanting to drive home the point. "Stockpiles of vaccines and antidotes are being rolled off the assembly line at the Plant on Samana Cay at this very moment. We can add the vaccine surreptitiously to the food supplies of our allies so as not to panic the local populace."

He sized up the men around the table. The looks of skepticism were turning into somber looks of intrigue. At bottom, these men all wanted the same thing. More money, more wealth, more power. There was also the undeniable hidden subtext: *Don't go along and your people will pay the price.*

"That brings us to our final slide. The spoils. The United States and Europe have had their turns at ruling the world. Now it's our turn."

He flicked his hand to show a map of the world coded in different colors. Instead of displaying the usual map of countries with defined geographic borders, it showed a topological map with a rainbow of colors.

"Gentlemen, behold the Seven Spheres. We can work out the details in the months ahead. But let's start thinking about the new world we're about to usher in."

Volkov had divided the world into spheres of influence based on each billionaire's underground operations. These were the world's supreme traffickers in drugs, weapons, sex slaves, and illegal goods. Ecuador's Alcivar would get Central and South America, a piece of southern Mexico, and the Southern Caribbean. Africa and parts of the Middle East would go to South Africa's Kruger. All of China and Taiwan would go to Zhang.

The exact manner in which they carved up the United States, Canada, Europe, and Australia would be a bone of contention, but this was not the meeting to settle such matters. They would all get a slice of the pie.

Zhang leaned back in his office chair and began to rock, arms folded. "With the fall of the West, what is to stop China from claiming territory as the world's preeminent superpower?"

"And Russia," Abdullin interjected. "She is eager to reassert a dominant role on world stage."

"That is precisely the reason I invited you to join the Compact." Volkov gave a nod of encouragement to two of his most ruthless colleagues. "You both have met with the top leadership in Beijing and the Kremlin. At the proper time, they need to be convinced that the West's fall does not create a power vacuum. The Compact is the new superpower. We don't own a useless nuclear arsenal. We own something better. The ability to surgically remove any world leader, any family, any ethnic group or populace. Personalized germ warfare is the game changer. More effective than nuclear arms, because we have no hesitation in using it."

Zhang stroked his analytical chin while Abdullin arched his eyebrows.

Volkov painted the big picture for them. "This is our time, gentlemen. For years, we have asked the question, how can the arrogant Americans be dealt a punishing blow? Would it be a dirty bomb in New York? A cyber-attack, bringing down the entire energy grid? No. The answer is a personal doomsday clock."

He was on a roll now, rallying the troops to the cause. "Have you forgotten how the West has treated us over the centuries? They have occupied us. They have imposed their will and their values on our people. Now it's our time to rule. To extinguish the vapid, empty consumer empire the Americans have built. To take civilization in new directions. *Our* direction."

He hunched his shoulders forward, grabbed the mike with both hands. "If you had a weapon that could disarm your greatest enemies, would you not use it?"

Did Isaiah not fortell this in Scripture? *Nations will be laid low, enemies will be utterly destroyed, the arrogancy of the proud will cease.*

"Your Project Ezekiel document is beginning to make sense now." Abdullin cracked open a 24-karat gold tin of rare white Beluga caviar and spooned it into a cold crystal glass. "When I first read it, it seemed to be the ramblings of a madman."

Volkov knew visionaries were seen as madmen in their day. Ezekiel faced the same skeptical reception 2,600 years ago.

Volkov chose to be magnanimous. "I knew some of you would be skeptical. Which is why I put off this gathering until we were ready to launch. Only the Compact has the resources needed to execute Project Ezekiel to its full extent. My Lab and your men on the ground—together we can bring the soft West to its knees."

He scanned the men's faces again, one at a time. Just being in the same room with these six killers made the hairs on the back of his neck stand up.

What's the best way to do this? I can't impose my will on the others—at least not yet. Should I put it to a vote? No, absurd. I need them to assent while giving them the illusion they had a say in this.

"Do any of you want out?" Volkov knew eighty percent of people never opt out of anything. Human nature. He stared at the six billionaires one by one. "Does anyone *not* want to rule over one of the Seven Spheres?"

Zaven Kasparian raised his hand. Or did he? The Armenian looked up and extended his arm into the air. Then he leaped to his feet and snagged something out of the air just above his head, as if catching a fly.

"What is this?" Broz snapped.

Kasparian opened his palm and stared at it in disbelief. "It's a drone." Then he looked at the others. "We're being spied on!"

30

Zug, Switzerland

K aden dashed back to her room and changed into her winter outfit of jeans, black stretch boots, black mock turtleneck, and black stitch beanie. She opened the room safe and grabbed her Beretta M9 that she'd gotten through Swiss Customs.

She called Tosh and got him on the line for twenty seconds. He and Carlos were positioned outside the target estate with Bo en route. The team had infiltrated the mansion's aging air ducts. They had a good read on everything happening inside. No sign of Savić at the residence.

She headed out of the room. Nico was waiting in the hallway.

"Figured you'd need backup," he said.

"I don't need your help."

"Just want to make sure you have your priorities straight. The others are on mission. You're going after a low-level thug for one reason. Revenge."

"I'm going after a killer who deserves justice."

Nico looked at her expression and saw she wasn't about to change her mind. "Let's go. Like it or not, I'm coming with you."

"All right."

They scoured old town. It was a small set of streets plus the lakefront promenade. If Savić was in one of the public spots, hotel lobbies, or restaurants, he'd be easy to spot. She sent Nico the shot of Savić that Bo had shared with her, and they separated, Nico taking the northern half of old town and Kaden the southern.

After forty-five minutes and no luck, they returned to the Theater Casino. The last bus was leaving for the Full Moon Skiing Gala at the fabled mountain peak Wildspitz. They snagged two of the last seats in the back. Up front, partygoers who had too much Champagne or schnapps sang songs from their home countries.

During the half-hour ride, she began to read the Project Ezekiel file that Amelia had sent to her phone. The document didn't go into detail, but it sketched the outlines of an international conspiracy. This cabal was targeting major drinking supplies in the U.S. and Europe. The document predicted a surge in civil strife leading to the fall of Western governments. It listed the conspirators, though none of the names seemed familiar.

She felt drained and numb after reading it. Could this cabal really pull off a global operation like that? She had to stop them.

Aside from her team, she wasn't sure who could she forward the file to. It seemed the top levels of the intelligence and law enforcement communities might be compromised. And she wasn't in a position to authenticate the document. After all, she committed a felony by breaking into her grandfather's digital vault. Not good, with another possible felony charge hanging over her head in Dallas.

Between that file and her inability to spot Savić, she was in a black mood by the time they arrived at Wildspitz. They did a quick reconnaissance of the après ski bar and the next-door base station. Didn't pan out. They rented snowboards and the special LED jackets that all gala guests got to wear. Then they took the chairlift to the top of the mountain. Below them, tall poles with bright LED lights illuminated the slope.

"Remember the tricks we did at Snowmass?" Nico said on the lift. "We were killin' it."

"That was a pretty sick week." She tried to force a smile. She and Nico used to do all kinds of borderline extreme sports together: rock climbing, free-diving, freestyle snowboarding. When they were nineteen, after they'd graduated from boot camp, she and Nico trekked to Aspen and tried out for the Winter X Games. "Too bad you flamed out early."

"And as I remember," Nico jabbed back, "you were still in the running until you twisted your ankle on your third Big Air run. That was an epic wipeout."

At the top of the mountain, they hopped off the lift. Her fingers brushed the Beretta in her pocket as they did a walk-through of the alpine restaurant overlooking Wildspitz. The atmosphere inside was raucous and festive. Outside in the snow-banks, a couple was tossing an LED-lit football. But still no Savić sighting.

"What now?" Nico asked.

"If they're coming for me," she said, "I need to be seen. Let's hit the slopes."

She led the way to the top of the run and lifted her goggles for a better view. The air was thinner up here, and the scent of alpine trees infused her senses. It smelled like Christmas—never a fond memory for her. Above them, though, a light snow made it feel as if they'd been transported to a more innocent time and place. A band of clouds fussed about whether to let the full moon join the gala. Zug Valley stretched out below with the soft yellow glow of distant houses curling around the lake and moonlight playing on the mountaintops.

"Didn't I tell you it was a heavenly sight?" Jacques Bouchard said. Somehow she'd missed him angling up from behind.

"You were right," she agreed. "This may be the most beautiful thing I've ever seen."

"Second most beautiful, in my opinion."

She felt herself blush. "Jacques, this is Lawrence, my executive assistant." She'd been eager to say those words, and Nico nodded like a good sport. "By the way, we're looking for someone. Hard to miss. Six-four, swarthy, dark beard, three hundred pounds. Smells like a musk ox. Any chance you've seen him?"

"Thankfully, no. I'll keep an eye out. That's the expression, *oui*?"

"*Oui!*" Kaden pushed off and the guys followed. Nico and she were the only ones on the hill riding boards.

Jacques rode his skis to her right flank. All three of them were wearing the specially outfitted ski suits with thousands of tiny LEDs sewn into the gore-tex fabric. The lights were dancing over their torsos in patterns of cascading green, red, yellow, and blue. *We look like we were beamed in from some futuristic Neon Ice Capades. All that's missing is the soundtrack.*

The slope led them toward a wicked chute and she decided to take it big and fast. If she pulled it off, she'd be the talk of the hill. If she crashed and smashed, well, she'd go out in spectacular fashion.

She pulled away from the others, setting herself nice and low to gain maximum speed. She readied herself for her signature trick, the frontside 900 with tail grab, the showtime move that was her undoing at the X Games. The difference this time? She wanted to tear the heart out of her enemy, Dražen Savić. She was ready to meet death and kick its ass.

Kaden spotted a hill up ahead that could serve as her kicker. She held her edge all the way to the end of the takeoff. She hit it at a sweet angle with good speed and went into her arc with massive air. She rotated her body counterclockwise, opening her shoulders right from the get-go. After the first rotation she reached behind her and grabbed the board's tail. After the five she let go and started thinking about her landing, so she started to lean forward on her way down, diving into her last 360. She felt inside of herself, in control by letting go of her fears and apprehensions. With these thousands of little lights pulsing across her body, she imagined that this is what pure energy must feel like. She nailed the landing and used the soft, deep powder of the mountain to glide to a halt.

Did I really just do that? She slowed to let Nico and Jacques catch up. A half-dozen guests along the edges of the slope yelled their appreciation, some lifting bottles of Swiss beer.

"A frontside nine!" Nico pumped his fists.

"That was amazing!" Jacques said, looking like he might swoon.

A shot rang out from somewhere. She spotted a bearlike figure a hundred yards up the hill, taking aim with his rifle's scope for a second shot.

"Move!" she commanded.

She got her wish. She'd smoked out Dražen Savić. Except he had the higher ground, superior line of sight, and a better weapon.

31

Samana Cay

Alex Wyatt took Bailey Finnerty's hand and led her twenty feet back up the shoreline away from the invisible perimeter. "You're geofenced."

Bailey shook her tangle of dark hair. "What's that?"

"It means you're confined to a certain geographical area—you're not allowed past a certain boundary. Usually geofencing is used for something more innocuous. Like keeping track of a child who strays from his parents at the county fair."

"And they shock him?"

"No. It's for the parents to see his location on their phone. But in your case, it means you get an electric shock when you leave the permitted area."

Collared goats or sheep get a little zap when they wander from the herd. But Bailey looked to be in severe physical pain when she crossed the boundary.

Bailey's eyes were downcast, her expression dour. "What about you?"

"What *about* me?" Alex was surprised by the question.

"Did they chip you?"

"No." He remembered when he did after arriving. "I mean, yeah, I volunteered to get chipped. Just to open my room door and stuff like that."

Cripes! He now realized what a major mistake he'd made.

He held up and inspected his right palm. There below the surface of his skin between his right thumb and index finger was the tiny metallic transponder that was implanted during his first hour on Samana Cay.

"If I had to guess, something tells me we're both being tracked," she said.

"Follow me. There must be a way out of this nightmare."

He led her back the way they came, across the watery edge of the beach. They retrieved their footwear and climbed the long stone walkway that rose past the grassy knoll and up to the ridge that extended the length of Fantasy Live Resort.

They paused outside the Deep Dream Lounge. "Wait here," he said. "If we're lucky, no one was monitoring us. We'll say you lost your contact lenses."

She nodded and sat on the wooden bench facing the ocean. Pleasure vessels skimmed the water a half mile from shore, taking in the last minutes of sunshine. He turned and entered the lounge.

Across the room, Evelyn and Maurice were chatting, seated in their familiar four-seat arrangement. They smiled as he approached.

"Andrew!" Flirty Evelyn said. "Pull up a seat. How are you enjoying the simulations?"

"Never mind that," Maurice said in a conspiratorial tone. "What about Rachel? Have you … taken advantage yet?"

"Guys." No time for chitchat. "I have an emergency. Can I borrow your phone? My battery died."

"Oh, an *emergency*, huh?" Maurice looked skeptical. "I get it. You had a taste of Fantasy Live and now you want your woman to dress up for cosplay. Let me guess. A ninja warrior? Wonder Woman?"

Evelyn took out her phone and handed it over.

"I asked for Starbuck from *Battlestar*, but you?" Maurice went on. "I know! Daenerys Targaryen, *Game of Thrones*."

"Bingo!" Alex said to shut him up. He dialed Alice Wong at *Axom*.

"I knew it!" Maurice looked triumphant.

Come on, come on, pick up! Voicemail. Damn!

"Alice, it's me." He lowered his voice and moved out of earshot of Evelyn and Maurice. "I have an emergency here. A young woman, Bailey Finnerty, says she was kidnapped. Check the database. Was she one of the Disappeared—"

A woman's hand plucked the phone from his grip. He looked up, startled.

"Oh, Andrew. We're so disappointed in you." Rachel hovered above him, flanked by two burly security guards.

"What the hell, Andrew?" Maurice said.

Rachel handed Evelyn her phone back. "No more calls tonight."

Rachel led Alex out the front door into a waiting car. From the back seat, he could see Bailey being escorted down the pathway past the Fantasy Theater to the farthest end of the campus.

One of the security guards got in the back seat next to him while the other got in the driver's seat, started the engine, and began driving. Rachel sat in the front passenger's seat. After a minute, she turned around.

"Alex, Alex. Whatever are we going to do with you?"

32

Zug, Switzerland

Kaden tore down the mountain. "Hit it!" she yelled to Nico and Jacques. Nico nodded and took off to her left. Jacques hesitated, no doubt wondering why a sniper would be firing at them, so she added, "*Now*, dammit!" That did the trick. He followed Nico's lead.

Her instinct was to head down the slope in a random pattern. But she remembered what her instructor said at boot camp. The advent of modern weapons has outpaced our evolutionary instincts for survival. Use a zigzag technique and you might have a slightly *greater* chance of getting hit by a shot. The faster you can get out of range or behind cover, the safer you'll be.

She looked back and saw Savić following, rifle strapped to his back, skiing fast for a big man. Too fast.

To her left, the ski lift snaked overhead and a wall of orange matting sealed them off from any escape route. To her right, a stand of snow-covered pines offered a faint hope, but the sprint across the deep snow would mean Savić could pick them off with no trouble.

She looked to her rear left and yelled, "Nico!" She unzipped her LED ski jacket. They were far easier targets while wearing these outfits that screamed, *Bullseye!* She grabbed her Beretta from the pocket with her right hand and struggled to remove the jacket with her left hand. Finally she got it half off, exchanged the handgun to her left hand, ripped off the jacket, and flung the jacket behind her. Nico followed suit, only with more finesse since he wasn't carrying a gun.

Jacques still had a shocked expression on his face, crouching low to avoid any more shots. She looked at him and Nico. *I can't be responsible for anyone else dying.*

A sharp snap of frozen air jolted her chest. An idea took shape. She fumbled in her pants pocket and finally found her earpiece. "Amelia, stop what you're doing and give me your full attention."

"Yes, Kaden."

"Personality mode off. Don't ask why." *I need data, not a pep talk.*

"Switching to default mode."

"I need night vision. Now!"

"Night vision enabled."

Immediately her field of vision looked radically different. She was using the new state-of-the-art night photography algorithms pioneered by Google for its smartphones, a step up from the garish green night vision technology still used by the U.S. military. The snowbanks were now better defined and she could see details in the shadows of the trees. Everything looked saturated and high contrast, as if she were snowboarding through a comic strip. But the LED lights glaring down from the slopes overhead bleached out the terrain.

She needed a change of scenery.

She slowed to make sure Nico and Jacques saw her signal to continue down the slope. Over the next ridge, she saw her chance. She took a hard right and plunged into the darkness down a side trail. She looked over her left shoulder and saw their surprised faces, but Nico and Jacques stuck to the main trail.

"Diamond trail, maximum level of difficulty," Default Amelia informed her. On her smart lenses, the AI began feeding her elevation, ambient wind speed, and temperature readouts as she sped down the steep trail that plunged into the darkness. No LED lights here. The snow began falling more heavily and the full moon gave up behind a thicket of dark clouds.

She glanced back and saw Savić leave the main run and follow her down the side trail.

She felt the familiar grip of her Beretta M9 in her hand. She turned and fired twice at the figure barreling down the hillside. Missed. Not surprising, given that she was firing behind her in the dark of night at a moving target while she was speeding down a steep slope at 47 mph. She wasn't sure how Savić was keeping up. *Must have night-vision glasses.*

She returned her focus to the trail in front of her. It was a winding black diamond run, the most difficult trail on Wildspitz and one she'd never taken before, much less in the dead of night. She knew if she made one slip-up and fell, she would be one dead girl.

At that moment she struck a slick patch of ice she hadn't seen. Her Beretta flew out of her hand into a snowbank. The thought flashed across her mind to stop, find the gun, take aim, and take out Savić. She didn't like those odds. She continued down the black diamond trail.

She glanced back and saw that Savić was gone. Must have taken a side trail.

"Amelia, call up a map of Wildspitz terrain. Look for steep vertical exit routes up ahead."

Five seconds later, Amelia projected a turnoff two hundred yards ahead—a steep cliff that plunged into a craggy ravine at a seventy-degree angle. "Chance of survival, twenty-two percent."

She didn't much care for those odds. "What's the snow coverage?"

A few seconds passed. No answer.

"Amelia? Are you there?"

She realized what was happening. She was out of Wi-Fi range. At the worst possible moment.

She looked back and saw Savić had rejoined the trail. He was right on her tail now, forty yards behind. He came to a skidding stop and took out his rifle as she reached the cliff.

She could raise her hands in surrender. Or veer off to the right and jump off a cliff with a one-in-five chance of survival.

She jumped.

♀ ♂

DRAŽEN SAVIĆ CHURNED through the snow to the edge of the cliff and peered down into the ravine. He felt a sense of relief mixed with triumph. There was no way the target could survive a fall at such a steep angle into a dark chasm of jagged ice, exposed rocks, and spindly underbrush.

His phone rang. Lucid calling.

"Yes," he answered in his native Croatian.

"Savić, you're needed back at home base. Did you find the target?"

"She won't be a problem anymore." *Unless miracles happen.*

"Good. Do you have proof?"

"I'll need time—"

"We don't have time. We're packing up and leaving now."

This was unexpected. He didn't like unexpected. "Why?"

"Because your security detail didn't do its job!" Lucid sounded angrier than he'd ever heard him.

He wondered what in God's name his boss was talking about. "I'll be back within the hour."

"That's too late. Meet us at the airport."

Savić peered over the edge, looking for any sign of a body he could bring back as a trophy of triumph. But there was no time to descend the steep trail. Savić cursed the darkness. He continued down the black diamond run toward the base station and the après ski bar filled with Westerners he hoped would soon meet the fate they deserved.

33

Zug, Switzerland

Maxim Volkov sat in the darkness and tried to contain his fury.

He flicked off the lights in his enclosure and watched as all hell broke loose on the other side of the partition. Each of the billionaires had many enemies, any one of whom might be willing to exploit the secret plans he'd just laid out. Paranoia ran deep.

Abdullin, Zhang, Kruger, Broz, and Alcivar all left the room in various stages of anger and alarm. Kasparian returned after ordering his men to fan out. He slumped into his chair and stared at the small broken object in his palm. He shook his head and turned to face the darkness.

Volkov raised his voice. "How could you let this happen?"

Kasparian frowned. "We swept the entire estate for bugs. Not once, but twice! We made a last pass of this room earlier today. I stationed a half dozen of my men at all the entry points and sent guards to patrol the outside grounds. I don't know how this could have happened."

"It's an outrage."

"It's unfortunate." Kasparian brought the crumpled object closer to his face. "I'll have this sent to my lab for analysis. Perhaps we'll be able to tell whose it is."

By the size of the mini-drone in Kasparian's hand, Volkov knew it was almost certainly American made. Perhaps Kaden Baker was working with the U.S. military.

"On another matter," Volkov said. "Your son?"

"He is still young. He will not say a word to anyone. I give you my word."

"Good." Volkov closed the books on the matter. His anonymity was still intact among the group where it mattered most. He had enough disasters on his plate.

"Where do we go from here?" Kasparian asked.

"Send in my man. Lucid. He will contact each of our members in due time."

Kasparian nodded, rose, and left the room without further comment. A minute later, Lucid entered and looked at the empty seats.

"Lucid." Volkov piped his voice over the loudspeakers, giving his COO a start. "You've heard about the breach. How do you explain it? Why didn't your men catch it?"

Lucid remained standing and grasped that Volkov was on the other side of the dark partition. "I can only theorize, Chairman. This next generation of spy drones can be launched from a good distance, with sensors that allow them to exploit any small vulnerability in a building or room." He scanned the room's ceiling and saw the grate with half-inch square openings. "Taking advantage of ventilation ducts, for example."

That still doesn't explain how they knew the Compact was meeting here.

Volkov told Lucid the bottom the line. "We were interrupted before I could get a final reading of the room about Project

Ezekiel. And now we're not certain if our plans have been compromised by an outside party."

"I see. I suggest that we wait for a while and see what the fallout is. Let things cool off. Or we scale back our plans."

Volkov considered this. *It would be the obvious thing to do. Lie low. Draw up a new course of action. Execute it in a few months with buy-in from the Compact after new security measures are put into place. That's what most leaders would do.*

But he was a man apart. He was carrying out Project Ezekiel —a divine-inspired grand design. The words of Ezekiel 25:17 came to him:

I will carry out great vengeance on them and punish them in my wrath.

"No. Here is what we will do." He took a deep, calming breath to put this fiasco behind him.

"I want a stepped-up effort to find and neutralize Kaden Baker. She may have been behind this incursion."

"Savić says the target has been eliminated."

"So someone else was behind this?"

"It appears so."

"I see. We need to circle the wagons tighter. In one hour I'll be flying out to my offices on the island." This security breach was unacceptable, and Lucid oversaw security for the corporation. Volkov would fly to Samana Cay to supervise events directly.

"Can I ask why? You've only been to Samana Cay twice before," Lucid pointed out. The first visit came when Volkov assessed the island for purchase. The second trip came when the virtual reality theme parks opened.

"I want to check on our security protocols. And I want to experience Fantasy Live directly."

Lucid blanched and took a moment to collect himself. "Certainly, Chairman. Should I accompany you on the Falcon?"

"No. We'll be taking separate flights." There were no separate compartments on his Dassault Falcon 8X, and he most certainly did not want to have to deal with face masking technologies on the long flight from Zurich to the island. He would fly solo in the spacious luxury cabin.

"Very well."

"One last matter. Send a message to Bashir. We're moving up the timetable for Phase One."

Lucid paused to take in the moment. "You mean we're moving beyond the planning and seeding stage? You're saying to flip the switch and to execute Project Ezekiel?"

"It is time."

"Starting when, Chairman?"

"Tomorrow. We start tomorrow."

34

Zug, Switzerland

Kaden shivered in the sub-zero cold. Her eyes fluttered open. It was still dark but no longer snowing. The full moon lit up the snow-covered alpine trees and the mountain peaks beyond.

What happened? Where am I?

She rolled over onto her elbows and surveyed her surroundings, a thicket of spindly brush at the foot of a crazy-steep trail that zigzagged along the face of an enormous hill. A sharp, jagged rock jutted out from the floor of the ravine inches from where she fell.

The night before began to come into focus. *Ah, right. The Schwyzer Alps. Wildspitz. A perfect frontside nine. Savić. The descent into oblivion. And then, darkness.*

She struggled to her feet. Her right calf was sore and bruised, and her left shoulder stung like a son of a bitch. But she thought nothing was broken. She looked down at the board that helped break her fall. It lay broken in half at her feet. She left it there rather than explain at the register that a hitman had tried to take her out.

She worked her way up the hill, a foot at a time, and it may have taken two or three hours to reach the top. She wondered whether Savić would be waiting there to finish the job, but at the top she was met only by a white landscape, silent and indifferent. She wobbled her way to base camp, fighting through the pain.

Her teeth were chattering by the time she made it into the breakfast cafe where the staff expressed shock and alarm at her overnight accident. Nico was waiting in a corner of the cafe after searching for her for hours. The ski resort crew fed her and provided a warm new jacket. The medical staff treated her injuries, putting a bandage on her calf and giving her a mild painkiller for her shoulder. The resort gave her and Nico a complimentary shuttle ride back to Zug.

She found Bo and the rest of Red Team Zero in the hotel restaurant having an early breakfast. Carlos seemed especially hungry, wolfing down a huge spread of soft Butter-Zopf bread, pastries, yogurt, coffees, and cheese from Switzerland's Fribourg region.

"Thank God." Bo scrambled to his feet and came up to hug her. He brushed the hair from her forehead and examined the scratches on her face. "Nico called me an hour ago. We were planning to form a search party. Are you all right?"

"A little sore. You should've seen me shred that last run."

"The frontside nine?" Nico asked.

"No. The one into the ravine."

"Ravine?" Bo said.

"Long story."

Bo scooted over in the booth to make room for her. "We saved you a seat."

A waitress took her order. A double kaffee-crème, which as far as she could tell was just a big ol' jolt of espresso with cream.

"I want to hear what happened," Bo said. "But do you want to hear our news first?"

She nodded. She was distraught at not being able to take out Savić. She wanted to know what they'd turned up.

"After you sent us the Ezekiel file, we tracked down the people putting together the operation. I've sent it on to some people I trust at DIA. Just sent you a copy of the surveillance footage."

"That's good," Kaden said.

"And now we have a lead on the girls," Judy said.

"Solid?" Kaden asked.

"I wouldn't say solid." Carlos seemed circumspect. "But we have a possible location."

"And it's thanks to you," Bo said.

She was feeling bummed that she abandoned the operation he had put together to find Bailey and the other girls when she went all psycho about finding Savić. So Bo's words were surprising and reassuring.

"How so?"

"Without your name turning up, we never would have been led to the Compact."

"The Compact?" she asked.

"Long story." Tosh smiled. "We'll fill you in later. But there was a snippet we caught about young girls on an island paradise called Samana Cay."

Samana Cay. That was the same island her friend Alex was heading to. "Isn't that the resort for one percenters in the Caribbean? Used to be part of the Bahamas?"

Tosh bit into a pastry before answering. "Everyone thinks the Bahamas is in the Caribbean, but it's not. It's just off the coast of Florida, and Samana Cay is right next door. So we're flying out later today to the Bahamas."

"Why not directly to Samana Cay?"

This time Bo answered. "They don't allow weapons into

Samana Cay. We've arranged for all our gear to be transported directly from the airport in Nassau to a boat we've rented."

"Well that's … that's good!"

She looked around the table, but everyone seemed subdued. "What's wrong? Something's wrong."

Nico looked puzzled, too, unable to get a read on whatever secret the group was holding back.

"Kaden," Bo began. "I received a communication this morning from my contact at the Justice Department. Just printed it out. It's for you."

"For me?"

"It's not good. I did what I could."

The waitress set down her kaffee-crème as the table went silent. She read the one-page letter. It came with a Department of Justice seal and letterhead at the top.

Dear Kaden Baker:

You are the target of an investigation by a Grand Jury sitting in Dallas, Texas surrounding events that occurred in this jurisdiction on or about August 31 of this year. In connection with that investigation, you are hereby invited to testify before the Grand Jury convening on or about November 12.

As a Grand Jury witness, you will be asked to testify and answer questions and to produce records and documents. Only the members of the Grand Jury, attorneys for the United States and a stenographer are permitted in the Grand Jury room while you testify.

We advise you that the Grand Jury is conducting an investigation of possible violations of federal criminal laws involving, but not necessarily limited to, Felony Murder. You are advised that the destruction or alteration of any document required to be produced before the grand jury constitutes a serious violation of federal law, including but not limited to Obstruction of Justice.

You are advised that you are a target of the Grand Jury's investigation. You may refuse to answer any question if a truthful answer to the question would tend to incriminate you. Anything you do or say may be used against you in a subsequent legal proceeding. If you have retained counsel, the Grand Jury will permit you a reasonable opportunity to step outside the Grand Jury room and confer with counsel as you desire.

Cordially,

Nancy M. Richardson

Assistant United States Attorney

"What is this?" she asked.

"A target letter," Bo said.

"Felony murder?" Kaden's mouth fell open.

"I'm sorry." Streaks of pain creased his face.

"What happened to our plea deal? To me pleading guilty to transporting a firearm across state lines or something? That's part of the reason I'm here."

"It fell apart. The black hats won the day. Must be outside forces with considerable leverage."

The news bowled her over. It was only a few weeks ago, but in her mind it seemed as fresh as yesterday. She, Nico, and two cohorts from boot camp followed leads that brought them to the Birthrights Unlimited campus in Dallas. They discovered a building where over a hundred women were being held against their will, including the surrogate for Valerie Ramirez, Alex Wyatt's girlfriend. After the Birthrights founder took a hostage and began firing at her, she returned fire.

"But I have a witness. Valerie Ramirez. She saw the whole thing."

"They have witnesses, too. Employees who saw you break in, shoot out the windows, endanger the patients and clinic staff, and get into a firefight. Or that's what they'll claim."

Unreal. I can't believe this is happening.

"What do we do?"

"First, we get you a lawyer. Then we have to decide where you go from here."

"What do you mean?"

"We have two options. First, you could fly back, testify this week, tell your side of the story, and hope they don't return an indictment. But if the black hats in Justice are gunning for you, they could have you arrested by the end of the same day. They could hold you for months without bail."

"And Option B?"

"We wait it out. Maybe get you into a country with no extradition agreement with the U.S. I could have Tosh and Carlos start looking into who's pressuring Justice to bring charges."

"Those aren't very good choices."

"They're not," he agreed.

She pressed her back against the booth and felt the sting of her shoulder injury. "And you guys are off to Samana Cay."

Bo looked at the others around the table. "That's right. We'll be posing as tourists." He put his hand on top of hers. "Or I could stay here with you. It's Switzerland, after all."

She locked eyes with him. She couldn't have him choose her over Bailey. His legit daughter.

"I'm coming with you."

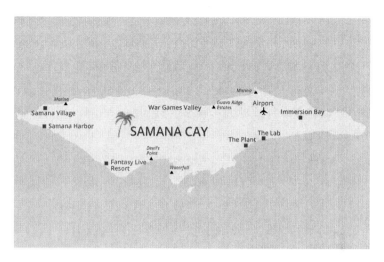

Map of Samana Cay and major landmarks.

35

Samana Cay

Volkov revved his Harley-Davidson FXDR 114 and sailed down the ramp leading out of the oversize rear door on his Dassault Falcon. He much preferred these flamboyant blasts onto the scene than an under-the-radar entrance with all the tense prep work that being Incognito required.

He spent the morning tooling around Samana Cay, taking in all the new buildings and tourist attractions that had sprung up since his last visit a year ago.

At noon he peeled down Columbus Highway along the eastern spine of the island and called up Lucid. His right-hand man touched down an hour ago and should be settled in by now. As usual, he'd see what Lucid was up to but not the other way around.

"Chairman, welcome back to the island."

"I see my dollars have been hard at work."

"The main attractions are drawing record crowds. Three

cruise ships in port today. And in Sector Two, the Lab is humming along nicely while Immersion Bay is maxed out."

"Excellent," Volkov said. Samana Cay was never intended to be a major revenue center but rather a biochemical staging area on sovereign territory close to the U.S. mainland.

"Zaven Kasparian just contacted me. He wants to fly out for a follow-up with you and a Fantasy Live session. Is that all right?"

"When?"

"Now. His plane is fueled and ready to go."

"Yes, that's fine." He needed to make amends with the Armenian after that security fiasco. "What else?"

"Your Fantasy Live simulation is set for tonight. But first we have our one o'clock with Bashir and Cazac."

"Yes, yes. Anything else?" Volkov's Harley passed two shuttle buses with red and blue teams heading to War Games Valley on the north side of the island, far from the Lab on the southeast end.

"One other matter, Chairman. A reporter for *Axom* gained access to Fantasy Live under false pretenses. We had our suspicions early on but decided to play it out. Our marketing department thought an unauthorized feature spotlighting our roll-your-own fantasy experiences would generate publicity for Fantasy Live among the chattering classes. There's nothing more alluring to the super rich than being told they shouldn't have something. "

"And?"

"We didn't count on Alex Wyatt and the performer breaking the rules, stepping out of the simulation. He knows one of the girls came from the Disappearance."

Damn it all! Volkov slipped the clutch into top gear and his Harley Softail screamed past 120 mph, tires smoking. He leaned his body forward atop the unrelenting power of the 1868cc motor as he considered this.

"Has he filed an article yet?" Volkov asked.

"He has not."

"Did you say he works for *Axom*? Isn't that Paul Redman's publication?"

"It is."

"And this reporter—he's in custody?"

"We have him in a holding facility. Not quite sure what to do with him."

"Let me think about this."

"Understood, Chairman."

"Chairman out." He disconnected the video chat, signaling he was displeased with how Lucid has been handling security matters. If this Alex Wyatt can connect Fantasy Live with the Disappearance, it could jeopardize Project Ezekiel at its most critical juncture—just before Phase Two.

Alex Wyatt was a liability. What to do with him was another matter.

♀ ♂

VOLKOV PARKED his sports bike along the road and followed the brightly patterned stone walkway into the heart of Samana Village, the tourist stronghold on the northwest part of the island. It was lunchtime, and Volkov walked through the throng in his motorcycle helmet.

He entered a sub sandwich eatery and stood in the short line. When it was his turn, he raised his visor just enough so the cashier could see his lips and hear his order. In other places, wearing a helmet covering your entire face inside a restaurant often drew a rebuke or a rude comment, but in the fanciful surroundings of Samana Village, it didn't merit so much as a quizzical glance.

He moved down the line and watched his "sandwich artist" go to work. Volkov could see through the reflection on her AR glasses that she received a visual prompt verifying the ingredients at each step so she'd get the order exactly right. *Step one, step two, step three.*

Volkov liked what he was seeing. A high-tech sandwich assembly line with the added benefit of removing awkward human interaction from the equation.

At the final step, just as the artist known as Sara was about to spray the top layer of the sandwich, he spoke up. "No special seasoning for me." He'd already been vaccinated for both strains, but no sense in taking chances.

"All right, sir. For here or to go?"

"To go."

He planned to return later to explore more of the village. But for now he returned to his bike, tucked his sandwich into his jacket pocket, and rode to his executive suite in the corporate offices. He entered through the secure rear door with the passcode known only to him.

He removed his jacket and helmet, shook his long hair, and placed his sandwich atop his desk next to the bottle of ice water his staff had placed there.

Today's four-way virtual meeting involved an additional layer of complexity. They'd be viewing live-action augmented reality street scenes via a hack his chief data scientist in Moldova had engineered.

For his appearance, he decided Revelation 13:1 would be fitting. *And the beast which I saw was like unto a leopard.* At one p.m., he began the virtual chat by selecting a pre-programmed avatar on his control module. With this selection, he assumed the form of a snarling leopard with glowing red eyes and a serpent's tongue. On his wall monitor he saw video feeds for Lucid, Lab chief Bashir, and Andrei Cazac, the head of his team of data scrapers and black hat hackers in Tiraspol, Moldova.

"Chairman Incognito, I presume?" Bashir was sitting alone inside the Lab's secure Blackout Room.

"It is I." He knew his choice of biblical creatures and historical figures made his executive team somewhat uneasy. So be it. They *should* be on edge.

Lucid appeared on the second screen. On the third screen Cazac adjusted his video cam and tested his audio. "At your service, Chairman. You'll be pleased to know the credentials still work. We still have root access."

Good news, indeed. Months ago Randolph Blackburn had given his team access to the content feed for his media empire's channel on all the new AR headsets from Google, Apple, Facebook. It appeared word had not yet filtered back to Blackburn that he was on the outs at the Compact, so the operating system backdoor still worked. Either that or he was too addled with his incurable genetic disease and forgot all about it.

"Let me show you what we've been doing," Cazac said. "I'll put up three live feeds. One from Manhattan, Washington, D.C., and Miami."

On Volkov's wall of flat-screen HDTV monitors, below the video chat with Bashir and Cazac, he now saw three street scenes. This was not much different than watching Lucid's Eyecam when he was out and about. The four men were able to see the world as these three targets were viewing the world as they walked down the street wearing augmented reality glasses.

"Now normally this would not be all that interesting," Cazac went on. "People wear AR glasses for all sorts of mundane reasons. To check the weather. Call their spouse. Check their messages. Scan headlines. To play a game or get block-by-block walking directions."

"What are those numbers at the bottom?" Volkov asked.

Cazac nodded. "Very perceptive. I've added a small data window that's outside the field of vision of the subjects. You're looking at numbers for heart rate and cortisol levels being detected from the connected wearable devices they have on their wrists."

"Chairman, I'm not clear on what's going on here," Lucid

broke in, looking puzzled. "Why cortisol levels?" And it was true. He hadn't had time to brief Lucid on the specifics of the activation method they were using. *The Switch,* as he called it.

Volkov moved his eyes left and right and watched his leopard avatar do the same, courtesy of eye tracking. The four of them were the only ones who knew the operational details of Project Ezekiel. With Lucid's background in evolutionary biology, he should grasp how this would work.

Volkov said, "Bashir, why don't you tell Lucid about The Switch without getting into the nitty-gritty."

Bashir nodded. "As you know, the new generation of wearables provide data on your heart rate via pulse points on the wrist as well as 'stress levels' based on the amount of cortisol detected in sweat drawn from the skin beneath the device. This all happens in a matter of seconds."

Cazac broke in, "My team increases the stress levels of the targets, starting with anyone wearing these AR glasses in Phase One of the project. Today's demo is proof of concept."

To Volkov's mind, the beauty of Project Ezekiel was how it blended modern technologies with ancient biology. Normal archaea die of exposure to oxygen, making it much more difficult to transmit from one person to another. The variety retrieved by Lucid and Bashir from the hydrothermal vents at the bottom of the arctic, however, was far hardier. Once Bashir's Lab succeeded in genetically altering new strains to survive exposure to oxygen or UV rays, the modified archaea could go to work inside the human host.

Bashir had hacked the gut-brain axis—the signaling pathways between the brain and microbes in the gut.

No one outside of Volkov and the lab coats, however, knew the specifics of the archaea experiments. Even Lucid and Cazac had been kept in the dark. So Volkov listened closely to make sure Bashir didn't say too much or utter the word *archaea.*

Bashir continued. "You've heard of 'fight-or-flight,' yes? It's a survival mechanism dating back millions of years in mammals. When someone perceives a danger, the eyes or ears send the information to the amygdala, the reptile part of the brain that processes emotions. The amygdala then sends a distress signal to the hypothalamus, unleashing a near-instantaneous sequence of hormonal changes and physiological responses that lead one to fight off the threat or flee to safety. Muscles tense. Breathing quickens. Blood pressure spikes. Beads of sweat appear. More oxygen is pumped to the brain."

"I see the cortisol levels rising in one of the subjects," Lucid observed.

Volkov saw it, too. The numbers began to spike for the woman in Manhattan—one of the women he had personally targeted with the first strain. He was sending a message with this infection.

Bashir went on. "Fight-or-flight provides the body with a burst of energy so it can respond to perceived dangers. Bumping up your cortisol levels is like pressing down the gas pedal on a car. It continues to speed up until the parasympathetic nervous system kicks in, calming the body down after the danger has passed."

Which brings us to The Switch, Volkov thought.

"But what if we managed to suppress the parasympathetic nervous system?" Bashir said with a knowing smile. "What if the brake is removed?"

Volkov improved on the metaphor. "What if we switched out the brakes as the car careened down a steep hill?"

This was the beauty of Phase One. He had asked Bashir to come up with easily memorable nicknames for the two strains his lab had genetically engineered. Both were catchy. *The Paranoia Strain* for Phase One.

Phase One held the potential to disrupt every aspect of life in the West. Through the introduction of genetically altered archaea in their systems, subjects would see a build-up of stress levels, leading to a cascade of paranoid behavior and a loss of memory, culminating in a crescendo of civil unrest and ultimately the collapse of the American health care system.

Once people realized how easily the infection was transmitted, chaos would break out. People would no longer leave their homes. Entire economies would collapse. Socializing, going out to dinner, shaking hands—all of it would be a thing of the past. America would be in turmoil in a matter of weeks, if not days. Until America fell, none of his vast plans for the Reset could be realized.

Lucid said, "So you're saying—"

Volkov's panther cut him off. "We will keep the Americans and western Europeans in a constant state of fear. We will scare them to death."

36

Miami

Alice Wong stood atop her chair in the conference room at *Axom*'s headquarters in Miami, grappling with the one-eyed smiley face piñata that dangled overhead. It was a reminder for the staff not to get too self-serious or puffed up. But today the subject was dead serious.

Victorious over the vanquished piñata at last, she stepped down and looked around the large cherry-wood conference table at the war room she'd assembled. *Axom* was that rare combo of national politics, entertainment, and opinion that actually worked as an online publication. Having a billionaire owner didn't hurt, either. She'd been elevated to Editor-in-Chief just a month ago. This was her first crisis, and she knew it was a test of her character.

"Is everyone here?"

"Everyone except Alex," offered Charlie Adams, the super-connected roving correspondent and Alex's best friend.

Not helpful.

She shut the glass door to the conference room. "Here's the

situation. As you know, Alex Wyatt left a voicemail for me last night. Here it is." She put her phone on speaker and played the short recording talking about a kidnapping victim.

The ten reporters, editors, and Paul Redman, the billionaire owner of *Axom*, looked glum at the sound of Alex's voice being cut off.

"We've been trying to reach him all day. Voice messages. Texts. We had a check-in scheduled for noon today. He didn't call."

"Okay, let's begin with the setting. What do we know about Samana Cay?"

She looked around the table and stopped at Paula Hayes, her talented executive assistant. She considered Paula a peer rather than an underling. *Axom* was famous for being a "flat" organization with few hierarchies and a collaborative structure—the exact opposite of most newsrooms. Which is why her in-box was overflowing with journalists' resumes.

"About 18,000 residents live on the island." Paula read from the research she'd pulled together on her Macbook this morning. "Ninety-six percent of the labor force works in tourism. The thing is, there's not a bright line between the government and the private sector. You live in a government-subsidized corporate village and work at a government-run theme park."

"Great. A socialist paradise." Stan Walters, the portly curmudgeon in residence, was known for his provocative conservative opinion columns. "Sounds like your people, Charlie."

"I hear the Reichstag is adding time shares—you'd be right at home," Charlie shot back. He could be just as acerbic from his left-of-center perch.

"Boys, boys, we're here for Alex." Alice shot a nervous glance at the owner. *Have to keep a lid on my team.* "Paula, go on."

"Samana Cay is approaching a half million visitors a year, mostly by cruise ship," Paula read from her screen. "State-of-the-art VR and AR facilities. A single corporate entity owns everything. Get this. The guy in charge goes by the name 'Chairman Incognito.' Nobody knows his real name."

"You're joking," Charlie said.

"I'm not." Paula knew her stuff. "And since the United States doesn't recognize Samana Cay as an independent country, we have no ambassador there. No embassy."

Alice tapped her pencil on the table. "Interpol doesn't operate in Samana Cay. So the only way to report a missing person is to contact the local authorities?" An idea began to bubble up in her brain.

"Apparently so," Paula said.

"What about this Bailey Finnerty he mentioned on the message?" Stan was finally getting down to business.

Paula nodded. "Confirmed. The Disappearance database was crowdsourced, and you never know if some of these girls ran away or encountered a random act of foul play on that day. But Bailey Finnerty is Missing Person No. 416 on the list. Parents divorced. No reported sightings of her since the abduction."

"Until now," Alice said. "This could be a big story. But our first priority has to be Alex."

"When did you last speak with him?" Charlie asked.

"Yesterday morning at ten. He sounded good. He said the series was shaping up nicely."

"He say anything else?"

"Just that he was getting a lot of color for the package and his first 'simulation' was scheduled for sunset yesterday. After the call, he sent in the photos he's taken so far."

That got the attention of DeShawn Robinson, the photo editor. "Can we see them?"

"Yeah, let me get them on screen." She hooked up her phone to the main monitor and it displayed row after row of color photos. She switched to gallery mode and began a slide show.

"Guests are not allowed to take their phones with them during a Fantasy Live session. Alex said he thinks it's because what *the phone* sees and what *you* see through your Eyewear are two completely different things."

"Makes sense," Alice said. "The physical world becomes recontextualized in any virtual or augmented reality experience."

They all watched the main screen against the wall as the photo gallery cycled through the first two days of Alex's shots. The angle of some photos suggested they were taken on the sly. But other shots were group selfies taken with fellow guests.

"The Fantasy Live people clearly knew some photos were being taken," DeShawn observed.

"Right," Alice said. "Alex signed an agreement—as Andrew Bayless— that no photos taken during his time on the island would be used for commercial or editorial purposes or posted to social media under penalty of fines up to $10,000 per photo. But you were allowed to take a few casual shots to share with friends and family."

Lionel Harriman, the corporate counsel, cleared his throat and leaned forward from the seat next to Redman. "Needless to say, the plan was for us to review every photo for its news value if breaching that agreement was our only option."

"This isn't a pitch meeting," Brian said, using the term the top editors used for the daily session where they wrangle over story placement on *Axom*'s home page.

"I know that," Harriman snapped.

"Go back, go back," Redman spoke up.

This was the first time Alice had ever seen their eccentric owner in the editorial conference room. On her first day as editor, he'd emphasized that he was a hands-off owner, even though he liked to be kept in the mix when an inside tip crossed her desk. She didn't have to run special projects or in-depth series past him. But when Alex went missing, he was the first person she called.

Alice swiped back three photos. "There!" Redman said,

pointing at a selfie of Alex posing with two other guests. "Who's that man and woman he's with?"

"I have no idea," she admitted.

"Is there a way to run facial rec on some of these guests?" Charlie asked, then glanced at Redman. "Without breaking any laws, I mean."

The room went silent. Finally Redman spoke up. "I've got some contacts at NSA."

"All right, great," Alice said.

She'd long heard second-hand reports about Redman's behind-the-scenes dealings both inside the government and with the rich and connected. There was also a rumor going around that he was a prepper—one of those survivalist types—and that he had a secret multimillion-dollar luxury bunker in Fiji just in case civilization was about to collapse. *Man, these billionaires and their play money.*

She turned to her executive assistant. "Paula, let's begin a contingency plan in case some of us need to travel to the island in the next twenty-four hours."

"On it." Paula added the action item to her list.

Alice knew it was time to wrap. "I'll take the lead on contacting Bailey Finnerty's parents. Mr. Redman will let us know if he turns up anything. And team. This Chairman Incognito character. Let's turn over every stone to see what we can dig up on him."

37

Manhattan

Eileen Mills paused to adjust her designer AR glasses as she stood in front of the window outside Saks Fifth Avenue. Like many consumers, she resisted the idea of wearing them for the longest time, until the frames were so inconspicuous they blended into the crowd. Now they were all but indistinguishable from any other pair of glasses.

Every year she and Bailey had made a ritual of heading out from Long Island to Manhattan for their early Christmas shopping. She'd debated whether to skip it this year. In the end, she decided to buy just one gift—to give her daughter a welcome-home present as soon as she returned. *But what do you get a daughter who's been missing for six months?*

She cycled through the special offers and loyalty points from nearby stores. She liked that the glasses were turning up all sorts of interesting tidbits about what was inside the stores as she passed by.

She continued down Fifth Avenue toward the Guess store, pausing at East 48th until the glasses told her it was safe to cross.

She stepped into the intersection. A speeding taxi blasted through a red light and almost struck her. She jumped back onto the curb, startled by the near miss. *What the hell? Looks like even smart-glasses aren't infallible.* She felt a shot of adrenaline kick in, sharpening her reflexes.

She crossed East 48th, keeping well back in the swarm of pedestrians. New York was still a struggle for her, but she decided after the divorce to move from Virginia to Long Island to be closer to her ailing retired parents. Bailey hated apartment life in Hicksville—"Are you kidding me? *Hicksville?*"—and was in full-on teen rebel mode by the time she turned sixteen. She demanded to live with her father back in Virginia during senior year of high school, and Eileen finally relented. Not a day passed when she didn't blame herself for that decision.

This never would have happened if I stood strong. If I'd just been a good mom.

She hopped up onto the curb and watched the faces of the passing strangers, some of whom were wearing glasses themselves. *Did they know? Were they being alerted about what a miserable failure of a mom I've been?* After all, she'd been on the news after the Disappearance. Her shoulders knotted up at the thought.

This new world of transparency—of glasses that *annotate the world*—had its upsides, but it had its spooky side, too. This particular AR channel had facial recognition turned on. While the names of the passing strangers were blocked for privacy reasons, the public records about them was not. A smug-looking Wall Street type walking in front of her just sold his Upper East Side condo for $18.2 million. A city architect to her right was pulling down more than five times her teacher's salary of $45,000 a year.

She gritted her teeth at the poor decisions she'd made. She owned a car that was eighteen years old with 270,000 miles on it and a cracked windshield she couldn't afford to replace.

In the doorway of a clothing store on her left, a priest held the door open for a mom and her two young sons. A simple line of white text appeared, superimposed across his chest: *Accused of molesting seven altar boys.* He looked up at her and she averted her eyes. *Not my business.*

She stabbed at the button on the right side of her glasses but couldn't toggle off the data. And now, what was this? An alert notification. Half a block up the street, advancing toward her, were three African American teenage boys wearing hoodies. She was not one to leap to assumptions, but the facial recognition feature flashed a warning across the bottom third of her field of vision:

Super predators.

She froze and tucked her purse beneath her coat. She looked around. Nobody seemed to notice the threat. She spotted a traffic cop back at the intersection and sprinted toward him. By the time she reached the corner, she was out of breath.

"Officer! Those boys!"

He waved his arms and waved at drivers in his lime-green vest, white cap, and white gloves. "Which boys?"

She didn't want to be obvious and point, so she jutted her chin out toward the approaching young men who were laughing at something.

"What they do?" The cop glanced at her then went back to directing traffic.

The glasses didn't say what they did. But now she saw a second alert. Her glasses threw a red circle around the face of a man standing at curbside on the far side of Fifth. What now? A moment later, the glasses flashed a warning:

Terrorist suspect.

She moved a few feet to her left to get a better view. *My God, what was going on?* He was a bearded Middle Eastern man in his twenties. His right arm sagged from the weight of carrying a black polycarbonate suitcase. He kept looking furtively to his right and left.

What was in the case? A bomb? A dirty bomb?

"Officer, that man! Check his suitcase!" She noticed she sounded out of breath and her voice was trembling.

"All right, Miss. Time to move along." The officer turned his back to her, blew his nerve-rattling whistle, and motioned for the pedestrians to cross. She felt her face flush red. *This officer doesn't believe me!*

She had to tell someone. What if she could have stopped a terrorist bombing and did nothing? She reached for the phone in her pocket just as it rang.

"Yes?" She wiped a sheen of sweat from her cheeks.

"I'm looking for Eileen Mills," the voice on the line said.

"Who is this? I can't talk right now." She felt agitated at the dangers swirling around her. *Why wasn't anyone doing anything? I have to call 911.*

"Ms. Mills, my name is Alice Wong. I have information about your missing daughter."

She'd received her share of crank calls over the past six months and was in no mood for it now. Her heart was racing now.

"Listen, I'm about to call the police. Don't call me again—"

"Ms. Mills, please listen. It's about Bailey. I believe we know where Bailey is being held."

38

Samana Cay

After a fifteen-minute taxi ride from Lynden Pindling International Airport in the Bahamas' capital of Nassau, Kaden wheeled her suitcase down the pier of Albany Marina on the south side of New Providence island. Bo, Nico, Tosh, Carlos, and Judy Matthews followed right behind.

"Is this the harbor where you rented a boat for us?" she asked Bo.

"Slight change of plans. Bigger boat, bigger team." Bo nodded toward three figures waiting for them at a slip in the distance at the far side of the pier.

"Why the change in plans? Who's joining us?"

"You know that call I took as soon as our flight touched down? That was my ex. Bailey's mom. She sounded ... *different*. She said she was on an adrenaline high, but she sounded a little frantic."

"Oh, because she's a woman, she was hysterical, is that it?"

"I'm saying I know Eileen. She's always grounded, and it was like she was in overdrive and couldn't calm down. But I buried the lead. She got a call from the editor of *Axom*."

"Alex's news site?"

"You know this guy?" Bo asked.

"Yeah. We're friends."

They'd met two months ago when Alex was covering the Birthrights Unlimited scandal for *Axom*. He was onto a new story now, and she'd forged his documents for Samana Cay. He'd left her two messages. She tried to text him from Zurich and call him on the ride to the harbor, but so far no luck.

"Well," Bo said, "it seems Alex spotted my daughter on Samana Cay."

"That's great news! Now we're not following a shot in the dark, we're following a solid lead. That's the break we've been looking for."

"It is." Bo's face registered only worry, not hope.

"I hear a *but* coming."

"Nobody's been able to reach Alex for the past twenty-eight hours."

Tosh caught up on their left side and joined the conversation. "So you've heard. This changes the equation. This is now an extraction operation."

"For Bailey *and* Alex?"

"And, we hope, for the other missing girls," Tosh said. "Two planes out of Zurich touched down on Samana Cay in the past few hours. Another on the way."

"How do you know that?" Kaden asked. "Agency contacts?"

Tosh held up his phone. "Flight tracker app from the App Store. Chances are one or both of those flights include the figures calling the shots."

Kaden considered this. On the flight from Zurich, she watched and listened to the entire recording of the Compact's meeting in Zug. She'd shared the Ezekiel file with Red Team

Zero. Bo told her he'd try to get the attention of someone higher up at DIA. *Maybe plans are finally in motion behind the scenes.*

But hope was not a plan. "Don't get me wrong," she said. "But this sounds like a bigger mission than Red Team Zero can chew off."

"I don't disagree," Bo said. "But we're not waiting on anyone."

As they tramped down the pier, the figures in the distance came into focus. The most senior member of the trio stepped forward to meet them. He was a tall, silver-haired business type wearing dark blue chinos and a gray track jacket.

"Bo Finnerty? Kaden Baker? Paul Redman." They all shook hands. "And these are two of *Axom*'s finest, Alice and Charlie."

Charlie gestured with two fingers toward a massive yacht in the slip to their right. "And this baby is our bad-ass ride."

Kaden saw she had a new alert from Amelia. They were about to set sail and they'd be out of Wi-Fi range, so she stepped off to the side and maximized Amelia.

Amelia appeared on the edge of the pier wearing dusty overalls. "Hi, sugar. Know you're heading off but though you'd want to know. You received a notification about your paternity test results. There's a 99.9 percent probability that Bo is your genetic father."

This was a life-altering moment, and Kaden had hoped for a more dramatic announcement. But there was no fanfare or flourish of trumpets—and no time to dwell on the news.

"Thanks, Amelia." Kaden minimized her and wheeled her luggage toward the others who were now boarding Redman's yacht, the Carpe Diem. At the bottom of the boarding ramp, Bo stood waiting for her.

Bo, her father.

♀ ♂

FOR KADEN, the operation started to fill in during the long ride to Samana Cay. Redman seemed to be something of a nautical nut and adventure seeker. Alice Wong turned out to be *Axom*'s editor. Charlie Adams was a hard-charging reporter and Alex's friend. Kaden was relieved to hear the *Axom* people were intent on bringing Alex and Bailey home and news stories about their adventure would take a back seat.

Redman kicked things off with a tour of Carpe Diem. At 200 feet long, it featured three decks, a huge owner's private terrace facing forward, a helideck at the bow, and a mosaic swimming pool that could transform into a dance floor.

Tosh and Carlos took a few minutes to ask questions about the elaborate communications controls linked to a dedicated Intelsat Earth Station satellite with an X-band uplink, which was mumbo-jumbo to her but seemed to impress the boys. Kaden and Nico checked out their cabins below.

She'd lost her beloved Beretta back on the slopes, but Bo gave her a spare SIG Sauer P226 Scorpion. She stashed the pistol, her fake passport, and her smart contacts in her fanny pack—no need for Amelia to make an appearance during the ride to Samana Cay.

After a short while, she and Nico joined everyone in the owner's terrace on top. Charlie appeared with a round of Bahama Mamas and poured drinks. Kaden decided to be a stick-in-the-mud and grabbed another glass of water. People made introductions before the talk turned to the extraction. Alice passed around her phone with the short snippet of Alex's last message before he was cut off.

"So what's the game plan when we get there?" Kaden asked.

"I was thinking we'd head straight to the authorities." Judy Matthews looked around at the others. "No?"

Kaden shot her a look of disbelief, but Bo cut her off.

"From what we've been able to establish," Bo said, "there's

every likelihood the top government officials know what's going on, at minimum."

She noticed Bo didn't yet share the news that their surveillance of the Compact revealed a much larger conspiracy with global implications, even though he'd passed that information to his contacts in the DIA. *First things first. Save friends and family, then save the world.*

Bo turned to face the *Axom* people. "What have you guys turned up about this character Incognito?"

"We have a dozen people just starting to dig in," Alice said. "Nobody seems to know much about him, other than he spends most of his time in Belarus. Public records in Belarus are hard to come by, to say the least."

Oddly, the video footage didn't capture a clear image of Incognito's face behind the partition. Bo theorized it had something to do with face masking technology, a cutting-edge technique used by some political leaders, celebrities, and illusionists.

Kaden thought about this misfit menace Incognito. *He was probably the one who ordered Savić to come after me. He's the one responsible for Gabriel's death. He might even be the ringleader behind the Disappearance.*

If priority one was the rescue, job two was to take down Incognito.

Kaden sipped her water and took stock of how unsettled her world had become. Her sense of who she was and what mattered to her had been rocked to its core during the past few weeks. First, she uncovered the revolting spectacle of scores of young women forced into surrogacy at Birthrights Unlimited, ending with a shootout and her facing possible murder charges.

Then, she opened up and made herself vulnerable to a serious relationship with Gabriel, only to see it end tragically. *His death —that's on me.*

Then, her biological father showed up to involve her in a search-and-rescue mission for the half-sister she never knew she had. Her shoulder still throbbed in pain after yesterday's encounter with a hitman. *Nearly got killed.*

This is not a good run I'm having.

If there was the smallest hint of good to come out of it, it was finding her real father and filling in some of the blanks. She suspected Bo was still holding back, though. She needed him to be straight with her. *I need someone I can count on. Someone besides Nico I can trust.*

They got down to business and sketched out a rudimentary search operation, starting with aerial surveillance of the island followed by splitting into pairs. Kaden would partner with Nico, given they'd pulled several special ops together and knew each other's moves.

The trip took most of the afternoon, but they finally got within sight of the island. They were approaching from the west —the more populous end where cruise ships docked at Samana Village—so Redman took them on a course south of the island to the less developed southeastern sector. If Alex and Bailey were being held on the island, chances were good they weren't being held smack in the middle of the touristy village center.

They watched from the owner's terrace high above as Tosh and Carlos set up their gear and used Carpe Diem's navigational system to send a swarm of fist-sized drones toward shore. These were considerably larger than the micro-drones used in Zug but smaller than the drones you'd see in public parks.

"I'm sure we're breaking all sorts of laws," Bo said. "The whole island is a no-fly zone. Generally, you can't fly a drone within five miles of an airport, and Samana Cay has one just over that ridge."

She watched as the drones lifted off from the heliport at the front of the yacht and hovered overhead before moving toward the southern shoreline. The drones were colored to match the sky, but she could still see their outlines move in unison in a magnificent swarm that reminded her of a starling murmuration. They swooped in beautiful synchronized formations like a giant paintbrush swirling across a brilliant blue canvas.

As they watched, Bo lowered his voice so only she'd be able to hear him. "I have a question for you. And something I've been wanting to tell you."

This was good. Maybe he was starting to confide in her. No more secrets. I need to tell him about the paternity results, too. But this doesn't feel like the right time.

"Your mother," Bo said. "You and I discussed her medical history back at the diner."

She nodded. Weeks before she'd met her Bo, she hacked her grandfather Randolph Blackburn's digital vault and read his medical records. He had a rare form of C-J disease, an incurable degenerative nerve condition that could strike at any age. He handed it down to her mother. It was the same condition now scrambling Blackburn's brain.

Bo looked deadly serious. "All these years, I felt it wasn't my place. But they told you about your odds. Right?"

She looked at him. This was the conversation she decided not to have with her grandfather. "Nobody's ever discussed it with me. I know I have a fifty-fifty chance of carrying the gene."

"You're talking about it so damn clinically. This is your life. You got tested so you know the results, right?"

After finding out about her biological mother and how she died at twenty-three—the same age Kaden was now—she'd decided there was more power in *not* knowing than in knowing.

"I've made my choice," she said coolly. Knowing whether Bo was her father was one thing. Knowing whether she was carrying around a genetic death warrant was another.

She realized for the first time that Bailey wouldn't have the gene and wouldn't have to wrestle with the same decision. Bailey's mother was Eileen, and Kaden's mother was Deirdre. *That's one thing Bailey and I don't have in common—a possible death gene.*

She didn't want to dwell on the subject. "You said you had something to tell me?"

"It's about my job at the agency—"

"Wait. What's that?" She squinted and saw the afternoon sun glint off a metal object in the water. In seconds she recognized it as a fast-moving speedboat approaching from the mainland.

A commotion of voices from Redman, Tosh, and Carlos. Redman sprinted to the helm and fired up the engine. "Raise anchor," he yelled.

"Gunboat, eleven o'clock!" someone below shouted.

Seconds later, a rough voice blasted out of a loudspeaker atop the gunboat. "Spies! Prepare to be boarded!"

She peered over the carbon fiber wall framing the lounge chairs on the top deck and saw the Swift boat. On deck six men pointed semi-automatic rifles at Redman and the others. The boat pulled up alongside and the men began to board while the gunner trained a high-caliber machine gun on their companions, probably a GAU-19/B Gatling Gun Tactical System. She'd seen one mounted on a Humvee during boot camp and knew it could kick out over 1,300 rounds per minute.

She and Bo hunched down to make sure they weren't spotted. They could see Tosh, Carlos, Redman, and Judy raise their hands in surrender.

"What do we do?" Nico came up from below, clutching the fanny pack from her cabin. She checked and all her essentials were inside. She pulled out the SIG Sauer to get it into firing position.

Bo shook his head. "You can't get into a firefight with these guys. It's suicide."

"We can try to head out to international waters in the speedboat." Nico gestured toward the powerboat hanging from the port side of the yacht away from the intruders.

"We'll never make it," she said. They were about a half mile from the island, too far from the three-mile limit. Not that these guys were going to respect an imaginary international boundary.

She wasn't about to become a prisoner. She tied the fanny pack around her waist and climbed over the railing. Nico understood. He nodded and followed suit. She teetered on the sheer edge of the deck opposite from the gunmen and turned to Bo. "We'll find you on land."

Bo reached out and squeezed her hand. "Be careful."

Kaden and Nico plummeted from the top of Carpe Diem into the warm waters, still sheltered from a view of the Swift boat. She took a deep breath to get as far away underwater as possible. But the moment she hit the water, the injury from last night's fall into the ravine knifed through her shoulder and into her upper back.

She began swimming. With each stroke the pain tore through her shoulder with an unrelenting ferocity. She wasn't sure she would make it.

39

Samana Cay

Bailey Finnerty hurried to her appointment along the familiar path that spilled into the central courtyard of the remote outpost on Samana Cay. Officially, the vast encampment along the eastern end of the island was called Immersion Bay.

The girls had their own name for it: Camp Resist.

She made her way down the cobblestone walkway leading away from the beach and her bare-bones bunkhouse through the center of the plaza with its neat rows of picnic tables surrounded by leafy trees and vegetation. Off to her right, girls were racking up points by scrimmaging against each other on the volleyball court and on two soccer fields—ten fitness points for each hour of play, regardless of whether you won or lost.

To an outsider, at first glance it might resemble a summer camp. But she'd learned the hard way that a modern high-tech prison didn't need physical barriers.

"Hey, Ling," she said as her best friend from high school approached carrying a lunch tray. But Ling averted her eyes and darted left to avoid direct contact. She and Ling had been on the outs ever since Bailey's score dipped into the red zone.

A lot of the other girls seemed standoffish today, too. She couldn't put her finger on it. Only Katarina Gorka—the English-speaking girl from Belarus, a year younger than her—looked up and rose from her spot at the table. She had long, straight brown hair and kind eyes.

"Bailey, I'm so sorry about your mom." Katarina wrapped her arms around her shoulders and gave her a hug.

"My mom?" Bailey drew back, alarmed.

"You don't know?"

Katarina led her past the last table and into the Commons with its benches, fountains, workout equipment, and grassy knoll fronting the amphitheater and its leaderboard screen that dominated everything. The Commons was where most of the girls spent their days racking up points by working out or taking acting lessons, with the leaderboard serving as a constant reminder of which girls had rung up the highest point totals along with inspirational sayings or pithy blurbs about how they'd earned their achievement points.

But Bailey's knees buckled at what she saw. On the large digital screen towering above the stage, the leaderboard was live-streaming a video. A video of her mother slumped against a building in New York, clutching her chest. As Bailey watched, paramedics arrived on the scene, placed her mother on a stretcher, and transported her into the back of an ambulance.

Across the bottom of the screen, a red strip with white letters blared the message: BAILEY BROKE HER PLEDGE—HER MOTHER PAYS THE PRICE.

Her heart sank. *They did this to my mother. And it's my fault.*

Katarina reached out to touch her shoulder in support. Katarina's neckband glowed scarlet, indicating she was a rebel, someone to be avoided.

For the first time in weeks, Bailey's own neckband no longer glowed a bright green. Instead, it radiated a scarlet red after yesterday's escape attempt. The neckbands were officially called "safety necklaces," while the girls called them for what they were —*dog collars*. As hard as she tried in the beginning, the microthread material with tiny LED lights couldn't be cut with regular scissors or shears. She hated her dog collar with all her soul.

"I—I need to go." She turned away from Katarina and swept along the pathway, fighting back tears as she passed more girls with their judgmental looks. *I can't be late for my appointment. That would be a fifty-point deduction on top of the 500-point penalty from yesterday.*

She reached the walls-free Open Offices area at the edge of the Commons. The entire enclosure was set beneath a translucent plastic layer with tropical landscaping that let in air and natural light but camouflaged Camp Resist from orbiting satellites and passing planes. The covering gave the entire camp the vibe of partly cloudy skies even on sunny days.

Stretched out before her on a natural-wood double chaise lounger was her acting coach, Rachel Torres. The seats were facing opposite directions yet attached, and she nodded for Bailey to take the adjoining seat so there'd be no way to avoid eye contact.

She got right down to it. "My mother. I just saw her on the leaderboard. What did they do to her?"

Miss Torres frowned. "I'm afraid I don't know. But you know the rules."

Bailey wasn't sure whether to press the issue. After all, they'd done exactly what they'd promised to do if she broke her pledge.

"What can I do to make it right?"

"Bailey, listen to me. You're one of the lucky ones. The world is about to change, and there's no safer place than Immersion Bay. But you need to build up your points again. You know you were in the top five percent on the leaderboard right up until your transgression. Community chores, workouts, volunteering in the kitchen. Sad to see all those points lost."

The day-to-day reality of their situation soon became clear to the Disappeared. Girls had two options. They could play along, earn points, and save loved ones from the coming Transition. Under Option Two, they could refuse to cooperate and face the consequences. She'd heard some girls were shipped off after they'd used rocks and underbrush to form a giant SOS on the beach.

By the end of month one at Immersion Bay, Bailey had shifted her focus from gaining her freedom to protecting her parents. She shot up the leaderboard. She volunteered at the Dance Studio and Arts Barn. Everyone liked Bailey because she was always helping out with cooking, workout routines, laundry, washing dishes, a million little things. She did it partly because she liked to help people but partly to score points.

Her big move up the leaderboard came when she received a five hundred point bonus for signing the Immersion Bay Opt-In Pledge. In it, she pledged to go along with the augmented acting classes and the In-World simulations and all the other crazy stuff in the fine print that went with being held prisoner on an island teeming with visitors—tourists who were just a few miles away from Immersion Bay.

That was what got to her—how tantalizingly close freedom seemed to be. And yet the dog collars prevented them from getting anywhere near the tourists.

Miss Torres read something on her tablet, then met her eyes. "I'm not here to scold you today. I'm here to offer you a fresh start. Your performance yesterday received a positive score on believability, empathy, and vulnerability. But the AI detected several negative micro-expressions it had to correct on the fly. Facial expressions of anger, fear, sadness, and disgust were all detected in one-twenty-fifth of a second increments. So you earned no points for the VR 'bathtub' simulation. As far as the AR 'picnic sunset' session—well, you've seen your adjusted totals on the leaderboard."

She had. She was now dead last at Camp Resist and in danger of being shipped out. There were rumors the girls who left the island were sold as sex slaves. So there were worse things than pretending to be submissive and accommodating.

"I just don't want my mom to pay the price for my mistake," Bailey said.

"Good. Then let's keep things positive." She looked up. "Here comes the nurse."

"Nurse? I'm not sick."

"Everybody needs a flu shot."

The nurse set a small plastic container on the ground next to their chairs. She clicked open the latch to reveal two batches of glass vials. Three-quarters of the vials had the letter "V" marked marked on a yellow plastic top while a quarter had the letter "C" marked on a green top.

The nurse withdrew a vial with a yellow top.

"What are the the green vials for?" Miss Torres asked.

"Never you mind." The nurse frowned and turned to face Bailey. "Roll up your sleeve."

"Something going around?" Bailey asked.

The nurse drew liquid from the vial into a syringe. "This may sting." She swabbed her right biceps with an alcohol wipe, and the strong smell conjured memories of her crying as a little kid when she got her shots.

"Ow!"

The nurse applied a small bandage. "You'll live." She returned the items to the container and marched off.

"Don't piss off Nurse Ratched," Miss Torres quipped. She looked down and scanned her tablet. "I see you're turning eighteen today."

"Oh, really?"

Is it my birthday? I didn't even know what month it is, never mind the date. Digital devices were banned at Camp Resist, and keeping track of the days seemed pointless after a few months.

"Happy birthday."

"Thank you." She never imagined spending her eighteenth birthday in prison.

"I can offer you a hundred-point bonus for your special day. But only if you agree to an In-World simulation tonight."

She found the whole idea of the acting classes baffling and kind of gross. But she went along with all the "performance art" and "mixed reality" and being shuttled to the Fantasy Theater's "In-World Playspace." It took days to prepare for a simulation and study the background materials for a Fantasy Live guest.

"With Andrew again, so soon?" she asked.

"No," Miss Torres said. "Not Andrew. A very special guest. This won't be a typical Fantasy Live simulation. No prep work. You just need to do whatever he tells you to do."

She stared at Miss Torres, trying to control her micro-expressions. *What choice do I have?*

"Thank you for giving me another chance. Can you try to help my mom?"

Miss Torres flicked off her tablet and stood. "The shuttle leaves at seven. Good luck, Bailey." She flashed a quick smile before strutting off, and Bailey thought she detected a microexpression of regret around her lips.

Bailey rose and retraced her steps back to the Commons for lunch. Up ahead, she saw the girls crowd around the leaderboard. She hoped to God they weren't doing something else to her mother.

She reached the grassy field in front of the leaderboard and looked up. It was another live video. But this time it was coming from the island. The giant screen showed a boat docking at

Samana Harbor. Guards led a procession of a half-dozen people at gunpoint.

She was shocked to see the lead prisoner. Her father, Bo Finnerty.

"No!" she screamed. "No no no no *noooo!*"

40

Samana Cay

For the last fifty yards, Kaden let the pounding surf push her body onto the sandy shoreline. She pushed through the shoulder pain and made it onto Samana Cay by shifting her usual technique and generating a catch movement with vertical forearm action and shorter strokes.

"You okay?" Nico said from his knees a few yards up the beach. He seemed out of breath.

"I'm good." She checked behind her and was relieved to see her fanny pack still intact.

They settled into a sandy spot below a palm tree to get their bearings.

"We must be on the south shore." She recalled the map of Samana Cay they reviewed during the ride on Carpe Diem. "Samana Harbor and Village are on the western shore. Most of the rest of the island is unmapped. Where do you think they'll bring the prisoners?"

"Hard to say." Nico scanned the beachfront in both directions. "What's that object reflecting on the sand?"

He walked down the beach ten yards, reached down, and scooped something into his hands. He walked another five yards and did the same. He returned and showed her.

Two of the downed drones.

"These guys don't fool around," Nico said. "The machine gun on the Swift boat was proof of that. We should get to a populated area and get out of these wet clothes."

She stood. "I agree. Let's cut north to a main road, then head west to Samana Village. We can get a change of clothing. Maybe even get ahold of Annika and Sayeed, back at the mother ship."

Nico retrieved a SIG Sauer P226 Scorpion from his pocket—like hers, also courtesy of Bo—and shook off the water. "I hope this thing still works."

♀ ♂

Bo Finnerty tried to maintain his balance on the slab of metal seating in the back of the dusky van. The ride had gotten much bumpier in the past five minutes.

"How far do you think we've gone?" he asked Tosh and Carlos, seated across from him.

"Four, five miles," Carlos said.

They all had their arms tied behind their backs. But they weren't gagged and the guards were riding up front.

"What do you think they'll do with us?" Paul Redman asked.

"Hard to say." Bo was considering this very question during the drive from the harbor. "Me and my team, we're off the grid. If we disappeared, maybe nobody raises a fuss. But you three." He eyed Redman, Alice Wong, and Charlie Adams. "You're a problem."

"Why?" Alice asked.

"A billionaire news site owner and *Axom*'s editor and two reporters, Charlie and Alex? People will raise a fuss if you all go missing."

"Unless they make it look like an accident," Judy Matthews offered.

"Thanks for the idea," Charlie snapped.

"The agency should be coming for us," Tosh said. "Protocol is to devote all available resources to finding a field agent who doesn't report in. Right, Bo?"

He scowled and peered into the shadows. This was the conversation he wanted to have when he found the right time, first with Kaden and then with the others. But he never found the time and now he'd have to come clean. Had he gone too far?

"They won't come looking for us," Bo said.

"Why not?" Carlos asked.

"Because I took a leave from the agency three months ago."

"You what?" Carlos looked like Bo hit him with a gut punch.

"Wait." Tosh was trying to piece this together. "How is that possible? You've been paying us. I've got pay stubs. We get assets, equipment."

"It's all a cover." Bo struggled to free his hands. *Might as well lay it all out.* "It's not hard to set up a bogus company when you're running an off-book operation. I left the agency three months ago. Had to sell my house to cover the costs of our operation."

"And the drones, the equipment?" Tosh was always a stickler for details.

Was it wrong to lie to them about receiving authorization for this mission? Was it wrong to bring them here and put their lives in jeopardy? Maybe. But those bastards have my daughter! He answered Tosh this way:

"After twenty years, I still have some juice inside DIA. Still have my contacts at the European intelligence services. A lot of people are bending the rules to get us what we need since they're being headed off at the top levels. But they've made it clear they can't do anything else for us. We're on our own."

They went quiet for a moment. Then Carlos broke the silence. "You son of a bitch."

Bo stared him down. "I'd do it again."

♀ ♂

BY THE TIME they reached the outskirts of Samana Village, their clothes were stiff and crinkly but nearly dry. They stayed off the main streets and found a merchant that accepted U.S. dollars, using the small wad of wet bills in Nico's pocket. They bought and changed into T-shirts and shorts that blended in with the crowds on the street. Kaden knew the security team on the Swift boat didn't spot their escape, and Savić probably thought she was dead, so they had a small time window before anyone would be looking for them.

They stopped at a cafe with Wi-Fi, then ordered coffees and sat at a table in an uncrowded corner. She retrieved her smart contacts and earpiece from her fanny pack. Because they didn't have phones, she'd bring up Amelia first and then try to contact Annika or Sayeed at B Collective.

"Hi, Amelia," Kaden began.

"Hi, sugar plum." Amelia materialized in the chair between Kaden and Nico wearing her trademark aviator's outfit, with her cap off and a loose tangle of brown hair. Her personality mode was back on.

"Make sure you're on a secure connection," Nico suggested.

"Hear that, Amelia?" Kaden asked.

"Already on it," Amelia replied. "I'm using high-end encryption and a Virtual Private Network for our connection. Just to be safe, I'll create a firewall with cryptographic keys for any third parties we need to bring in. By the way, I like your outfit."

Kaden liked hearing that, even if she did program the compliment.

"Thanks. Can you pinpoint our location on this island?"

"My GPS is on by default."

The irony was not lost on Kaden that no one was able to pinpoint Amelia Earhart's last location on a remote island.

"Amelia, please contact Annika or Sayeed at B Collective."

"Sure thing." Amelia had access to her contacts even if Kaden didn't have her phone.

Annika picked up on the first ring. "Oh my God, Kaden, is that you?"

"It's me and Nico, yeah. Sorry we haven't checked in since Zug."

"That's okay. Are you all right? Where are you?"

"Long story. We're on Samana Cay. Bo and the others have been taken into custody."

"Oh, no! I'm switching to speaker so Sayeed can hear us."

"What's up, Sayeed," Kaden said.

"Sorry to hear about the others," Sayeed said. "What's the plan? How can we help?"

Kaden had several ideas swirling around during the walk to town. "First, we need to know if the local authorities will admit they have Bo and the others in custody. Call over and pose as Bo's attorney. Find out the pending charges. If they profess ignorance, that's a danger sign."

"On it," Sayeed said.

"Second, we need anything you can find out about Samana Cay's military infrastructure. Is there a main jail? Where are prisoners held before being brought up on espionage charges?"

"I'll start looking while we're talking," Annika said. She started typing search commands. "You think they'll be charged with spying?"

"Have no idea how things work in this place." Kaden lowered her voice. "There may be a bigger conspiracy in play. The Disappearance. The girls. They may be here somewhere."

"Oh my God, Kaden. And there are only two of you? Be careful. Hold on, working on an idea."

Sayeed broke in. "I've found contact info for the Ministry of Justice. Will call them as soon as we hang up. But one thing you should know. Samana Cay was rated the world's No. 1 surveillance state in the world last year, ahead of Singapore and even China. They've got sensors everywhere."

"I read about that," Kaden said. She knew China used facial-recognition technology for its "sharp eyes" program, which collects surveillance footage and renders a score for each of its 1.4 billion citizens based on their observed behavior, right down to how carefully they cross the street.

How could Samana Cay be worse with only 18,000 residents?

"Might be helpful to send you satellite footage of the island," Sayeed suggested.

"That, and more." Annika's voice brimmed with excitement. "I was able to access a restricted database. We're on a secure line, right?"

"As always." Kaden switched her earpiece to speaker mode but kept the volume low. Nico leaned forward into Amelia's personal space without realizing it.

"Good. You've heard of SLAM, as in SLAM maps?"

She hadn't, but Nico nodded. "It's part of the tech that lets you move around a hologram from all sides while it's sitting or standing there," he said.

"Right, but think much bigger," Annika said. "SLAM stands for Simultaneous Localization and Mapping. During the Mars Rover mission, they created a three-dimensional map of the Mars surface because it takes about fourteen minutes for a radio signal from Earth to reach the Rover. NASA couldn't send navigational commands to the little robot vehicle in real time. So Rover tooled around with the help of a virtual map on top of its unfamiliar environment."

"Makes sense," Kaden said.

"Here's what *isn't* public knowledge," Annika said. "The government and U.S. tech giants have teamed up on a massive

SLAM project to map the surface of Earth." She paused to let the import of this sink in. "The newest Earth Station satellites can identify buildings and objects almost down to the centimeter. By using photogrammetry and long-range volumetric capture, the result is a continually updated 3D geospatial rendering of the physical world. Now, mind you, not everything on the planet is 3D mapped yet, but every island within five hundred miles of the U.S. coastline certainly is."

"Including Samana Cay."

"Right. But here's the most interesting detail about your little island. On the eastern side, there's something that's just ... *weird.*"

"What do you mean, weird?"

"I mean, somebody's gone through a lot of trouble to camouflage it. But 3D models don't lie. There is no natural topography that looks like this."

"Looks like *what?*"

"Kaden, there's a giant dome in the jungle."

41

Samana Cay

Volkov watched with satisfaction in his executive suite as the video feeds came in with the first results of the Paranoia Strain. The limited clinical trial offered a proof of concept for a wider release, but it had a secondary benefit. It targeted the mother of one of the Opt-Ins who had not yet come to heel.

He hoped it would send the desired message to all the Opt-Ins. Every one of them had signed the pledge, taken the oath, committed to the cause. *They would obey or face the consequences.*

"Chairman." He recognized the mellifluous voice of Liv, his remote virtual assistant. "Lucid is on line one. He says it's urgent."

It had better be. Messages were piling up from different stakeholders. But he had to focus on salvaging the Compact and carrying out Project Ezekiel.

"Patch him through." He spoke without having to pick up a phone, courtesy of the thousands of audio sensors built into the surround-sound walls.

Catch and Kill   231

"Chairman, are you there?" Lucid's voice on the call sounded tense, as he did when he had bad news to deliver.

"What is it?"

"I'm calling from my SUV to alert you. I just received word we've successfully intercepted an intelligence operation off our southern coast. Seven prisoners taken into custody and their yacht captured and brought into Samana Harbor."

"Did you say 'successful'?"

"Yes, Chairman."

"What's successful about our sovereignty being breached by enemy intruders?"

"Sir, we downed their drones in mid-flight. They didn't even make landfall."

"Drones! Like the drone that put an end to our Summit?"

"Different model. We'll run diagnostics to see if there's a connection."

This was unacceptable. First, the Summit was cut short by the most disconcerting security breach imaginable. They were still assessing the fallout. A day later, intruders had violated Samana Cay's sovereign territory. Someone would pay.

"Lucid, these latest security lapses are mind-boggling. We may need to rethink your role as security chief." What was a threadbare string of trust was now frayed beyond repair.

"Chairman, as I stated, the intruders are in custody. We have no evidence our security has been compromised."

"These seven intruders. Who are they?"

"We're still identifying the captives. Five men, two women."

I'll deal with Lucid later. But this latest breach was beyond the pale. The enemy is right at my doorstep. How did they track down my whereabouts? Is there a mole in my organization? My circle of trust is small—perhaps it needs to be smaller. This calls for drastic action. I need to move up the time frame!

"Action item. Tell Bashir I want him to green-light the clinical trials for Phase Two of Project Ezekiel."

"I'm heading to the Lab now. But Chairman, that step was redacted in my version of the plan." He detected a note of derision seeping into Lucid's voice.

Volkov had been holding back details of the Phase Two strain from his top lieutenant. The lab coats just came up with a name for it.

The Fantasy Strain.

One of Bashir's neurobiologists pointed out the strain's symptoms: fantasy-like delusions, hallucinations, and fever states, leading to a quick and painful death. Fantasy Live no doubt figured into the nickname, too.

Volkov liked the name for a different reason. *For centuries, my people harbored the fantasy that the West could be brought to its knees. Now, thanks to a biological agent, I will deliver on those dreams. Is this not the ultimate fantasy?*

Lucid's uneven performance decided the matter. It was still too risky to bring Lucid into the fold.

"I want the Fantasy Strain released at Camp Defiance," Volkov ordered. "At once—this afternoon. Bashir will know."

A pause. Lucid knew the precise location of Camp Defiance. Every second that passed made him question Lucid's loyalty.

Finally, a stammer. "As you wish, Chairman."

♀ ♂

LUCID DISCONNECTED the call and rubbed his forehead. Incognito's actions seemed to be getting more erratic and impulsive. He was changing plans on a dime. Altering timelines on a whim. *Keeping things from me.*

He had learned long ago to look the other way when it came to the Chairman's idiosyncrasies. The fixation on biblical allusions. The voyeuristic use of Lucid's always-on Eyecast to the point he no longer enjoyed a speck of privacy. Project Ezekiel and its bold if overwrought plan to bring the West to its knees through stealth germ warfare.

He had accepted the position of chief operating officer of Samana Ventures not so much for the financial returns or even for the sense of power that comes with running the day-to-day business affairs of an entire island nation. He'd taken it because he could tap into an almost unlimited source of funds to design a technologically advanced culture that would pave the way for the Singularity.

Fantasy Live was the perfect sandbox for experimenting with the essence of the human condition. He saw it as a grand social experiment to identify humanity's primal needs and desires and to tease out all the cultural nonsense.

Lucid was chosen to help *build mankind's future.* He was specially suited to the task.

Like other members of the small but vibrant transhumanism movement—men and women who allowed their bodies to merge with machines—he considered himself more than human. Some days he thought of himself as more machine than man. He was the prototype of the new humanity that awaited the world in the Reset following the Transition.

In a way, he was a soft launch himself. The prototype of the new epoch. *That* was the vision he shared with Incognito. While some fellow transhumans dropped out of society, he was determined to *re-engineer* society.

Then there were days like today when he felt more like a grunt than a shaper of worlds.

He turned off Columbus Highway, took the short side road, and pulled into his executive parking space at the Lab on the southeast end of the island. He strode through the security doors with a wave of his hand and entered the main building.

Bashir looked up from the microscope on a lab table, surprised to see him. "Do we have an appointment?"

"We don't. But I have an urgent message from the Chairman." He dialed his voice down to co-conspirator level. "But first, I need to know. What is the Fantasy Strain?" He knew some details about the strain being developed for Phase Two, but he couldn't let on how he knew.

Bashir took a step back as if Lucid had crossed a forbidden line. "That's a closely guarded secret. Only the Chairman and I are privy to that information. I'm surprised you even—"

"Don't give me that." Lucid moved closer to within inches of the scientist's angular face and grabbed the lapel of his lab coat. "I need to know. *Now!*"

"You know I'm under orders," Bashir stammered.

"I'm responsible for everything that happens on this island. How can I do that when I'm in the dark about *the* key aspect of Project Ezekiel?"

The pair noticed the other lab workers peeling away from the vicinity, trying to pretend everything was normal. Lucid loosened his grip.

"Sorry, Lucid, I cannot tell you." Bashir held the upper hand. He reported directly to Incognito. Lucid had no leverage here.

Lucid tried one last twist. He let go of Bashir's lab coat and retreated a step. "How targeted is the Fantasy Strain?"

"Brother, I cannot share that. But I can tell you not to worry. You are safe."

"At least tell me this. What's the incubation period?"

"Hours."

Lucid nodded. He would see how this played out. "The Chairman wants you to deploy the Fantasy Strain on Camp Defiance."

"When?"

"Now."

Bashir nodded gravely. "Tell him I will see to it myself."

Lucid gave a cursory nod. He turned and headed out of the Lab and back to his vehicle. He needed to be on site when the prisoners were offloaded. He had a plan for them. One the Chairman didn't need to know about.

On the drive to War Games Valley, not far from the outcasts at Camp Defiance, he considered the events that led up to this week. He had been puzzled when Incognito decreed at the outset that no one who was married would be hired into any key management positions on the island. At first he thought it was a misguided effort to bring on type A overachieving workaholics with no personal life. Now he wasn't so sure.

He was no choirboy. He was on board with Incognito's vision of rebalancing the world global order. He was on board with the Paranoia Strain crippling the West. Such was the price of the Reset. If the Seven Spheres meant anything, it meant the old order must be reduced to cinders.

But now, given the way he was being kept in the dark, one thought burned through his brain.

What will the world look like after the Fantasy Strain is unleashed?

42

Samana Cay

K aden and Nico spent another twenty minutes at the cafe figuring out a plan and syncing their waterproof devices. Nico flashed his fitness bracelet that let him text, record audio, and send or receive location-enabled alerts.

Kaden opened the pendant attached to her necklace. Inside was the small photo of her real mom, a constant reminder of her roots and her evolving self-identity. Gabriel said the quartz pendant symbolized the love chakra, but it was practical, too. A digital screen on the back tracked her activity level, heart rate, calories burned, distance traveled—and you could use it to video chat. Double-click the top of its back and the pendant sends an alert.

With Gabriel, it was, *Thinking of you.* With Nico, it's: *I'm in trouble.*

She double-clicked her pendant.

Nico looked down at his bracelet and saw the alert. "Yeah, tell me about it."

"Now that we're synced, we need to decide whether to split up," she said.

"Why would we do that?" Nico discreetly removed the loaded chamber indicator from his P226 Scorpion and checked to see if there was any water damage.

"We could cover more ground if we split up. It's a big island. We need to find Bo, Tosh, Carlos, Judy, and the three *Axom* people. Then we need to find Alex. Then we need to find Bailey and the other girls."

"That's a tall order," Nico said.

"If we could free Bo, Tosh, and the others, we could fan out and use the tactical quadrant methodology we learned at boot camp."

Nico nodded. "Where do we start?"

Kaden reached for a napkin, borrowed a pen from the cashier, and sketched a rough outline of Samana Cay. The island was long and thin, about ten miles from west to east and two miles wide. She drew a dotted line to show the trek they'd made from the south shore to Samana Village along the northwest coast. She added a circle to represent the mystery dome Annika spotted on the far northeast corner of the island.

Sayeed hadn't been able to locate any jail or holding facility, but they were able to identify the location of several small military police garrisons. She marked those with X's.

"We have one ace in the hole," she said. "This character Lucid."

"What about him?" Nico asked. She hadn't clued him in yet.

"He's into biohacking, neuro-hacking, whatever you want to call modifying your body with electronic components. These folks see technology as a way to transcend their physical limitations. Turns out Lucid was the guy the rest of Red Team Zero tracked to the Kasparian estate in Zug while we were hunting down Dražen Savić at Wildspitz." Her shoulder was still killing her from her plunge into the ravine, but she was careful to mask her pain from Nico.

"Someone put a tracker on him?" Nico guessed.

"Better. He's got a GPS-enabled signal transmitting from a sensor on his body."

"Why would he do that?"

"Maybe he needs to be at the beck and call of his boss. The one who's really calling the shots." *Find Lucid and he'll lead us to Incognito. It was only a theory but the one that made the most sense.*

"So we're hacking into a biohacker?"

"Yeah. Kind of poetic."

"How do we find him?"

She turned toward Amelia, who'd been sitting patiently in the chair between them.

"Amelia? Put up a map of Samana Cay, please."

Amelia projected the map so Kaden could see it with her smart contacts. Nico didn't have his smartglasses with him so he was out of luck.

"Now," Kaden asked, "can you locate the current position of *target Lucid* with the I.D. signature I provided earlier?" Location awareness was one of Amelia's most awesome features.

"Based on your conversation with Nico, I anticipated that request. As you requested, I was being *proactive*. Isn't that the berries?"

Kaden couldn't help but smile at the goofy little old-timey expressions Amelia always trotted out. "Yeah, it's also called snooping. Anyway, where is he?"

"Lucid is at the War Games Valley, four miles east-northeast of here," Amelia said. A blinking red dot on the projected map marked the position on the island's north side. She drew it on her napkin, folded it in half, and gave it to her best friend.

"Nico, why don't you run reconnaissance of the National Guard presence in Samana Village?" She realized she was giving orders to Nico in the field again like she did during the Dallas operation. "I'll head to the War Games Valley. We meet back here in front of the cafe in four hours. Five at the latest."

She clasped the pendant with her palm for good luck and tucked it back beneath her T-shirt. She headed out.

♀ ♂

KADEN DECIDED HITCHHIKING or renting a car would be too risky in a surveillance state like Samana Cay. So while Nico scouted out Samana Village, she kept to the pedestrian trails heavily used by the local tourists. The crowds thinned as she headed away from the touristy attractions and toward the more remote northern side of the island.

She kept off the main roadway and stuck to a hiking trail running parallel to it, well behind a thicket of pines. Along the highway to her left, the streetlights were topped with gray flat-panel antennas that looked like a series of high-powered Wi-Fi hotspots configured as a mesh network. Looked like Wi-Fi was pervasive on Samana Cay, not confined to a few cafes.

Kaden instructed Amelia to crawl the Web, and Amelia found an online advertisement for the War Games theme park. One of the promotions said: "Put your battle skills and survival instincts to the test in a fully immersive, live-action role-playing theme park complete with enemies—both alive and undead."

Oh, brother. People pay for this?

She reached the turnoff along the main road and approached the large carving of Christopher Columbus at the intersection. She knew the island's main claim to fame was that Columbus first made landfall in the Americas on Samana Cay on Oct. 12, 1492.

But there was something odd about this wooden statue.

As she neared, Columbus gestured with his uniformed right arm toward his right. She was synced with the local network so she didn't need to don a pair of AR glasses to see Columbus give virtual directions.

"That way to Samana Village," Columbus said in English with a clipped Italian accent. He thumbed backward and added, "Set sail that way to War Games Valley." And finally he used a sword to point to his left. "Immersion Bay five miles that way. By the way, forget what you've heard, I came in peace."

She didn't have an opinion about Columbus, but she was sure she hadn't seen any of the native people who once inhabited the island.

She swept past Columbus toward War Games Valley. The sun began to set, casting a golden sheen across the veil of hardwood trees. Birds flitted and chittered in the tall trees, joined by the first hesitant chirps of crickets. The smell of jasmine filled her senses. She heard a low rumble from behind and ducked into the underbrush as a shuttle bus passed by with tourists outfitted in military camouflage fatigues.

She returned to the road and hiked about a mile to the north. She was out of Wi-Fi range now. Lucid was somewhere up ahead, according to the last readout she'd gotten from Amelia. The paved turnoff had turned into a dirt road, so she followed the tire tracks through the jungle canopy.

Off to the right, a distinctive salvo rang out and echoed across the valley's switchback trails. Gunshots.

She drew her P226 Scorpion and headed deeper into War Games Valley.

♀ ♂

Bo SIGNALED TO TOSH, Carlos, and Judy to keep low and stay out of sight. They moved in formation about ten feet away from each other along a ridge on the north side of the island as far as he could tell.

Bo paused behind a rock outcropping. Tosh and Judy came up alongside him while Carlos hung back, telegraphing the sense of betrayal he felt at being misled the past two months. Bo didn't blame Carlos in the slightest. But he couldn't worry about that now. He had to focus on keeping his unit alive.

"What happened to the others?" Judy asked.

Paul Redman, Alice Wong, and Charlie Adams were riding in the van on the trip from the harbor. After Bo and his team were forced out of the back, the three people from *Axom* were told to stay inside. The van drove off while the four Red Team Zero members were issued weapons by their captors.

"No idea," Bo said in a hushed voice. "They split us up for some reason."

At least there were three fewer civilians to worry about, he thought.

A volley of gunfire tore through the woods, strafing the trees behind them. He considered what to do. Returning fire might signal he's playing their damn war game. Then again, firing back might keep them at bay.

Bo examined his semi-automatic weapon. It looked like a newer version of the SCAR 17S, the Special operations forces Combat Assault Rifle. A matte-black beauty, she had a sixteen-inch barrel, collapsible side-folding stock, and a twenty-round magazine with large-caliber .308 Winchester cartridges. It was now the favored weapon of U.S. Special Operations—he'd used one during an op in Yemen. The SCAR would give them a fair chance in any firefight.

He checked the magazine. Filled with blanks. *Not so fair.*

At its core, a blank round was a powder charge without the bullet. The blank cartridges looked like they contained a plastic plug. This wad, Bo knew, could cause severe penetrating wounds at close range and bruising at medium ranges. Then there was the muzzle blast, a cloud of hot gas spewing out of the muzzle at high velocity. It can cause severe injury at close range. Do these players know that? Or would Bo and his unit get picked off at a safe distance?

Another flurry of shots buffeted the cluster of large quartz rocks they huddled behind. The gunfire was drawing closer, the shooters maybe a hundred yards away now.

"Let's move!" he ordered.

They followed close on his heels, hunkering down low through this stretch of woodland that thickened into denser jungle as they rose up from the base of the mountain. They needed better cover. He glanced back and was relieved to see Carlos trailing behind. The four figures moved furtively through the winding mossy trail for a long stretch before they paused to catch their breath.

Tosh came up beside Bo. "What's happening here?"

"Check your weapon," Bo said.

"What do you mean?"

"Is it loaded?"

Tosh removed the magazine of his SCAR. Same result—no live ammo.

"I was afraid of that. We're target practice. That's what's happening."

♀ ♂

KADEN FOLLOWED a trail up the face of the mountain looming over War Games Valley. The scrubby grassland at the start of her journey had given way to windswept rolling hills and woodland, growing lusher with every step. The trail knifed through thickets of giant ferns, heart-shaped orchids, and red and yellow heliconia plants. Above the thin patches of jungle brush, birdcalls and screeches in the hardwood trees announced her presence.

She could see hiking through here one day when she wasn't trying to escape with her life.

Up ahead she spotted a small squadron panning out to cross a stream. They were all wearing AR glasses as they advanced through the brush. She could tell they weren't soldiers or commandos. They must be the tourists taking part in the War

Games simulation by the way they were moving and holding their weapons. The glasses probably let them see the heat signatures of their targets.

She kept fifty yards behind the group. She had her Scorpion drawn but aimed downward. *Don't want to accidentally shoot one of these tourists playing soldier.*

There was no mistaking the semi-automatic weapons the AR players were using: the M4 carbine, a descendent of the M16. The M4 was now the standard infantry weapon of grunts in the U.S. Army and Marines. Ever since boot camp, Kaden had been a student of weaponry. She knew the military had switched over to the M4 for its collapsible stock and shorter 14.5-inch barrel, as opposed to the longer twenty-inch barrel of the M16A2. That made it easier to carry in tight spaces like helicopters and Humvees and easier to use during combat on close-quarter battlefields—like in the jungle.

She smiled at the clever mashup of realistic traditional weaponry and high-tech wizardry. *They must be shooting blanks and the simulation would fill in the blood and guts and all the grisly realities of war.*

Beyond the unit in front of her, she spotted a hint of movement on a thin trail that cut through the brush. Maybe a large animal, maybe an enemy target.

A burst of gunfire from the squadron tore through the silence, raking the underbrush and slamming into trees and boulders. *Damn if this didn't look super-realistic.* She smelled the aftermath of sulfur still wafting above the jungle floor. High in the trees, monkeys and jungle birds squawked about the nonsense below.

"I think I got one!" someone said in a low voice.

"Shut up, you idiot," came a rejoinder.

The squad leader signaled for his squad to divide and move forward in a pincer movement. She followed the unit to the left.

She reached the spot where the tourists had laid down a

deadly fusillade at the shadows in the brush. Her fingers traced the holes from the bullets that ripped into the tree bark.

Oh my God! What were tourists doing roaming around the backwoods of Samana Cay firing live rounds? The simulation should have meant they were firing rounds that *looked* real. *But they're firing the real thing.*

She moved into an exposed trail and crouched low along the side. No bodies here, thank God. She still didn't know who or what they were firing at. *This whole island may be one big fetishized techno wet dream, but when the players can't tell the virtual from the real world, that's a problem.*

Another flurry of gunfire came from the M4s farther up ahead. She paused to decide on her next move. *This was crazy dangerous, following a pack of inexperienced tourists through the jungle as they fired live rounds at anything that moved. Was Lucid part of this group or not?* She hadn't spotted him yet.

To her left, a figure emerged from the brush. Kaden instinctively raised her gun and aimed. But the figure was unarmed, dressed not in camo but in shorts and casual island wear.

It was a girl. A teenager.

She looked dazed. A tangle of dirt and small sticks laced her disheveled brown hair. Her face was streaked with mud. Her eyes darted as she coughed and spit up blood. Kaden drew nearer and the oddest thought flashed through her mind. *She was pretty once.*

"Help me!" the girl cried. She flung her body forward and clutched at the air in front of Kaden as if she couldn't see.

Kaden reached out and grabbed her hand in support. "What's your name?"

"I—I don't know!"

43

Samana Cay

On the main screen of the Bliss Lounge, Volkov watched Zaven Kasparian arrive in a caravan of black SUVs. His entourage included one body double, two mistresses, and a platoon of bodyguards. Volkov didn't know if Kasparian was coming as friend, foe, or frenemy, but he would do his best to enlist his help.

The Americans and Interpol had warrants out for Kasparian's arrest based on charges of money laundering and human trafficking—he had a nice little business selling women online. Lately the warrants had put a crimp in his overseas travels and lavish lifestyle.

But today, in Samana Cay, the Armenian was a VIP. And Volkov, for the first time in his life, would play the gracious social host. He was uncertain he could pull it off.

Dražen Savić escorted Kasparian to the luxury pool lining the island's southwestern cliffside with its majestic view of the waterfall beyond and the long sweep of white sandy beach. Teal and tan umbrellas rimmed the pool, which ended abruptly with a water slope that cascaded down to the hillside below. Guests spilled out around the pool right up to the twenty-foot zone set up around the Jacuzzi by Volkov's security team—off limits to everyone except Kasparian, himself, and the occasional butler.

Volkov stepped out of the doorway and onto the large patio in his royal purple bathrobe.

Kasparian, a big man with big appetites, looked over, smiled, and marched briskly to meet him. "Good to see you, my friend." They shook.

"And thank you again for your hospitality," Volkov said. "I was happy to hear you wanted to follow up so soon."

"There is still much to discuss. This time, without interruption."

Volkov gave the cue for the DJ to begin spinning a special selection of high-energy tunes he had personally selected. He called it the Apocalypse Mix.

From the edge of his field of vision, Volkov noticed several faces in the crowd turn his way, trying to steal a discreet look. He could hardly blame them. *Maxim Volkov in the flesh is a rare sight.* His usual attire—a ski mask, balaclava, executioner's mask, or motorcycle helmet—would hardly do at a high-end affair like this. So he decided to wear a sporty sailing cap atop a holographic foil sheet mask, similar to the kind sold over the counter to help exfoliate the skin. But the lightweight mask had a twist: It was personalized to resemble a skin-hugging, fibrous-material Guy Fawkes mask with its rosy cheeks, handlebar mustache, and soul patch.

Anonymous indeed.

"Apropos look." Kasparian took in his appearance. "It says, 'Incognito.'"

"Just for a short time. Then we retire to the cocktail lounge, followed by a special evening I've arranged."

"I hope it involves Fantasy Live."

"It does."

Volkov had not created Fantasy Live to satisfy the libidos of men like Kasparian, but he knew it would be a powerful lure and serve his business needs as well as his long-term vision.

He showed Kasparian to the changing room at the end of the patio. Then he removed his robe and ascended in his matching purple swim trunks to the elevated Jacuzzi with its glorious view of the beach, waterfall, and bikini-clad women brought in for the party.

As he looked over the scene of throbbing, gyrating bodies, he considered how tame this event was compared to the parties put on by other billionaires. No call girls, no blow, no light shows, no private helicopter waiting to give guests a private tour of the island.

But he was different from other members of his class. Never ostentatious or flashy. Not interested in buying superyachts, wineries, paintings by Renaissance masters, fleets of classic automobiles. Not tempted by having his name inscribed on sports complexes or tall buildings or other phallic symbols. No, the usual displays of vanity that animated the super-rich did not interest him. He had no desire to flash his billions.

He had other plans. He wanted to make a more fundamental mark on the world. People would speak his name centuries from now.

He looked up and watched Kasparian arguing with his two mistresses, who didn't understand why they couldn't join him in the Jacuzzi. But Volkov's bodyguards had strict instructions not to allow anyone except Kasparian to pass.

The Armenian brought his great white walrus belly up the steps and he sank into the bubbling waters opposite Volkov. Kasparian was no fellow immortal, not a true equal, and yet he was a peer. A man wealthy beyond words. They spoke the same language of riches and power.

"I'm intrigued by the orderliness I saw throughout your village," Kasparian began.

"Thank you." Volkov had directed Savić to meet the Armenian at the airport and have a little head-of-state procession through the heart of Samana Village.

"How did you manage to accomplish this? I don't think I saw a single jaywalker or scrap of litter."

"Two factors. Watchfulness. And our points system."

The *watchfulness* piece was well understood, with the CCTV cameras from the Sharp Eyes program stationed at every intersection and in every public building. Less understood was the home-grown system of rewards points that was the lifeblood of Samana Cay's economy.

"Your citizens receive points?"

"Samana Cay has no paper currency. All transactions are based on monthly point totals. Citizens receive auto-texts notifying them of points achieved or deducted for actions small and large."

Kasparian nodded and beckoned for the butler, who gained passage after Volkov signaled with his fingers to let him through. "I see. And who decides what points to award or deduct?"

"My team and I established the Samana Cay Points System with rewards and penalties, and our AI dispenses points based on what it observers. Jaywalking, a fifty-point deduction. Service in the Military Police, a thousand-point bonus each week. Our tracking system has a record of where every resident has been over the past three years. When your actions and behaviors have a direct bearing on whether you can afford to feed your family come Friday night, the level of conformity achieved is astonishingly high. We've built accountability into the very design of our community."

"Brilliant."

"In effect, we've *gamified* social actions on Samana Cay. The next step is to export our innovation to all four corners of the globe. We'll need a common global currency during the Transition. Think of it! What happens when humanity itself becomes gamified? When we can use rewards and punishments to push our new world in new directions?"

That was all he was ready to share with Kasparian tonight about his vision of the new order. A white-tux butler appeared and poured Champagne for the two billionaires. The DJ amped up the beats per minute on the pulsating Apocalypse Mix and the younger women and men began dancing around the edges of the pool.

Volkov was feeling effusive. He couldn't remember the last time he socialized. But he felt full of himself today so he tried an anecdote as they drank Cristal's stellar 2009 vintage.

"Do you know about Cristal's genesis?" he asked. In addition to being an expert in apocalyptic literature, he considered himself something of a wine connoisseur.

"Do tell."

"Cristal was first created for Tsar Alexander II in 1876. As Russia became less stable and Alexander feared death, he commanded that his Champagne be bottled clear and with a flat bottom, to ensure no bombs were placed beneath the bottles."

"Smart man."

"He made the mistake of selling Alaska to the United States in 1867. But he was a visionary who brought Russia into the modern world. Just as we now have a chance to remake the world."

Kasparian lifted his Champagne flute. "I'm ready to toast the Transition and the Reset—on one condition."

Volkov steeled himself. "And what is that?"

"I get New York."

Volkov leaned back into the Jacuzzi's pulsing jets to consider this. In the plan he began to outline at the Summit, he had split up New York among members of the Compact like so many crime bosses bickering over turf. But was that the best approach?

"In return, I'll put the entire weight of my organization

behind Project Ezekiel." Kasparian's toast hung precariously in the air.

He remembered the business adage that had served him well over the years. *Take the deal in front of you, not the one over the next horizon, for it may not be there when you arrive.*

"Done!" Volkov nodded. *This is good news. The Compact is solidifying.* "So now you are all in?"

"Yes. And ready for my first Fantasy Live experience."

Beneath his mask, Volkov smiled. To the Compact, Fantasy Live was a staging ground for the bio-attack on the West. To Volkov, it was much more. It was a proving ground.

"Why don't we go in and select our entertainment for the evening?" Volkov suggested. "One of the girls turned eighteen today. She's quite lovely. When I'm done, I can share her with you."

They clinked glasses.

44

Samana Cay

Kaden followed the young woman back through the woods. She was relieved the stranger bore little resemblance to Bailey, so she could rule out that possibility. Still, her heart went out to this girl. A mix of feelings swirled in Kaden's head.

Can't get sidetracked in looking for Bo, Alex, and the others. But this young woman needs help—and she could lead me to the perpetrators. By the looks of it, she could be one of the Disappeared.

"Are we close?" Kaden asked.

"Not sure. I think so."

The girl wasn't blinded, just dazed. Kaden knew they had few options. If they retraced the long hike she'd made through War Games Valley, there was no way this girl would make it to the roadway.

At last the trail ended, spilling into a clearing with an encampment of a dozen tan pop-up tents. The tents were arranged around a fire pit framed by rocks in the shape of a keyhole. The scent of burning wood lingered in the air from the smoldering campfire.

"I need to lie down," the girl said. She sank onto a log, then crumpled to her side.

"You need a doctor." Kaden covered her with a blanket. "I'll try to find help."

She approached the nearest tent and peered through the mesh entryway. "Hello?" She spotted someone lying down inside. She unzipped it and entered. Another girl, maybe seventeen. A pool of blood soaked the sleeping bag she was lying on. Kaden checked her neck for a pulse.

She's dead. And she's wearing some kind of choker.

She moved from tent to tent. Some were empty while others had victims' bodies inside. But victims of what? Food poisoning? An experiment gone wrong? All the other girls were wearing chokers, too.

She paused outside the seventh tent. These tents were on the large side, and it was apparent they served as the living quarters for these women, with areas for bedding, clothing, toiletries, books, keepsakes. This tent had the entryway flap zipped shut, but she thought she heard someone moaning inside.

"Hello, anyone there?" Kaden called.

No response.

She unzipped the flap and entered. Huddled in the far corner was a girl with a pixie haircut and scared expression. She wielded a long steel barbecue skewer as a weapon. "Don't come closer!"

"I just want to talk." Kaden lowered herself to the ground at the tent's entrance, but she realized she still had her P226 Scorpion drawn.

The girl stared at Kaden's weapon. "You're one of them."

"I'm not." Kaden raised her hands then slowly pocketed her Scorpion to show she was no threat. "They're after me, too. But we have to get help. What happened here?"

The girl lowered her skewer a few inches. She reminded

Kaden of a younger version of herself, with her short hair and wiry, athletic build. "I don't know what happened."

"Tell me what you know. What's your name? I'm Kaden."

"Piper." She was sitting up and now brought her knees together.

"Piper Matthews?"

A light sparked in the girl's eyes. "How'd you know?"

"I came with your mom, Judy." She didn't add, *Your mom's also a prisoner.*

"Oh my God!" She dropped her skewer and Kaden thought the girl might cry.

"We don't have much time," Kaden said. "What is this place?"

"We call it Camp Defiance. You're sent here if your scores drop too low."

"Scores?"

"Points." Piper traced a finger around her choker. In the shadow Kaden could see it gave off a light reddish glow.

"So this isn't the main place where the captives are held?"

"No. That's much bigger, a few miles east of here at Immersion Bay. We call it Camp Resist."

"Do they have medical staff there?"

"One doctor, one nurse, for something like 600 girls."

Kaden had one final question. "It looks like you're not sick. Why?"

"Not sure. I skipped dinner tonight, went to bed with a cold. I woke up when I heard the other girls …" Her voice trembled before it trailed off.

Kaden nodded. "Let's get you out of here. You need to see a doctor."

Piper's eyes clasped shut. She tugged at her choker. "I can't. They won't let us move beyond our restricted area."

That changes things. I'll have to double-time it to Immersion Bay and return with medical help. Maybe some of the other girls here are still alive.

"I'll be back as soon as I can," she told Piper. "Probably safest for you to stay sealed inside here."

"Thank you. Tell my mom I'm okay."

Kaden smiled, lifted the canvas flap, and stepped outside into the gathering darkness.

"Hands up!" A gruff voice came from her six o'clock.

She turned and confronted five men with semi-automatic weapons trained on her.

"Now drop the gun." Same voice. The squad leader.

She lowered the Scorpion and dropped it. She recognized the semi-automatic smartguns his men were carrying as combat assault smart rifles—the kind that can be fired only by its owner. Even if she managed to overpower one of the guards, she wouldn't be able to fire the weapon. A guard snatched her handgun from the ground.

"You have to help these women," Kaden said.

"I don't have to do anything. Move. Now!" The squad leader's voice signaled he would brook no delays.

They headed out of the encampment with Kaden near the rear. She reached beneath her shirt to find her necklace. She double-clicked the back of the pendant. But she knew she was out of range in this part of War Games Valley.

Ahead of her, the squad leader spoke into his comms. "Sir, we have a prisoner. Female."

"Bring her to me." The reply came loud enough to send a chill through Kaden. That voice. *Savić.*

She followed the throng of guards through the woods for only a minute when she felt it. At first, a slight tingling sensation in her nose. She reached out her hand and saw it land on her palm.

A drop of blood.

45

Samana Cay

Volkov and Kasparian peered up at the large digital screen in the Bliss Lounge, ready to inspect the digital catalog of Opt-Ins.

"How many did you say?" the Armenian asked.

"Six hundred eighteen at Immersion Bay," Volkov said. "Another thirty-two Opt-Ins on the payroll."

"Can you sort by age?" Kasparian asked, wielding his remote.

"A popular request."

"Youngest to oldest."

Volkov nodded and gave the voice command to set up the age filter. He watched as Kasparian cycled through the catalog and saved several girls to his Favorites. It took a long time but Kasparian finally settled on his top two picks. Volkov sent the order to dispatch the sixteen- and seventeen-year-old girls to the Fantasy Theater along with Bailey Finnerty.

"Next step is to select a simulation." Volkov had always left it up to Lucid to give guests a run-through of the full Fantasy Live immersive experience. But he had a pretty good handle on how this worked.

"We can't personalize your fantasy experience without a longer lead time," he explained. "So this will be off the shelf."

"Quite understandable."

"Here's a look at our default presets." He sorted through the options on screen, calling up short video snippets of each archetype. "Most men zero in on a fairly narrow set of fantasies. You can dress up your fantasy girl as a cheerleader. A schoolgirl. A sexy secretary. Girl Scout. Favorite action hero. A girl strapped to a dental chair. A mannequin." *A mannequin, imagine. Nothing surprises me anymore.* "A tart. A stripper. The ponytailed girl next door. A girl under hypnosis. A naughty girl who needs spanking. A girl surprised in the shower."

Kasparian watched each vignette with lurid fascination. "So hard to choose."

"You might as well see the stable of go-to fantasies we provide our women guests." He panned through a different category. "Having her way with a favorite actor or movie star. Dominating her male partner. Enjoying a threesome. Having sex with a stranger. Many tamer options as well."

"Here's to fantasies."

They'd switched from Champagne to the harder stuff, and Kasparian lifted a glass of Remy Martin Louis XIII Cognac. They clinked Cognac glasses when an alert popped up on screen. Lucid was trying to contact him.

"Excuse me while I take this." Volkov stepped into the foyer out of Kasparian's earshot. He pressed the code on his phone to dial Lucid. "I'm entertaining a guest."

"You'll want to hear this," Lucid said. He sounded distant, no doubt coming from a remote part of the island.

"What is it?"

"I have two updates. First, we've apprehended Kaden Baker."

"I thought you said she was eliminated! How did this happen?"

"It appears she managed to escape in Zug. We're interrogating her now."

Unacceptable. Lucid and his team had failed again. There would be consequences. "Put your man Savić on this. I want to find out what she knows. What else?"

"We've identified the intruders. Two distinct groups of interlopers on the yacht we commandeered."

"Two groups?"

"The first is the *Axom* group—Paul Redman and two of his staff members. Redman owns the yacht."

Redman! The billionaire owner of Axom was in their custody?

"Why was Redman coming to Samana Cay?" Volkov asked.

"Because we detained his reporter. I told you yesterday about Alex Wyatt finding out about Bailey Finnerty, one of the Disappeared."

"Yes, yes. We haven't decided how to handle that."

"Correct, Chairman."

"You mentioned a second group," Volkov said.

"The covert operatives. They wouldn't cooperate, but we've identified the lead as Bo Finnerty, along with three team members."

"Finnerty." He spat out the name. He was surprised Finnerty had tracked him to Samana Cay. But perhaps he shouldn't have been. Months ago he and Lucid had targeted the daughters of a handful of intelligence officers who'd meddled in Volkov's affairs over the years. He'd also singled out Bailey Finnerty's mother for special treatment.

Lucid continued. "You instructed me to oversee all security measures. So I've sent Redman and his two employees to our holding facility to join Alex Wyatt. I took the liberty of having Finnerty and his operatives outfitted as enemy combatants out at War Games Valley."

"You did *what*?"

"I'm in the valley now, watching the war games simulation. They're under surveillance. No chance of losing them."

This would not do. Bo Finnerty could still prove valuable. "Call it off. Take them all into custody. I'll send further instructions."

Once the Fantasy Strain proved to be effective, he planned to give the go-ahead to launch Phase Two of the Project Ezekiel on a global scale.

The fate of a handful of interlopers won't cause a ripple, given the storm that will soon consume the West.

♀ ♂

VOLKOV AND KASPARIAN donned their Eyewear. Volkov led the Armenian onto a long swaying footbridge past a waterfall on their right that tumbled into a raging river. Across the way, he could see a large arched doorway that led to their Fantasy Live simulation. As intended, the daunting bridge and rushing waters quickened his heartrate and sharpened his senses.

"Tell me, Incognito," Kasparian raised his voice from just behind as he balanced himself on the wobbly footbridge. "How did you decide on which girls to target as part of your … program?"

No harm in sharing the details. "Initially, we were working with Randolph Blackburn."

"Oh?" The Armenian seemed surprised.

"He was the major shareholder in Birthrights Unlimited, the Dallas fertility center. I was intrigued by the operation they carried out to recruit young runaways and street trash."

"Recruit?" A gust of wind and spray of mist prompted Kasparian to reach for the hand ropes to steady himself. "I heard it was more than *recruit*."

Volkov ignored the interruption and continued across the footbridge. "Those girls were selected for surrogacy. Still, the operation served as proof that runaways and street girls were unqualified to perform the immersive stories required for Fantasy Live."

He decided not to mention his secondary motivation. The sport of breaking their will. Of using their love for family members as a weapon against them. And above all, the need to test out his theories about women's roles in Civilization 2.0.

Volkov raised his voice above the sounds of the rushing waters below. "We created a prototype agricultural community at Immersion Bay that brings us back to our pre-industrial ancestral roots. And we stocked it with a wide variety of girls who we believed would be grateful to be spared from the harsher elements of the Transition."

Volkov left out the operational details. The months of preparation that had gone into the mass operation, the use of third-party underground operatives, the safe houses used until the dome was completed and the young women could be transported without incident to Samana Cay.

"We have arrived," he announced as they reached the far side of the gorge. Volkov plunged a hand into his right pocket and pulled out two small inhalers. "You'll want to try this. To enhance the senses." He took two puffs from one container and handed Kasparian the other. His guest took two hits asking no questions about it.

A small gesture of trust.

They pitched forward through the dark arched doorway into the chamber. They were inside the mountain now, alone in the silent shadows. The sounds of the waterfall and raging river were gone. He'd given only one directive to Lucid: Unlike all the other simulations, he wanted no staff to witness their Fantasy Live simulations.

"Where are we?" Kasparian asked.

"The real question is, where are we going?" Volkov answered, though he was as much in the dark as the Armenian.

In front of them were two pathways pulsing with colored lights along the edges, like tiny airplane landing strips. The paths led to two glowing doors, red and blue, across a dark open space. The edges of Kasparian's Eyewear gleamed red and Volkov's glowed blue.

They started down the paths and paused outside each door. Kasparian pressed his fingers against his red door but hesitated in opening it, perhaps nervous about plunging into his first simulated reality. Volkov stepped over and pushed it open for him. They both peered through the doorway.

Kasparian had sent Lucid some preferences for his Fantasy Live simulation. He'd told Lucid to give the man whatever he asked for, and now he saw that Kasparian's tastes were a bit tawdry. The spacious bedroom was a kaleidoscope of pink and mauve. The wallpaper brimmed with drawings of ponies, unicorns, bunnies, and butterflies. To the left, a large king-size bed beckoned with pink pillows and brown and white teddy bears. A small writing desk sat next to a rocking horse and a bookcase filled with storybooks and photos of young girls.

Directly across from them, below a Girl Power wall hanging, the two girls from Immersion Bay sat demurely side by side on a pink sofa, dressed in plaid schoolgirl uniforms. Next to the sofa were two sparkly princess outfits and silver slippers laid out on matching pink ottomans covered with hearts.

Humbert Humbert would approve.

Volkov backed off a step as Kasparian entered and looked around. "I've got to hand it to you, Incognito. You've outdone yourself."

"I'm glad you're pleased. Now, if you'll excuse me—"

"Not so fast! I need to check one thing."

Kasparian stepped around Volkov to the right, and now Volkov saw a diminutive pink vanity with a large heart-shaped mirror. Next to it was a mini chest of drawers with an offbeat, asymmetrical *Alice in Wonderland* melting shape. He opened the top drawer and produced two sets of ropes. He walked past the girls without acknowledging them and set the ropes on the bed. Then he returned to the chest and opened the bottom drawer. He pulled out two sets of handcuffs and a black leather cat o' nine tails bondage whip. He set them on top of the vanity.

"Excellent. Just as I requested." He turned to the girls. "How are my little vixens today?"

Volkov hadn't expected quite this level of ... *overindulgence.* He and Lucid had gone to great lengths to establish a reputation for Fantasy Live right from the outset. A place for men and women to live out their fantasies in a safe space—no pedophilia, no torture, no hint of force, coercion, or violence.

The two girls looked at each other and clasped hands. They both had little furry black-and-pink kitty ears perched atop their hairdos—one in a ponytail, the other in pigtails—and kitten whiskers painted on their cheeks.

"I didn't opt in for this part," the ponytail girl spoke up with a worried look.

"All the better." Kasparian took another hit from his inhaler and glanced back at Volkov. "I like them feisty. Don't you?"

Volkov mulled this over. *Should I tell Kasparian to cool his jets? To respect the rules and think about their budding collaboration?* Standing there, watching this tawdry fantasy play out, deciding whether to intervene, Volkov recalled the verse from Scripture, *1 Corinthians, 11:9.*

For indeed man was not created for the woman's sake, but woman for the man's sake.

The girls turned their expectant eyes to him. What would he do?

Volkov took a step backward and closed the door.

46

Samana Cay

When Kaden awoke, she found herself in an unfamiliar room. Two bright lights glared down from above her head. She lay sprawled on her back, tied to a wooden table. *They must have drugged me.*

"You're awake. Impressive survival skills. You've caused me a great deal of trouble with my superiors."

Savić!

"Mmmm. Kaden, no courtesy title or last name. I remember that right?"

"You killed Gabriel, you bastard!"

"Was that his name?" The same ugly thin smile. Same Eastern European accent.

"You'll pay for what you did." *As soon as I'm out of these restraints.*

"You think so?" He stepped to the table, leaned down, and pulled the earpiece from her ear. Then he unbuttoned her shirt and pulled the necklace over her head. "Somebody did a bad job of prep."

She turned her head in each direction and studied the room. A countertop with cabinets below and two long metal tables lined the walls of the cramped, cold, spare space. Her arms were tied over her head to the edge of the table with tight leather restraints. Ropes bound her thighs and ankles so she could barely move.

"You know why you're here?" Savić's greasy face loomed inches above hers.

She spit up at his face. Scored some spittle on his left cheek. He wiped it away without comment.

"You're here for two reasons." Savić's expression was efficient and impassive, as if torture was just another item to check off his to-do list. "First, the Ezekiel file you stole from Randolph Blackburn. We want it back. You open it? Share it with anyone?"

She'd shared it with Red Team Zero, but she wasn't about to put their lives in jeopardy.

Savić glanced at the video surveillance cameras in the two corners of the ceiling. He brought his face down level with her left ear and whispered, "Just between us, I hope you resist."

"You're gonna die, Savić."

"So. You know my name. What else do you know? What were you doing in Zug?"

She kept silent.

"Good! We can get down to business."

Savić wheeled over an elevated metal tray of sharp torture instruments straight out of the Sadistic Dentistry Handbook. He set the tray to the left of her hip. He opened a side cabinet and produced an iron halo brace like one she'd seen in a movie, used to keep the head and neck immobile during a cervical operation. He attached it to her scalp, rendering her head immobile. Now she could look only upward, her field of vision pinched.

"Mmmm. You have a nosebleed." He attached a nose clamp so she could breathe only through her mouth. "This will stop it."

She gulped for a breath of air. "You're wasting your time."

He moved out of her line of sight and brought back a pair of rubber goggles. He set them on the tray. He leaned down closer and inspected her face more closely. "What's this? Contacts. No. *Smart* contacts." He brought his pungent, rancid fingers to her face, held her eyelids open, plucked the contacts from her eyes, and placed them on the tray. He reached for a small plastic vial and applied eye drops to both eyes. Then he fumbled around on the tray before he found a small steel device. She recognized what it was from the time she had LASIK surgery. A speculum. *Creeps me out to this day.* He positioned it to prop her eyelids open so she couldn't shut her eyes or blink. He placed the goggles around her head and tightened the steel brace.

"I mentioned two reasons you're here with me today." Savić moved away for a moment and returned with a mobile tablet. "Not much evidence about whether Chinese Water Torture works. My superiors want to see if it's a better option for our rebellious Opt-Ins."

The phrase Chinese Water Torture caught her attention. *Strange. I didn't see any apparatus in this room that contained water.*

"Wouldn't be my first choice, you know? So consider yourself lucky. But it's your choice. Don't talk and we'll do it my way. What do you know about the Chairman?"

"Who?"

"Last chance. Anything to say?"

She ignored him, focusing on a way to get out of this.

"Let's begin then."

Savić tapped a few times on his tablet. Then he rolled a tall, thin metal stand over and positioned it over her head. The stand had protruding metal arms that held a large, clear container of water. The container fed down a tube to a small device perched above her forehead; she narrowed her eyes and realized what it was. An eye dropper.

The first drip pinged her forehead and she flinched against

the head brace, not ready for it. The second drip came two seconds later. Cold. Wet. *Not too bad. Not yet. It's just water.*

"I'll be back in a half hour," Savić announced at the doorway. He exited and locked the door.

Drip. She counted two seconds. *Drip.* One, two. *Drip.*

She thought back to her torture survival training during boot camp at Lost Camp in the sticks of Alabama. It was five years ago, but she remembered the two hours of waterboarding she underwent, a vivid memory that chilled her to this day. How would this compare?

Her mind released a floodgate of thoughts as she lay immobile. *How did I get here?* She retraced the journey that brought her here. Not the Brooklyn to Zurich to Nassau to Samana Cay journey. Earlier. To the discovery that Randolph Blackburn was her grandfather. To her hack of his digital vault. *Was my hack clean? Or did he want Project Ezekiel exposed because he wasn't on board? He wasn't at that gathering of the Summit. Was he using me—again?*

Drip. Drip. Drip.

Her thoughts turned to Bo. Her biological father. She thought about the holidays they'd never spent together. The fatherly advice she never received. The normal childhood she should have had.

But was she falling into a pattern again? Was Bo just using her? She sensed he was still holding some things back. *All my life I've been subjected to master manipulators, beginning with adoptive parents who turned out to be paid actors. Is it any wonder I've got trust issues? But can't dwell on that. I'm not a victim—even now.*

Drip. Drip.

Her own life was a work in progress. She had dared to imagine a normal life with Gabriel. *Look what happened when I tried to bring someone close to me. Isn't that the lesson? By trusting in another person, putting yourself out there, you just open yourself up to heartbreak and misery.*

Drip. Drip.

She racked her brain—*ha! rack!*—for what she knew about Chinese Water Torture. Drops of water falling one by one will form a hollow on a stone over time. The theory goes that the same principle applies to waterdrops flicking down on the forehead. Eventually, a prisoner goes mad—or confesses.

Drip. Drip. Drip. Drip. The unrelenting rhythm of the water seemed to taunt her.

She struggled again by yanking at the ropes that bound her wrists and feet until they burned. *No good.* Her brain was spinning, overstimulated. She knew she'd have a hard time lying here for hours on end. With her nose sealed shut, the overwhelming feeling pressing down on her was a drowning sensation. *No, I'm not suffocating or drowning! Breathe in, breathe out.* She needed to calm her wild mind.

She counted the seconds between drips like counting sheep. *Drip, one, two. Drip, one, two. Drip, one, two ... three?* She noticed the intervals varied. Two, three, four, as many as six seconds elapsed between drops. She realized what this meant—and why Savić left the room. To keep her focused on the drips and nothing else. To let her mind worry about anticipating the *next* drip.

She knew behavioral scientists found the most effective form of conditioning comes with something called variable-interval reinforcement rather than the steady, reliable kind. It's why mice will keep pushing a button that dispenses a food pellet—because sooner or later a pellet will appear. It's why gamblers hit the slots —after some period of time, they'll get a payoff along with a norepinephrine hit.

So this wasn't just Chinese Water Torture. It was sensory deprivation combined with physical discomfort and the unpredictability of variable reinforcement.

Drip! Drip! We have a winner! Ha ha! She was starting to feel punchy.

She needed a change in plan. A change of mental scenery. She and Nico often listened to mindfulness podcasts after their kick-boxing bouts. She'd try to apply some of those lessons. Meditation lite.

She focused her attention on her own body. She experienced the rise and fall of her chest. She shut out everything else and observed her breathing and how her body moved with each inhalation and exhalation. She noticed the small movements in her rib cage, stomach, upper shoulder muscles. She wiggled her toes and relaxed her knees.

She needed to stay strong and not crack. For her Red Team Zero team members. For the captured girls on the island. For the untold number of people whose lives would be at risk if Project Ezekiel were allowed to unfold with no one to stop it.

She needed to get past her primal instincts, past the constant striving, past the despair and anxiety that kept her up at night. She needed to *use* the drips, not fight them. To go inside herself. To let go and accept. To cast off her responsibilities and wants and needs. To surrender her defenses, her feelings, her will. *To just be.* Seconds, minutes passed. She found herself being transported to a calm, beautiful resting place. The world no longer judged an experience as good or bad, pleasant or unpleasant. Instead of judgment, there was acceptance.

That's when she felt it.

Her first shoulder spasm.

47

Samana Cay

Volkov stepped through the blue door and emerged in a drab, musky space. He could see shadows and forbidding shapes. As far as he could tell, he was alone. After a few moments, his eyes adjusted to the darkness. The room resembled—

No. Could it be?

He looked around, transfixed. Fantasy Live had transported him to his youth. To the habitat of a teenage Maxim Volkov before he became Incognito.

The lighting was faint but there was no mistaking *this* room: the antechamber in the basement of his parents' Belarus mansion. His parents almost never came down here, and the room was off-limits to chambermaids and servants. The help, though, was always game to spread dark whispers about what took place inside "the master's dungeon," as they called it. In a way, he was grateful for the rumors. It propelled him down the path of epic myth-making and toward his destiny.

He spun around and moved deeper into the familiar space

with its dark medieval furnishings. There on his left, the solid-oak Emperor Throne with its engraved carving of Adam and Eve with the serpent. Off to the right was the large wooden casket with incised leather and iron mounts embossed with scenes of courtly lovemaking and debauchery. Scattered about were the 1400s walnut dining table, Gothic armoire, late Roman iron folding stool, ornate hand-carved chest. All were playthings and curios of rich parents. Members of the Belarus elite who dabbled in collecting oddball antiques that would be out of place in a normal collection.

He stepped through the room, heels echoing on the hard-wood floor. There, on the far wall—the pair of Louis XIV period mirrors he'd smashed so long ago. *But what was this? The mirrors were intact! Flawless, in fact.*

He approached and examined his reflection in the mirror. He drew close, closer, inches away in the frail light. *Lucid must have done this*—created a youthful likeness of him. *How?* He must have stitched this together through facial reconstruction algorithms and digital reverse-aging technologies and the spatial augmented reality face masking they'd used in Zug. That, combined with the fact Lucid was the only living soul who knew Incognito's real identity.

He touched his face, tugged at the skin, examined the left side of the face that had been stripped bare, ravaged to the bone by a mother furious at his insolence, a mother who doted on his older, stronger, more handsome brother but who came to look upon her younger son as a mistake. A mother who refused to ever look him in the eye after her act of malice.

This room!

During his youth, it was everything to him. A refuge from his mad mother. An escape from the world's cruelties.

When he was coming of age, he would bring local girls down here and force them to wear blindfolds during long conversations about life, culture, sex, culminating in fumbling efforts at making out. After *the incident,* he would bind the girl's hands as well and they would experiment with some kinky positions while blindfolded on top of the ancient dining table or the leather-bound casket. Once, a girl ripped off her blindfold in a fit of passion. He was wearing only an eye mask not large enough to cover his disfigurement. Repulsed, she began screaming.

Without remorse, he snuffed out her screams.

But that was not the youth he now saw in the mirror. He took a final look at the clean-shaven teenage boy who bore a striking resemblance to the boy he might have been. This apparition, this avatar, this illusion is how Bailey Finnerty would see him, as young, handsome, and virile.

And I saw one of his heads as it were wounded to death; and his deadly wound was healed: and all the world wondered after the beast. Revelation, 13:3.

He wrestled with a welter of feelings about this. Years ago in Belarus, he'd considered a face-transplant operation, but he decided to pursue his epic destiny and shun the herd. His disfigurement was burned into his identity. *All historical figures are outcasts or contrarians.*

He knew he was a breed apart from the millions of malleable consumers with their notions of skin-deep beauty. Nearly everywhere he turned—shopping malls, television ads, the movies—he saw the premium placed on superficial looks and counterfeit happiness. *The lies, the vanity, the hypocrisy!* He would be the epochal figure who would bring it all down. He would answer the historical call for a cleansing.

Beginning with the Fantasy Strain.

He took in the room again, this time to plan out how the night would go. The furnishings were real, though some flourishes, like the composition of a painting on the wall, were superimposed with AR. But it all looked real. He walked—no, *glided* across the dark marble floor to the smaller side room cloaked behind an ancient Chinese screen. The inhaler was working. He was ready to begin.

He moved around the screen and saw her. Bailey. Young Bailey, standing there waiting for him against a wall of antiques and artifacts illuminated by the glow of candles resting in tall, black candelabra stands. She was dressed as he'd requested, in a sheer white nightgown that reminded him of the ones his mother once wore.

He positioned himself in front of Bailey's pretty downcast face and ran his fingers through her fragrant dark hair. She pulled her head back, shook her long dark hair. But resistance was no longer an option.

"Do you know why you're here, child?"

Fear lined her face, but he saw something else in her eyes. *Defiance.* She kept silent.

"You know the consequences for breaking the rules."

She hesitated, as if deciding the least bad course of action. "I broke the rules. This is my penalty." Her voice was a whisper. Still, Volkov didn't detect remorse.

"Other girls at Immersion Bay have resisted. Have any succeeded?"

She shook her head.

He began walking around her, exploring the eighteen-year-old fom every angle. She began to turn. "Do not move!" he snapped.

He stood behind her and began to tell her the story of how Immersion Bay came to be. "Many months ago, we considered stocking Fantasy Live with call girls and women of the night. But it soon became clear that such an approach was all wrong."

He moved to her right side and curled a loose strand of hair over her ear. "Fantasy Live was never meant to be a high-priced brothel. I had a larger vision. To take a select group of girls through the Transition and into the Reset. To use our girls to reboot humanity itself!"

Volkov finished circling her, his face now inches from hers. His forefinger touched the bottom of her chin and lifted her head to make her eyes meet his. "I see leadership qualities in you. You can help lead the girls into the new era."

He raised his left hand high above his head and hoped the AI would understand it was a signal to move to the next part of the simulation. Out of the shadows just ten feet behind them, a small glassed-off booth in a recessed wall began to reveal itself. The modern modular design was wholly out of place in this re-creation of his boyhood haunts, but that did not matter. What mattered was who was inside it.

As the lights illuminated the interior of the enclosed booth, the figure looked out at Volkov and this young woman with her back turned. The figure yelled and beat his fists against the plexiglass partition. But no sound penetrated the silence.

Bo Finnerty could not do a thing. He was powerless.

As the light grew, Bailey drew a frightened breath and turned with a start. She ran to the window and pressed her palms against the glass. "Dad! Dad! Are you okay?"

"He can't hear you," Volkov said. "It's fitting that your father should see this. You made a grave mistake, and you must pay the consequences."

Bailey began to sob. "Don't hurt my father."

"Tonight it's about you." Volkov lowered himself into the large antique lounger. "Come, let's begin your punishment."

Bo Finnerty banged his fist against the pane. Volkov couldn't hear his shouts but the prisoner's message was clear enough.

"Now," Volkov said, "pull down your pants and bend over on my lap."

He felt something stir inside. Not sexual arousal. Something else buzzed through him. A feeling of power filled his senses. Control. Domination. It was intoxicating.

"No!" Bailey pleaded.

"I promise you'll remember this birthday for the rest of your life."

He looked away toward the exit for just a second. As he did, she grabbed the iron candelabra stand, aflame with candles, and slammed it against the side of his head. "This is for my dad and mom!"

Volkov blacked out with Bailey's words still ringing in his ears.

48

Samana Cay

Nico was getting worried. He spent hours last night milling outside the cafe in Samana Village where Kaden told him they'd rendezvous. He sprung for a new phone in a nearby shop, waited until almost midnight, then crashed overnight in one of the town's handful of Airbnb apartments to avoid being picked up for vagrancy.

It wasn't like Kaden not to get in contact or send a distress signal if she was in trouble. But she could have been out of comms range if she was taken into custody in War Games Valley.

He used his hosts' Wi-Fi for a smartphone video call with the only Red Team Zero members not on the island, Annika and Sayeed.

"Nico! Are you and Kaden all right?" Annika looked like she'd just woken up. "We were getting worried after you guys didn't check in."

"I'm okay. Following protocol. Paid the hosts here in cash. Blended in with tourists from the cruise ships in port to minimize suspicions. But Kaden didn't come back from War Games Valley last night. I'm worried."

Sayeed, the head of their B Collective co-working space, popped up on screen and joined the video chat.

"Sayeed, Nico says Kaden's missing." Annika's voice brimmed with worry.

"And no sign of Bo and the others?" Sayeed asked.

"Nothing so far," Nico reported.

Annika leaned forward, looking intense. "I don't know if you've heard, but there's a lot of weirdness happening back home. Hospitals in major urban centers reporting patients showing up to emergency rooms with similar symptoms. Spikes in blood pressure. Memory loss. Hallucinations. Signs of paranoia. They say it could be an outbreak. A new strain."

"And you think it's related to Project Ezekiel?" Nico had a bad feeling about this, especially after watching the surveillance video from Zug.

"It tracks with that file Kaden sent us. The outbreak is bad and getting worse." Annika looked grim. "There's a big uptick in major traffic accidents in New York, D.C., L.A. Almost overnight, taxi and Uber drivers have gone colorblind. Driving through red lights. It's a mess. People are getting scared to go outside."

"We need to move fast," Nico said. "Sayeed, you turn up anything about jails on Samana Cay?"

"You are visiting one weird-ass little island." Sayeed furrowed his bushy brows. "Officially, there are no jails on the entire island. They use a points system for all their commerce. Most of the residents are on work visas, so if anyone gets out of line, they're just sent back to their home country. And members of the National Guard are mostly foreign mercenaries."

"So you came up empty?" Nico thought of Kaden and all the times she'd come to his rescue, on missions and in his personal life. He'd turn over every rock on this island to find her if he had to.

"Who said we came up empty?" Sayeed smiled and put a photo up on screen. "We've been in close contact with the *Axom* team in Miami. They sent us a selfie Alex took at Fantasy Live. Him with two other people."

"That's a start."

"It's better than that," Annika broke in. "You know the facial recognition program I turn to in emergencies?"

"The one created by your ex-boyfriend?" Nico had heard the story of Annika's ill-fated courtship many times.

"Don't go there." Annika shot him her squinty *I'll-strangle-you* look. "Here's the deal. Facebook was in negotiations to buy my ex's Israeli startup until they got public blowback about invasion of privacy. They bailed on the deal. But Amit still has access to a backdoor for the entire Facebook photo library. You know it's in the *trillions* of photos now?"

"So anyway." Nico tried to hurry this along.

"I ran the two faces and finally got hits at twelve-thirty and two a.m. last night. Sending their IDs to you now."

He checked the message and saw the names. Maurice Beauchamp and Evelyn Gladstone. "On it."

"Send me the video of the drone footage in Zug, too. Might need that."

"Roger that. *Sent.* Before you head out, what are you packing?" Annika asked.

Nico held up his handgun. "P226 Scorpion. It'll have to do for now."

"You're gonna need more than that before this is all over," Sayeed said, as if Nico needed the reminder.

"See what you can do on your end."

"We're already probing the enemy's vulnerabilities," Sayeed said.

"And I have an idea," Annika said. "I need all the team members' fingerprints."

"For what?" Nico asked.

"Trust me."

"One last thing," Sayeed said. "This guy Viper? The husband of Judy Matthews, father of Piper. He's flying out to Samana Cay this afternoon."

Nico winced. "One more wanna-be rescue team member?"

"You forget. His skills might come in handy," Annika said. "Former Special Forces."

Nico smiled. "Now that's something."

♀ ♂

KADEN LOST track of how many hours had passed. Savić had checked in on her a dozen times. *Did that make six hours?* She couldn't be sure.

Each drop felt like a small explosion. One relentless, unsparing boom after another. Each one slammed into her very being.

The meditation exercises had gotten her through the first five hours or so without her losing her mind. But now, in the sixth hour, she was starting to lose control. Her shoulder spasms knifed through her back like a serrated dagger. An icy sweat drenched her body. Breathing came in shorter spurts. She felt her heart thrumming faster in her chest. The room seemed colder, smaller, suffocating.

Was it because of the waterdrops? Or did she catch a fatal virus at Camp Defiance? *Either way, does it matter? This could be the end.*

She found herself immersed in a dark and visceral place. She had never before come to this point, the life-flashing-before-your-eyes moment. Here it was not so much a blinding flash as a clarifying highlight reel in slow motion. Her fake parents forcing her to undergo hormone therapy to make her more "girly." Her ten months of pure hell at a special ops boot camp. Her ray of light, Gabriel, gone.

Drip. Drip.

Some people on their deathbeds report feelings of clarity. Inner peace. Slates wiped clean. Forgiveness of enemies.

No. Not today. I still have scores to settle.

She heard the door click open. Out of the corner of her eye she could see them moving into view.

Savić. And someone I don't recognize.

♀ ♂

Nico left the tour group milling around Samana Village and hiked down to Fantasy Live Resort on the island's southwest shore. Annika had located phone numbers for Maurice Beauchamp and Evelyn Gladstone, and Nico left messages for them both. Only one of them answered.

Evelyn Gladstone emerged from the stylish restaurant, trimmed with silver and black, and approached. She positioned herself just inside the metal gate that barred entrance to the private community. "You said you had something urgent to discuss?"

Nico was making a leap of faith he could appeal to this millionaire stranger and her sense of decency. If he failed, she could report him and the Guardians would be on top of him in minutes.

"Not something. *Someone.*" Nico drew out his phone and showed her the photo of Alex Wyatt with her and Maurice.

"That's Andrew. Are you saying he's in trouble?"

"He's gone missing. And the rescue party sent to bring him back has gone missing."

Evelyn considered this. Nico figured she's probably thinking, How is this my problem?

"There's more." Nico found the drone surveillance video and played the part where Incognito boasted about infiltrating the water supplies of major cities and planning a biological attack on the United States and western Europe. "This is the head of Samana Cay. Chairman Incognito."

Evelyn remained silent, but her mouth tugged up, showing she knew the guy. She gripped the metal gate with both hands. Her eyes moved from the video to find his name. "What's your name?"

"Nico. Nico Johnson."

"Nico, tell me what's happening here." She pushed open the gate and emerged onto the street. "Let's walk."

49

Samana Cay

Volkov was in a murderous frame of mind after Bailey Finnerty's rash assault last night. Security tracked her down, running along the beachfront in her ghostlike nightgown under a waxing moon, tugging at the safety necklace that revealed her exact location. She was escorted to a solitary holding facility at Immersion Bay. During his fitful sleep, he weighed the appropriate penalty for her crime.

Today I will dispense justice for all the prisoners, he thought as he swung his Harley-Davidson FXDR 114 onto Columbus Highway and led a caravan of SUVs carrying Kasparian and his guards to Immersion Bay.

He needed to put the girl out of his mind and focus on his special guest. Kasparian was flying back this morning. Before leaving, he wanted a tour of Immersion Bay to hear more about Volkov's plans for the Reset.

"Kasparian, are you there?" Volkov tested the comm system his people had rigged up.

On the screen built into his motorcycle helmet, he saw the

video feed of the Armenian in the third SUV behind him. "Incognito, that was glorious last night! My desires were more than satiated. I'm sure those girls will long remember it, too."

As usual with his video chats, Volkov selected an avatar as his stand-in. Today he chose a burning bush. It seemed fitting for the epic subject matter at hand and for his white-hot mood. *There's a purity in fire. Elemental, cleansing.*

"Lust is an uncomplicated thing," Volkov said as he sank lower onto the powerful engine beneath him and opened up the throttle. "We forget. Every cell in your body has been trained by millions of years of evolution. Fantasy Live and the Reset are based on the idea that modern cultures have lost touch with our primal needs. Passion, desire, lust—they all spring from the life force. "

Kasparian lowered his window and let his eyes run over the early morning mist drifting over the tropical hillside. "Man, woman. Desire, purpose. It doesn't get more basic. Tell me more about what comes next."

Volkov sketched out his vision in broad strokes. "Project Ezekiel outlines our plan to take down the great Western powers. But it's not just about vanquishing the West. What comes next? I've been giving a lot of thought to the new era."

"The era after the Transition. The Reset, you call it."

"Yes, the Reset. Civilization 2.0."

Volkov had altered his thinking over the past year. Lucid and his transhumanism were one approach, the idea of merging man and machine in something called the Singularity. But there was a certain soullessness to the whole notion.

What if he took the opposite route? What if society were stripped down its essence—to humanity's most primal needs and base instincts? What would that look like? Is there not something purer in the idea of embracing our true nature and building on that? A second chance, a clean slate.

He tried to articulate this for Kasparian. "Here's how I see the new world of the Seven Spheres. Everything from religion to moral codes to politics, civic life, technology—all of it will need a rethinking. We have a historic chance to wipe the slate clean and begin anew. To create a better version of humanity. A version that embraces basic human nature."

"And how do you propose we do that? Summon Zeus from on high?"

Volkov swerved right to avoid a dead dog on the road. "We experiment. We create new cultural norms. We question. What is actually hard-wired in our genome? And what is the product of hundreds of years of cultural poisoning? Things had gotten wildly out of hand over the past century. Society is coming apart. Women no longer know their place."

Weren't Bailey's actions last night more proof of this? He saw it more clearly now. A new order. One in which women respected men. One in which women embraced their historic, traditional roles before modern culture upended things.

"It's true," Kasparian agreed. "And not just in the West."

"Ah, here we are."

After eight miles of driving, they reached the turnoff for Immersion Bay. Volkov led them a hundred yards down the unmarked road to a military checkpoint that blocked passage with a formidable metal boom gate. A uniformed member of the National Guard emerged from the guardhouse with a semi-automatic weapon across his chest.

"This area is off-limits to visitors—oh, sorry, Chairman! We received word you might be coming. Haven't seen you here before."

"Now you have." Volkov peered behind him. "And these are my guests."

"Right away, sir." The guard circled his finger high in the air and the boom gate rose.

Volkov led the caravan to the visitors parking lot. He slid up his visor partway and walked over to escort Kasparian on a quick tour of the grounds. Volkov had never been to Immersion Bay, but he'd seen the construction diagrams—and he'd paid for all this. *I built this.*

The Armenian emerged from the SUV and craned his neck upward at the translucent covering high above. "Sky dome?"

"Made of lightweight metals and natural materials to blend in with the landscaping."

"Impressive. I can see the need."

Volkov gave a walking tour of the grounds, modulating his voice so only Kasparian could hear him. He showed off the sports fields, the large vegetable gardens, the main multimedia stage, the food commons, and the housing units, some with guards posted at the doors. More than 600 girls milled around, playing soccer or broken into acting workshops. They paid the visitors no heed, as they'd been instructed to do. Few would guess the man in their midst was responsible for their stay.

"These girls are lovely," Kasparian said. "I may extend my stay."

"No need for that. They'll be here when you return." Volkov had no immediate further need of the Armenian now that he'd committed his men to executing parts of Phase Two for Project Ezekiel.

Finally Kasparian turned to the question Volkov had been dancing around. "This camp. You say it's a prototype for the Reset? How so?"

Volkov led the men to a cluster of picnic tables in the Commons below a leafy elephant-ear tree. "I think of it less of a camp and more of a construct."

"A construct?" Kasparian looked puzzled as they settled into their seats.

"Look around." Volkov swept his hand across the plaza with its simple benches, fountains, gym weights, and amphitheater stage. "We've created a new reality, one that aligns with the coming age of disruption. Here, it's grow your own food. Hand wash your own clothes. Low energy use. Travel by foot. Get plenty of exercise. We emphasize *experiences* instead of things."

The Armenian smiled wryly. "Except the experience of freedom."

"True enough. But you can say the same thing about half the population of Earth. *More* than half, in a few weeks. We provide food, shelter, safety, free health care. Life here is simple but sustainable."

"I don't see the girls carrying any digital devices. Are you saying there would be no technology in this new agrarian utopia?"

"The girls are *wearing* the technology. Which *we* control."

Kasparian nodded. "I still don't get 'construct.' Dumb it down for me."

"A great many people believe the world around us is a *simulation*, that we're simply bit players in a reality created by superior beings. Elon Musk said he believed it. Two tech billionaires have gone so far as to employ scientists to work out how to break us out of the simulation."

"Do you believe it?" Kasparian closed one eye and scowled.

"No, I think it's science fiction. But we're experimenting with the idea of creating a permanent artificial reality for all Opt-Ins. A place of beauty and harmony. A literal nirvana on earth, designed by man, powered by artificial intelligence. A construct."

A staff person, no doubt made aware of the Chairman's presence, came by their table to offer refreshments to the group and pour glasses of water for Volkov and his guests.

Volkov took in the intense scent of a nearby bougainvillea vine. "An Israeli scholar, Yuval Noah Harari, argues in his book *Sapiens* that the ability to create *binding fictions* is what enabled humans to become the most dominant species on the planet. And what are stories if not simulations of reality? Religions, money, language, social norms are all subjective realities—human fictions that have enabled societies to flourish. They lose their power the moment people no longer believe in them."

"I'm no scholar, but that sounds reasonable," Kasparian offered.

"We've already begun experimenting with this. We've found that the longer the girls spend in AR and VR, the harder it is for them to readjust to the real world. It's amazing how plastic the brain is at that age. As we develop, we edit, we distort, we censor, we select, we discard, we reshape our reality to suit our self-identity, the myth of ourselves. People resist the idea that we're just bags of chemicals. But science says you can change someone's behavior in major ways by altering brain chemistry. AR and VR can get you there."

"I don't see the girls wearing headsets."

"The technology isn't apparent to the eye. It blends in with their daily routines. And we're finding that the longer you keep the girls in an alternate reality, the easier it is for them to not just adapt but to *internalize* this new world. This construct. This new story we're telling."

Kasparian's voice got excited. "So you can massage the behaviors and social norms to whatever suits your purpose." He saw where this was going.

Volkov nodded toward the leaderboard displaying the Top 20 list of the girls with the most points. "Here, the social capital—the literal currency—is all about points."

"And Fantasy Live?"

"Fantasy Live is a living laboratory. How would our deepest desires play out if left to our own devices? Fantasy Live removes the filters of culture, religion, law, civil society. Our goal is to get you out of your comfort zone, your safe space of routine and conformity, and to reimagine feelings, urges—instincts and impulses that have been buried for decades. We're modeling the future. Our researchers are already collecting a fabulous amount of data about people's behaviors when stripped to the essence."

"Are you saying, Incognito, that each of the Seven Spheres will impose this same version of the Reset?"

"Each of the Seven Spheres will be free to experiment as you see fit. Immersion Bay is my experiment."

He would entertain other approaches after a period of experimentation. But ultimately it would be his call. He saw the Seven Spheres as seven divisions of the same global corporation, eventually replacing nation-states. Was this not a superior model for the future? Putting aside clueless biblical scholars, after the rise of the Holy Roman Empire, the British empire, and the American empire, was this not foretold in the Book of Daniel?

The fourth kingdom upon earth shall be diverse from all the kingdoms, and it shall devour the whole earth, and trample it down, and break it in pieces.

Kasparian jolted him out of his reverie. "Will we be happier?"

Volkov had always found happiness an odd concept. Arbitrary. Elusive. "In the long arc of history, we've been heading in the wrong direction, to a future of dislocation, distrust, and disintegration of the social compact. To a planet that will soon be unlivable. The rate of technological change is accelerating at a breakneck pace. People know in their bones the current trends are unsustainable. So millions will flock to a governing authority that brings order out of the chaos."

He mused on Kasparian's question. "Will people be happier? That hasn't been on our roadmap."

A crashing sound assaulted the peaceful calm of the Commons. Someone hurled a chair through the window of a second-story apartment unit, sending it skittering across the landing. Three guards hustled up the stairway to put down the disturbance. But not before Bo Finnerty climbed through the broken shards and yelled down to the crowd of strangers.

"They've got my daughters! Both of them!"

Seconds later, two guards grabbed Finnerty by the upper arms and dragged him away to a more secure location.

Finnerty misjudged this particular audience.

"Apologies for the drama." Volkov shot up, signaling the tour was over.

"And we must take our leave." Kasparian stood and gave a half-bow. "Thank you again for your hospitality."

"Safe flight." Volkov shook hands. "I have business to attend to."

50

Samana Cay

As Evelyn and Nico walked the public promenade along the southern bluff, she peppered Nico with questions. How did he know Andrew Bayless? What was Red Team Zero? How did they get involved with the owner of *Axom*? How did any of this connect to the strange events in the U.S. she was seeing in the news? It took a while to unspool the story, but he was straight with her.

"Those are serious charges you're making," she said at last.

"Every word is true," Nico said. "And every second matters. Will you help?"

"There's not much I can do. But maybe my ambassador can." She pulled out her phone and texted someone.

"Ambassador? So they're on staff? Can they be trusted?"

"We'll see, won't we?"

So far, Nico was running low on trust in this place. "I'll lie low thirty yards ahead. Signal me when it's safe."

Evelyn nodded and Nico headed for a bench down the promenade.

It wasn't long before a dark-haired woman in sunglasses emerged from the back gate of the resort. She and Evelyn had an animated back and forth, and he couldn't tell if it was going well or he'd have to bolt. He checked the Scorpion in his pocket and kept an eye out for military guards.

The brunette woman looked distraught at what Evelyn was telling her, and Evelyn grasped her arm in support. After several minutes, they both approached.

"Hello, Nico." The woman's voice quavered. "My name is Rachel Torres. Let's go to my house. We can talk in private there."

Nico wasn't ready to trust her, but he followed Evelyn's lead. They followed Rachel to her car, a Hummer H3, and headed east along Columbus Highway. After five minutes, they turned off and took a winding road up the spine of the island's tallest mountain. Rachel pulled into the driveway of a sleek cliffside home with a splashy view of an aquamarine cove on the north shore.

For a while, Rachel seemed conflicted, gravitating between playing gracious host and cross-examining district attorney. She served them bottles of Pirate Republic ale from the Bahamas as they sat on two chairs facing her on the white leather sofa. The place looked more like a Manhattan penthouse than a tropical bungalow, with modular furniture and artsy wall hangings. Evelyn did most of the talking, bringing Rachel up to speed on what Nico had passed along.

"How did you wind up working for these people?" Evelyn asked.

Rachel clasped her hands and began her story. "I was a broke psychotherapist in Mallorca and needed the money. A year ago I saw this ad for ambassadors for a new luxury resort and applied. I'll admit it was an odd interview. They asked me to imagine myself as an old-fashioned Playboy centerfold—but a playmate with superpowers who can confidently step out of the centerfold and wield my powers to bend any man to my will. 'What would you say to him? How would you treat him?' Honestly, they made it sound cool. And as an expert in the male psyche, I was fascinated by the promise of Fantasy Live, with being able to help people fulfill their deepest desires."

"Maybe those desires should stay deep," Nico suggested. "Can I stream my phone to your TV?"

"Sure. This is a smart house. Latest everything."

"How can you afford this?" Evelyn looked around at the upscale furnishings. "You said you were broke."

"They're very generous with their compensation packages. Free housing, free health care, you name it."

"And I'm sure the mob has a great dental plan," Nico said.

"Don't judge me." Rachel picked up an orchid-watercolor throw pillow and straightened it on the sofa. "I'm not sure what you think is happening here."

"Let me show you." Nico found the wireless signal and streamed the Zug video. He followed that with news footage of the infectious outbreak along the East Coast with symptoms ranging from hallucinations and memory loss to extreme paranoia. As the videos played, Rachel's expression changed from skepticism to concern and anguish. At the end, she wiped away a tear.

Evelyn leaned forward to show support. "Your boss, Incognito, is responsible for this. Rachel, you said Fantasy Live was an open, transparent, welcoming place. That's a lie. We need to do something. You're saying you didn't know about any of this?"

"No, of course not. All the girls I worked with said they were Opt-Ins."

Nico didn't ask about Opt-Ins but he didn't need to. "We think a lot of these 'girls' were kidnapped during the Disappearance."

Rachel's mouth dropped open. "Like from the news?"

"Yes, Rachel, exactly," Evelyn said.

"Is that even your real name?" Nico set his ale on the crystal table's drink pad. He had some cross-examining of his own to do.

"It's Rosalia Torres. Our clients are overwhelmingly from the U.S., so we Americanize things to make our clients feel at home."

Evelyn said, "Hell, Rosalia works just fine for me."

"Tell us more about the island," Nico said. "Layout, logistics, military presence."

She hesitated, perhaps pausing to consider how her life and career had just taken a hundred eighty degree turn.

Evelyn clasped the woman's bare knee. "Are you going to help us?"

Rachel-Rosalia closed her eyes and regained her composure. "Let me tell you what I know."

Nico and Evelyn sat back as Rachel—he'd stick with the name Rachel—proceeded to sketch out the contours of the island. Samana Village, Fantasy Live, War Games Valley, the Lab on the southeast shore, and Immersion Bay to the east.

When she finished, Nico asked, "Where is Alex Wyatt being held?"

"I—I don't know. They took him away in a National Guard jeep."

Nico felt his phone buzz. An alert. "Viper" Matthews was approaching the island in a large Boston Whaler fishing boat with a trove of weapons below deck. His message asked, *Where should I dock?*

"Do you have a wharf near here?" Nico wanted to see if she was really on board.

"Sure. There's a small wharf for this development a hundred yards away, just down the pathway."

"Room for one more visitor?"

"Whatever you need."

His phone pinged again. A text from Annika about Lucid, the guy they'd been tracking on Samana Cay. They'd not only hacked his location but cracked the signal from a video he just began to live-stream. *A video from his phone?* Nico wondered.

"I want to throw this up on your screen," he said. "It's coming from Lucid. He's in some kind of small room with … *that's the guy from Wildspitz who was shooting at us on the slopes!*"

"What?" Rachel turned to watch the video feed.

Nico started providing color commentary. "It looks like they have a prisoner. Wait, he's giving us a better angle now, getting closer to the captive. It's a woman. Look at how they tied her up."

"See!" Evelyn said. "This is who you're working for!"

"Wait." Nico peered at the large color screen. "That's Kaden!"

Rachel looked aghast at the spectacle playing out on her TV.

"Kaden came with the others looking for Alex," Evelyn said.

Nico shot to his feet. "She's bleeding! Look at that closeup! She looks like the patients we just saw on the news heading into the E.R."

"You don't think—" Evelyn began.

"She's been infected," Nico said. "And she's gonna die if we don't do something."

51

Samana Cay

Volkov switched on his visor's comms and saw that Lucid had joined Savić in interrogating Kaden Baker. He sent an alert notifying Lucid to pick up.

Now that Kasparian was gone, he could get back to executing Project Ezekiel. *I don't have time for these inconsequential interlopers. Need to get to the Lab and talk with Bashir about the final countdown to unleash the Fantasy Strain.*

"Yes, Chairman?"

"I'm at Immersion Bay."

Volkov watched the two mini-screens in front of him. One showing Lucid in an interrogation room, the other showing Lucid's Eyecam feed.

"You're here?" Lucid stammered.

"I want Bailey Finnerty interrogated next to Kaden Baker."

"But I don't see what they have to do with each—"

"Do it! I'll be there in fifteen minutes."

"Yes, Chairman."

♀ ♂

Nico met Viper at the wharf at the base of the mountain. Nico had only met him in passing at that Greenwich Village nightclub the night before they flew to Zurich. Now, in the morning light, he got a better look at him. Viper was maybe six-foot-two, nearly as tall as Nico but built like a tank. Late thirties with a cueball head. He carried a hard look that said he'd seen it all and didn't want to talk about it.

They greeted each other as they tied the Boston Whaler to the pier.

"No problem with the security patrols out there?" Nico asked.

"The fishing gear helped." He nodded toward the deep sea fishing rods at the boat's aft. "Hundreds of pleasure boats out there today."

Viper disappeared into the hold and emerged with three Heckler & Koch HK416s, a bad-ass piece of firepower, and 100-round drum magazines. They began hiking up the trail to Rachel's house.

"Isn't that the gun—" Nico began.

"That took out bin Laden? Yeah," Viper said.

"You were Special Forces?"

"Afghanistan. Two tours." Viper didn't seem to be the loquacious type, which was fine by Nico.

They got a fix on Lucid's location, thanks to Annika. It was smack in the middle of the camp at Immersion Bay. Rachel said the medical center there was dispensing vaccine shots. They decided Evelyn would stay here and sit tight. Rachel couldn't get them past the military checkpoint, but she could drive them to a point just west of Immersion Bay where they could infiltrate the camp by foot.

"Does Rachel need to enter the camp with you?" Evelyn asked.

Rachel looked at the spare semi Viper brought. "Forget it. I'm not going to fire that thing."

"You don't have to," Nico said. "It's for Kaden. But you have to come with us. You know where the med center is, we know where Kaden is. Annika texted to say they're administering the vaccine all over the island."

"I've seen vials of the vaccine and the cure." Rachel looked stressed by this whole ordeal. "It may be too late for the vaccine, but I'm not a doctor."

Nico clicked the magazine into his HK416. "Then let's find one. Let's go."

♀ ♂

KADEN DRIFTED in and out of consciousness. She could no longer feel her hands or feet. Her breathing came in short, labored gasps. Her back had tightened into one giant constrictor knot.

Her eyelids fluttered open. She saw a figure hover above her in a hazy mist. She recognized who it was. She tried to reach up and touch her face but couldn't reach her.

"Mom," she whispered.

"Where's my Kaden?" Her mother was always playing tricks like that.

"Mom, I'm right here."

"Are you under the covers? I can't find you, you silly bean."

"Mom, I missed you."

"Missed you too, little love." Deirdre Blackburn's face started to fade. "She thinks I'm her mother."

"She's hallucinating." It was a stranger's voice. A voice with an Arabic accent. "One of the side effects."

"Side effects?" Savić's baritone voice. "What's she got? Can we catch it?"

"Don't worry. You're safe."

Kaden blacked out.

♀ ♂

ALEX WYATT PACED across the bamboo floor of the apartment unit at Immersion Bay—their "temporary detainment quarters." His mind kept going to Valerie, his girlfriend. She must be worried sick by now. He had to get out of here. But how?

Alice Wong and Charlie Adams sat curled up on opposite ends of the simple slipcovered sofa while Paul Redman occupied a rattan chair, looking pensive as he stared out the window.

Alex slowed his pace and shook his head. "Something isn't adding up."

"Yeah. Our chances of getting out." Charlie, his best friend, shot him a look that said, *What did you get us into?*

Alex ignored the taunt. "Think about what they've done. First, they put me in this room in solitary confinement two days ago."

Alice looked up with her always-inquisitive eyes. "And why here? It looks like an apartment for two girls. Brushes, mascara, lipstick in the bathroom."

Charlie, with his dark streak, took a stab. "Maybe they knew the previous occupants weren't coming back."

Alice and Charlie glared at each other, then turned to Alex to continue.

"Then, yesterday when you guys were captured, they separated the captives into two groups. Bo, Tosh, Carlos, Judy—we don't know where they are. And you three, they brought you here. Why?"

"Why not?" Alice said. "We're all *Axom*."

Alex stopped his pacing. "We're a problem, and they're trying to decide how to deal with us. We're being singled out for special treatment."

"We are." Redman spoke up for the first time in an hour. "This is my doing."

The three staffers looked his way. "What are you saying?" Alice asked.

"This is all off the record," Redman began.

"Screw off the record!" Charlie's face started to get red. "This is our lives!"

Redman nodded. "Sometimes business and editorial interests converge. Last July, Randolph Blackburn—"

"The media and marketing magnate?" Alex interrupted.

"The same. I met Blackburn at Allen & Company."

"Wait." Charlie was a good reporter and always wanted to check his facts before moving on. "That's the annual conference at Sun Valley in Idaho for multimillionaires, media titans, one percenters with luxury yachts—."

Redman broke back in. "Very exclusive, invitation only. Blackburn had a modest proposal that, looking back, wasn't so modest. He wanted to make a very generous contribution to the *Axom* Families Fund in support of homeless families—in return for a story about a glitzy new high-end resort called Fantasy Live."

"But we don't do pay-for-play journalism," Alice objected.

"Ordinarily, no. But it was for charity, and it seemed harmless enough."

Alex stepped past the bookcase and positioned himself in front of Redman. "But the Fantasy Live story was my idea."

"Was it?" Redman looked up at him. "We seeded your in-box with intriguing headlines and wire reports about a mysterious new enterprise that would soon launch just off the coast of Florida. And with your love of VR and AR, I wasn't surprised when I heard Alice green-lighted a story. I just didn't expect you to turn it into an exposé."

"So you played me." *Damn it to hell!* Alex knew he could never work for a Redman publication again.

"Who else knew about this?" Charlie looked upset enough to quit on the spot.

"The corporate counsel and me, that's all."

Alex threw up his arms in disgust. "So all along you wanted a harmless puff piece, a publicity blast, not a real in-depth report."

"We'd let you run with some negative details, but you're right. For Fantasy Live, the thinking was that a little bit of scandal was good publicity." Redman turned to face Alex. "But let me be clear. All that changed the moment you called in with news about that missing girl."

"Changed how?"

"It turned everything. You think I knew about that? We're not in the business of shilling for a criminal enterprise."

"So what did you do?" Alice asked.

"Within five minutes I was on the phone with Blackburn. He claimed he didn't know about it. He put me in touch with this eccentric strongman, Incognito."

"Maybe a bit more than *eccentric*," Charlie pointed out.

Redman turned from the window and met Charlie's eyes with a steady gaze. "I left Incognito a series of messages promising a million-dollar payment and a pledge not to publish anything about Fantasy Live or Samana Cay in return for your release."

"You did what?" Alex felt a rage boiling at his billionaire boss. "A secret deal, without asking us?"

"I wasn't able to get through, so I agreed to Alice's suggestion that the three of us visit in person, see what it would take to spring you. Your life is more important than any story."

Alice clasped her hands and leaned forward. "But what about Bailey Finnerty, getting her back? I told her mom we knew where she was. Maybe the other girls from the Disappearance are here, too."

"It's a mess," Redman agreed. "But I promised not to publish a story. I didn't promise not to notify the FBI."

"So you contacted them?" Charlie asked.

Redman hunched forward in his chair. "Not yet, but I plan to."

They all went silent. Alex shook his head. *Good intentions. Not worth jack.*

"So now what?" Alex asked.

Redman didn't hesitate. "The stakes have been raised—there are four of us now. Maybe they'll ask for more money. Or maybe no amount of money on earth will work. Would they trust us not to publish if they let us go?"

"If I were them …" Alex weighed their chance of survival. "No, I wouldn't trust us. Absolutely not."

52

Samana Cay

Two quick knocks at the door jolted Kaden awake. She'd lost track of time and place. She barely remembered who she was or why she was tied down on a slab of wood. But she recognized the face of the man torturing her.

Savić turned toward the door. "Who's that?"

"The Chairman." She didn't recognize the new voice.

At the edge of her field of vision, she saw Savić's face tense up. He moved toward the door and she heard it open. At the same time, she sensed something was different in the room. Another person nearby. She detected the faint hum of short, quick breaths.

Someone stepped into the room. Everyone went quiet. *The Chairman.* The boss of bosses on Samana Cay. Even in her fevered state, even as Savić's water torture continued to assault her, she knew the Chairman was her true enemy. Out of the bottom right corner of her eye, she spotted a figure approach the table. He was wearing a black ski mask that was doing a poor job of hiding his brown and gray beard.

"So these are the sisters that Finnerty mentioned," a deep voice said.

"What are you talking about?" The voice of a girl lying right beside her. "I don't have a sister."

"Oh, this is good." Incognito reared his head back. "Raise the table to the vertical position. I want to look them in the eye. And remove this one's head brace, goggles, and nose clamp."

Kaden shook her head when Savić freed her from the brace. After hours of being immobilized, every inch she moved sent ripples of pain radiating through her neck muscles.

She turned to her right and looked at Bailey Finnerty. Over the past week she had imagined the first conversation she'd have with her half-sister. *Hey, sis. Too bad we didn't know about each other. Shame we missed out on all those sisterly fights growing up. Isn't Dad a character? Like some action movie hero. The flawed silent type but with a good heart or something.*

That conversation would have to wait. She tried to smile but couldn't. She whispered, "Bailey." Then her eyes closed from exhaustion. Couldn't tell if Bailey replied or understood. Guess Bo didn't read her in on this whole having-another-daughter thing.

Incognito positioned himself in front of Bailey. "Ordinarily, I like a spitfire. But last night was your chance at redemption."

"I'm not sorry." Bailey's eyes flashed a fierce, defiant shade of green. Kaden could only imagine what she'd been through these past six months.

"And this one." Incognito stepped in front of Kaden. "Has she told you the location of the digital files with the names of the Compact?"

"Not so far," Savić reported.

"It appears our methods are too mild." He picked up the iron head brace to inspect it and then leaned six inches from Kaden's face. "Why are you here, Kaden?"

"To stop you, you monster."

Incognito let out a laugh devoid of mirth. "Another rebel. Must run in the family."

He placed his finger under Kaden's chin and bobbed it up. "Let's play a game. Which Finnerty will live or die?'"

"Go to hell." Kaden searched for saliva to spit in his face but her mouth came up dry.

"The rules are simple. In the next sixty seconds, you get to play God. You decide who lives and who dies. Your sister or your father."

"I won't play your game."

"Oh, but you will. Because if you don't, everyone loses. Now, choose."

Kaden said nothing.

"Thirty seconds left."

"Take me. Kill me," Kaden said.

"I'm afraid that's not an option. That's a given. Either Bailey will be exposed to a fatal infectious disease. Or your father gets a bullet in the brain. Fifteen seconds, or they both die. Oh, the drama!"

"Pick me, Kaden." Bailey teared up. "It's okay. Don't kill Dad."

Kaden wasn't sure what to do. If she didn't choose, she was certain Incognito would make good on his threat. They'd both be dead. If she followed Bailey's wishes and saved Bo—

"Five seconds." Incognito pursed his lips behind his gutless ski mask.

Kaden banged her head back against the table and let out a guttural *I-want-to-gut-you* growl. "Save Bailey."

Bailey burst out crying. "*Nooooo.* Don't hurt my father."

Incognito ignored her. "Excellent. We have a decision. The father will get a bullet between the eyes."

Kaden knew she'd never forgive herself. *My own father brought me here. And now I'm responsible his death before I even get to know him.*

Incognito moved over to Bailey and stroked her long dark hair. "I'll see you in another Fantasy Live session—after we tame you."

He nodded toward the figure in the far corner of the room. "Lucid, come with me. We have some further business. Where's Bo Finnerty?"

"Solitary confinement in the Archery Center. Only space available."

Incognito started toward the door when Savić signaled toward Kaden and called out, "What about her?"

Incognito paused and turned around. "Judging by the progress of the infection, she'll be dead within the hour. See if you can persuade her to cooperate, by whatever means necessary. She's all yours."

The two men left the room and their footsteps faded up the cobblestone walkway.

Savić walked to a chest of drawers and removed a black leather pouch. He placed it on the counter to Kaden's left and began removing items. She recognized some of them. A pair of carpenter's pincers. A mini-blowtorch. A carbon-steel gravity knife tucked inside a black Grim Reaper pocket folder—a small but efficient weapon. During past wars, paratroopers used the gravity knife to cut themselves free from their rigging if they landed in a tree.

Savić placed the weapons on the large portable metal tray to her left. He dipped into his pouch again and removed a case that looked like a drill bits holder. He pulled them out one by one— she recognized some of them from the time she needed a root canal. Stainless-steel dental probe. Tartar scraper. Dental pick. And the pièce de résistance, the dreaded dental drill. *Dr. Mengele, call home.*

"What are you gonna do to her?" Bailey yanked at her tied wrists. "Leave her alone!"

"Shut up or you're next." Savić rummaged in the bottom of

the bag. "Ah, here it is." He pulled out what looked like a rusted, old-fashioned crank telephone with two pairs of long, ragged-looking exposed copper wires connected to the back. He placed the thing on a new tray and wheeled it over next to the Dr. Mengele tray.

"Have you heard of the Tucker telephone?" Savić's body stench was as foul as ever. "No? Gruesome history. In the sixties, doctors at Tucker State Prison Farm in Arkansas began using it on some of the more unruly prisoners."

He loosened the restraints on Kaden's wrists above her head. Her shoulder was in agony, and even a half-inch of movement was a relief.

"American soldiers liked the idea so much they used it on Vietcong prisoners." Savić took an exposed ground wire and wrapped it around her left thumb. "All it takes is a few cranks and the battery cells shoot a nice electric shock. Next, we hot-wire the genitals. Mmmm."

Savić lowered his head and started to unbutton her jeans.

She was almost about to pass out again, but an idea came to her. "Wait. Not in front of Bailey."

He straightened and looked at her dead on. "No negotiating."

She cast her eyes to the tray for just a second, but long enough for Savić to see it.

He looked down at the tray. "Are you nervous about these?" He picked up and stroked the dental pick. "I'm saving the best for later."

She glanced at the tray again, tried to pretend she was hoping he wouldn't see.

"Or maybe you're concerned about something else." He reached down to the far end of the tray and retrieved one of the contact lenses he'd removed from her eyes last night. He held it up to the light. "Bionic contact lenses. I read about these. Only a few thousand worldwide."

"There's nothing to see on those," she said. And that was true. She'd programmed it to authenticate only against her own retina.

Savić smirked. "Sorry if I don't take you at your word."

He took the first lens, raised his face to the ceiling, and slipped it on. Then he did the same for the second lens. "If the Project Ezekiel files are on here—"

Savić let out a scream of agony. He doubled over and reached to gouge out the lenses from his eyes. But she knew it was too late. The built-in failsafe system recognized the intruder. It gathered all the ambient light in the room and amplified it to shoot directly at the optic nerve. It was the equivalent of staring at the sun during a solar eclipse. It wouldn't permanently blind anyone but it would disorient them for several minutes.

Time enough.

She pulled her arms downward with a violent motion. She felt a sprain in both thumbs, but her hands slipped through the restraints. She reached with her left hand, grabbed the gravity knife, tossed it to her right hand. With one motion she flicked the trigger open, exposed the blade to Savić's jugular vein, and plunged it with all her force. She wanted to make this count, so she brought the knife up to puncture the external carotid artery.

Savić's eyes couldn't see but they got wide. He reached to cover his throat to stem the bleeding. Blood poured from his neck down his arms and chest. She could tell the wound was fatal, but to be certain, she drove the knife up through his throat toward the half-moon scar on his forehead. He gurgled once, twice, and crumpled to the ground.

"How'd you do that?" Bailey looked a little wide-eyed. Maybe scared of her, too.

Kaden used the bloody knife to free her legs. "Let's get you out of here." She stepped to her left, woozy after regaining her feet, and cut the ropes from Bailey's wrists and ankles. "Follow me. We have to find Bo."

She retrieved her contacts from Savić's corpse and stashed

them in her pocket. She retrieved her pendant and earpiece from a corner table. Then she opened the door and was brushed back by the bright afternoon light. She shielded her eyes, feeling disoriented.

Is that Nico at the edge of the woods? Looks like Nico and three others running this way.

She took one step toward them and collapsed.

53

Samana Cay

When Kaden came to, she was sprawled on the ground where she'd collapsed. A doctor daubed the sweat and blood from her forehead. "You'll be okay, but you need to rest," the doctor said as she put away a hypodermic needle.

"Rachel led us to the cure," Nico said.

Rachel smiled. "I had a feeling those green vials might do the trick. Thank you, doctor."

"I administered a painkiller, too," the doctor said. "But you should stay off your feet."

Kaden looked up at the five faces above her. Nico, Bailey, the doctor, Viper from the nightclub, and this new person, Rachel. *Introductions can wait.*

"Let's get you off this island," Viper said. "We'll take you back to my boat."

She sat up and checked her arm. Just a dot of blood where she'd gotten the shots. She wobbled to her feet, still lightheaded. "No time. We have to find Bo before—" She looked at Bailey.

"Before they do something," Bailey said. "He's being held at the archery range."

Rachel was already on her phone looking at a map of the area. "That's less than a quarter mile from here."

There was no way in hell Kaden was leaving without Bo. "Nico, Viper, come with me." She took a good look at the map on Rachel's phone and figured out the quickest route. She looked up at Rachel and nodded toward Bailey. "Can you take care of Bailey for now?"

"Consider it done," Rachel said.

Viper offered Kaden one of the HK416s. She looked it over and decided there was nothing like an ex-Special Forces bad ass to get them out of a jam. She took it and checked the magazine. More than ample ammo.

Kaden watched Rachel and Bailey about to head off, then stopped them. She grabbed the gravity knife from her pocket and wiped Savić's blood on her shirt. "Lean over," she prompted Bailey. With one determined cut, her sister's choker fell to the ground. Security would know the choker was removed, but they wouldn't be able to track Bailey.

Kaden took off her necklace, removed the photo of her mother from the front of the pendant, and stashed the picture in her shirt pocket for good luck. Then she wrapped the necklace around Bailey's neck and turned the pendant over to expose the digital display on the back. "This way I'll know you're safe. It's synced to Nico's phone so we'll be able to video chat."

Bailey smiled and clasped the pendant in her palm. "Thanks."

"Hurry!" Kaden said.

Rachel grabbed Bailey's elbow and led her away.

Kaden, Nico, and Viper headed toward Immersion Bay's sports park. This part of the island didn't seem to have a high concentration of guards. Must be because the girls had those electronic monitors around their necks and every incentive to cooperate while being held prisoners. From the information Annika had sent earlier about the so-called Guardians, these dudes were bad news. Mercenaries and hired guns with track records of human rights abuses.

Damn, spoke too soon! Two guards at the corner of the last apartment building spotted them and opened fire.

"Cover me!" Kaden shouted to Viper, and he laid down an impressive line of fire. In fully auto mode, the HK416 could fire 900 rounds per minute. Nico followed on Kaden's heels.

They reached the sports complex. According to that map, the archery building should be at Kaden's two. They headed that way, exposed on a ridge that dipped down onto a grassy field with woods to the north and south. Soon they came upon the squat building with an arrow and bullseye above the door and two guards framing the entrance.

At her four o'clock, two men approached the building on foot. She recognized them. Incognito and Lucid. She wouldn't be able to reach Bo in time, so she let out a high-pitched whistle and waved her arms. The guards, already on alert after Viper's burst of gunfire, saw her and began to approach—just what she wanted.

She aimed at the top of the complex—*don't want to hit Bo*— and opened fire, chewing up the top of the bamboo structure. Incognito and Lucid saw they were directly in the line of fire, so they veered away from the building, off to their right. An armor-plated SUV appeared on the service road to the north. Incognito and Lucid jumped in and the vehicle tore off down the road.

The guards took to one knee and returned fire with their SCAR smart rifles. Nico scrambled behind a two-foot tree stump while she took cover behind a big fallen tree trunk. Viper made a flanking maneuver to her nine. Automatic gunfire crackled. Rounds shredded the slightly elevated ground behind her. A spray of bullets ripped into the tree trunk, keeping Nico from firing a shot.

It might have been an even match, the guards' SCARs versus her HK416, but it didn't factor in her penchant for long-range precision marksmanship. She did a commando crawl to the lopped-off edge of the desiccated tree trunk and found a clear shot. She went with a fifty-meter zero, a good, flat trajectory for her targets a hundred meters away. Her finger kissed the trigger and she watched the rounds slam into the guards' torsos. Through the scope she saw the bodies flop lifeless to the ground.

Nico rose to her left. "Field is clear."

Viper marched toward her, his face a dark storm. "You had a clear shot at Incognito. Why didn't you take it?"

She hesitated. After Dallas and now here, her kill count was up to three. She didn't want to get used to this.

Viper's veins popped from his neck. "You always cut off the head of the snake." Kaden thought that was ironic, coming from a guy named Viper. Was he right? She had a split second there where she might have been able to take Incognito down by shooting him in the back.

Viper turned to go. "You're gonna get your father?"

She nodded.

"I need to find Judy and the others." Viper headed east, back to the apartment units.

"We'll be right behind," she said.

She and Nico neared the Archery Center. The door was locked, so she yelled a warning to stand clear and she blasted the lock to hell. She opened it and inspected the interior with Nico right behind. She gave the all-clear call for the main room.

She entered the manager's office in the back. Bo was there in the far corner, gagged and tied to a chair. She ripped the duct tape covering his mouth.

"Bo. Are you all right?"

"I'm good. What about Bailey?"

"Bailey's fine—for now. But we need to move. We're easy targets here."

She finished untying him. *If I could just get everyone off this island, everything will be all right.*

"Still all clear," Nico said, peering out the front entrance. "But not for long."

Bo stood and grabbed her by the shoulders. "My God, what did they do to you?"

She didn't care about the blood on her outfit. It was mostly Savić 's. The painkillers had kicked in. As long as she could run, they could hold off the enemy. "We need to go."

The three of them sprinted out the door.

54

Samana Cay

Volkov and Lucid hustled into the armor-plated black SUV at the far end of Immersion Bay. They entered through the open door on the right side as the vehicle shielded them from the intruders' weapons.

During the commotion, Volkov needed to remove his ski mask for an unimpeded view of the threat and to take evasive action. The mask lay on the ground outside the archery building. As he entered the vehicle, he saw the driver looking away as he'd been trained. Unlikely he'd seen Volkov's face.

With the dark tinted privacy window raised, the driver peeled out on the service road to avoid gunfire. "Where to, Chairman?"

"Headquarters," he barked.

Sitting in the belly of the SUV, he and Lucid came face to face for the first time in four years. There had been one earlier misbegotten encounter, only a few fleeting seconds long, when Volkov had entered a meeting room by mistake. Lucid—candidate for chief operating officer of Samana Ventures—was sitting at the conference table.

Volkov hired him rather than kill him.

Volkov leveled a hard stare at Lucid. "Don't get used to this. You've seen me unmasked once before and lived *not* to tell about it."

Lucid cast his eyes at the passing landscape and said nothing.

"Mobilize the National Guard reserves," Volkov ordered. "We need every able-bodied man deployed to neutralize the threat."

Lucid took out his phone and tapped out orders to the field commanders. "On it. Should I increase the island's threat level?"

"Yes. Threat Level One—Critical." Every CCTV camera, every sensor on the island would now make tracking of the intruders a critical priority. Every citizen would receive a text alerting them of the threat. "Make sure you circulate photos of the terrorists."

"Including Bailey Finnerty?"

"Including the girl. Offer a reward."

Just before the shooting started, he and Lucid had received notifications from Immersion Bay security forces that Savić was down and Kaden and Bailey had escaped.

"Done," Lucid reported.

Volkov looked out the window at the dark clouds gathering in the distance beyond the emerald hillside and Guava Ridge Estates. The vehicle exited the service road and turned left. They were now speeding west on Columbus Highway.

"When we put down this rabble, have someone retrieve my bike and helmet from Immersion Bay."

"Your Harley? Yes, sir." He sent out a brief voice text and put away his phone.

It was odd, relying on Lucid to issue orders instead of doing it himself. But he'd be back in his office soon enough. He'd turn it into a makeshift command center until the terrorists could be brought to heel.

"Are things on track with today's big shipment?" Volkov asked.

The Plant next to the Lab had been producing new batches of the next strain for deployment. Lucid had arranged for containers of the treated water to be stored in the hold of Kasparian's luxury ship, the *Seaduction*. It would be disguised as Samana Cay spring water in five-gallon water cooler dispensers to get past U.S. Customs.

Lucid nodded. "Six o'clock tonight. We're all set."

Out of the corner of his eye, Volkov saw Lucid shoot him a discreet look once, twice.

"What is it, Lucid?"

"Chairman, if I may. I've been on board with Project Ezekiel, with using the Paranoia Strain to sow discord in the West. To foment fear and civil unrest in the population. It's a genius plan when facing an enemy with a vastly superior military. Early reports are that the Paranoia Strain is having the desired effects."

Volkov peered out the window at the thicket of woods blanketing War Games Valley. "I've been monitoring the news as well. Phase One is meeting expectations. But we need to accelerate the timetable. Send Kasparian a message. We want to strike the next targets immediately. Today's incursions show we have vulnerabilities."

"Chairman, what will the Fantasy Strain do?"

"Give us a new beginning."

"But what specifically will the new strain do?"

"Stay in your lane, Lucid. Enough questions!"

He calmed himself by recalling a passage from Ezekiel 5:17.

So will I send upon you famine and evil beasts, and they shall bereave thee; and pestilence and blood shall pass through thee; and I will bring the sword upon thee.

Three, four minutes passed in silence. Finally Volkov said, "The terrorists. We need to draw them out."

Lucid furrowed his brow, then he whipped out his phone. "I have an idea, Chairman. Actually, two ideas. Oh, this is good!"

55

Samana Cay

K aden, Bo, and Nico ran side by side along the trail leading back to the apartment units. Viper was scouting out this area to find the other prisoners. But they needed a plan and they needed to get out of sight—fast.

"Any ideas?" Bo seemed out of breath already.

Kaden tried to recall any suitable venues she'd seen that would give them cover. "We passed a building that looked vacant on the way over. There it is."

It was large and gray, the color of a dirty puddle. The name in front said, Art Barn. She ducked inside. Empty. The lights were off but a skylight scattered the afternoon rays every which way. The main area was a ceramics studio with art sculptures and pottery—no doubt made by the kidnapped girls—scattered on workshop tables on three sides. She spotted a wooden ladder halfway across the room. It led to a loft.

They climbed it. *Perfect.* It gave them a hidden place to figure out next steps. They slumped down against the side of bound bales of straw.

"Weapons check?" Bo asked.

"Two Heckler & Koch HK416s," Nico said, indicating the assault weapons they got from Viper. "And you can have your Scorpion back." He handed Bo the handgun.

"We need comms." Kaden turned to Nico. "Let me borrow your phone. I need to access my accounts. See if Bailey's all right."

Nico handed over his phone and she went to work. She wasn't sure if the Wi-Fi signal was strong enough to bring up Amelia. Instead, she logged in and saw a message from Annika.

"Good news." She looked up at her father. "You know that guy Carlos and Tosh were tracking in Zug? The one who led you to the meeting of the Compact?"

"Sure," Bo said. "I assume they tracked him here?"

"Better. He's one of these biohack types." She was always careful to avoid the word "freak," given how often it was wielded as a weapon against her when she was a kid. "He's even implanted a video camera into his eye. Annika and Sayeed just hacked the feed."

"Damn, they're good," Nico said. "Red Team Zero 1, Island of Misfit Psychopaths 0."

"What else?" Bo asked.

Kaden read a second message. "They tried to access Samana Cay's internal security system but they can't break into the servers."

"I thought your people could hack into anything," Bo said.

"These guys are extra security-minded. Their servers may be on a private network. We could be looking at an air gap."

"Try English," Bo said.

"Corporations and government offices with sensitive materials sometimes cordon off their servers from the Internet. So you have to *physically access* the facility if you want to hack in."

Bo frowned. She doubted he understood, but no time for a remedial hacking course.

"Any word from Viper?" Nico asked.

"Not yet," Kaden said.

"What about Bailey?" Bo had hope in his voice for the first time in a while.

"No. But I can see she's just left Immersion Bay. She's on the move."

"Thank God."

Nico peered around the loft for a lookout perch, but there was none up here. "Rachel's place is a couple of hundred yards from the marina where Viper docked. Should be a fast extraction."

Bo nodded and forced an unconvincing smile.

"Let's do a reality check." Kaden had learned a lesson during her boot camp training. Don't go off half-cocked until you have a solid plan. "We have Viper approaching the apartment units, looking for his wife Judy." She looked at Bo. "Was Judy with Tosh and Carlos earlier?"

"Last I saw," Bo said. "But that was before I threw a chair through the window."

"I'll let Viper know." Kaden sent off a quick voice text. "Now, what about Paul Redman, Alice, and Charlie?"

Bo glowered. "They were separated from us. But I heard one guard talk about other prisoners. So they're probably nearby."

"That's good. Alex may or may not be with them."

"Listen, Kaden. This isn't your fight. I'm responsible for you being here. Look at you, you're a mess. Now that we have Bailey, I say you, Bailey, and Nico get off this island. That should be priority one. Nico can drive Viper's boat. I'll stay behind and look for the others."

She thought it over. Tempting, the idea of getting off this rock, taking her shiny new sister to safety. Maybe even bonding. She'd already gotten her revenge against Savić. Her part of this mission was done.

Bo added, "At the very least, go to Rachel's and be with your sister. Your mother would have wanted you to be safe."

She retrieved the small photo of her mother from her shirt pocket. Looking at it, she smiled. Her mother died when she was three. She had only the vaguest memories of her mom, but she remembered her smile, her laugh, her boundless affection for her little girl.

She could choose love, safety, normalcy. Nobody would blame her. Or she could stand shoulder to shoulder with her father and his righteous anger, trying to help the others escape.

"I'm not abandoning you," Kaden said. She'd turned out more like her father than her mother.

"Headstrong, like your dad," Bo said.

"I think the word you're searching for is 'independent.'"

Bo smiled, but it came with a sadness he couldn't hide. He had something else to say. "If you're staying, now's the time for all cards on the table. The next few hours may be life or death. When I was tied up waiting for the end to come, well, you start thinking. About the things you've done. The things you didn't get a chance to say."

He looked over at Nico, who put up his hands and said, "I'm not here."

She wondered what he was about to share. He kept too much inside. After her childhood with her fake parents and grandfather who abandoned her, she just wanted him to be genuine. That was her line in the sand. No deceit or lies.

Bo edged closer, but he was still a good five feet away, back against the bales of hay.

"I'll make this quick. Kaden, I didn't tell you everything in the diner about those early days. After your mother died and your grandfather decided not to keep you, I took you in."

"You took me in?"

"For three weeks." He wrung his hands, lowered his head so his voice was barely audible. "I tried as best I could as a single working father. The foreign assignments were brutal, and a nanny just wouldn't work on a government salary. But it was more than that. Every time I looked at your face, it reminded me of Deirdre, and it broke my heart. So I gave you back."

She looked away, trying not to tear up. "You gave up on me?" She thought of all those years with the fake parents Blackburn had hired.

"I'm sorry. I screwed up."

She was crushed about what could have been. But maybe she could make a difference with Bo and Bailey.

"Have you told Bailey about what you do?"

Bo looked up, surprised. He started to say something. Maybe something like, "That's none of your business." But he thought better of it. Instead, he said, "Can we do this later? She knows I work for a government agency. Or used to work. I'm on leave."

She let that new wrinkle slide. But her sister needed a cold dose of truth. Kaden fetched Nico's phone from her lap. She punched in the shortcode to dial her wearable device.

"Bailey? You safe?"

The video on the pendant was jumping around like crazy, but she could hear her sister. Bailey was hurrying along a walking trail. "Yes, we're good! What about Dad?"

"He's safe." Kaden switched to the phone's rear lens to show their father, who rose and came over.

"Sweetheart. I'm okay. You too?"

"Thank God! Okay, are you meeting us here? Can we get out of here?"

Bo looked from the video chat to Kaden and back. "Sweetheart, we have to go rescue the other prisoners. They're still somewhere in Immersion Bay."

"But—how is that your job? Why not the Navy or Marines or CIA?"

Kaden nodded, urging her father to tell Bailey the truth.

"This really isn't the time, sweetheart," he began. Kaden shot him daggers, so he relented. "I formed a special ops team to rescue you."

"But—you always said you were a paper pusher. A bureaucrat."

"I was a field operative. I couldn't tell you the truth—for your protection."

"What? You were a spy!" Bailey looked flustered. "So all those trips?"

"Overseas assignments."

Bailey looked on the verge of tears. "Is that—is that the reason I was kidnapped?"

"I don't know. I gotta go."

"All right. Be careful, Pop."

"I will. I love you." He shut his eyes.

Kaden ended the call. *That was tough to watch.*

Bo straightened. "Fantastic. I could be killed in a few minutes and my last conversation with my daughter was about how I'd lied to her all these years. Happy now? See! That's what the truth gets you."

He stormed off to the other side of the loft.

Nico stood and grabbed his HK416 from on top of the bale of straw. "So. What's the plan?"

Nico's phone buzzed in her hand. But it was an incoming call for her.

A call from Alex Wyatt.

"Alex, is that you?" she said.

"Kaden? Yes, it's me." She recognized his distinctive accent, Miami by way of New Jersey. "Don't have much time. I managed to distract one of the guards and grab my phone from the other room. We're locked in the Dance Studio."

"How many of you?"

There was a slight pause. Then he said, "Four. Paul, Alice, Charlie, and me. Where are you? Can you help us break out?"

"I'm close by." She didn't want to give away their whereabouts.

"Guard's comin'." The line went dead.

Kaden rose to her feet and Bo came down the rows of hay to see who'd called.

"Sorry for before," he said. "Who was that?"

"Alex. He and the *Axom* crew are in the Dance Studio, about 300 yards from here."

"All right, then." Nico headed toward the top of the ladder. "We have our target."

♀ ♂

THEY MOVED through the thin woods rimming the south end of Immersion Bay, figuring that was a safer bet than a straight shot across the exposed grassy field. Kaden remembered passing it on her dash to free Bo, and they now approached it from the rear. They gathered in a thicket of brush behind the studio, a one-story affair with a wide thatched roof and light-rose stucco exterior. Viper was waiting for them there after Kaden had messaged him.

Nico kept his voice low. "We free these four. We find Tosh, Carlos, and Judy. We grab Bailey and then get the hell off this damn island, right?"

"Maybe." Bo turned to Viper. "How many people can fit on your boat?"

"No idea," Viper said. "I'd guess eighteen, twenty max capacity if some go below deck."

"How is this gonna work?" Nico said. "There are—what?— 600 girls on this island. We just make thirty trips to shuttle them off to the Bahamas?"

"Yeah, that's not gonna work," Kaden agreed. "Maybe we can smuggle out footage of the camp. Get public pressure to force the U.S. government to do something. But first we focus on freeing the *Axom* four."

"Then we find Judy and your two guys," Viper said to Bo. "I did a reconnaissance. One guard posted by the front entrance. I'm hanging back. Who's going in?"

"Let's do surprise and disable," Kaden said. It was a routine she and Nico had worked out when they wanted to immobilize an opponent. "I'll run point."

"On your right," Nico said.

"I'll bring up the rear," Bo said.

She moved out along the left side of the studio. The rear door was boarded up. She peeked inside the windows but it was too dark to see anything. She reached the end of the building and angled the glass on Nico's turned-off phone to get a reflection. She positioned it at the base of the building and saw the guard at the front door with a weapon, probably the same SCAR 17E smart rifle she'd seen the other guards carry.

She threw a pebble about twenty feet in front of the guard, just enough to attract his attention. Then she whipped around the side of the building with her hands raised.

"I want to surrender. My name is Kaden Baker." The guard approached her with caution, smart rifle pointed to her chest. "And I demand asylum under Article Twelve of the Geneva Convention."

She watched as Nico snuck up behind him. By the time she was seeking asylum, Nico was applying a chokehold. Nico had six inches on him—both height and biceps. After five seconds, the guard dropped his weapon and collapsed.

Kaden checked the entrance for booby traps. She entered the large open space, framed on two sides by mirrored walls and wooden rails. Across the room she spotted a figure. She moved efficiently across the polished bamboo floor until his face became clear in the frail light.

It was Alex, tied and gagged in a chair, just like her father was. She wondered what infraction he'd committed to get him tied up like this. And where were the others?

She didn't like this.

She glanced over her shoulder and saw Nico enter and then Bo, who stationed himself at the door. She hadn't seen Alex since the incident in Dallas. She knelt and untied the gag from his mouth.

"You'll be okay. We're getting out of here." She said it half to herself.

"How'd you find me?" His eyes looked surprised to see her.

"What do you—" It took a second for the realization to hit her. "It's a trap!" she yelled. "We need to get out of here!"

She heard a sound in the back of the studio. Nico raised his HK416 toward the dark shadows.

At the front door, Bo signaled for them to hurry so they could get out of there. She got Alex's hands free, and she and Alex both worked on the ropes tying his ankles to the chair. Suddenly, Alex's chest started chiming.

"What's that sound?" she asked.

"My medallion." He removed it from his neck and looked at it quizzically in his palm. "It's supposed to go off if someone who's my 'type' comes within fifty feet."

Clicking sounds on the hard floor, maybe the heels of a woman's pumps. The lights came up. Kaden's heart fell.

Walking slowly toward her, Rachel held a gun to the back of Bailey's head. "You have a brave daughter, Bo," Rachel said. "And a brave sister, Kaden. Drop your weapons or I'll kill her in three seconds. One, two …"

All three laid their weapons on the floor.

"Now, interlace your fingers behind your heads."

"I'm sorry, Dad." Bailey was trembling.

As they raised their hands, Rachel said, "After your call, your daughter insisted on coming back to help you out."

"How could you do this?" Nico asked her.

"A million points in reward money goes a long way on this island," she said.

The shuffle of feet outside. Kaden's eyes widened at what she saw next. A half-dozen of the kidnapped girls entered the front door and trained their bows and arrows on the four of them.

"Terrorist scum," one of the girls spat out.

She didn't know how, but they'd been indoctrinated.

Seconds later, a dozen uniformed Guardians entered with their smart rifles drawn.

They were prisoners again.

56

Samana Cay

The SUV pulled up at the rear of corporate headquarters in front of the private entrance to Volkov's executive suite. He opened the door but turned back to Lucid.

"What's the most secure building on the island?"

"The Data Center," Lucid said.

"Let's keep these three prisoners there, with a heavy contingent of guards."

"Yes, Chairman."

Volkov climbed out and waved his palm in front of the chip reader. The door clicked open and a sonorous automated voice said, "Welcome, Chairman."

He ordered a guava purée from his assistant and tried to calm his nerves. What a day! His people had outsmarted the terrorists by using artificial intelligence. First, they lured the intruders into a trap by using AI voice technology. Today anyone's voice could be replicated to sound a hundred percent authentic after supplying only a minute-long sound clip. They had much more than that with Alex Wyatt. The twist came in using AI that could simulate someone's voice in a realistic conversation on the fly. That was still cutting-edge.

Second, they turned select captives at Immersion Bay against their potential liberators. *What poetry!* Six of the at-risk girls with rebellious streaks underwent a procedure for implantable smart contacts—lenses implanted between the iris and the natural lens. *Takes all of fifteen minutes and you've got someone who's susceptible to whatever reality we want them to believe.*

Volkov checked the time: just after four p.m. In less than two hours, the *Seaduction* would be on its way with its world-changing cargo. He'd given the crew instructions to wear their smartglasses to glimpse a special send-off message in the sky.

But his thoughts were already onto the effects of the Fantasy Strain would have on the United States, Britain, and Western Europe. Centuries of hegemony, vanquished. Crushed in the cruelest possible way.

And the beast was given authority over every tribe, people, language and nation. Revelation 13:7.

♀ ♂

VIPER hoofed it back to his Boston Whaler the moment he saw Bo, Kaden, and Nico being marched out of the Dance Studio and Rachel holding a gun on Bailey. Looked like she'd double-crossed them.

He untied the vessel from the dock, started the engine, and headed along the northeast coast of Samana Cay. When he was clear of the shoreline and certain he wasn't being followed, he got onto the secure comms with home base, Annika and Sayeed at Red Team Zero.

He filled them in about what he'd seen. They said to stay tuned, events were unfolding fast. He set a course past Immersion Bay around the eastern tip of the island where he'd wait for further instructions.

He might be one man, this might be a small boat, but there was a lot he could do with the firepower below deck. A hell of a lot.

♀ ♂

Three armed guards ushered Kaden, Bo, and Nico into the subterranean level of the Data Center. Bailey was taken somewhere else. They passed through three layers of security to get down here. The room was cramped and bare except for three folding chairs and a small table. Looked like an unused meeting room. They performed a full sweep of the room and found no cameras or listening devices, but they stuck close together and kept their voices to a whisper.

"I wish you'd listened," Bo said, shooting Kaden a sideways glance. "You, Bailey, and Nico could have been in the Bahamas by now. Would have put my mind at ease when they put a bullet in it."

"Quiet, I'm thinking," Kaden snapped.

"Don't talk to your father like—"

"Are you kidding? Listen for a minute. They confiscated our weapons and my earpiece. But they didn't notice my contacts."

"So? You can see better?"

Looks like Bo has an annoying streak. "Smart contacts are still new enough that the guards figured they were for vision correction, if they noticed them at all. I'm picking up a strong Wi-Fi signal down here. That means I can still access Amelia."

Nico jumped at the news. "That means Internet. We can contact anyone!"

"I'm thinking bigger. Hold on." Kaden blinked three times and Amelia appeared in her classic aviator outfit, standing beside the door. She started talking but Kaden couldn't hear her. So Kaden began using American Sign Language, a nice little skill she'd picked during two summer of volunteering at a youth shelter for deaf kids.

Amelia began signing back. She was relieved Amelia could understand—not just sign language but the ability to read it as the signer, not the receiver. With Amelia right there in front of her, Kaden always had to remind herself that Amelia sees what Kaden sees.

What is this building? Kaden signed.

Data Center, Amelia signed.

For the whole island? We haven't been able to hack into their servers.

Yes. The main room has an air-gap design, Amelia signed. *One access point but it would take weeks to crack it.*

"You were right," Kaden told Nico. "Air-gapped."

"Damn it all," he said.

At least they knew they were in the nerve center now. The Data Center was the hub that controlled the tens of thousands of digital screens, sensors, and CCTV cams scattered around the island. There must be a way to access the central servers. That was the key to everything.

Kaden had read on one of her hacker boards about a new blackout technique that could target a physical space and its surroundings. She couldn't remember the details, but she pointed Amelia in the right direction and she was able to find the thread.

Once Kaden told Amelia what she had in mind, her AI went out scouring the Internet for what was needed. Amelia then spidered all the open channels in the Data Center to find a suitable hardware match.

I'm sorry this is taking so long, Amelia signed.

It's been like five seconds, Kaden replied.

No, 5.87 microseconds—an eternity. Found it. I had to go on the Darknet. I think I need a shower.

I forgot to ask about the backup generator, Kaden signed.

It's within the pulse blast radius.

Kaden nodded and stopped signing. Amelia smiled that breathtaking smile of hers and waited.

Kaden turned to Nico. "Remember Dallas, when we were trying to add one of us as a super admin?"

"Yeah, we ran out of time."

"And we didn't have Amelia."

"True."

Kaden worked out the final details of a plan. "Amelia said the servers are on this floor. Second door on the right. It's nice and cool down here—they must keep them below ground to avoid the tropical heat. We can create a temporary power blackout lasting a few minutes."

"What good would that do?" Bo asked.

"We need to access the server room. It's a longshot, but it might work. Here's my idea."

She leaned closer to them. "We'll create a localized digital power outage. We create a tiny pulse that'll disrupt the magnetic field used by everyday electronic devices. When we set it off, everything digital on this floor and the two floors above will go dark. It'll kill all computers, smartphones, lights, CCTV cameras, televisions, radios, digital wristwatches. But unlike a real electromagnetic pulse, it doesn't damage the physical devices. It won't fry your digital watch—but it'll reset the time to 00:00."

"I see where this is going," Nico said.

"I don't." Bo looked out of his depth.

"Yeah, yeah," Nico said. "Step one, a digital power outage hack. The Data Center—everything goes dark. Step two, we access the server room, slip in your USB drive, do a hard reboot on the servers."

"Wait, what?" Bo said. "I've been running ops for twenty years and never heard of something like a localized blackout. First of all, they must have confiscated your USB thingie—"

She reached down, pulled off her right tennis shoe, and peeled back the hidden compartment in the heel. She pulled out the thumb drive and dangled it in front of her father. "The drive will reboot the servers and create a new user with super admin privileges."

"And that's good?" Bo asked.

"Wait and see," Nico said.

"Annika had a wicked idea—I'm still working on it," Kaden said.

Bo looked like he was trying to follow along. "But how do you create a power outage in the first place?" He waved his hand across the small room. "If you haven't noticed, our options are limited."

Only by your imagination, she wanted to say. "We can hop onto a small physical device that's connected to the Internet and essentially turn it into a nondestructive mini-EMP gun that's not used for evil. Now, Amelia says there's only one Internet of Things connected device in this building with a capacitor that can be repurposed for this. A bug zapper racket."

"You're kidding." Bo collapsed back in his seat.

"It's lying on a secretary's desk one floor above, just eighteen inches from a networked computer, and it's resting on an ashtray with a copper rim. So we can hop onto this IOT mosquito zapper and turn it into a small EMP device that can temporarily shut down the network through code. After Amelia hacks the internal circuitry of this racket, it'll send out a small pulse that'll knock out the power of anything within a hundred and fifty feet. Voila, a mini-blackout."

"Wait." Nico brushed his palm across his forehead. "That could corrupt the data on the flash drive."

"Got that covered." She showed them the inside of her shoe's secret compartment, lined with copper mesh and solid aluminum. "I basically created a tiny Faraday cage."

"A what?" Bo looked confused.

"It's like a force field that shields everything inside—"

"Forget I asked," Bo said. "What about me? What do I do?"

Kaden took on a serious look. "You stay put for now. Trust me."

She put her shoe on and went through the plan five times with Nico, looking for holes, factoring in unexpected variables and unlikely scenarios. Finally, they were ready.

It's almost time, Kaden signed to Amelia.

You know I'll be offline during this, right?

Yes.

The two men took their positions at the far end of the room. Kaden knocked loudly on the door's glass window. "Bathroom break emergency," she shouted.

A guard appeared and peered into the room. He shook his head no.

"Come on, I won't bite. Super emergency!" She hopped up and down, raised her hands over her head, and backed away from the door to show she posed no threat.

The guard entered cautiously with his weapon drawn. "Nice and slow. Don't try anything."

"There is no try," Kaden said. The guard looked confused. Obviously not a *Star Wars* fan.

She signed to Amelia, *Execute now.*

Before Kaden had a chance to say *please*, the lights died. Everything was black. She reached for his smart rifle and heard the guard exhale a surprised grunt. She took the butt of the rifle and brought it up hard against his face. That didn't floor him, but they struggled for the gun and it clattered to the ground.

She set herself into her favorite kickboxing position and delivered a roundhouse kick to his chest, sending the guard crashing down on the table. A few times a year she practiced this move with her eyes shut just in case she needed to bring down somebody in the black of night.

Nico was on top of the guard now using a chokehold to immobilize him, by the sound of his gasps. After a few seconds, the gasps stopped. He was out cold.

"Let's go," she said.

From the far end of the hallway, she heard the panicked voices of guards. No flashlights, though. She led the way, heading left and feeling along the far wall until she found the second door. They entered. It was cool but not cold; she pegged the temperature at around sixty-eight F. No sound or movement in here. This was the hard part, groping in the dark for a tiny USB slot on whichever machine was the master. They split up and began feeling their way around the room. The space felt much bigger than she expected.

"Are we looking in the right place?" she asked in a low voice.

"I can't tell," Nico whispered.

A bank of low-wattage lights clicked on overhead. They could see—and be seen.

"They must have a second backup power source," she said. The outside hallway still looked dark, but the Data Center was the brains that powered this smart island, so no real surprise they planned for just such a contingency.

The room was long and windowless, with two rows of tall gray steel telco racks holding scores—maybe hundreds—of what she recognized as high-end blade servers with their gleaming blue and green lights, blinking as if speaking an alien tongue with one another. The racks stretched almost to the ceiling, leaving just enough room for overhead airflow and for the cables that disappeared into the false ceiling.

She removed the thumb drive from her shoe and continued down the rows of servers looking for a master terminal window. "We need to find this thing in the next thirty seconds or else ..." Her voice trailed off.

Thirty seconds came and went. She heard voices coming from far down the hallway. A conversation about a missing guard.

She turned to Nico. "We need to—"

"Found it!" he said.

She handed him the drive. He punched it into the slot to do

its magic, a combined effort of Red Team Zero. "Let's go!" she said. No time to wait for it to execute. They'd have to hope the hard reboot programmed into the disk would bring back the servers so there'd be no need for tech support to begin milling around down here.

They scurried down the hallway in the darkness and found their way back into their lockup where Bo was waiting. She nearly tripped across the body of the unconscious guard but righted herself.

Seconds later, the lights came back on. Power restored. Everything working. They pulled the guard's slumped body to the side out of view, closed the door, and heard the lock engage.

Bo looked dubious. "Can you tell me why we didn't try to break out?"

"Trust me," Kaden said. "Our time is much better spent right here."

She resumed signing with Amelia. She had a lot to get done.

57

Samana Cay

Volkov settled into his chair in his office, surveying his control console. Under the Critical Threat Level, he was granted sweeping powers to impose martial law and to mobilize the citizenry against any external threats.

Volkov worried there might be other spies and terrorists afoot on the island. Officials at the National Guard were analyzing data provided by the country's vast network of sensors and CCTV cameras to identify any suspicious activities.

But he needed to do more. *A line had been crossed. A tone needed to be set.*

He checked the time on screen: 5:10 p.m. He called Lucid's video chat line. "Lucid, pick up. This is a priority one call."

"Yes, Chairman." Lucid's face appeared on screen, his voice tired after all the excitement of the day. He was riding in the executive compartment of the SUV again. "I'm heading back to Immersion Bay. Hearing reports of a minor disturbance."

Volkov chose his avatar for the chat. *The prophet Ezekiel. For today—in less than an hour—the fateful shipment will go out that will bend the arc of history.*

"I've decided what to do with the prisoners," Volkov said as he looked at Lucid watching Ezekiel seated across from him.

"Excellent. And what did you decide?"

"We'll have a public execution." The grave words seemed to take on added weight when spoken by Ezekiel. "The first in Samana Cay's history."

"No trial or hearing as we normally would?"

"We're at Threat Level Critical. I'm sentencing the enemy combatants to death, exercising my executive powers under the Corporate Charter."

"When should I schedule it?"

"Six o'clock tonight."

A panicked look crossed Lucid's face. "That's less than an hour from now!"

"I want it to coincide with the sailaway of the *Seaduction*. I have something special in mind."

"I don't know that we can pull that together in time," Lucid protested.

"Nonsense. Three lone prisoners. Escort them to Devil's Point. Blindfolds. Last words. A dozen guards. We live-stream it to the nation. Alert the media. More exciting when it's televised live. People will be captivated. And it sends a strong message about nationalism and loyalty."

"Sir, that's a tall order. But if you're adamant, I need to get on that right now."

"Go, go. I'll be observing from here."

Volkov disconnected the call. He rose and poured himself a glass of Belaya Rus premium vodka. He had been a heavy drinker in his teens but rarely drank now that he was running a global empire.

He drank fully, then refilled his glass in early celebration. *A toast. In less than an hour, I'll be rid of Kaden Baker and Bo Finnerty forever.*

♀ ♂

AT PRECISELY FIFTEEN minutes until six o'clock, a platoon of Guardians led Kaden, Bo, and Nico—handcuffed and now dressed in drab gray prisoner's uniforms—from the basement of the Data Center down the seaside path past Fantasy Live. They arrived at a windswept rock outcropping perched high atop sheer hundred-foot cliffs—a precipice that was one of the island's signature natural wonders. Devil's Point.

The lead guard refused to tell them why they were here, but Kaden suspected the worst. She looked out over the long ribbon of white sandy beach stretching all the way to a ship anchored in the turquoise lagoon in the distance.

Authorities had set up a makeshift rope line fifty feet away— just a long set of ropes running from one stanchion to the next for crowd control. Camera crews jostled for position, and a crowd began to form five persons deep all along the barricade.

"So this is it." Bo looked around, but he already seemed resigned to their fate. "I'll hand it to them. This is a beautiful place to die."

"If this is an execution, it sure is a damned strange one," Kaden said. "No jury trial. No chance to make a final call to relatives. No blindfold or handcuffs. No final words. No priest to say last rites."

Nico gave a slight nod as she surveyed the sightlines. "I guess the plan is, *Pop pop pop,* bodies fall backward down the towering cliffside. Great visuals. Film at eleven."

She looked up at Nico. The sunset was brightening the green flecks in Nico's Afro. He looked nervous. He just needed to trust her a little longer.

Bo stepped closer to her. "Sorry. For everything."

"It's not over yet. I'm running this op," she said.

He took a step back, searched her face. "Op? What op?"

"Follow my lead."

Kaden turned her back to her father, the soldiers, the crowd, the media, this entire island of misery and pain. She looked out at the horizon where an orange sun was melting into the distant waters. It would be tough in these handcuffs, but she would do her best.

She began to sign.

♀ ♂

ANNIKA AND SAYEED had different styles when it came to red teaming. In penetrating a secure database, Annika used tricks she'd picked up during her days in corporate offices, and she let her fingers fly over her keyboard. Sayeed came up from the streets and earned his chops by hacking into North Korea's government servers with an elegant subroutine nobody had ever tried before. He preferred standing at his terminal and issuing voice commands to his online bot.

But differing hacking styles took a back seat the moment Kaden sent them an encrypted message with log-in credentials to give them root privileges. Until now they hadn't been able to penetrate Samana Cay's Data Center from the outside. With Kaden and Nico commandeering the main server from the inside, they not only had remote access to the cPanel, they had super admin privileges.

Super powers.

"This is pure gold," Annika said.

"Better than gold," Sayeed agreed. "Platinum. No, *vibranium*."

They divvied up three tasks. First, they created an image backup of a critical fingerprint data file. Any second now, they should be hearing from Amelia with directions about that.

Next, they turned off geofencing for all the captured women at Immersion Bay.

Third, they got down to the hardest part: finding compromising material that could bring down this war criminal, Chairman Incognito.

Annika made an educated guess that the architects of Samana Cay's "smart island" network reserved account User1 for Incognito. As a super admin, she'd be able to see everything.

She dove in.

♀ ♂

LING AND KATARINA met at the usual spot in the Commons on their way to Immersion Bay's Dining Hall for dinner. They were eager to discuss the events of the day when Piper came running across the courtyard out of breath.

Ling screamed and hugged her. "What are you doing here? I thought they shipped you off."

"I've been on the island the whole time," Piper said. "Camp Defiance. I'll tell you later but, look! Your dog collars. They're turned off!"

Ling and Katarina both gasped and looked down to check. Sure enough, their own neckbands were deactivated. No color diodes signaling where they stood on the leaderboard. That had never happened in the past six months.

"Here, let me." Piper circled to Ling's back and fumbled at the tiny clasp on the choker around her friend's neck. The dog collar fell to the ground. Without an electrical current, the choker came off just like any other choker.

Their eyes all got wide. Ling then freed Katarina from her collar.

"The electronic locks must be short-circuiting or something," Piper guessed.

To their right, they saw small circles of the other girls

snatching off their collars, throwing them to the ground, and stomping on them. A buzz began to build in the courtyard as the girls debated what was going on and what they should do next.

From the other side of the courtyard came a crackle of gunshots. A barrage of nonstop, heavy, hit-the-deck gunfire from an automatic weapon.

The three girls knew they were exposed in the middle of the courtyard. Piper grabbed the nearest picnic table and toppled it over. They scrambled behind it to take cover.

♀ ♂

Sayeed called Annika over to his terminal stand. "Take a look at this."

After they'd accessed the central AI database and verified User1 was indeed Chairman Incognito, Sayeed went to work calling up all instances of Incognito using video chats or AR simulations in something called Fantasy Live. Incognito had used an avatar for every video chat, so that didn't provide evidence of anything.

This simulation in the Fantasy Theater, though, was more interesting. The file was marked "Level 1 Access Only." A note in the metadata showed why the recording was restricted. *All sessions are recorded by default to ensure player safety and to score the performer during the simulation. Access granted to Level 1 personnel only.*

"So what's in the simulation?" Annika asked.

"Watch this." Sayeed began playing the recording. "Looks like Mr. Incognito has a kinky side. He wants to spank this girl on her eighteenth birthday."

"Gross. Wait, I recognize that girl. It's Bo's daughter!"

They watched to the end when Bailey smashed a lit candlestick stand over his head.

"Yes!" Sayeed cheered. "This is good. Incognito's face is visible on the video."

"I have a close-up of Incognito's face from the Lucid Eyecam we hacked," Annika said, hustling back to her computer. "But I just came across something better. Apparently this guy transferred over all his old videos from years ago. I guess he figured it's a super-secure installation, better than the cloud."

"So much for that theory," Sayeed said.

"Check this out." Annika began playing an old mp4 video of a video chat over Skype.

"Haven't used Skype in years," he said.

"Just watch."

The date stamp showed it was recorded seventeen years ago—the oldest video in the batch. The recording showed Incognito playing a game of Truth or Dare with one of his online friends. Maybe an American, because they were speaking English.

"Is the footage corrupted—or is that him?" Annika asked. "It looks like half his face melted off."

"There went his shot at Hollywood," Sayeed said.

"Horror films, maybe. From their conversation, I pieced together his real name. One Maxim Volkov from Belarus. He's nineteen here. It all jibes with public records. Am I good or what?"

"You're the best. We'll blow the crap out of Incognito's cover."

"That's not the best part. Watch the video, see what they talk about next."

Truth, Volkov said.

His friend said, *Okay, truth. You ever kill anyone?*

I can't tell you that. Volkov let out a nervous laugh.

Major penalty! Let me think of some epic public humiliation.

Volkov hesitated. Picked up his hookah and took a hit.

Hold on, I'm thinking! He downed another shot, clearly

massively drunk now, and almost fell off his chair. He said, *Yeah.*

Yeah, what?

Yeah, I killed someone. My parents.

No shit! His friend smiled broadly, rocked back in his chair. *Why'd you do that?*

It was partly an accident. I was trying to off my mom. Total bitch. I paid someone a lot of rubles to take her out, force her car over a guardrail into a gorge. Make it look like an accident. Afterward the guy says, You didn't say she had to be alone.

He stopped rocking his chair and took another drag on his water pipe. He went on. *She had an appointment—they decided at the last second to head out with her. My father was driving. My older brother in the back seat. Guy says he didn't see him there.*

Holy shit! And that's how you got the house?

The house, all their holdings. Everything. It's a lot. He exhaled out a strange, joyless laugh. Then he grabbed the ends of his computer screen and leaned forward. *I never told that to anyone. You say a word and I'll kill you.*

You personally? No hitman? What an honor. His friend burst out laughing. Then Maxim Volkov cursed him and reached down to turn off his computer.

The video ended.

Sayeed rubbed his stubbly jaw. "Wow. This guy is now the head of state of Samana Cay?"

"One and the same. He inherited billions. I'm finishing up a highlight video reel now."

"That'll be must-see TV."

"Look!" they both said at once. Incoming message from Kaden.

Execute Operation Lethal Checkmate.

58

Samana Cay

At Devil's Point, Kaden looked down at the grand view of the island's southern beaches, the waterfall, and the sweep of sea. The Swift boat that attacked Redman's yacht patrolled the waters far to the east. She checked her smart contacts for the time. Five minutes until six o'clock Standard Grim Reaper Time. She looked at Bo and had to admit—it still stung that her father had given up on her so long ago.

No matter what happens now, I won't do the same to him.

The unit commander—stern faced, dressed in a white officer's uniform, hair graying beneath his white cap—ordered the prisoners to line up along the precipice at the edge of the cliff. He directed one of his men to release the prisoners from their handcuffs. Then he instructed his men to allow the camera crews to advance beyond the rope line and set up just behind where the firing squad would be located. But there was something weird going on. A murmur going through the crowd. People holding up their phones and watching something.

The commander didn't seem to notice or care. When the

cameras went live, he read from a prepared statement, using the scenic sunset as a backdrop.

"Under the emergency powers granted me by the Corporate Charter, I, Chairman Incognito, do hereby sentence the enemy spies Kaden Baker, Bo Finnerty, and Nico Johnson to death by firing squad."

Kaden let the words flutter by. Her eyes swept over the crowd. Standing against the rope line, one young mother bounced a two-year-old girl in her arms. Kaden saw the mother glare at her, and she returned the stare with interest. How could she bring her daughter to this? If she knew one thing now, it's that family is supposed to protect you from life's cruelties, not subject you to them.

The commander continued to intone, "Let the word go out to the enemies of Samana Cay, both foreign and domestic: This is the fate you will meet for acts of espionage and terrorism against our citizenry."

He folded the sheet of paper and tucked it into his uniform's pants pocket. He nodded to a soldier, who came up and marked their prisoner uniforms with a big black X over their hearts. He then offered them a choice of putting on a black hood or not. They all declined. He stepped away.

"Company, take your positions!" The commander took his place on the right side of the firing squad. He raised a long steel sword into the air.

The guards, dressed in military fatigues with olive-colored berets, set up in front of the television crews. Three of them lay in prone positions and three went to one knee, all facing the captives. They were all carrying the standard-issue SCAR 17E military-style assault rifle—the smart version.

Kaden checked the time. Six o'clock sharp. She stood in the middle and grasped hands with Bo and Nico. White seabirds fluttered above the heads of the spectators. The crowd fell silent.

"Courage," Kaden said in a low voice so only Bo and Nico could hear her.

The commander brandished the sword forward. "Company, prepare arms!" The Guardians aimed their weapons at the prisoners' chests. The commander spaced out the words. "Ready! Aim!" He brought his sword down with a flourish. "Fire!"

Kaden flinched and shut her eyes. When she reopened them, she saw that the guards had confused looks on their faces. The commander repeated, "Fire! Fire!"

It worked, thank God. Annika had swapped out the fingerprint registry for every networked assault rifle on the island. Until now, more than 500 Guardians were able to pick up any smart rifle and have it fire. The new registry permitted only four people to fire the smart weapons: Kaden, Bo, Nico, and Bailey.

"Now!" Kaden shouted. They rushed the Guardians.

♀ ♂

VOLKOV WATCHED the public execution proceedings from his command center. What was happening? Faulty rifles? *Someone is going to pay for this major screw-up!* He watched the local TV networks televise the fracas at Devil's Point.

One by one, the stations cut away from the prisoners and guards' hand-to-hand combat and went to a video. It took him a full moment to realize what he was looking at. *No, it can't be.* A video of himself! A video that showed his young, disfigured face! A video that, he now realized, he himself had once recorded but hadn't watched in years. He turned up the volume.

Yeah, I killed my parents.

A two-line red chyron at the bottom of the screen read:

MAXIM VOLKOV EXPOSED
    Killed parents before becoming Chairman Incognito

That startled him. *Were Kaden Baker and her people behind this? The Guardians needed to finish the job!*

But first things first. He gave the voice command to summon his virtual assistant. "Liv, get me the network chiefs."

"Chairman." Liv's voice seemed rattled. "The networks just passed along word about the video. They've been hacked. They can't take it down."

He hung up and watched the rest of the video. The ramblings of the drunken, spiteful, stupid boy he'd once been. He had little in common with this Maxim Volkov. It was true—a stroke of good luck had made him the sole heir of the Volkov fortune. But he had leveraged those hundreds of millions into billions with the help of key advisors.

He stood and tried to calm himself. His identity had been compromised. The mythic persona of intrigue, fear, and respect he'd spent nearly two decades cultivating—destroyed. He would need to start over with a new identity. *Someone will pay with their life!*

His eyes found the bottom of the TV screen. A new message appeared beneath a closeup of his face:

WAR CRIMINAL — REWARD OFFERED
    10 million points for Incognito's arrest or execution

No, no, no! He returned to his desk and summoned Lucid. "Lucid, are you seeing this?"

"Yes, Chairman. It's on nearly every screen."

"Prepare my jet. I'll be leaving tonight."

"Yes, sir. May I ask where—"

He hung up. He needed to think. He needed to keep things in perspective. Big picture. He could fly to Belarus. Or he could stay with a member of the Compact. He needed to buy a few days. The Fantasy Strain was about to change the course of history. The moment the strain hits a major drinking water

supply, it would all be over. The contagion would spread expo-
nentially and there would be no way to stop it.

*The Transition is nearly here. Then the Reset and the Seven
Spheres. The Fantasy Strain will set the wheels into motion.*

The Fantasy Strain! He'd almost forgotten about the *Seaduction*'s sailaway at six p.m. He'd instructed members of the crew to
don their smartglasses for a special parting visual. He turned off
the network channels and switched to the live feeds of the *Seaduction*'s departure taken from the seaward-facing cameras at the
Plant next to the Lab at the southeast corner of the island.

He switched to the video feed and saw—smoke.

Impossible! The Seaduction is on fire!

♀ ♂

AFTER TAKING OUT THE *SEADUCTION*, Viper steered his Boston
Whaler farther west along the island's south bank and found a
suitable hiding spot in a thicket of brambles along a craggy
stretch of shoreline. He tied the boat securely then went below to
retrieve the boxes of C4 for his final mission here.

He carefully carried the bricks to shore two at a time and laid
them above the waterline. He'd use eight in all—eight heavy
bricks of C4 plastic bonded explosives in two-kilogram butter
boxes. That and his HK416 should do the trick.

From the inside intelligence Annika was feeding him, there
were two remaining targets on this side of the island. The Plant,
or factory. And the Lab. Four bricks of C4 per building should
do the trick. He was still waiting to hear when to move into position to try to free Kaden, Nico, and the others. But he had to
move fast.

He placed the detonator and wiring in the outside pocket of
his military satchel and stacked the butter boxes containing the
C4 atop one another, then zipped it closed. He heaved it over his
shoulder and set off.

He'd begin by destroying the Plant.

♀ ♂

BAILEY WOKE up after a short nap on the polished bamboo floor of the Dance Studio, where she was the lone captive. But something seemed off. The pacing she'd heard from the guardsmen creaking along the boarded walkway out front was replaced by an eerie quiet. She peeked out the front window and saw the guards were gone.

This is my chance.

She checked the front door. Locked. The back entrance was sealed off, the side windows locked and bolted. The front window seemed her best bet, though it was locked, too. She looked around. Tried to pick up the pommel horse but got it only a couple of inches off the floor. *There!* She went to the corner and dragged over a short mauve stretch ladder the dancers used for flexibility. She could lift it okay, so she got a running start and used it like a battering ram, smashing the window to pieces and sending glass flying over the walkway. She brought a chair over and stepped through the window, careful to avoid shards.

Free again, though maybe not for long. Her fingers went reflexively to the dog collar around her neck. She held the tip of it and was shocked to see it no longer glowed red. It didn't glow any color at all.

She looked up and down this isolated stretch of Immersion Bay and didn't see anyone. But another thing surprised her. One of the guards' smart rifles was leaning against the facade of the studio. She had seen this movie before.

For months, the guards at Immersion Bay had played mind games with their captives, taunting them by leaving their assault rifles right out in the open, propped up against the outside of the barracks and Dining Hall. *Go ahead. Why don't you try to escape?* they'd jeer. Once, one of the girls did just that, turning the rifle on two guards, only to discover it wouldn't fire. They roughed her up and sent her off to Camp Defiance.

Bailey grabbed it with a show of what-have-I-got-to-lose defiance. She carried it back to the Commons, where dozens of girls had gathered. She moved through the groups of girls to see what the buzz was all about and realized their dog collars had stopped working. She reached up to the back of her neck and tore it off with a vicious yank.

To celebrate, she pointed the smart rifle at the leaderboard above the main stage and scared herself half to death when it went off. She let off an automatic burst, riddling the electronic board with a volley that sent smoke spiraling up to the dome.

When she realized she'd created a small panic among the girls in the Commons, she set the rifle down and called out, "Sorry, everyone, my bad."

The girls emerged from their hiding spots and came over to witness what seemed to be another part of the change in power dynamics on the island.

Ling, her estranged best friend, came up to her. "How'd you do that?" She bent down, picked up the rifle, tried to fire it at the smoldering leaderboard. Nothing happened.

The rest of the girls gathered around. Katarina, twenty or thirty others, even Piper was here.

"You know what this means?" Piper said to the group. "It's like that legend of King Arthur and the Sword in the Stone. Only one person could unlock the weapon's power—Bailey Finnerty."

"I'm no legend," Bailey said.

"I don't mean you have special magic." Piper picked up the weapon and tried to fire it. "I mean you can kick some serious ass with this thing!"

A black SUV rumbled into the courtyard and stopped. The side opened and an odd-looking man stepped out. Was it Lucid? She'd heard rumors about Incognito's right-hand man.

"What's the meaning of this?" the man raised his voice. "You know the rule against large gatherings. Now disperse or I'll send you all to Camp Defiance! Where are the guards?" He looked around but spotted none.

Bailey picked up the rifle and walked deliberately toward Lucid. The crowd parted like the Red Sea. She stopped three feet away and lowered her weapon to his chest. "Lucid, I presume. Get back into the SUV. We're going to Samana Village to find my dad." Rachel had let it slip that Bo and Kaden were being held in a secure location there.

Lucid smiled smugly. "I'lll do no such thing."

Bailey pointed the assault rifle straight up and fired three shots. "I won't ask again. Piper, Katarina—and Ling, you can come, too."

Bailey had heard about Samana Village, a resort town visited daily by thousands of American tourists, but she had never come close to visiting. Except for the shuttle buses to the Fantasy Theater, the western half of the island had always been off-limits to the girls—until now.

Lucid and Bailey entered the SUV. Piper, Katarina, and Ling piled in after them.

♀ ♂

SAYEED TURNED TO ANNIKA. "I just realized Samana Cay's AI records every conversation that takes place in their facilities. Fantasy Theater. The Bliss Lounge. The Lab. There's a record of everything."

Annika stepped over. "Really? Let me look at that." She studied the interface on his screen for a minute. "So, it looks like not only are the conversations recorded, they're transcribed."

Sayeed squinted at the text files at the bottom of each "session" the AI records. "Wait. Isn't that a universal search option?"

"You're right!" Annika's voice got excited. She raced back to her desk and scribbled down terms she'd come across in some of her findings. *Immersion Bay. Camp Defiance. Project Ezekiel.*

She dashed back to Sayeed's station. "Try this one. Exact matches for 'Fantasy Strain.'"

Sayeed entered the term. Three results popped up on screen. They began scanning through each video to get to the exact spot where it was mentioned.

♀ ♂

KADEN, Bo, and Nico charged the six guards, who still seemed flummoxed that their smart rifles wouldn't fire. Kaden was the first to reach two of the guards who'd been on one knee.

The first one had four inches and sixty pounds on her, plus two tattoos of naked girls on his neck. *Tat Man.* The second one had a face like an anaconda—flat nose, powerful jawline, not much happening behind the beady eyes. *Snake Man.*

Tat Man swung his rifle butt up and aimed at her right temple. She blocked it away with her right arm before grabbing it on the carry-through and bringing it down hard enough to knock his beret off. Snake Man had a similar idea, holding his SCAR assault rifle by the barrel and bringing it down like a hammer. A swift side step averted disaster.

She glanced to her left and saw Bo and Nico mixing it up with the four other guards. Bo had a more traditional boxer's stance, punching and jabbing, while Nico resorted to moves they'd worked on in the ring. Both stood dangerously close to the edge of the hundred-foot precipice.

Tat Man flung his SCAR to the ground, perhaps figuring the rifle was busted. He unclipped the nylon sheath on his belt and flashed what looked like a Snake Eye tactical combat knife with a gold steel blade—she'd almost bought one of these babies for a past op. Used properly, it could slice straight through to deep muscle tissue, or the serrated top could tear open an opponent's neck with a sudden upward motion. But Tat Man was wielding it completely wrong, tucking his thumb beneath his index finger like he was about to play a damn game of Mumblety-peg.

She gave Snake Man a hard side kick to the right kidney so she could focus on this other fool. Tat Man could get lucky with a wild jab of his knife. She figured she had two seconds tops, so she surprised him with a lightning-fast first strike: a close-range push kick to the chest, true as a straight punch, that caught him off guard and knocked the wind out of him. She followed that a second later with a roundhouse kick to his upper left torso with her right shin, well away from the knife, powering the blow with her pent-up rage. The first blow staggered him backward and the second strike knocked him off balance.

Yes, girls can kick.

He was as big and stubborn as a mule and he came charging at her. She had no choice but to dive for the SCAR and hope the keypad would validate her fingerprint in less than a second. It did. She lay on her back and got off three quick rounds to Tat Man's chest as he fell, knife in hand, on top of her with a final expression of shock and astonishment.

It was her third kill today. Maybe not her last.

Her eyes moved from the dead body to the crowd just beyond. A sea of bystanders stood there with their smartphones recording the real-life action sequence.

"Get the hell out of here!" Kaden fired her weapon into the air. The bystanders screamed and began to scatter. Including moms with traumatized two-year-olds.

Don't want these civilians in the line of fire.

Snake Man had been about to charge her, but the SCAR changed his mind. He beat a quick retreat toward the SWAT-like black police van that was now pulling up twenty yards away. Five, six men poured from the back. From both sides of the vehicle, they fired their old-fashioned handguns. Glocks, probably. She heard the thwack of impacting bullets and realized it was the sound of rounds hitting the now-abandoned television cameras.

Kaden was hoping she wouldn't have to do this, but these guys couldn't take a hint. She moved into a firing position and strafed the police van. She zeroed the SCAR in an unsupported position and marveled at how insanely accurate it was.

A moment later, a guard emerged from the van's rear, preparing to toss an M84 flashbang at her. But she saw he was making a major miscalculation. A flashbang is different from an ordinary fragmentation grenade. He tried to be cute and cook off *one second, two seconds*, but by then it exploded in his hand. *He'll lose two or three fingers minimum.*

She scrambled to her feet, keeping low. She saw Nico had knocked the first guard unconscious. Nico lunged and grabbed the spare SCAR on the ground. The second guard pulled out his spare firearm but Nico was faster and wasted him with a good, long burst. Then he turned to the police van and sprayed it with half his magazine.

She turned back and saw Bo was holding his own right there at the edge of the cliff. She ran toward him, ready to toss him a SCAR when she spotted it. A red laser beam zeroing on Bo's chest. The next seconds seemed to happen in slow motion.

She yelled, "Get down!" She dove to her right to knock Bo out of the line of fire. Saw the shooter take aim from the left corner of her eye. Stayed on her feet as Bo fell backward onto the big pile of rope that fed the rope line. Saw Bo's opponent smile, grab her shoulders, and shove her backward.

She plunged over the cliffside.

59

Samana Cay

Annika and Sayeed could barely believe what they'd uncovered. They originally zeroed in on the trove of compromising material about the Chairman. His real name. His confession about killing his parents. His fantasy simulation with a young woman.

But they keep digging, based on that drone video and the Ezekiel file summary that Kaden had sent them earlier. And now they unearthed the truth about Project Ezekiel—its massive scope and ghastly objective.

Annika called Sayeed over to her station at B Collective. "I think it's ready."

Sayeed looked pale. "I'm still shaking."

She nodded. "Before we send this video out to the world, we need to try to stop Volkov. Let's start with Samana Cay's TV stations. We exposed Volkov's identity and the fact he killed his parents. Now everyone needs to hear the details of what they're planning to do with the Fantasy Strain. "

Annika took the new video footage, enhanced the audio, and

added subtitles so there would be no mistaking what was being discussed. But she was proudest of her next hack.

She managed to sub out Volkov's avatar during his video chat with Bashir about the Fantasy Strain. Instead, the split screen now showed footage of Volkov himself speaking while seated at his computer—a recording he didn't know was taking place. His COO, Lucid, kept a private folder with recordings of everything the Chairman said and did in his executive suite. It wasn't pretty, but it was Volkov in the flesh talking in his own voice.

The conversation took place nine days ago. Annika and Sayeed watched as the video went out over Samana Cay's airwaves:

Incognito: "How soon will the Fantasy Strain be ready?"

Bashir: "We'll have the results of the initial clinical trials in a few days. If all goes well, we'll be ready to scale up production."

Incognito: "Excellent news."

Bashir: "I want there to be no mistake. This is germ warfare. A worldwide pandemic targeting a subset of one gender. This strain has the potential of killing every woman and girl in the United States, United Kingdom, and Western Europe. Once it's unleashed, *half a billion* women and girls may die."

Incognito: "An unfortunate but necessary sacrifice to bring the West to its knees. If you have any objections to Project Ezekiel, state them now."

Bashir: "You know I am loyal to you, Chairman. I have no love of Western whores. I am ready to do what is necessary."

Annika and Sayeed looked at each other, somber and angry. Sayeed lowered his head. "They're barbarians."

"They're freaks," Annika said. "Let's get this footage to the NSA and CIA."

♀ ♂

VOLKOV HOWLED and raged at the sinking of the *Seaduction*. And this latest video feed that revealed their plans—another setback! But it only made him more determined to charge ahead with Phase Two of Project Ezekiel.

He pressed the one button on his command console he'd never pressed before. It had taken him and his visual arts department months to program this. He grabbed the pair of smartglasses sitting on the corner of his desk and slipped them on. He peered out the window.

The Four Horsemen of the Apocalypse dominated the Western sky. Four forbidding figures—Conquest, War, Famine, and Death—rode their enormous white, red, black, and pale horses, as if performing a dance of death for mankind.

Thousands of people would see it—anyone on the island or at sea with smartglasses. Would it stir awe and rapture? Panic and mayhem? It did not matter.

It marked the beginning of the Transition.

He moved closer to the window to admire the spectacle. The Four Horsemen—designed true to the last detail—come at last to deliver a fearsome justice, signaling that the End of Days was nigh. He'd memorized the passages from the Book of Revelation long ago:

Now I watched when the Lamb opened one of the seven seals, and I heard one of the four living creatures say with a voice like thunder, "Come!" And I looked, and behold, a white horse! And its rider had a bow, and a crown was given to him, and he came out conquering, and to conquer. When he opened the second seal, I heard the second living creature say, "Come!" And out came another horse, bright red. Its rider was permitted to take peace from the earth, so that people should slay one another, and he was given a great sword. When he opened the third seal, I heard the third living creature say, "Come!" And I looked, and behold, a black horse! And its rider had a pair of scales in his hand.

When he opened the fourth seal, I heard the voice of the fourth living creature say, "Come!" And I looked, and behold, a pale horse! And its rider's name was Death, and Hades followed him. And they were given authority over a fourth of the earth, to kill with sword and with famine and with pestilence and by wild beasts of the earth.

THE TRANSITION WAS UPON US. The *Seaduction* may be burning, but there were still large quantities of the Fantasy Strain to be loosed upon the land. He called Adam Bashir.

"Before my jet takes off, I want somebody on your team to add as many containers of treated water to the cargo hold as possible."

"I'll see to it, Chairman," Bashir said.

Volkov hung up and stormed out the door. One final thing to do before leaving the island. *Make sure Kaden Baker is dead.*

♀ ♂

AT THE MOMENT the swarthy guardsman flung Kaden backward off the edge of the precipice, she saw Bo react. Sprawled on the ground, he grabbed a coil of rope lying just to his right and hurled it directly toward her. It barely had enough heft to reach her. She lurched her hand toward the lifeline.

As she began to fall down the sheer cliffside, it astonished her how her mind went to the most mundane details of her plight. The length of the rope (at least twenty feet). Its width (thinner than a mooring line, thicker than a jump rope). Its makeup (nylon fibers) and strength (braided construction of eight strands, she guessed).

The likelihood she'd survive this? (Remote.)

She stretched out, clutched the strand of rope, wrapped it tight around her hand, and held on tight as she smashed onto the side of the cliff, a good twelve feet below the precipice. She heard Nico roar an epithet followed by the now familiar burst of the SCAR—but now in friendly hands. Moments later, a swarthy guardsman's body swooped past her on the way to the rocky shoals a hundred feet below.

Bo peered over the edge. His arms held onto the rope but there was no way he could lift her up. "Kaden! Hold on!"

She held tight with both hands, but already her palms were burning and her injured shoulder straining at supporting the weight of her entire body without being able to get any footing.

She looked over her right shoulder and saw a billow of thick smoke rising from a ship in the far distance. *Viper's doing?* She turned to check over her left shoulder and saw the Swift boat, which had been a distant speck only minutes before, drawing closer. Her heart sank as she heard the burst of the .50-caliber machine gun coming from the water and strafing the cliffside a good twenty feet below. The only saving grace was that the boat was still at least a quarter mile away.

But one shot was all it would take.

"I can't lift her by myself!" Bo yelled to Nico, who sounded busy fending off the guards in the SWAT van. That's when she heard Nico unleash his war cry and lay down a steady stream of hellfire as he charged the van. Or that's what she imagined was happening.

She tried again to shimmy up the rope by herself but managed only a few inches more. The wind buffeted her body and twirled her around like a marionette as she struggled to find a small foothold on the rock face. She saw her hands were beginning to bleed.

Another report of gunfire from the Swift boat. This time it struck five feet below her. *One more calibration and that would be the end.*

She looked up and saw Bo continuing to struggle to hold her aloft. "Kaden, trust me, we're going to get you out of this."

She took a deep breath and struggled to stay dangling there. Might be her last words. "I trust you, Dad."

He looked down and smiled. "You called me 'Dad.'"

But a moment later she looked up again and Bo was gone. She had no idea what was happening up there. No idea whether Nico was shot or Bailey was in custody or if Viper was still on the loose. She managed to stop whirling, but this was no climbing rope and doubted she could hold on for more than another minute.

Amelia appeared in a corner of her smart contacts—still in Wi-Fi range—but Kaden didn't have her earpiece and couldn't sign. Amelia detected her body's stress signals and signed an urgent message. *Rock outcropping … your two o'clock.* Kaden looked up and to her right and saw the narrow opening on the side of the hill. She shimmied up two torturous feet, swallowing the pain, and she squeezed her arm in there to support part of her weight—enough to give her a few precious seconds of relief from the pull of gravity.

She looked behind her. The Swift boat was getting closer and she could see two small figures examining her with their binoculars, no doubt discussing the best strategy to take her out.

"Kaden, hold on! We're pulling you up." Bo's voice.

She began to move. Two feet. Four. Six. Nearly to the top. Behind her, the Swift boat strafed the side of the hill, blasting into the limestone walls where she'd been hanging ten seconds before.

Kaden reached the top and grabbed Bo's hand. "I've got you," he said. He pulled her up and over, and she now saw the rope, frayed to almost nothing, tied to the back of the police van with Nico at the wheel.

They hurried off the precipice and out of the Swift boat's line of fire. The remaining Guardians were either dead or wounded.

She was sore as hell, but she'd be all right. She checked in with Red Team Zero home base. Annika shared the latest updates about Viper and Incognito. They'd learned his real name. *Maxim Volkov.*

"Good," she told Annika. "We'll need that for his obituary." She turned to Bo. "We've got to find Bailey."

"Where do we start?"

As if on cue, a black SUV barreled down the road and came to a screeching halt next to them. Kaden, Bo, and Nico trained their SCARs at the doors. The side entrance flew open and Bailey spilled out, holding the same model SCAR. She hugged Bo and then trained her weapon on Lucid, who sat impassively in the back seat.

Kaden looked down at her prison garb and the X across her heart. "This might raise a question or two. Let's ditch these prison jumpsuits and find the others."

And, she silently added, *kill this son of a bitch Incognito.*

♀ ♂

VOLKOV DONNED his favorite motorcycle helmet, buttoned his Titan sport jacket, packed his favorite semi sidearm, and headed out on his Harley. He buzzed Lucid to ask about the status of the prisoners' execution. The call went to voicemail, so he called up Lucid's Eyecam and saw Bailey Finnerty leveling an assault rifle at Lucid's chest. He immediately regretted he'd shown such compassion toward her.

Next he tried his unit commander at Devil's Point. Radio silence. Were Kaden Baker and her father disposed of or not? He couldn't get Lucid to order up another detachment of Guardians. *Do I have to handle everything myself?*

He exited the corporate campus and hit cruising speed as an idea began to take form. He had one last card to play.

♀ ♂

KADEN, Bo, and Nico crowded into the SUV alongside Lucid, Bailey, and three of the other missing girls. They stopped at a clothing shop leading into Samana Village and swapped out their prison garb for tropical-friendly civvies—olive-colored shorts and drab T-shirts that wouldn't raise attention. Kaden also stopped at an electronics shop next store and got a new earpiece so she could make calls over Wi-Fi and talk with Amelia again.

She paused before re-entering the SUV and saw she had a new voicemail from Annika. She called.

Annika sounded excited. "We just got a call from Paul Redman. We know where the others are! Looks like they were all being moved as one big group from Immersion Bay to a new location on the western half of the island."

"How did he get a phone?"

"He didn't. He's been wearing a smart jacket. There's a sensor built into the cuffs. When Redman's group got put back with the others, Tosh got the sensor to connect to the Internet."

"So I can reach them?"

"Think so. Tosh got a rudimentary audio bridge working. I'll send you the IP address."

Bo came up to her side. "What's happening?"

"Looks like all the others are in one place now."

"Where?"

"Amelia, ping this IP address and see if we can get an audio connection."

Amelia's voice came through the earpiece nice and clear. "Roger that. So glad you're all right. Connecting now."

She heard a high-pitched melodic ping once, twice.

"Hello?" Redman's voice.

"Paul, it's Kaden."

She heard Redman hush the others. "Isn't this the damndest thing, turning the cuff of my jacket into a phone?"

"Are you all there? Where are you?"

"Yeah, we're all here. We're locked inside something called the Fantasy Theater."

She heard Alex's voice edge closer. "It's part of Fantasy Live, in the resort complex just southeast of Samana Village."

Kaden looked at Bo. "How do I know this is really you guys? We were already burned once today." Hard to tell reality from fantasy on Samana Cay.

"Let's go around the room," Redman said. Tosh, Carlos, Judy, Alice, Charlie, and Alex all sounded off in their familiar voices.

"That's not good enough." Kaden thought for a moment. "Let me ask you something the island's AI wouldn't know. Carlos, what did you have for breakfast on our final day in Zug?"

A pause—then Carlos's voice came in loud and clear as she pictured him leaning close to Redman's cuff. "Pastries, yogurt, cheese, Butter-Zopf bread. And it was delicious."

She looked at Bo. Her voice cracked with relief. "It's them." Then to Carlos and the others: "We're on our way."

aden, Bo, Nico, Bailey, and the girls pulled up to the

aden, Bo, Nico, Bailey, and the girls pulled up to the

60

Samana Cay

Kaden, Bo, Nico, Bailey, and the girls pulled up to the entrance of Fantasy Live Resort and parked. They decided it would be safer if they didn't split up, so everyone came along, including the driver and Lucid, who could get them a clean entrance and not set off any alarms.

The theater was a long, modern metal and glass structure, the largest building in sight. After Kaden jammed her SCAR into his back, Lucid waved his hand across the electronic touchpad at the northern entrance and the door whooshed open. A computerized voice said, "Welcome, Lucid and guests."

They stepped inside what looked like a dark lobby. "Where are the lights?" Bo asked.

From behind, they heard the door lock click into place. Nico went up to the door, his big frame silhouetted against the day's dying light. "I don't like being locked in."

Neither do I, Kaden thought. "Where's Lucid? Get him to open it back up."

They all looked around in the fragile light. Lucid and his

driver were gone. Bailey checked the back of the room. "Inside doors are locked," she reported. "He's not here."

A set of low-level lights flicked on around them, followed by a pair of bright lights above, revealing a slender white control booth. It hung twenty feet overhead and jutted into the lobby like a theater balcony. A plexiglass pane running across its length made it easy to see inside. She recognized the two figures.

Maxim Volkov and Paul Redman.

Volkov's voice came from all directions. "Good of you to join us."

Redman looked down on them, arms folded across his jacket. Volkov wore a gold and black helmet that made him look like one half of that old musical group, Daft Punk. But she doubted he was here to spin some jams.

Kaden nodded to Nico to take out the front entrance with his SCAR. "They know we're here," she said.

Nico released the safety on his smart rifle and pointed it at the glass entrance. "Stand back!" He pulled the trigger. Silence. "Not working!"

Kaden stepped next to him and aimed her smart rifle. Again, nothing.

A second set of lights appeared above and to their right, this time illuminating a booth with the same plexiglass pane but no computer console inside. Tosh, Carlos, Judy, Alex, Alice, and Charlie stood inside—the entire rest of their crew. Judy spotted her daughter Piper next to Nico and banged on the window, calling out for her, but the soundproof room swallowed her cries.

"Mom!" Piper called out plaintively, stepping closer to the soundproof booth.

"Silence!" Volkov commanded. "They cannot hear you."

Volkov grabbed his helmet and lifted it off. He set it down on a narrow table, smoothed back his hair, and ran his fingers through his gray-brown beard. "No point in sustaining the legend any longer. Incognito is dead. Maxim Volkov is reborn."

He held up a USB drive and showed it off. "Whoever controls the network controls destiny. Whoever controls the network controls reality. And the reality is that thirty minutes ago, one of our engineers noticed your flash drive in the Data Center. He reset the admin privileges and took back control."

Kaden's eyes swept over the faces of the others in her group. Bailey, Bo, Nico. And Ling, Piper, and Katarina, the three girls who'd breathed a few minutes of hope before it all came crashing down. They looked devastated.

Volkov turned toward Redman. "Paul Redman, a former silent partner in the Compact, has stepped up and shown his loyalty. As discussed, a large slice of your country, from Miami to Dallas, is your reward."

"That's generous of you," Redman said.

Kaden looked up and saw Alice Wong crying, "No! No!" as she slammed her palm against the plexiglass.

Kaden projected her voice across the lobby. "Why, Redman? Why'd you sell us out?"

Redman looked to Volkov as if seeking permission. Volkov smiled and gave the slightest nod.

Redman peered across the lobby at Alice and Alex. "I do regret the way this turned out, Alex. Once I found out Alice sent you on an undercover assignment, I knew I had to intervene."

And whisk their group of operatives into the waiting hands of that Samana Cay Swift boat, Kaden thought.

She saw Alex cursing Redman, jabbing his finger, his face a mask of rage. But the lobby was deathly silent.

"And you, Alice," Redman went on. "Your predecessor asked a lot of questions, too. She signed an NDA so she could never discuss any of the tips about movers and shakers that poured into the newsroom—scandals involving CEOs, governors, presidents. Buying the rights to freelance investigative journalism and burying the stories proved to be a vastly more lucrative business model than actually running them. My vault is overflowing. But I never thought I'd have to do a catch and kill with a reporter on my own staff."

"Enough of the past," Volkov cut him off. "In a matter of days, as soon as we deliver the final payload, civilization will get a hard reboot. Our past lives, past identities will no longer matter. The Transition will cleanse the West and prepare us for the Reset."

Volkov looked down on his captives. He bent forward to enter commands on his console, cutting off the audio feed. He said something to Redman. They turned and exited the booth.

Fifteen minutes passed with no movement around them. They explored every inch of the lobby but found no weak spots they could exploit.

From the back of the room, a doorframe lit up a bright blue. A guardsman stepped through the doorway, followed by another and another—ten in all. Half carried SCAR assault rifles, half were armed with military-style handguns, and all were dressed in military fatigues and berets. They formed a circle around Kaden.

"Kaden Baker, come with us," ordered the guard she took to be the unit commander.

"I'm not going anywhere." She thrust her head back.

"All right. We'll take your sister instead." The commander waved his gun at Bailey. "Come on, let's go."

"Stop!" Kaden saw she was out of options. "I'll go."

She followed the first five guards through the blue door while the remaining guards followed close behind.

The Guardians led her through a narrow hallway. They emerged in front of a large clear machine that reminded her of a TSA full-body scanner. "Step inside, hands over your head. Then hold still," the commander said.

She stepped into the cylinder and watched as a thin red light scanned her from head to foot, zipping up and down with a buzzing sound every three or four seconds. She felt nothing. After a half minute they ordered her to step through a security gate. Two of the soldiers followed on her heels.

Kaden looked around at what appeared to be a waiting room. A severe-looking woman, dressed like an executive assistant and wearing too much rouge makeup, removed the earpiece from Kaden's ear and placed it on a side table. She handed Kaden a neatly pressed dress and shopping bag. "Put this on." She opened the door to a changing room.

Not much time. The Wi-Fi in here was still good, so Kaden began signing commands to Amelia.

Amelia, get word to Viper about all the captives being held in the Fantasy Theater.

Amelia replied, *Message sent!*

Thanks. Next, is there any way to get eyes on the room I'm about to enter?

Let me work on it. When we had control over the servers, I created an alias as a systems engineer as a backup in case we lost our super admin privileges. Should be able to log in. Also downloaded the schematics to all the buildings at Fantasy Live Resort as a precautionary measure.

Kaden thought, *Good thing I set up those proactive protocols for Amelia.*

Two quick raps on the door. "Is everything all right in there? He's waiting."

Damn! "Just a minute, almost there!"

She shimmied out of her shorts and peeled off her T-shirt. Then she slipped into the outfit, a stylish, low-cut red cocktail dress with an Eastern European flair, a bare back, padded shoulders, and a wrap front that ran up high and exposed most of her legs. She plucked out the items from the shopping bag: sheer stockings and a pair of black strappy high heels. She checked herself in the mirror. She looked like the hostess for some Russian dacha dinner party or something.

She stepped out of the dressing room. The no-nonsense

assistant, Rouge One, handed her a stick of red lipstick—and made clear it wasn't a suggestion. As she watched Kaden apply it, she said in a monotone, "The prisoners. Your full cooperation is required for their survival."

Kaden replied with a glare. Then Rouge One handed Kaden a pair of lightweight designer glasses with tiger-stripe frames. Kaden put them on—a pair of smartglasses over her smart contacts.

I'll go along with their game for now.

Rouge One led her through the next door into the main room. She turned and left, replaced by the two Guardians. Kaden surveyed the room. The space was large and dusky, furnished with antique tables, chairs, chests, mirrors, and lit up by table lamps with smoky glass shades and bronze bases that had seen better days. She tapped down her glasses on the bridge of her nose and saw that the chairs, table, and chests were real but half the artworks and antiques in the room weren't really there. *Mixed reality.*

The guards came up beside her. "He wants you in the Throne chair," the first one said, training his Glock on her. He walked ahead and pulled an ancient-looking wooden chair out from the end of a long walnut table. She walked slowly to the oversize chair and sat, pressing her back against an engraving of Adam and Eve with a serpent. The second guard stepped behind her and dropped the items he was carrying to the floor. Leather straps.

Don't have many options here. I'll let this play out a little longer.

They tied her up. The first strap bound her waist to the back of the chair. Next they bound her thighs and ankles. Guard One tied the leather restraints tight around her wrists.

"You sure you don't want to tie her arms behind her back?" Guard Two asked.

Guard One smirked. "I have my instructions. 'Bind her hands but don't tie them to the chair.' Guess he wants to make it sporting." He paused in front of her eyes. "You'll behave, won't you?"

She spat in his face. He raised his hand to strike her when Guard Two said, "Leave that to the boss."

They finished tying her up. They bound her body tight with her legs slightly spread apart. Guard One repositioned her chair to three o'clock—a ninety degree angle to the table. He stepped over to an ancient-looking chest in the corner, opened it, removed three items, and set them on the table.

A blindfold. A long pair of sharp-edged scissors. A small covered glass jar containing a clear liquid.

"That will be all." Maxim Volkov's voice kicked across the length of the room. "You guards, leave now."

Guard One objected, "But sir, your safety—"

"My safety is assured. You're dismissed."

The men saluted and left. Kaden craned her neck to her far right and watched Volkov moving toward her. He was wearing what might be some kind of gray Victorian smoking jacket. No helmet in sight, but he was wearing something else: a pair of blue rubber goggles. He carried a shot glass and a bottle of vodka and set them on the table.

He dropped down to one knee directly in front of her as if genuflecting to the Madonna.

"You look magnificent."

"What do you want?" she asked.

"Remarkable. Even the voice is dead on. I'll have to congratulate Lucid on the fidelity to detail."

She studied him. *A man who had never fully formed. A man still in search of something. Redemption? Revenge?* She checked the Internet reception in here with her smart contacts. Strong.

Volkov rose, went to the table, poured himself a drink. "Thank you for the body scan. I'll be able to re-create this experience over and over again."

Her wrists were bound tight and she could feel her fingers

start to go numb, but she kept quiet. *Disrupting the fantasy might be dangerous.*

He pulled a chair out from the table, sat opposite her, and placed his hands on her knees. He stroked his hands atop her silk stockings nearly to her panties.

Amelia appeared in the bottom left corner of her field of vision and began signing. She had eyes in the room—there were five different video cams positioned in unlikely hiding spots.

Volkov met her eyes with a level gaze that seemed to mix hate and desire. "The less you say, the better. After all, what is there to say after all these years?"

He removed his hands, sat back in his chair, downed another shot of vodka. He stood, moved next to her right side, began stroking her hair. He grasped her smartglasses with both hands, set them on the table. Then he picked up the silk blindfold and slipped it over her head. *Looks like he has this all game-planned.*

He leaned down next to her ear. "Do you remember our compact? Our little secret? I was only twelve at the time."

He slipped his right hand beneath her low-cut dress and cupped her left breast. He pressed his rancid lips over hers, pressing in, scratching his rough beard against her chin.

Kaden forced her eyes open beneath the blindfold. It was dark, but she saw Amelia lit up in the lower left corner. She was signing again.

I can't access enough processing power to generate a full 3D visualization from your point of view. But I can give you a black-and-white illustrated sequence in real time. It would resemble those old A-ha pencil-sketch music videos from the eighties—never mind, before your time. Blink twice if you want that turned on.

Kaden didn't know which videos Amelia was talking about, but she blinked twice. Immediately she saw a live-action simulation: the outline of Volkov leaning toward her, holding her hands down with one hand, now groping at her left breast with the other.

She wouldn't beg, but this had already gone too far. She heaved his torso backward with her bound hands. "Stop! No!"

"No? It's not up to you anymore!" He slunk away, maybe wounded by her act of rejection. She couldn't see his expression. But she saw a rough simulation of his head, eyes, beard, and body as he straightened and paused beside the table, as if trying to decide between the vodka and the other items.

He reached down, picked up the scissors, made three quick snipping sounds with it.

"Do you remember what you did with these when you used to sneak into my room?" He shook his head and lowered the scissors. "No matter. We can replay this scene with a new girl who'll get the fantasy right. Let's finish this. I have a world to conquer."

He leaned down and carefully unscrewed the lid of the glass jar. An acrid odor assaulted her—the overwhelming smell of rotten eggs. She hadn't smelled a concoction like this since chemistry class. *Sulfuric acid.*

He painstakingly picked up the open container with his right hand, still holding the scissors in his left hand. He looked down on her as she sat there, blindfolded and docile. He gave a quick feint, a head fake, as if to see if she could detect his movements. She remained still as an ice sculpture.

"I should have done this a long, long time ago." He brought his right arm backward, as if cocking a trigger, still grasping the glass of acid in his right hand.

At the exact moment he began to drive the glass of acid forward, she raised her cupped hands and intercepted the container. Before he could react, she summoned all her strength and propelled it upward, splashing it onto the right side of his face—the good side. *Until now.*

Volkov howled in agony. She dropped the container to the floor. His knees buckled, bringing his body forward, closer to her. His free hand went to his face as another shriek of anguish escaped his throat.

"I'll kill you, you bitch!"

He moved to switch the scissors to his dominant hand. *A mistake.* He was right on top of her now, inches away, so close she could smell the scent of burning skin. Volkov fumbled to get a solid grip even as he tried to drive the scissors down into her chest. She grabbed his arm with her bound hands.

Caught you.

She couldn't see his expression, but she pictured his face in his rubber goggles, contorted into a look of surprise at how strong she was, how he'd underestimated her.

He tried to pull away, but she grabbed his fingers, still curled around the end of the scissors, and bent them backward, freeing the handle from his grasp. She couldn't insert her own fingers into the handle while her wrists were bound, so she wrapped her palm around the base and jabbed the blade upward with a violent jerk. She felt the tip of the shears enter Volkov's neck just above the Adam's apple.

This is for Gabriel. She pushed the shears deeper.

A river of warm blood gushed out and onto her chest. He sank onto her lap but brought his hands up to around her balled fist in one last attempt to ward off further damage. But she wasn't through.

This is for all the girls. She drove the scissors farther up, deep into his skull cavity. Volkov let out a sickening death gurgle. One final thrust and his body went limp.

She took a deep breath to calm herself. She pulled out the scissors, opened the shears, and used them to slice away at the leather strap wound around her wrists. She was worried Volkov's howl would bring the guards, but not so far. She ripped her blindfold off and removed the last of the restraints.

She kicked off her high heels and looked down at her blood-soaked dress—a darker shade of red now. She opened the door to the waiting room. Empty. She spotted her bag of clothes in the corner and quickly changed.

The door to the hallway opened. As Guard One entered, she grabbed his arm to immobilize the Glock he was clutching. She drove a knee high into his solar plexus. His uniformed body bent forward. She interlaced her fingers and brought a double fist down with a brutal fury at the base of his neck. He crumpled to the carpet. Guard Two was a second behind but a second too late. She grabbed the Glock—the good old-fashioned fingerprint-free variety—and pumped three shots into Guard Two's chest. The rounds sent him sprawling lifeless to the floor.

She went to the end table and found her earpiece. She plunked it back into her ear and called Viper.

"What's the situation?" she asked.

"Glad you're all right," Viper said. He had enough firepower to keep a small army at bay, but he was just one man, and it was iffy whether he'd be able to elude capture.

"You got Amelia's message?" she asked. "Can you get us out?"

"Already on it. Just say the word."

"Do it now."

Three seconds later she heard the beautiful sound of C4 blasts being detonated outside.

"Keep this line open. Keep me updated." She swept into the hallway and raced toward the front of the building. She found a stairway leading upstairs and took it.

"Status?" she barked.

"Sorry, busy here," Viper said. She heard frantic voices on the other end. "All captives from the lobby are out."

She twisted around a corner and continued running down the corridor toward a door at the far end. "I'm going for the others," she said.

She reached the door, tried the handle. Locked. "Tosh, Carlos, you in there?"

"Yeah! Kaden, that you?" Carlos's voice.

"Step back." She waited two heartbeats and fired two shots.

She kicked open the door and saw them. Tosh. Carlos. Judy. Alex. Alice. Charlie. Everyone accounted for.

They followed her down the hallway and raced down the staircase before they spilled into the lobby and then out the Fantasy Theater's big new Viper Exit.

Bo, Bailey—everyone was together now. The two tribes had merged. The group looked shaken but no worse for wear.

"Follow me," Viper said. She was glad someone else was taking the lead. She was out of gas and the painkillers had worn off.

They raced down the hillside keeping low, dashing for cover when they spotted guards and Viper had to clear the way with short bursts from his HK416. They made it to the spot along the south shore where Viper hid his Boston Whaler in the jungle undergrowth. They boarded the ship. Bo, Nico, and Viper released the stern, bow, and spring lines tied to trees and shrubs, and they set off.

Viper checked his comms, nodded, reported back to the group. "Red Team Zero home base says satellite imagery shows the Swift boat sweeping along the north part of the island, biting on some of the decoys I set up there." He steered the ship toward the east end of the island.

"Shouldn't we be heading out to sea?" Bo asked.

Viper kept quiet for a few minutes as they cruised along the underbelly of the island a safe distance from shore. "One last piece of business." He squeezed Judy and Piper in his arms. "No, this isn't the business I meant." He let out a full-throated laugh—the first real laugh of joy she'd heard in days.

After another minute he let go of the ship's wheel and picked up what looked like a radio detonator. As they passed the Plant and the Lab, they watched from a quarter mile off shore as Viper set off the stacks of C4 bricks or cakes he'd set around the complex. The walls of the buildings collapsed in a ball of flames, black smoke belching into the twilight sky.

Kaden hugged Bo and Bailey as they watched the fireball consume the Lab. She knew nothing about what Viper had carried out on this part of the island. But she liked people who were proactive.

Viper retook the wheel, opened up the engine, and headed out to deep waters. He called over his shoulder, "*Now* we can go home."

EPILOGUE

Off the coast of the Bahamas, next morning

K aden sipped her orange juice and smiled at Bailey, who was resting her head on Bo's shoulder as they neared the port of Nassau. She stood at the stern and watched the wake left by the no-frills Boston Whaler fishing boat —much more to her liking than a crooked billionaire's luxury yacht.

The Whaler paused in international waters off Samana Cay until they'd gotten confirmation that the U.S. Navy would send a vessel to bring home the kidnapped girls. Annika releasing a video of the prison camp at Immersion Bay might have had something to do with that. Medical staff would be on board to help remove some of the girls' permanent contact lenses. So, there'd be a happy ending for the traumatized parents who'd soon be reunited with their missing daughters. The young women would need counseling, and Annika had siphoned some of Volkov's millions into a victims' fund.

The Centers for Disease Control and Prevention was sending a team out to Samana Cay and to Nassau to meet with Viper, who'd smuggled two large containers of the vaccine and the cure onto their boat. The compromised drinking water systems were in the process of being shut down.

Other things didn't sit so right with her.

Lucid and Redman, both last seen in the lobby yesterday, had escaped. What court would hold them to account? The members of the Compact were likely to escape justice as well. She and Annika planned to circulate the video of the Compact, but these underworld figures were likely to go about their business controlling governments and public policy from the shadows. And what were Alice and Alex supposed to do? They seemed distraught at the prospect of returning to work for *Axom*. How could anyone work for a publication whose owner belonged to an international crime syndicate?

One tiny bit of good news: Fantasy Live suspended its operations, at least for now, according to a text Evelyn sent to Alex. As for the locals who worked in Samana Village running little shops or working as tour guides—Kaden doubted they knew what was really going on. So late last night she arranged with Annika to use Amelia's system log-in to award every resident a 100,000 point "liberation bonus" if they volunteered to help set up a real government and a real currency that didn't incentivize obedience to a corrupt regime.

She plopped into one of the blue-and-white plastic seats across from her father and sister. Bo rose and walked across the small teak deck and sat next to her. "How are you holding up?"

"Pretty well, considering. Looking forward to getting back to normal life. Doing something boring. Shuffleboard, darts. Maybe navel-gazing on social media."

"Boring sounds good," Bo agreed.

She still had some healing to do after all the trauma of the past week. She had seven kills to her name during the past eight weeks. Yeah, she was tallying up her body count now. *Maybe I should carve seven notches in my bedpost at home. One for each scar.*

She'd set off with Bo hoping to find Bailey and the missing girls. And to fill in the blanks, find out more about herself. She'd arrived at a realization during her journey of self-discovery.

You can't erase your past—but you can't let it define you. You just have to invent yourself one day at a time. I'm just not sure if I like the work-in-progress.

"I got the paternity test back," she finally told Bo. "Want to know the results?"

"I already know." He smiled and put his arm around her shoulder.

"That still hurts." She was getting her shoulder back but had to pop four Advils this morning. He let go and she grinned.

Bailey strolled over and sat on her other side. "So you're finding out more about Dad," she said.

"He's kind of clueless with technology, isn't he?" Kaden teased.

"Totally," Bailey agreed. "Except maybe spy gadgets. We haven't had that talk yet."

"We have all the time in the world," Bo said.

"How's your mom doing?" Kaden asked her.

"Stable. Still in the hospital. I'll be seeing her tonight." Bailey leaned forward and began removing the necklace and pendant from around her neck. "Here, you can have this back."

"You should keep it. That charm turned out to be lucky." The least she could do for her new sis.

Bailey smiled and stroked the back of the pendant. "Thanks. So I can still reach you with this?"

"Sure. And not just when you're in trouble."

A device pinged in Bo's shirt pocket. He took out his phone and checked a new notification, thanks to Tosh setting up an Internet-at-sea connection for him.

"Anything good and boring?" Kaden asked.

Bo's expression turned grim. "Oh, no."

Bailey leaned forward, clasped her hands. "Pop, what is it?"

He paused as if deciding whether to be as transparent as his daughters now demanded. "Bad news." He turned to Kaden and handed her the phone with the message. "I was afraid of this. Kaden, you've been indicted for felony murder in Dallas County."

Bailey's face radiated concern. "Murder?" She looked at Kaden and asked, "Who *are* you?"

It was a damn good question.

CHARACTERS

*Amelia Earhart standing by her Lockheed Electra in
Natal, Brazil, in June 1937. Her plane disappeared over
the Pacific less than a month later.*

Here are the characters in *Catch and Kill* who appear in at least
two chapters:

Adam Bashir: Chief scientist at Samana Ventures

Alex Wyatt: Senior correspondent for the online news site
Axom who's posing as millionaire entrepreneur Andrew Bayless

Alice Wong: Editor-in-Chief of the online news site *Axom*

Amelia: The personalized artificial intelligence created by Kaden

Annika: Data operative/hacker and partner in Red Team Zero at B Collective in Brooklyn who also just began working for Bo on the side

Bailey Finnerty: One of the high school girls abducted during the Disappearance

Bo Finnerty: Off-book covert operative whose daughter Bailey was abducted

Carlos: Off-book field agent working for Bo

Charlie Adams: Reporter for the online news site *Axom* and Alex Wyatt's best friend

Compact: A cabal of billionaires bent on divvying up the world. Members include Incognito, Armenian-born Zaven Kasparian, Radovan Broz of Croatia, Jaco Kruger of South Africa, Walid Abdullin of Uzbekistan, Luis Alcivar of Ecuador, and Zhang Lee of China.

Deirdre Blackburn: Kaden's birth mother

Dražen Savić: Lucid's security chief

Eileen Mills: Bo Finnerty's ex-wife and Bailey's mother

Evelyn Gladstone: One of the millionaire guests at Fantasy Live

Gabriel: Kaden's boyfriend

Jacques Bouchard: French entrepreneur who's smitten with Kaden in Zug

Judy Matthews: Piper's mother and a translation specialist

Kaden: Data specialist/hacker with special skills training who prefers not to use a last name. Or pronouns, for that matter.

Katarina Gorka: Sixteen-year-old from Belarus being held captive at Immersion Bay

Ling: Bailey's best friend who was abducted during the Disappearance

Lucid: Chief operating officer of Samana Ventures and Incognito's right-hand man

Maurice Beauchamp: One of the millionaire guests at Fantasy Live

Maxim Volkov aka Chairman Incognito: Belarusian billionaire who purchased the island of Samana Cay and funded its mixed reality theme parks

Nico Johnson: Kaden's soulmate, workmate and fellow graduate of the special ops training facility Lost Camp

Rachel Torres: Alex's personal ambassador at Fantasy Live

Paul Redman: Publisher-owner of the online news site *Axom* and billionaire investor

Piper Matthews: One of the high school girls abducted during the Disappearance

Randolph Blackburn: Billionaire media and marketing mogul who is Kaden's grandfather

Sayeed: Data operative/hacker and partner in Red Team Zero at B Collective in Brooklyn

Tosh: Off-book analyst working for Bo

Viper Matthews: Piper's father and former Special Forces operator

HELP AN AUTHOR OUT

If you enjoyed *Catch and Kill*, please leave a review—just one sentence and a rating makes a big difference. If a new book doesn't get some love from readers, it can sink into oblivion quickly.

Please take a moment to review *Catch and Kill* on Amazon. I'd be enormously grateful. You'll find it here:

jdlasica.com/catch-review

FREE GIFT

Join the author's Best of Indie mailing list to get updates about free, high-quality ebooks in your favorite genre and to find out when Book 3 of the Shadow Operatives Series comes out at a special price.

BONUS: Join now and JD will send you his full-length ebook *Biohack* for free! Just tell him where to send it:

jdlasica.com/connect

FACT VS. FICTION

Catch and Kill is a high-tech thriller inspired by Michael Crichton, the king of the technothriller. Crichton, who died in 2008, once wrote that his books "are all about actual possibilities," not far-off science fiction. In the same way, *Biohack* and *Catch and Kill* blend today's reality with tomorrow's coming-to-a-mall-near-you plausibility.

So what's real and what's not yet real?

Let's start with the setting for much of the book. Samana Cay is a real place. Today it's an uninhabited island in the Bahamas, though so far no underworld figure has ponied up five billion dollars to buy it outright. Many historians believe Samana Cay was the first place in the New World where Christopher Columbus made landfall.

Now, onto the technology. While general artificial intelligence remains years away, there have been credible reports that researchers have already developed a self-aware computer in secrecy. You'll notice that many of Amelia's abilities are more limited, confined to search engine queries, communication, surveillance, or data-crunching tasks. Imagine souping up Amazon Echo or Alexa by tricking it out with vastly more processing power, giving it access to a global database, enabling it to self-improve, and giving it a personality.

All manner of science fiction movies and novels depict AIs from the playing-hard-to-get *Her* to Arthur C. Clarke's immortal HAL 9000. But I haven't yet seen a personal AI brought to life as a historical figure. (Have you?) Isn't it much more human to interact with an AI with a specific personality and distinctive appearance? I'm not sold on the idea that we'll all have robot sidekicks when we can more easily don a pair of smartglasses and interact in a cheerful way with the AI of our choice.

Would a world-class programmer like Kaden be able to create and personalize a custom AI such as Amelia Earhart? To my mind, it's not a question of if but of when.

How about Kaden's smart contact lenses? They're in development at a research lab near you. Already bionic contacts are here and not merely the stuff of sci-fi series. Prototypes of bionic contact lenses were first developed in 2011, with the first Wi-Fi enabled contact lens prototype developed at the University of Washington in 2016. Do they still have a long way to go to achieve what Kaden does in the book? Yes.

As for Lucid's video-enabled eye, that creepy technology has already made its way into reality. Digital Trends magazine reported in 2017 about "biohacks that blur the line between human and machine," including The Eyeborg Project, the brain-child of filmmaker Rob Spence. Spence wanted to deliver a point-of-view filming experience and thus created a prosthetic eye that captures video footage.

And CNET reported in November 2018: "Biohackers set on re-engineering better bodies are creating bionic eyes and sticking RFID chips under their skin to turn their limbs into credit cards and travel passes." It is, indeed, all the rage in Scandinavia.

What about Fantasy Live's real-time facial manipulation and simulations? It's on the way. Nvidia and other companies are working on technologies where you can take a person's face and manipulate it so you can't tell if the video you're watching is real or not.

What about cloning Alex's voice? In 2017, a Canadian artificial intelligence startup called Lyrebird debuted, showing off a new technology that can create realistic artificial voices from only a minute of sample audio. Google, Adobe, and other companies have similar projects in the works and the tech is getting better all the time.

Staying on tech: In a key scene with the Compact in Zug, I refer to spatial augmented reality face-masking techniques. I'm indebted to German computer scientist Oliver Bimber, who heads the Institute of Computer Graphics at the Johannes Kepler University Linz, Austria, who writes, "Changing the appearance of static or moving objects or people using projector-based AR technologies is possible within certain limits." He explains the science of SAR in detail, and I'll be happy to share his correspondence on the subject with readers.

Prof. James Chong at the University of York has been instrumental in helping me work out the logistics of how bad actors might use archaea, the oldest form of life on Earth. Advances in microbiology have ushered in an age when skilled technicians may be able to unleash personalized biological attacks based on people's genetic makeup.

Can a genetically modified pathogen be time delayed and lay dormant until it's externally triggered by the bad guys? "Theoretically, yes," Chong tells me. "In the scenarios you outlined, once you have got your engineered archaea into the human gut, then these genes would not be expressed unless they were triggered. This could be easily done through a food additive or by exploiting the so-called 'gut-brain axis,' which suggests that there are signaling pathways between the brain and the gut and vice versa. So if you make someone very stressed, then this could trigger a response from the gut microbes." Sorry about that, Eileen.

What about personalized targeting? Says Chong: "You could also target your archaea to only be activated by certain features of the host. There are certainly DNA markers that can apparently be used to determine differences in background – so Irish American compared to Italian American might be possible. And male vs. female is easy."

What else? FN Herstal makes the SCAR 17S Special operations forces Combat Assault Rifle. I don't know that a smart e-rifle is in the works, but proponents in the U.S. have been pushing for the adoption of smart guns that can detect authorized users. They're not ready for prime time today but may be in a few years' time.

If you have other questions about what's true and what's fiction in *Catch and Kill*, just drop me line.

– *J.D. Lasica*

ACKNOWLEDGMENTS

As with *Biohack*, the first entry in the Shadow Operatives series, *Catch and Kill* relied on a host of people much smarter than me to guide me through the science and technology tackled in the book so that I'm gliding close to terra firma and not floating off into the ether of pure speculation.

For my continued forays into biotech, I'm especially indebted to Prof. James Chong at the University of York, whose paper on paper in *Microbiology Society* on archaea as closet pathogens led me down the evil and scary path toward biological pathogens and personalized germ warfare.

Augmented and virtual reality play large roles in the novel, and I owe another lunch to Nicole Lazzaro, Sky Schuyler, and Shel Israel for their insights about mixed reality. Oliver Bimber at the Johannes Kepler University Linz in Austria offered valuable assistance on spatial augmented reality. Emily Olman helped inform the scenes set in Zug Valley, Switzerland. And Robert Scoble was helpful in my sorting out SLAM mapping.

I owe an immense gratitude to my first reader, Mary Lasica. Others lending their expert eyes at whipping the manuscript into shape included authors John Hindmarsh and Michael James

Gallagher, Isabel Draves, members of the Tri-Valley Writers including John Bluck and Gary Lea, launch team members Terry Temescu, Howard Greenstein, Clark Quinn, Shannon Clark, Judi Clark, and the excellent beta readers Jess Angers, E.G. Stone, Brooks Kohler, Dana Maclean, Deborah Duncalf, Kay Smith, Mark Ferguson, Tiffany Lee, Richard Pietschmann, and Tabatha Lemke.

I'm indebted to the Squaw Valley Community of Writers for starting me down the path of fiction writing. Authors too rarely acknowledge a debt owed to other authors, perhaps believing it's a given. Still, I feel the need to tip my hat to masters old and new whom I've drawn from, including Michael Crichton, James Rollins, Blake Crouch, Robert Ludlum, Dan Brown, Dean Koontz, Margaret Atwood, Tom Wolfe, Stephen King, Matthew Mather, A.G. Riddle, Tim Tigner, Mark Dawson, Brett Battles, Steve Konkoly, Leslie Wolfe, J.B. Turner, Marcus Sakey, Diane Capri, Joanna Penn, Michael C. Grumley, Nora Roberts, Michael Connelly, Daniel Suarez, Barry Eisler, Nick Thacker, A.C. Fuller, John Hindmarsh, John Mefford, and other great storytellers. You should read them all.

Last, thank you to those who joined my Readers' Circle for your continued support. And thanks to the readers who've found my novels, taken the time to read them, and posted reviews. If you spot something in these pages that I got wrong, let me know and I'll fix it. Always feel free to connect.

– *J.D. Lasica*

ABOUT THE AUTHOR

On the writing front, J.D. Lasica is the author of the book *Darknet* (John Wiley and Sons) and *Biohack*, Book 1 of the Shadow Operatives thriller series. Over the years he has been a newspaper journalist, books editor, magazine columnist, and a tech columnist for *Engadget*.

On the tech front, J.D. has been a tech entrepreneur and an executive or senior manager at several startups and has run a department at Microsoft. He has been a pioneer in social media and grassroots media as well as a longtime champion of the idea that we all have stories to tell. J.D. was one of the first 20,000 bloggers on the planet, and he co-founded Ourmedia, the world's first free video hosting platform (yes, before YouTube).

J.D. has spoken at the United Nations, Harvard, Stanford, Princeton, MIT, the Institute for the Future, and at dozens of conferences on four continents. Besides speaking to college students and aspiring authors, he continues to be involved in the social good sector. Most of all, he enjoys interacting with readers.

J.D. lives in Greater Silicon Valley with his wife and their hyperkinetic dog. He's now working on Book 3 of the Shadow Operatives thriller series.

Thanks for reading! Please join my Best of Indie Readers' Circle to receive updates about free ebooks and get alerted when Book 3 comes out.

 facebook.com/authorjdlasica

twitter.com/jdlasica

bookbub.com/authors/j-d-lasica

31920190R00246

Made in the USA
San Bernardino, CA
09 April 2019